IMPURE BLOOD:
"Great plot, appealing hero, glorious setting plus taut writing – a real winner"
Martin Walker, author of the bestselling Bruno Courrèges novels

"Impressive… will delight fans of international crime"
Booklist

FATAL MUSIC:
"Pulls you along like an iron bar to a magnet. Crime and mystery readers will consume every last morsel of this book"
Criminal Element Magazine

"The road to the logical solution is full of surprises"
Publishers Weekly

BOX OF BONES:
"An accomplished piece of crime fiction. Captain Paul Darac has become, without doubt, my favourite foreign detective created by a Brit since the late Michael Dibdin gave us Aurelio Zen"
Award-winning critic Mike Ripley, Shots eZine

"The plot, filled with enough twists and turns for a corkscrew, is intriguing while never losing touch with either reality or humanity"
Crime Review

KNOCK 'EM DEAD:
"Pin sharp... A winner from page one"
Dagger-winning author Jim Kelly

"The best Darac Mystery yet! Peter Morfoot's jazz-loving French detective will once again delight his readers"
Fantastic Fiction

ESSENCE OF MURDER:
"While the many subplots and numerous characters might hamper a less-gifted writer, Morfoot's fluency ably carries the reader through the always intriguing complexity of the investigation and these intertwined lives"
Bruce Crowther, Jazz Journal

To Barbara,

A DEATH IN TIME

with every good wish,

Peter Morfoot.

Captain Darac Mysteries

A DEATH IN TIME

A CAPTAIN DARAC MYSTERY
#6

PETER MORFOOT

G

Galileo Publishers, Cambridge

Galileo Publishers
16 Woodlands Road
Great Shelford Cambridge
CB22 5LW UK

www.galileopublishing.co.uk

Distributed in the USA by:
SCB Distributors
15608 S. New Century Drive
Gardena, CA 90248-2129

ISBN: 9781915530868

EU Authorised Representative: Easy Access System Europe - Mustamäe
tee 50, 10621 Tallinn, Estonia, gpsr.requests@easproject.com

Printed in Poland

For Floss and Vi

CORE CHARACTERS

The Brigade Criminelle of Nice
Agnès Dantier: Commissaire
Paul Darac: Captain
Roland Granot: Lieutenant
Alejo 'Bonbon' Busquet: Lieutenant
Yvonne Flaco: Officer
Max Perand: Officer

Francine 'Frankie' Lejeune: Captain, Vice Squad.
Jean-Pierre 'Armani' Tardelli: Captain, Narcotics Squad

Forensics
Raul 'R.O.' Ormans: Senior Forensic Analyst
Erica Lamarthe: Principal Technician

Pathology
Deanna Bianchi: Chief Pathologist
Carl Barrau: Deputy Chief Pathologist
Djibril 'Map' Mpensa: Pathologist
Lami Toto: Technician
Patricia Lebrun: Technician

Other Officers
Astrid Pireque: Sketch Artist
Jean-Jacques 'Lartou' Lartigue: Crime Scene Co-ordinator
Serge Paulin: Beat Officer
Alain Charvet: Duty Officer
Wanda Korneliuk: Patrol Car Driver
Farid Haloud: Narcotics
Charlie Presse: Narcotics

Judiciary

Jules Frènes: Public Prosecutor
Albert Reboux: Examining Magistrate

At The Blue Devil Jazz Club

Eldridge 'Ridge' Clay: club owner
Pascal Malata: doorman
Khara Oliveira: waitress
Roger Oliveira: chef

The Didier Musso Quintet★

Didier Musso: piano and bandleader
Maxine Walda: drums
Luc Gabron: bass
Paul Darac: guitar
Dave Blackstock: tenor sax
Trudi 'Charlie' Pachelberg: alto sax
Jacques Quille: trumpet

★ It is something of a running gag at the club that Didier Musso's group of high-quality local musicians is always billed as the Didier Musso Quintet irrespective of the number of players on board at any particular time.

Tuesday March 18th

2014

ONE

Narrow, labyrinthine and hazardous, the path through *Le Bois Empoisonné* had fallen into disuse decades ago. These days, few were aware it had ever existed and fewer still recalled where it had once led. The boys knew nothing of its history. They just knew that, twisty, scary and best of all their secret, the path led somewhere really special.

The riskiest part came near the end. First, they had to squeeze through a gap in the fence directly opposite the gateman's caravan and if the miserable old sod happened to look up from his paper at that moment, their game would be over before it began. If he didn't, the cover provided by the long stand was their next objective, yet safe passage was not guaranteed even there. The stand consisted of just three tiers of open seating clustered in groups with aisles in between. At the penultimate aisle, the boys had to break cover again as they crossed the athletics track that encircled the pitch. If the gateman spotted them at this stage, it would still take him a good five minutes to limp his way to the far end of the ground and boot them off. Their aim though, was to get as much pitch time as possible.

This morning promised more fun than usual: the boys were in possession of a brand-new football, and as if that weren't enough, they had barely glimpsed the pitch itself when an even more thrilling prospect presented itself.

'Nets!' the smaller boy blurted out, unable to stay his excitement. 'They've got the nets up!'

'Quiet, Shit For Brains. Arsehole will hear us.'

But Arsehole, it seemed, had seen or heard nothing and with the threat of red cards receding with every stolen step, the older boy was soon booting their new ball as high as he could towards the goal. The pair sprinted on to the forbidden turf, jinking this way and that like foals let out on Spring grass. The ball bounced with a thump, climbing as if weightless into the clear blue sky and as it fell once more, the older boy, adjusting the angle and speed of his approach, met it on the full.

'Benzema shoots…'

The ball arced towards the target. The older boy froze. Would it, would it..?

'Ye-es!' Mimicking his hero's moves, he saluted the crowd as the ball whipped and fizzed around the net. 'He scores! Benzegoal, Benzegoal!'

'Me, me now! I'm Yaya Touré. You go in goal.'

'Shh, Yaz.' Shielding his eyes against the early morning sun, the striker-turned-keeper scanned the area for signs of trouble. All appearing quiet, he collected the ball and rolled it invitingly towards the penalty spot.

In the caravan, Eric the gateman took a sip of his third mocha of the morning, rubbed his bad leg and glanced towards the far end of the ground.

'Ah.'

He smiled, touched that there were still football-mad youngsters prepared to risk a tongue lashing or worse for the dream of playing on a proper pitch. Three-and-in to win the World Cup before school – why not? And to give some substance to those dreams, although Le Stade Walter Vallain's tired old 2,000-seater could never be mistaken for Le Stade de France, Wembley or the Maracanã, it did boast a near-perfect playing surface. Indeed, some believed it superior to the swish new Allianz Riviera up the road, the top-flight 37,000-seat stadium which was home to "*Le Gym*," the city's top-flight team, L'OGC Nice.

Seeing the kids were enjoying themselves even more than usual this morning – the magical effect of the nets – he decided to give them another five minutes before shooing them away with threats of consequences should they ever return. Not that he would admit it to the stadium's management, but he knew the kids would take no notice. And he was glad of it.

The older boy must have been, what... Ten? Yet Eric could tell he would make a decent player in time. But it was the younger boy – his brother? – he was the one. A natural. A natural, though, who had just missed an open goal.

'Go get it!' the keeper shouted, as the ball skidded away towards the athletics track.

Eric grinned as he watched the younger boy tear after his quarry only for his brother to charge up behind him, turning the chase into a footrace. Had junior intended to land the ball in the steeplechase water jump set into the track's infield, he couldn't have taken more perfect aim and sure enough, it plopped in just as the pair arrived too fast to avoid a watery conclusion to their sprint. Eric couldn't help laughing as, splashing into the jump, the boys lost their footing and fell in headlong. In scrambling to their feet, they fell over one another again but finally upright, they stood transfixed. Eric's smile faded. A cry rent the air and as they turned to run, the old man set down his coffee and made as quickly as he could for the door.

'Hey! What's up, boys? Don't go! You've left your ball!'

By the time Eric had taken off his slippers, put on his boots and locked up the caravan, the boys had already gone. At the jump, the first thing he clocked was the abandoned ball. But something else had found its way into the water. Something bulky. He'd read in *Nice-Matin* that fly tipping was an increasing problem and for a stupid few seconds, he wondered who on earth would have considered this a suitable site.

Then he saw the body lying prone in the water, and the battered, bloody mess that had been the back of its head.

TWO

Over in the old town, bells competing to toll the Angelus drifted across Place Saint Sépulcre in a slippage of pitch and rhythm that had once so inspired the jazz musician in Paul Darac, he'd used it as the dominant motif in a piece he composed for his group. This morning, the dog-tired detective in him felt quite differently about things. And if it was too early in the day for clanging dissonance, in or out of time, it was certainly too early to be taking a right uppercut to the nose. Especially on his day off.

'Breaking,' he said sleepily into his wife's ear. 'Your daughter has just pasted me a good one on the schnozz.'

Drawing up her knees, Frankie turned languorously on to her side. 'Did you, Lily?' she murmured, her eyes still closed. 'Good girl.'

'Good? Attempted patricide at 7 o'clock in the morning?'

'Came out wrongly. I hope she showed remorse. That's what I meant.'

Nestled in the crook of her father's arm, Lily burped, giggled and, changing her point of attack, mounted a concerted double-footed barrage.

'Only if remorse means an all-out assault on the ribs,' he said, though a pair of tapdancing butterflies would have done the job just as well. 'She's a hard case, this one. Aren't you, sweetie?' He kissed Lily's forehead. 'I blame the parents.'

Over a leisurely breakfast, the pair discussed the day ahead as any parents of a seven-month-old baby would. Broadly, at least.

'You any closer on the Port Lympia strangling?' Frankie

said, sipping a mint tea while scrolling her mobile.

'If you'd asked me a couple of days ago, I would have said there were some pieces of the jigsaw missing...' Making a game of it, papa successfully teased a spoonful of apricot rice into Lily's mouth. '... But that it was all coming together. Trouble is, the source picture keeps getting bigger.'

'Ah.'

'In some ways it reminds me of the... What was he called? Citroën? The mechanic who clubbed his father to death with a tyre iron? About this time a couple of years ago, it was.'

'Up in Fabron Supe?'

'Yes.'

'It was... Sateille.'

'Sateille – that's it. What had seemed routine at the beginning became quite a complex case in the end.' Darac scooped up the last of the rice. 'Into the tunnel, Lily-belle. Heee-re we go.' Mission accomplished, he glanced at his watch. 'March 18th. Why does *that* date stick in my mind?'

Frankie made a face at Lily, making her chuckle.

'Got it. It's a year ago today that Bonbon had his greatest triumph.'

Frankie looked away from her phone. 'The Saint-André poisoning case? That was the previous summer, wasn't it?'

'March 18th was the day the case opened in court.'

'Ah, so it was. Remarkable scenes. Unprecedented, even.'

'Despite everything we had, it would still have gone down but for Bonbon.'

From doorstepping potential witnesses to conducting complex lab work, the Saint André poisoning investigation was one in which everyone involved had made a significant contribution and when, in the run-up to the trial, poisoner Alain Daillier as good as admitted his guilt, securing a conviction seemed odds-on. But at the 11th hour, everything changed. On the advice of his counsel, Daillier decided to plead not guilty to a crime everyone in the investigative team knew he had committed.

Step forward Lieutenant Alejo "Bonbon" Busquet. As Alain Daillier entered the dock on that first morning, he scanned the courtroom for Bonbon, the officer who had formed such a tight bond with him throughout the investigation, he'd come to believe he was the only person who had ever understood him. Bonbon had promised to be in court but when their eyes met, he looked away, stony-faced. Daillier knew why: his broken promise over the plea. Longing for a reassuring smile, a look – anything – Daillier's eyes bored into his one and only friend. But nothing came back. The more he willed Bonbon to acknowledge him, the more obvious it became that it would never come. And so, needing more than anything to re-establish their bond, Daillier announced to a stunned courtroom that he was changing his plea to guilty, made a full confession and was rewarded with a nod from his fake friend.

'Bonbon,' Agnès had said to him as the killer was led away. 'I will never forget this moment. I've witnessed some remarkable "good cop" performances in my time but you've just taken it to a whole new level.'

'A year ago today,' Darac said, wiping Lily's mouth. 'For some reason, it's gone by quite quickly, hasn't it, sweetie?' He lifted her out of her high chair and dandled her on his knee. 'And you? How's the Manzano case looking?'

'We think we've got *all* the girls to safety now. And I do mean girls and not young women.' Frankie tapped in a number on her phone. 'But as for nailing the gang? We've got some leverage on one of the two minders we collared and he just might spill but I wouldn't bet on it.' She tickled Lily's foot while she waited for her call to pick up. 'Good progress on the bestiality case, though. Ah, Mariette. Hi.' She listened. 'We're very well, thanks although Lily had a disturbed night and so of course did we… Yes, it *is* good we are both off today. But listen…'

As Darac and Frankie were required to work a set number of hours per week, organising a childcare rota should have been a straightforward matter in theory. In reality, the peculiar demands of their lives as police detectives meant that the daily distribution of those hours could vary widely, making sudden revisions to the rota inevitable. The mainstay of their team of nannies – *nounous* – was Mariette Bélanger, a switched-on and sweet-natured former nurse in her late 40s. Mariette had worked as a *nounou* for police and fire service families before and came highly recommended by friends and colleagues. Contracted to look after Lily up to nine hours a day three days a week, Mariette was well used to calls advising her that a late hand-over was on the cards or that a member of the back-up team would be showing up in the parents' stead. It was clearly essential that these arrangements worked perfectly on both sides and so far, there had not been a single hitch.

During her pregnancy, Frankie had spent many hours considering the timing of her graduated return to work. As Captain of Nice's Vice Squad, her days were spent confronting everything from the pathetically squalid to the pitilessly brutal. With this stark truth in mind, when Lily was just weeks old, Darac had asked Frankie if not continuing in the role when she returned to work, or perhaps extending her maternity leave, was something she had considered. 'If that's what you decided,' he'd said, 'I would be with you all the way.' Her reply would stay with him. 'I'm already upside down in love with this little mite,' she'd said, stroking their daughter's cheek as she lay asleep at her breast. 'And what could be lovelier than to be with her every step of the way up to *Maternelle*? But it's precisely because of the power of these huge emotions that I *have* to get back to work as soon as it feels right. The number of trafficked youngsters my group encounters, Paul.' She shook her head. 'They *may* have been wanted and loved just like our Lily here. But whether they were or not, I've always felt a deep responsibility toward them. I feel it more strongly than ever now.'

The question was settled there and then and Frankie had been working three full days a week for some three months now.

She finished her call. 'Our disturbed night? Mariette wonders if it was a first sign of teething.' She felt Lily's cheek. 'Not overly warm. Open up, darling. Tha-at's it. No, her gums look… gummy. She is a little behind with her teeth, you know.'

'I think all her energy has gone into growing her hair. Give it a couple of months and you'll be booking double appointments at the salon.'

'I don't think precociousness in one area rules out progress in another, Paul. As you should know, Monsieur Poète Policier.'

'Ah.'

'But in any case, our nocturnal woes last night had nothing to do with hair, thick or thin.' She eyeballed him accusingly. 'I think it was that lullaby you played her.'

'No, no. She loves Grant Green's stuff, don't you, sweetie?'

As if carefully considering the question, Lily frowned and then, wagging her tiny fists in the air, grinned excitedly.

'See there?' Frankie said. 'Air guitar. Your take on Monsieur Green's work was just *too* stimulating.'

'If it was, I'd better keep Django a secret a little while longer.'

Once a year, Darac's group, or as many of its members as could make it, forsook their regular Thursday night spot at Nice's Blue Devil Jazz Club to spend a week or so on tour, sometimes abroad. This year, club owner and the group's nominal manager Ridge Clay had secured them four dates on alternate days in England. With Lily's arrival, Darac had offered to miss what Frankie knew was an annual treat for him but she wouldn't hear of it and so in six weeks' time, Darac would be joining the three to eleven other available members of the Didier Musso "Quintet" – a deliberate misnomer – and it would be *au revoir* to Nice, and *bonjour* to jazz clubs in Canterbury, London, Cambridge and then back to London for the closer.

'So what are you going to lull Lily to sleep with while I'm away? That silky contralto of yours is just made for the classic American songbook, you know.' One of Darac's dreams was that Frankie might join him onstage for a couple of numbers with the DMQ one day. 'What do you think?'

'Singing her to sleep?' Frankie said, sidestepping the further point. 'I find humming works better.' She leaned in and took Lily in her arms. 'While rocking her gently like this.'

'That would work.' He smiled. 'Though I don't think it would send me to sleep.'

'Tiger? Down.'

'Copy.' He began clearing the table. 'Remind me what you two are doing this morning?'

'Off to the La Turbie house to check it's still standing. And so we can look down on the filthy rich from above.' She stroked Lily's back. 'Aren't we darling?'

'Burp once for yes; twice for no,' Darac said.

Lily obliged in the singular.

'There we go. She's all for it.'

'And we're also seeing a couple of my former neighbours for brunch. Be back early afternoon, though.'

'Good – same here.' He glanced at his watch. 'Didier's due to ring in a minute. If he's been able to dig out the Mingus scores he wants for the tour, he'll be coming round for a few hours. Whatever happens, I shall be free from lunchtime so the world will be our oyster.' His mobile groaned. 'Speak of the Blue Devil…' But the caller display read "Duty Officer's Desk" and, sharing an all-too familiar look with Frankie, Darac took the call.

'Morning, Charvet. You do know I'm off today? In fact, we both are?'

'I do but Public Prosecutor Frènes has detailed you specifically.'

'I'm still working on the case he *specifically detailed me to* last Saturday.'

'I know. Sorry, Captain.'

'O-K…' The sigh was long and deep. 'So where is the bastard sending me now?'

'Le Stade Walter Vallain.'

FOUR DAYS EARLIER

Friday, March 14th

THREE

In the heart of a university city several hundred miles to the north of Le Stade Walter Vallain, two women in their mid-20s had spent the past hour ensconced at a café table they liked to think of as their own: a corner spot by the window on the first floor of a Cambridge institution almost as venerable as the college to which they were attached. Afternoon tea at Bobby's was always something of an occasion but today, the pair had something special to celebrate and not just that it was the last day of term. On the white linen tablecloth, a stack of crumb-pocked plates stood both as a monument to the baker's art and gave evidence, if evidence were needed, that the pair had been away from their rooms for longer than posted.

A people-watcher concerned solely with appearances might have deemed Sue Talbot and Inès Laborde an unlikely couple. Wearing jeans and a roll neck pullover-gilet combo, Sue was a chirpily expressive, slender girl-woman with straight fair hair tied back in a short ponytail. Fuller of form and clad in an assortment of designer and charity shop items that somehow worked as an ensemble, Inès's olive-toned skin and dark eyes spoke of more exotic climes.

'O ye of little faith, Innie,' Sue said, indicating the view outside with a glancing header. 'It's clearing, look.'

Inès's shoulder-length black hair fell away from her face as she turned towards the window. It had indeed stopped raining and a weak sun was doing its best to highlight the finialed spires foresting the roofscape opposite.

'So let's go before it starts binning it down again,' she said, a trace of Sue's regional accent inflecting her own. 'We were due back 15 minutes ago, anyway.'

' "Binning it down"? I've taught you well all these years.'

It amused Inès to think of it now but she had initially found Sue's accent so incomprehensible, it had taken some days into their first Lent term together to realise English was the native tongue of that cute, funny and talented music student who seemed to have taken a shine to her, too.

The pair drained their tea cups, donned their cagoules and, leaving a cairn of coins in the lee of their crumpled napkins, made for the stairs. On a table at its head, a splay of the day's newspapers all led with the same story, each employing a variation of the headline: "Same sex marriage now legal in the UK". Anticipating this day for some time, Inès and Sue had planned a range of celebrations to mark it, afternoon tea at Bobby's being just the opener.

At the newspaper table, a beetle-browed old codger wearing a sodden knee-length cycling cape reacted to the headlines as if they were a personal affront. As the pair headed off down the creaky wooden stairs, Sue couldn't resist a parting shot. 'Wonderful breakthrough, isn't it?'

'You think so, do you?' The Caped Crusader strode to the rail. 'Well, I think the whole thing's ungodly. Dirty. Filthy, actually!'

'Oh, me too, pet,' Sue called back over her shoulder. 'On a good day, that is. Right, Dolores? Tell the man.'

'You already have.'

Perhaps it was because Inès was facing far more important and difficult conversations on the topic that joining in a spot of routine bigot-baiting held little interest for her just now. The first of those conversations would not be to inform her parents that she and Sue planned to take advantage of the new legislation and marry. Having fluffed the opportunity to bite the bullet on many previous occasions, Inès would first have to come out to them. She knew it was a situation she should have tackled years before but the way things were between them just hadn't permitted it. Or that was what she told herself.

A curious mixture of fragility and prickly obstinacy, her mother Zoë's take on things was something Inès didn't always share but if their bond wasn't absolutely the strongest, she did love her mother and respect the way she had carved out a niche for herself in a traditionally male metier. Had Zoë ever suspected the truth about her daughter's sexuality? At times, Inès sensed she had and if that were the case, she hadn't seemed unduly concerned about it. Her father, Gilles? Different story. A huge scene was inevitable, one that would upset her mother deeply and that was a prospect Inès couldn't bear.

Gaining the ground floor somehow seemed to help Inès turn her thoughts away from the ordeal to come. With new customers filing in while those leaving were still gathering up their things, progress to the door was slow. 'Picture this scene before the advent of breathable, waterproof fabrics,' Inès said over a buzz of voices. 'Imagine what it would have been like on a warm, wet day like this. All that soaked woollen cloth, steaming.'

'And through fuggy Cambridge town,' Sue sang, as they picked their way to the door. 'The sun was shi-ning everywhere.'

'Exactly.' Inès cast a weather eye outside. 'Shining for the time being. Did you just make that up?'

'Me? Think George and Ira Gershwin.'

'Who?'

Sue rolled her eyes. 'Oh, just a couple of guys I know from the pub. *Who*?! You scientists don't know squat. You've never heard "A Foggy Day" before?'

'No, but I tell you what I have heard. Something Dag told me in the lab yesterday. The Norwegians have a name for this.'

' "This" being?'

'The periods of sunshine between rain showers. "*Opplett*" they call them.' She spelled it. 'Lovely word, isn't it?'

'*Opplett*? Sounds dead Geordie,' Sue said, exaggerating her accent. 'We got a lot of our language from the Scandies.' They arrived at the door. 'Just be a second. One of these brollies is mine. Or that new porter's, to be exact.'

As Sue began sorting through the umbrella stand, Inès cast a fond eye around the tables. 'Sounds stupid but I might just choose this as my happy place, you know.'

'Why not? If the prospect of a Bobby's bun or two ever loses its lustre for me, book me on the first available to Zurich.' She pulled a likely looking candidate out of the stand. 'One-way.' She scrutinised her find, declared it a ringer and slotted it back.

'One-way? Certainly.' Inès essayed an indifferent smile. 'Plane or train?'

'Train!' Sue gave her a reproving look. The pair had already spatted about the return Stansted-Nice flights Inès had booked for the following day. And the mode of travel was not the only bone of contention about the trip.

Inès joined in the search. 'So where's *your* happy place?'

'Now I've been here a bit, I'm going quite gooey over these brollies.'

'Seriously.'

'Polite society? The Backs. Carpeted in crocuses in the spring.'

'And the real you?'

Sue pulled out another possible. 'This is the one. The real me?' She smiled sweetly as she reached for the door handle. 'The luxuriant glade between your legs. At any time of year.'

'Shh!'

'Listen to little Mademoiselle Prim-All-Of-A-Sudden! No one can hear, anyway.'

'Little *Doctor* Prim-All-Of-A-Sudden, if you don't mind.

But you're right, Sue. Sorry. Stressed to shit.'

The door tinkled cheerfully open and, taking each other's hand, the pair set off along puddled pavements back to college. At the street corner ahead, a party of tourists was gathered around the Corpus Clock, a fabulous creation in gold whose construction reflected the history of time from the Big Bang to the present moment. It was the monstrous grasshopper-like creature surmounting the clock face that most caught the public's imagination. Dubbed the Chronophage, the beast appeared to gobble up each minute as it passed – a graphic reminder of the finite nature of existence, a somewhat morbid theme continued elsewhere in the design. The size of the gathering indicated the clock was about to strike the hour.

'So when are you going to break the good news to ma and pa? After their anniversary do is over and done with, presumably?'

'I'll give it… what's the phrase? I'll give it *a day's grace* in between.'

'Uh-huh.' As if she had a further question she couldn't quite bring herself to ask, Sue nodded circumspectly, gave Inès a sideways look and nodded again. But then she asked it. 'Innie, are you *sure* you'd prefer me not to be there? I wouldn't have to show up at your parents' place until the day of the inquisition itself. I don't have any supervisions until next term and I could reschedule my private piano students. It's not too late to book.'

The proposition clearly discomfited Inès. 'Buying a Eurostar ticket for tomorrow will be expensive. And SNCF is prone to striking at the drop of a… cap? No, hat. Besides, we've made up our minds, haven't we? It's better if you keep the fort here.'

'*You* made up our minds, you mean. And you don't keep forts, you hold them.'

'Better if you *hold* the fort, then.' Although Inès didn't have a particularly expressive face, her Gallic shrug and moue combination was the genuine article. 'Alright?'

'You know, Innie, the only reason I'm not *really* fighting you over this is that when it comes to it, I sense it won't be as difficult as you've been imagining. You suspect your mother knows anyway and when it comes to sexual politics, I'm not sure your father is quite the dinosaur you think.'

'Really?' Inès halted them. 'Look at me. What do you see?'

Sue made a show of scrutinising her. 'Leaving aside your voluptuous gorgeousness and your maddening way of dressing cheap as chips but still looking ultra-*chic*, I see a woman who grew from a shy but promising undergraduate into a confident and brilliant postgraduate, and is now blossoming into an academic who's going to have a long and distinguished career. How'd I do?'

'Beautifully,' Inès began, but then her black eyes hardened. 'I'll tell you what my father sees. He sees an overweight...'

'Innie...'

'Listen! He sees an overweight, plain-looking couch potato who would never have amounted to anything if it weren't for the accident of being born with a brain that works better than most.'

'OK, he's a body fascist. What do you expect from a guy who does what he does for a living?'

'No, no. You don't understand the scale of it.'

Inès made to move off but Sue held her.

'Then explain it to me. Here and now. It's about time you did.'

Inès hesitated. The better she made her case, the more determined Sue might become to make the trip. But she was right, wasn't she? It *was* about time. 'Alright... let's start with my name. My mother wanted me christened Inès after a favourite aunt of hers. My father said OK, you can have it but only as a second name. He *insisted* my first name be Jackie. Maman can *really* dig her heels in at times, but after many heated rows about it, Jackie it is. You've seen my passport.'

'Yes, and when I ask you about it, you don't really answer.'

'Alright – Jackie was the forename of a woman my father regards as the greatest female athlete of all time. A black American named Jackie Joyner. All through school, despite my father's efforts behind the scenes, I was the last to be picked for any sports team, right? Flat last. But this unbeatable, perfect physical specimen Jackie J was my role model. Talk about falling short. And don't be fooled into thinking that giving his white daughter a black role model was progressive of him.'

'I was looking to salvage *something* from the wreckage.'

'Don't bother. Father votes Le Pen at every opportunity. Something he keeps from the black athletes in his squad, obviously.'

'What a bastard.' Sue's brows lowered. 'You know, having met them both, I get what your father sees in your mother, but what does she see in him? Apart from his looks or is that all that binds them?'

The Gallic shrug once more. 'She loves him.'

'But how did they get together in the first place? Your mother isn't remotely interested in sport, is she?'

'That *is* how they met, actually. At a local *VTT* event.'

'*VTT?*'

'*Vélo Tout-Terrain*. Mountain biking. She hasn't done it competitively for decades but she was pretty good at one time. Still enjoys the occasional pedal.'

'Ah. I'm surprised.' Sue took a moment to marshal her thoughts. 'Look, it's true that you are not an athlete in the normal sense of the word, especially an elite one like some of the specimens your father works with. But you *are* a high flyer in a different kind of elite set-up, aren't you? Surely that registers with a fiercely competitive animal like him? When I spoke to him at your PhD do, it seemed clear that he was proud of your achievements here.'

'Apart from giving him, what do you call it... bragging rights over some of the other parents in their circle, it doesn't mean a thing to him. He would much rather I'd striven to become the best athlete I could be, even if I turned out to be mediocre, than to have made a mark in the academic world. I've been nothing but a huge disappointment to my father. And I'll tell you partly why. It's because I haven't needed one single second of his time and expertise to get where I have and he can't stand that. With the guidance of some remarkable teachers at home and here, I went "faster, higher and stronger" all by myself.' Her face crumpled. 'That's *my* Olympics.'

'Hey, hey. Come here.'

'I'm not going to cry.'

'Come here anyway.'

The women embraced and it was some moments before they continued on their way.

'Right, so you're a disappointment to your stupid father. But, he is *also* a disappointment to you, too, isn't he? And rightly so. He doesn't care about what you've achieved academically? In a sense, he's given up on you? Then he isn't going to care about revelations of your sexual preferences, or me, our getting hitched, or anything, is he?'

'You have a point and if he were a rational being it would be a cogent one. But I'm telling you now that when he knows what I am and what we're planning to do, he will see it as not just another failure on my part, he will despise me for it.'

Sue let go of Inès's hand and put an arm around her shoulder. '*He* is the failure here, Innie. He is the loser. His one and only child doesn't love him. That's a whole career's worth of L for Lose in the league table. I tell you, if I were in your shoes, I wouldn't give a shit what a wanker like him thinks.'

'You can say that because your parents and your brothers are so different.'

'No argument there. But my point holds.'

'And you're forgetting the worst aspect of all. On the few occasions it's happened in the past, my mother really hated it when he and I went at each other. With this, I worry she might... I don't know. Sob her heart out, probably.'

Neither seemed aware of it but the pair had reached the Corpus Clock just as its celebrated hour-striking routine was beginning. As phone cameras recorded every move in the sequence, LEDs went into a crazy backwards dance around the dial. Adding to the melodrama, the timepiece to end all timepieces emitted two macabre sounds, one after the other. The first was a rattling of chains.

'It's not just that I don't love my father. I sometimes wish...'

'What?'

The second was the sound of a hammer walloping a coffin.

FOUR

Frankie had never been able to fathom how frequently "going shopping" appeared in surveys of the nation's favourite leisure activities. Shopping was a chore pure and simple, wasn't it? But how things had changed. With Lily beaming contentedly back at her, even pushing a trolley around a crowded *C'est Ici!* could be a wondrous thing. Today, managing a cross and screeching Lily was making for a less than cheerful outing. Fortunately for Frankie, her stepmother-in-law, Chantal, was on hand to help.

Widowed for over 20 years, Paul's father Martin Darac had given up hope of ever finding a second true love of his life when, enjoying a few days in Lisbon the summer before last, he met widow Chantal Lantosque at an exhibition of contemporary tile art and they had hit it off immediately. Things moved quickly and Chantal was soon introducing *parfumier* Martin to her two daughters, both professional women in their early thirties. Although approval for their marriage had not been explicitly sought, it was resoundingly given.

There remained just one obstacle to a happy transition into married life. With ample justification, Martin's son Paul had long experience in the role. In the event, Martin needn't have been nervous: Paul took to Chantal immediately. And now here she was shopping with her stepdaughter-in-law and her little one. A particular pleasure was that as part of Frankie and Paul's back-up roster of carers, Chantal sometimes had Lily to herself – if she could prise her away from doting grandfather Martin.

'You're right, Frankie,' Chantal said, as they came to a standstill. 'For a city-centre supermarket, the quality's excellent here.'

'So you'd come again? Despite the trolley-jams?'

'Definitely.' The hold-up proved temporary. 'Fish now?'

'Far corner.'

'Very kind of your friend Noëmi to offer her fridge. She'll definitely have room?'

'Unless we turn up with a couple of basking sharks.'

'Damn. They're my favourite.'

At the counter, someone had been overly zealous with the mister.

'Are there any fish down there, do you think?' Frankie said, trying to pick out the day's catch like a pilot peering at the sea through cloud cover. But then a shoal of perfect silvery beauties loomed out of the gloom. 'Ah – sea bass. God, they look good.'

'Gorgeous.' Chantal sought Lily's opinion. 'What do you think, sweetheart?'

Lily's eyes were closing. At last.

'No comment, it looks like. What's your favourite sea bass recipe, Chantal?'

'*En papillote.* Over a bed of roasted tomatoes.'

'Ah, yes – lovely. Haven't done that in a while.'

'I'm going in. Monsieur?'

While she put in her order, Frankie exchanged routine messages with *nounou* Mariette and by the time the fishmonger had finished demonstrating his filleting skills, Chantal was asking for Frankie's tips on preparing a dish she knew formed a significant part of her culinary heritage.

'*Gefilte fisch*?' Frankie smiled. 'Used to help prepare it more or less every Saturday, growing up. If you use only boned white fish which was my grandmother's preference, it's easy to do and can be fabulous to eat. If you go hardcore – deboning pike, adding carp into the mix and so on – my mother's take on it – yes, it works but let's put it this way, every chance I had, I spent Saturdays with Grandma and Grandad.'

'One day, I'm going to give it a try. Grandma's way. I love pike but deboning them? As my Uncle Jean used to say, "Screw that for a game of soldiers." Whatever that means.'

Frankie chuckled and the fishmonger seemed amused too as he handed over the order.

'Thank you, Madame.'

'Monsieur.'

Chantal put the wrapped sea bass in the trolley and they turned away. 'That's me finished. You?'

'Yes, let's go.'

Chantal moved to head back the way they had come but local expert Frankie had a different thought on the matter.

'Oh, not the Garibaldi exit, Chantal. Check-out queues are always shorter this way.'

A little way to their right, a woman wearing a hearing aid perhaps caught the tip because she turned abruptly on her heel and fell in behind them as they made for an exit signed AVENUE SAINT-SÉBASTIEN.

'Are they still with us, Frankie, your grandparents?'

Lily began to stir.

'No but they're with *me*,' Frankie said, a touch on the cheek sufficient to calm her baby. 'Always.'

Chantal smiled. 'Ah.'

FIVE

As Director of Athletic Performance at the University of the Côte d'Azur, Gilles Laborde had been offered one of the grander offices at the recently built Faculty of Sports Sciences, *STAPS*, an impressive complex located in the *zone sportif* on the left bank of the Var in the west of the city. But he had turned it down. This, despite the fact that of the university's many campuses, *STAPS* was the closest to both its principal track and field facilities in which he spent most of his time: the up-to-the-minute 8,000 seat Stade Charles Ehrmann; and the rickety old Stade Walter Vallain, scene of many an illicit kick-around Gilles and his mates had enjoyed as kids. Instead, he had opted to keep the office he'd called home for the past 16 years, a modest room in the Department of Letters and Human Sciences building a few kilometres to the east.

The reason he always gave for not having upped sticks was simple: he saw no reason to do so. Besides, it made it easier to keep "a protective eye" on those members of his current 30-strong squad who both studied in the building and were housed in the *Résidence Baie des Anges* immediately behind it. Gilles's eye was focussed on two athletes in particular: postgraduate literature student Julien Baille, and final-year undergraduate in language sciences, Grace Nahili. Excited by their raw potential from Day One, Gilles had tailored their training regimes specifically to them, applying the principle of improvement by small, incremental gains so assiduously, he had taken their performances to levels that had surprised even him.

At the previous year's World Student Games, Julien had

won a bronze medal in the 3,000 metres steeplechase; Grace, a fifth-place finish in the heptathlon. After these landmark performances, Gilles's meticulous approach had continued to reap benefits and he was sure that if the WSG were an annual rather than biennial event, Julien would be favourite for gold in his event, Grace a likely medallist in hers.

But there would be other peaks to climb this summer and they were loftier still.

In two days' time, the French Athletics Federation was due to announce its senior track and field squad at a press conference to be broadcast on *France Info*. The names of Baille and Nahili were sure to be on the roster, the first Gilles Laborde-coached juniors to be awarded senior international vests.

Had the press conference been scheduled for any other day, Gilles would have relished attending the celebration his team had organised in anticipation of the news. But he would be there in spirit, and possibly, albeit briefly, by a live video link. As to what form the celebration should take, Gilles had given explicit instructions to the team's captain, shot putter Emil Arcot, that the drinking of alcohol be strictly enforced. The decree had surprised many but, drawing on his long experience, Gilles knew that elite athletes seldom drank to excess when given the green light to do so; and also that to have not relaxed his rules on drinking for such a prestigious occasion would have been the quickest way to destroy the esprit de corps he had worked so hard to build up. And if a couple of his lesser lights rendered themselves legless? Come the following evening's training session, they would certainly wish they hadn't.

As one of the co-stars of the wedding anniversary celebration slated for the same day, declaring open season on champagne was something he himself would be observing. He glanced at his watch. Still plenty of time before he needed to pick up daughter Jackie from the airport. In readiness, he had already pushed the passenger seat back a couple of notches.

Except for his thinning sandy coloured hair, 52 year-old Gilles had the appearance of a man at least a decade younger, and a keen-eyed, super-fit specimen of manhood, at that. A pair of scales lay propped in the kneehole of his desk and once a week, he weighed himself as close to one hour after lunch as was practicable. The wall space in his office was covered in photos of the teams and individuals he had trained over the years, hundreds of pairs of eyes looking on. But on the desk itself, just two faces gazed back at Gilles as he stepped on to the scales. One was his co-star for Sunday evening's wedding anniversary bash. Wearing mud-spattered cycling kit and holding a modest trophy, wife-to-be Zoë was 19 when the shot was taken. Gowned and hooded in scarlet, pink and blue silk and holding her doctoral certificate, the photo of daughter Jackie had been taken the previous year. Both winners. Of sorts.

On the eve of his wedding 30 years ago, Gilles weighed 72.2 kilos wearing his regular garb: trainers, shorts, jockstrap, tracksuit bottoms, short-sleeved polo shirt, sports wristwatch. He checked the read-out on the scales today. 72.4. Well within the acceptable range. Regulating his weight was just one aspect of the monitoring regime that had stood him in good stead all these years. No one knew better than he did that at 52, he would not be able to match the levels of performance he had achieved at a younger age. But his bench press reps, sled push times, and vertical jump stats were all within 90% of what they had been back then, and that was a higher percentage than anyone could have reasonably expected.

Zoë's numbers, should she ever submit to such an assessment, would not have remained in the acceptable range.

Acceptable, that was, to Gilles. He had never once let his thoughts on the matter show. Or so he believed. To have done so would have been unkind and more importantly, counterproductive. As for Jackie? The answer, Gilles was sure, was for her to find the right sort of partner. Over the years, Cambridge had produced scores of top performers in a range of sports, especially rugby. The right man alongside her. That was all she needed to rectify her BMI issues.

Following a useful catch-up session with his PA, Monique Azzani, Gilles was concluding a phone call with the sports desk at *Nice-Matin* when Zoë dashed into the office, slipped a laptop out of her shoulder bag and, mouthing *two minutes* at her husband, began tapping away at the keyboard.

'Yes, we're naturally very excited about Julien and Grace's prospects,' Gilles said, blowing his wife a kiss. 'But Ben, I must also mention two other members of my squad. Both have surpassed all expectations over the indoor season and in their different ways express what we are all about here. And you can quote me. First, our team captain, club man extraordinaire and the kind of guy you'd want by your side in a fight – Emil Arcot.' He listened. 'Shot-putt, yes. Final year engineering.' He listened once more. 'As *two* oxen, that's right. And secondly, the newest member of my squad, 800 metre-runner Samira Padar from Bangalore or whatever they call it these days.' He listened. 'Is it? If you say so…. No, not this campus, unfortunately…' The journo's response made Gilles grin. 'She's over at Saint-Jean d'Angély. Studying for a Masters in Contract and Administrative Law.'

As Gilles continued the call, Zoë finished the invoice she was typing and by the time she heard one of the printers in the adjoining office spitting out a copy, she was already tapping in the details of another job she had completed that morning.

'No, you won't have come across Samira yet, Ben – no one

in the media has.'

Once they do, Zoë thought to herself, she would stick in their minds, alright. Short in stature but blessed with looks that wouldn't have appeared out of place in a Bollywood romance, Samira made quite an impression. Her athletic potential? "Lane fodder" had been Gilles's tart assessment. "If she knuckles down."

'When Samira came to me just last October,' Gilles continued, 'she was an occasional hockey player who had never trained for athletics in her life, let alone run competitively. Now, her personal best times improving with every session, she is approaching selection for university-level meets this summer.'

Zoë's ears picked up. Judging by sounds out in the corridor, Samira was not only approaching selection, she was approaching the office. And if Zoë weren't mistaken, the temperamental talent that was Julien Baille was with her. Zoë had mixed feelings about the skinny white boy from Grenoble. Since Gilles had become senior coach to the team, he had given unstintingly of himself to each and every student who sought to improve their athletic performance. When it came to coaching the gifted Julien and Grace Nahili, he had practically sweated blood. Both owed him. The difference was that the ebony-skinned young woman from the Ivory Coast was grateful to Gilles for everything he'd done; Julien, equally as obsessive as his coach, saw it as no more than his due.

Zoë knew that, different in so many ways, Julien and Grace shared one thing absolutely: left-wing political beliefs. Both hated everything the far right Marine Le Pen stood for and had they been aware of Gilles's secret support for her party, both would have been incredulous, then furious, then... what? Like Zoë herself, she suspected, Julien's resolve to have it out with Gilles would flare up briefly, then fade into disappointed acceptance. A furious Grace, she was sure, would come out swinging with both fists and keep swinging until real damage was done.

As Zoë routed the second invoice to the printer, her thoughts turned to Sunday's big event. A wedding anniversary was always a time for taking stock, of evaluating how things were once and are now. And how would Gilles and Inès get on with one another this time? *Inès*... In the sanctuary of her own mind or when just the two of them were together, Zoë dumped the name Jackie. Of all the irrelevant, idiotic... *Jackie*, for God's sake! As her due date had approached, she had done her best to persuade Gilles against it but had caved in eventually. You had to pick your battles, a friend had told her. Pick them? What a luxury.

Gilles hung up as Samira and Julien knocked on the open door and although she smiled in welcome, Zoë hoped they wouldn't stay long. Part of the reason for her dropping in en route to another call was to discuss a change for the night of the anniversary party.

'Come in you two, come in,' Gilles said. 'Just been talking about you.'

The four exchanged greetings but Samira's face had lit up on clocking Zoë and as the men went into a huddle, she took her on one side.

'Madame Laborde, I'm so glad you're here. I was going to call you.'

'Samira, I think you've known me long enough to call me Zoë.'

The Samira smile, Zoë reflected, really was a thing of beauty. 'Thank you. *Madame* Zoë, perhaps?'

'I... like it. Done.' She offered her hand and well-schooled in European manners, Samira shook it. 'You have some sort of problem?' She pictured the young woman's antique laptop. 'I can guess.'

Samira confirmed that the machine given her by brother Dilip on arriving in the city last summer had all but died and she had purchased a brand-new replacement.

'I just got it. And I went for the specification you stipulated when we talked about the likelihood of needing a new one soon. I know how busy you are, Madame… Zoë but…'

'You need it setting up, all data transferred from your old machine and so on.'

Samira waggled her head in the style of her native region back in India. 'Yes, exactly.' And now a French face: eyebrows high, mouth turned down at the corners. 'But…'

Zoë had heard it all before. 'You need it yesterday.'

'Well, I didn't need it then but… Oh, I see.' She laughed and made a silly face. 'Sorry. I attended the French Academy school in Bengaluru from age 7 and they taught core French brilliantly. They stopped short at more inventive usage, though. Yes, I *would* like it done as soon as possible.'

Zoë indicated Samira's day sack. 'I don't suppose you have both of them on board, do you?'

'Only the old one. The new one's in my apartment over in Riquier but I have a meeting with my brother shortly and then classes until six.'

'Hang on a moment.' Zoë consulted her phone. 'Ah, yes… Strictly speaking, I'm not free until… Let me think.' She stared off, tapping the phone on her palm. 'So how's this? You'll be attending tomorrow night's training session, I take it?'

'Oh yes.'

'Then pack both laptops and hand them over to Gilles at the Stade. He'll pass them on to me when he gets home. I can get the ball rolling overnight and by the morning… What's that phrase everybody is using? The new one will be *good to go*. And so will Gilles. He's coming in to see you all on Sunday morning, isn't he? To say a few words about your big evening do.'

'I believe so, yes.'

Samira thanked Zoë profusely and, promising to post a 5-star review on her website in due course, hurriedly said her goodbyes.

'We've finished, Gilles?' Julien said, watching Samira disappear out of the door.

'Yes, that's all.'

'See you tomorrow, then.' A parting glance in Zoë's direction. 'Madame.'

'Julien.'

He shot into the corridor and wasn't quite out of earshot when he called out: 'Sam? I could've set up your new laptop for you.'

Zoë gave Gilles a knowing look.

'Those two. Did you notice anything?'

For a busy alpha male used to calling the shots, Gilles could look surprisingly childlike at times. 'No,' he said, warily. 'What?'

'Oh, nothing.'

'Don't do that. Tell me.'

'Alright. Julien the big star is clearly besotted with exquisite little also-ran Samira and Lord, you can see why. But I've got news for him. Trotting around after her like an adoring dog isn't going to work.'

'Good,' Gilles said, losing the defensive look. 'For athletes, sex and training do not go together.'

Zoë could have added that the same appeared to apply to their coach, too. It had been some months now, after all. Instead, she scrolled the notepad on her phone. 'Quite a list. We need to push on. Took a call from Guillaume. He and Anna can't make the do. She's come down with some sort of bug and he wouldn't feel right leaving her at home. Or so he says.'

'No Anna? That will ease pressure on the wine stocks.'

'That's right, make fun of her alcoholism, why don't you?'

'I was just speaking the truth. I can't help it if she's turned into a lush.'

Marriage to Gilles's cousin would drive anyone to drink, Zoë believed but there were more pressing matters to discuss. 'Pal-Mas now. They've been in touch about the flowers…'

Gilles was already switching off. He had taken several calls of his own this morning. And one of them, he remembered with a smile, would need acting on in person.

SIX

Samira Padar's brother Dilip was managing director of the only firm in the city tailored to the needs of companies trading with the Asian sub-continent. Or that was the spin he put on being a one-man operation geared solely to the Padar family's modest silk exporting business. When he had taken over the French end of the operation back in 2005, Bengaluru was still called Bangalore and there were three Padars handling things in Europe. From the earliest days, the Côte d'Azur gave Dilip everything he had ever wanted and now he was the last man standing, he was determined he would not go the way of his two cousins recalled to India. Recalled in disgrace, too, though neither had been remotely responsible for the decline in the firm's market share in the EU.

It hadn't taken long for Dilip to realise that he appeared exotic enough to the locals in his adopted city without sporting what some considered to be the more vulgar trappings of his heritage. And so, item by shiny item, he began de-blinging his world until only two statement wristwatches, three gold chains, a top-of-the-range home cinema set-up, and his Mercedes convertible remained – objects any self-respecting local A-lister might own. In more recent times, circumstances had continued this asset-stripping process all by itself.

They spoke in their native tongue.

'Take a look at this, Sam,' he said, picking up the remote for the TV.

Samira joined him on the sofa as an image filled the wall space opposite and it took her some moments to appreciate exactly what she was seeing. On the screen, a ground-level camera was filming a line of crouching women from behind. Ahead of them, a flight of hurdles looking impossibly high from such a low angle was merely the first of ten such barriers stretching in what seemed like infinite regress into the distance. On the call of "set" eight pairs of hips rose in concert.

'Why are you showing—?'

'Just watch.'

The starter's pistol was fired and the women sprang forward, sprinting hard away from the camera. As the angle changed to a side-on view, the field was already spearheading from the centre and it was the ebony-skinned athlete in Lane 5 who rose first, clearing it in one fast, fluid movement.

'That's Grace,' Samira said. 'Grace Nahili.'

By the time Samira had identified that the 100-metre hurdles race they were watching was a heat in the previous year's World Student Games heptathlon competition, Grace had already crossed the line in a close second place. Puzzlement shading to wariness, Samira turned to face her brother.

'Dilip, you never do anything without a reason…'

'Does anyone?'

'So why are you showing me this?'

On screen, the athletes were recovering in a variety of attitudes: some leaning forward, hands on knees; one or two, chests heaving, lying flat on their backs. Breathing normally, Grace stood tall, smiling as she embraced the winner. Samira was new to competition athletics but she recognised this as a ploy as much as a pleasantry; what Gilles meant by "the inner game." '*There's a lot more to come from me, girl*,' is what Grace was telling her opponent.

'Father emailed me yesterday,' Dilip said, rewinding to the start of the sequence. As the athletes rose in their blocks, he froze the image. 'You know what I'm going to say.'

Samira's pulse speeded up a beat or two. 'All those scantily-clad bottoms sticking up so invitingly? I know it gets you horny. Is that it?'

Eyebrows raised in supreme self-satisfaction, Dilip nodded. 'Exactly. You've made my point for me. Some lawyer, you're going to be.'

Samira took in the sort of deep breath she usually reserved for the start of her own event, the two-laps of the 800 metres.

'Sam, listen. Pa *and* ma do not want you to disport yourself in such an outfit. It will lead to trouble.'

'They've seen me play hockey. Showing my legs.'

He pointed at the screen. 'These girls show everything they've got. Look! I've seen thongs with more material in them.'

'I'll bet you have.'

'Listen! It's not decent, right? And you couldn't blame any man for…'

'Oh yes, you could! And so would the courts. In this country, at least. But our dear ma and pa have no need to worry, Dilip. You can tell them that *my* event begins with a standing start and although *no one* has the right to tell me what to *fucking* wear, I prefer to run in shorts, anyway. If you'd ever bothered to come and see me training, you would know that.' Her dark, expressive eyes bored into him. 'Will you tell them?'

Dilip was stone-faced as he considered the point. 'Alright.'

'Good. Is that all?'

He brandished the remote. 'No.'

On the screen, games coverage switched from the opening round of the women's heptathlon to the final of the men's steeplechase. As the camera ran along the competitors lined up at the start, Dilip zapped the screen with a backhanded flick. The image froze on one face in particular and now it was his turn to fix Samira with a look.

'Who's that?'

'I'm not playing this game.' Samira got up to leave but Dilip's gold bracelet jangled against her wrist as he grabbed it, preventing her. Digging in her nails, she pulled back.

'I know who it is,' Dilip snarled, pulling Samira to heel. 'And I know you're screwing him!'

For Samira, the words rang in the air like a bell at the end of a round of boxing. Hostilities would resume but for the moment, she needed to regroup. How did Dilip know what she did? What else did he know?

'Let go of me and we'll talk. If you don't, I won't and I'll never speak to you again.'

'Alright, but none of your lies, Sam. I want the truth and the truth only.'

She nodded; he released her and, fighting an urge to slap him hard, thought it safer to sit down further than arm's length away.

'I won't need to restrain you again,' he said. 'I hope.'

'Piss off.'

Dislodged in the fracas, a silk cushion the colour of a ripe cherry lay on the floor. Samira picked it up and, hugging it to herself, opened her defence. 'How do you know what I do in my private life?'

'You should thank God every day that it is I who is looking out for you and not some private detective! Our father has suggested this several times and, on each occasion, I have assured him that it is neither cost-effective nor necessary.'

'I am grateful,' she deadpanned, hugging the cushion more tightly. 'I repeat. How do you know what I do in my private life?'

He shrugged. 'I've seen you together. But there's more. I had reason to call in at the Riquier apartment last week when you should have been in college studying and I heard you in the bedroom. Do you deny it?'

Samira sighed. Although renting an apartment owned by her brother was advantageous financially, she had known almost from the first that it had been a terrible mistake not to have found her own place. And now here it was biting her again. As to answering his question, a number of possible responses vied with one another in her head.

'How do you know it wasn't Carole?'

'*Tcha*! What's your flatmate doing screwing in your bedroom?'

'Her own was full of placards, posters and stuff for International Womens' Day.'

'I know. I saw what state it was in. But I also know your voice when I hear it. Even through a closed door. The truth, I said, Sam.'

'I didn't lie. I just asked what made you think it wasn't Carole in my room.'

Dilip sighed.

'Alright,' she said. 'I do not deny it.'

'You do not? I was hoping… Don't you realise, my dear baby sister, that by screwing that boy, you are screwing *all* of us!'

Samira wasn't having it. 'You sanctimonious arsehole. How many lovers do you have? Eh? How many?'

'*I,*' he said, jabbing himself in the chest. '*I* am not the prized virgin beauty who is going to save our company. Save it by one simple act.'

While not technically an arranged marriage, a covenant of union had long been agreed between Samira's father Sanjay Padar and fellow silk exporter Anil Ratmanath. Far more beneficial to the Padars than the Ratmanaths, the union would nevertheless help to safeguard the future of both companies.

'The simple act of saving myself for that turgid fart Jai

Ratmanath?' The cushion's silky feel suddenly abhorrent to her, Samira threw it hard into the far corner of the room. 'It's too late for that now, anyway, isn't it, Dilip?'

'We can hide the truth providing the affair stops right now and you don't get pregnant.'

'How many times do I have to say it? Our mother and some of our aunts may have grown up using sanitary cloths, burying them and being forbidden to enter the kitchen when they're menstruating but we are not living in the middle ages anymore! I am a modern woman, Dilip. With all that goes with it.'

Dilip clearly found the remark distasteful but it seemed to give him something he could use. 'Yes, I know. And it is precisely because of your own... sanitary arrangements that makes hiding the truth possible.'

My bathroom now? Samira thought to herself. He's been snooping in there? 'I want to give up the apartment, Dilip. Find somewhere else.'

'You ungrateful... No! And as a law student, you should know better. Look at your agreement. By the time your notice to quit is up, you will have passed your Masters and you will be heading back home to marry.'

Samira could feel her anger rising. 'No. *That*, I will not do!'

The stand-off lasted no more than a couple of seconds but it occasioned a change of tack from Dilip. He looked rueful. He extended a comforting hand. But a docking manoeuvre between spacecraft would have been more easily accomplished and he withdrew it.

'Listen, Sam. Just marry Jai, huh? Have his kid, and so long as it's a boy, you can leave him soon after. It'll be a year out of your young life. Two at the most – that's all.'

'One year, two? Yes, why not? What does my young life matter?'

'Sam, Sam. It's for the best.'

She needed a moment to regroup. With every passing day since her arrival in Nice, Samira saw the plans that had been made for her back home in starker relief. They belonged in another world, one she had well and truly left behind. Like Dilip, she had found her feet in Europe and had absolutely no intention of walking back into the past. Progressive thinking and practices did exist in the sub-continent and she knew her experience was by no means that of every young middle-class Indian woman. So why her? What was all this virgin princess sell-off crap for? It was a business move, that was all: an attempt to shore up a once-flourishing family concern weakened not by unavoidable global or local pressures but by her father's sheer ineptitude as a businessman. But he had one priceless asset left: the beautiful Samira herself. That her value to the family lay not in her burgeoning legal competence but in the quality of her looks and in the status of her vagina infuriated Samira beyond words.

'And what if I had a girl, Dilip? And then another girl? And then… Don't you see that what's being asked of me is wrong? I am not, repeat, *not* going through with this.'

Dilip looked uncomfortable suddenly and for a moment, Samira wondered if he might even be about to express some long-overdue solidarity with her over the issue. Instead, he got to his feet. 'I'll just be a second.' When he returned, he was holding a newspaper clipping. As if chewing over whether to show it to her or not, he hesitated for a moment but then handed it over.

'It's from home. She… was a cousin. Ma's side.'

Samira scanned the page. Dated three weeks ago, the report was headlined: MURDER OF TEACHER WAS AN HONOUR KILLING SAY POLICE.

The paper slipping from her fingers, Samira stared blindly ahead. On the TV screen, a frozen Julien stared back at her.

SEVEN

After the delight of wheeling a trolley around a crowded supermarket, Frankie's next port of call was Noëmi and Armani Tardelli's place a few streets away. Noëmi was yet to meet Frankie's stepmother-in-law Chantal and as both were members of Lily's back-up childminding team, it was considered high time they did. But as they turned off the avenue into rue Pastorelli, a call from an elderly neighbour dispatched Chantal back to the Darac seniors' family home in nearby Vence and the meeting was put on hold.

The Tardellis lived in a top-floor apartment overlooking Place Wilson. Flanked by a quartet of busy and buzzy streets, the park at its centre was a pleasant, tree-lined space complete with a playground for little ones.

'One day,' Frankie said to Lily as they waited at the street door for Noëmi. 'You and Fabi will be able to play on these slides and spinny things, won't you, sweetie?'

Kisses of greeting were accompanied by the news that young Monsieur Fabien Tardelli was in a foul mood this morning and would Frankie and Paul like to take him for the rest of the month?

'One of those mornings, eh?' Frankie said, grinning.

'And *then* some. I'll pay big money.'

As they disappeared into the apartment house, a woman on an entirely different mission faded back into a doorway on the adjoining rue Gubernatis and took out her earpiece. Aged perhaps in her mid-50s and dressed in quality garments that had seen a lot of wear in previous decades, the woman had the look of someone for whom the past may have been another country but at least she had lived life to the full there.

Ballpoint at the ready, she rummaged around in her handbag and took out a notebook, coverless and dogeared. Separating the heavily creased hanks of paper, she found a pair of blank pages and flattened them out. But what to write? She had been told never to make any written notes but if she didn't, she knew she would never remember the details. She – Dédé Dubreuil – whose memory had once been the envy of her colleagues! In a half-cocked attempt to comply, she decided to keep things cryptic, using initials for full names and titles. MT and SM would do the trick. The pen's sticky nib made a messy entry on the page but, satisfied it was legible, the woman put the pen and notebook back in her bag and fished out the mobile he had given her. It rang immediately Was he watching her? It wouldn't be the first time.

'So?' he said, his voice conveying all the easy-going warmth of a slamming cell door. 'Remember what I told you. Be careful.'

'I was just about to call you. We're still OK. So that's me finished for the day, right? You can tell... *Don't say Cassie's name...* our friend not to come.'

'She's en route. Stay where you are until she arrives.'

'I just want to go back to the flat. I'm tired.'

'Wait there, I said! And we'll meet again tonight. As arranged.'

'But I—'

'Tonight. *Where* we said. *When* we said.'

Before Dédé could reply, the line went dead.

Saturday, March 15th

EIGHT

The Laborde family home was a neat three-bedroomed villa in La Ginistière, a settlement laid out along the western end of one of the higher ridges that formed the backdrop to the city. Lacking the steepling drama of a *village perché*, La Ginistière attracted few tourists and that was a boon to its residents. But if the village were not a spectacular sight in itself, the views in all directions from it certainly were. On the Laborde villa's raised patio, a slow pirouette was all that was needed to take in the region's two topographical wonders in one movement: the Alpes Maritimes massif to the north, and to the south, its eponymous azure coastline.

And there were other pluses. In his often-used phrase, Gilles Laborde considered the village both "close but not *too* close to everything that mattered." To him, that was. For her part, Zoë's IT business would have been marginally easier to run from a more central location.

Inès's flight had landed a couple of minutes early which she knew her father would have appreciated. He was a busy man, after all. As she merged into the tide of humanity disgorging into the arrivals hall, she was also certain of two other things. Whatever might have held him up, he would have made the receiving line in time; and he would not address her by her preferred name.

'Jackie!'

He broke ranks the moment he saw her and as they walked away after the rituals of hugging, kissing and entreaties to allow him to take her bags were over, Inès entertained a familiar thought: the pleasure he'd expressed at seeing her had all been on the surface. She had always been prone to making odd connections between entirely disparate things and for a moment, she felt an affinity with Sue's execrable concept of toast: doorstep-thick doughy white bread scorched on the outsides, untouched by warmth on the inside.

Even as he was hurrying towards her, Inès could sense her father was running a critical eye over her shape and she knew what his conclusion would have been. She also knew he wouldn't mention directly anything about her failure to lose weight since they were last together. Indeed, she had put on a couple of kilos. But that was nothing to what was coming. Disappointment in her? Wait until the anniversary shenanigans are over, papa. Then you'll really have something to chew on.

Traffic on the complex of roads around the airport was lighter than usual and they were soon filtering out on to the broader boulevards that ran parallel with the Var river on their way north. But first, Inès had to run the gauntlet of the *zone sportif*, backdrop to a thousand tedious monologues on the theme of her father's many coaching triumphs over the years. But today, as its various stadia, courts, tracks and pitches came and went, Gilles confined his comments to just two members of his current squad.

'Julien Baille and Grace Nahili. Remember those names, Jackie. They're going to be stars. They were always talented, of course. Julien, especially. But God, they've worked hard to maximise that talent. As have I, in my small way.'

Has it never occurred to you that I had to work hard to "maximise" *my* talent? Inès thought to herself. Why don't you think *that* worthy of comment? Inès's visits back home always began like this. It was one thing thinking about her relationship with her father from afar; quite another to be exposed directly to the microclimate of disdain he created around him, a phenomenon which, appearances notwithstanding, chilled her to the bone. Reflecting that she would become acclimatised to it in a day or two, her thoughts turned to her mother. Was this how things had gone for her in recent years? Being constantly reminded, sometimes in words *un*spoken, that she had dipped below the standard? The standard others achieved.

As they passed the striated glass and concrete confection that was the new police station at Les Moulins, Boulevard Paul Montel gave way to Avenue Simone Veil and Gilles trotted out the first of the two comments he always made at this point in the journey.

'Avenue Simone Veil, huh? I still think of it as Avenue Sainte Marguerite.'

Should I? Inès asked herself. Should I say what *I* always say in response to that? Say it in the hope it might start a proper conversation between them? One last try. 'It's a French proclivity, I've discovered – renaming streets, squares, parks *etc.* They don't do it much at all in England.'

'They're extending the tramway to run along here, you know. Going to terminate all the way up in Saint Isidore, eventually. Short jog from home.'

'Uh-huh,' Inès said, giving up. 'Everything in place for tomorrow?'

Gilles began by listing who could and couldn't make the party, went on to outline the saga of the cut flowers Zoë had ordered "by the bucketful" for the occasion, and finished by declaring that having their daughter with them on the big night would be the best thing about it.

'That's sweet,' she said, only half returning his smile. 'Alright if I do myself some toast when we get in?'

'Toast? Uh… I suppose so.'

'For some reason, I fancy a couple of slices. Because I missed lunch, I guess.'

'Mistake, there. But you would be far better off…'

With an antioxidant-rich, kind-to-the-gut salad, obviously. But it interested Inès that he had seen fit not to complete the thought.

'Of course you may have it. Won't be able to join you, I'm afraid. Work to do. However, unless she's had an emergency call-out, Maman will be at home.'

'Excellent.'

'And just to say, I'm training the squad this evening, too. Back at about 11.'

Whatever else she may have felt about her father; his work ethic was something to be admired. 'Ever thus,' she said.

'Afraid so.'

'Oh, I've brought a little anniversary gift for you both,' she said, hoping the Moorcroft vase she had bought had survived the journey. 'A little fragile. Sounds as if it might come in handy.'

'If it's champagne,' Gilles said, failing to make the connection to Zoë's fight with the florist. 'It will certainly not go amiss. Though we've laid in decent stocks, I think.'

'And what will you be giving Maman on the day?'

'Ah, ah, ah.' He smiled. That's a secret. No spoiler here!'

Go on, thought Inès. Say you know how we women talk.

'I know how you women talk!'

'Uh-huh.'

They had reached the stretch of Avenue Simone Veil lined on both sides by car dealerships. With one very notable exception. On every other trip home in recent years, Inès had studiously avoided commenting on the building they were about to pass on their left-hand side. Had it been possible to avoid the task of coming out to her parents on this trip, and, into the bargain, giving them the added shock that she and Sue planned to marry under the UK's newly passed law, she would certainly have done so. But it wasn't possible and who knew where the three of them would stand at the end of it? Perhaps it was the sure and certain knowledge that, whatever the consequences, the truth was going to be told at last that emboldened Inès to raise a topic about which she knew her father held precisely the opposite view.

'Back in Cambridge, I watch *TF1* news online sometimes.'

'Keeping in touch with home?' He smiled. 'That's good.'

'Last week, they did a piece on our new mosque here. Well, not so new these days.'

No smiles now. 'Uh-huh.'

'Despite the Council of State ordering the mayor to open the mosque for worship, he still hasn't, has he?'

'He knows the score.'

'It was 12 years ago that permission was given to build the place…'

'I know how long ago it was, Jackie.'

Was this the time to insist he called her Inès from now on? No. One step at a time. 'The building was completely finished two years ago yet the mayor and his corporation are still fighting it.'

'We have a strong tradition of defying Paris in the regions. Have since 1789. Thought you would have approved.'

'But that's not the argument, is it? And think of the injustice. The new mosque can accommodate 900 worshippers but they're not allowed to use it. Yet people complain about Muslims from that tiny little prayer room on rue Genève having to pray on the street when it's full inside. How would that make you feel if you were a Muslim?'

'Listen, our powers that be here know things we don't know, Jackie. Alright? These mosques are hotbeds of radical thought. And when that lot are allowed to congregate, the next thing is that places go up in smoke. We're talking terrorists here.'

'I think this would be a perfect time to build bridges

between the communities, not destroy them. *That*, is what will lead to terrorism here.'

'I disagree.'

Convincing Gilles of her argument was clearly a hopeless task but at least, Inès reflected, they were stating their positions without rancour. 'Actions have consequences, as we know, and so do attitudes.'

'Meaning?'

'Take this new tram line they're constructing along here. Assume for a moment that they put in a stop close to the mosque which, by the way, will open fully one day, however much the mayor and his cronies hate the idea. What do you think are the chances of them naming that tram stop *Mosquée*?'

'Why *should* they name it that?'

'Tradition demands it, doesn't it? Think of the *Cathédrale - Vieille Ville* stop on Tramline 1. Or the countless bus stops named after nearby churches.'

'May I remind you that this is France? Jackie – the Muslim problem is of their own making, OK? It has nothing to do with… attitudes.'

'May I remind *you* of one particular Muslim? Your distance athlete from a few years back, Muhammad Al…' She could picture the smiling young medical student but the remainder of his name evaded her.

'Muhammad Al Zeriya. I loved the man. Still do. And if your point is that Muslims can be nice people who use their talents both to advance themselves *and* the society to which they've been extremely fortunate to become part, I of course know that. But he, and those like him from *any* background are the exceptions to the rule.'

'That background was as a refugee from bloody conflict abroad, wasn't it?'

'I repeat. Maz is an exceptional human being.' He made a

chopping movement with his hand. 'And that's all I have to say on the matter.'

As their progress north continued, a less than companionable silence turned into an exchange of banalities and pleasantries on familiar themes and by the time they turned off the Chemin de la Ginistière on to the gravel-laid driveway of Inès's first and only home in her native country, a degree of cordiality had been restored.

'I'll bring your luggage.'

No point in trying to gainsay him. 'Be careful with the pull case. The fragile gift I mentioned?'

'Oh yes. I'll carry it.'

As Gilles moved briskly to the rear of the car, Inès reflected that while one part of today's airport pick-up conversation had been a first, everything else had stuck to the usual script. She had wondered if obtaining her Cambridge doctorate might have changed the balance of their relationship. In her undergraduate days, she had tried on a number of occasions to interest Gilles in her studies – there were overlaps between the natural sciences and sports science, after all. But it hadn't taken then and it still hadn't. The conclusion seemed clear. When it came to pedagogy, however far she went in her subject, her role was to listen to her father, not to try to teach him anything.

'Maman!'

The women embraced, kissed, embraced once again and still holding hands, stood moist-eyed and smiling facing one another.

'Happy anniversary!'

'Thank you, darling.'

'Jackie missed lunch,' Gilles said, sweeping past. 'She would like some toast.'

'No, no,' Inès said. 'I just went off the idea.'

Her mother leaned in to her. 'Just as well I made a

pissaladière, then.'

'You had time? I was *so* hoping you would.' Her eyebrows rose enquiringly. 'And might there by any chance..?'

'Be meringue kisses to follow?' Zoë smiled. 'I know my eater-ship.'

Linking arms, the pair strolled in Gilles's slipstream to the door.

'So how is your teaching going? And your research? And your friend Susan – how is she? Oh, we'll have time to discuss everything.'

For one mad moment, Inès wanted to say that Susan was just fine, sends her best and that when a suitable date could be found, a wedding invite would be in the post.

'We will, definitely. And how are *you*, Maman?'

'Oh, fine.'

But Inès sensed a different truth behind the smile. 'Don't believe you. What is it – the work-life balance thing we talked about in Cambridge?'

'Now and then I still have to run just to stand still but on the whole, that side of things has improved, I think.'

'So what is it?'

Gilles was already returning.

'Nothing.' Zoë squeezed Inès's forearm against her own. 'I'm fine but definitely *all* the better for seeing you.'

That, Inès did believe.

'So sorry, ladies, but I have to run.'

And not just to stand still, Inès reflected. Forwards as fast as possible was the only kind of running Gilles recognised.

Kisses of parting were exchanged and as mother and daughter walked on into the house, Inès wondered if they both had things they would rather not discuss.

NINE

Samira had asked Julien Baille to meet her at *Haricots, Baies et Jus*, a scrubbed-wood wholefood café she didn't much care for but she knew he did. The likelihood that there would be fellow students around would make things easier for her but just in case, she had asked her flatmate Carole along as insurance, instructing her to appear at a specific time. An ardent feminist studying for a Masters in International Human Rights Law, Carole was a self-determined young woman not given to being told what to do but, as with so many others, where Samira was concerned, she was biddable.

Samira couldn't remember which character from her secondary school Shakespeare course was possessed of a "lean and hungry look" but whoever it was, Julien appeared to be his natural heir. Talented and ambitious, he was a young man who was clearly going places. But it was equally clear to everyone around him that he would get there quicker if he were able to blunt the hair trigger mechanisms that controlled his emotions. Despite Coach Gilles Laborde's best efforts, Julien was gaining a reputation on the circuit as a touchy, even explosive competitor. At a recent training session, heptathlete Grace Nahili had remarked to Samira that if Julien were to keep winning, his explosive temperament would make him box office gold. If it began to trip him up, he would become a pariah. Who knew where that may lead?

Knowing all this wasn't making breaking up with him any easier.

'I've told you the position I am in, Julien. It can't go on.'

He grasped her hand. 'You are the most beautiful thing I

have ever seen. I love you. You know I do.'

She withdrew her hand. 'I know that if you love someone, you don't wish them dead.'

He bristled with all the energy of a trapped animal set to fight its way out of a corner. 'I'm going to see Dilip.'

'You're not thinking. It will only make matters worse. Don't you see?'

'I don't lose, Sam. Understand? Not without giving it…'

'No!'

Samira's look held him for some moments and then, anger vying with despair, Julien jumped to his feet and hurried away.

Samira's eyes stayed on him as Carole flickered into view through the beaded curtain hanging in the doorway behind him, a *pointilliste* image come to life. Julien shouldered her aside without a word.

'Arsehole!' Carole called after him but he was already out of sight.

In the café, a few heads turned but no one seemed unduly concerned at what had just happened, or at the disagreement which had presumably preceded it. Looking entirely serene, Samira waved Carole over to her corner table for two.

'What was that about?'

'Are you alright? He really barged you.'

'My shoulder? Stronger than his, I should think. But enough of that. How did it go? As if I didn't know.'

Samira produced a classic head waggle. 'He took it well, considering.'

'Considering?'

As if to say "all in good time", Samira smiled and then, looking into Carole's eyes, held the look as she took a slow sip of cranberry juice. 'Would you like something?'

'Ideally, a double espresso.'

'Let's get out of here, then. Café Suarez is just around the corner.'

Once outside, Samira hooked her arm in Carole's and said, 'I went to see my brother this morning.' Horrifying her flatmate with every new development, she gave a full account of her meeting with Dilip. 'That's what passes for brotherly love in my old circle.'

'Alright, Sam, we're calling the police. Apart from all the other misogynistic shit he came out with, the bastard practically threatened your life! Honour killing? Fuck! If ever there were a misnomer.'

'Carole, you are sweet, but you don't understand. Yes, all the stuff before that was misogynistic, coercive, hypocritical *caca*. But have me killed? No. Nothing like that will happen to me. I can assure you.'

'You can?'

'I can. One hundred percent.'

Carole seemed relieved but she was still spitting angry. 'We should definitely call the police and other bodies, too. There are organisations I'm in touch with who…'

'No!' Samira released Carole's arm. 'Leave this to me. Promise?'

They had reached Café Suarez but for the moment, they went no further.

'Alright. I do promise. But look at what you've just done, Sam. You've broken off with your boyfriend because your brother ordered you to.'

Gathering in Carole's arm once more, Samira smiled. 'Did I?'

'Well didn't you?'

'Let me tell you something. It was over weeks ago. Julien couldn't see it but I've finally told him flat. All the rubbish Dilip came out with had nothing to do with it. But it was convenient.'

'Why convenient?'

Samira smiled. 'It spared me having to tell Julien the truth.

There's only so much TLS a girl can take, you know.'

Carole looked blank. 'He made you read the Times Literary Supplement?'

Samira threw back her head and laughed and it was some moments before she leaned in to Carole and whispered, 'TLS - Tiny Lingam Syndrome.'

It wasn't just the delicious experience of feeling Samira's warm breath on her ear but Carole felt lighter suddenly. 'You mean..?'

Samira crooked her little finger. 'I've had more fun in bed with Levallier's *Public Sector Disputes and Settlements Volume 3.*'

Now both women laughed but as they disappeared into the café, Carole reflected that if Samira's relationship with Julien had been over some time ago, with whom had she been having far from boring sex in the past month?

TEN

Darac's shadow fell over the Blue Devil's pay table. In the background, the silvery horn of Clifford Brown was doing its best to remind everyone what genius was.

'Kick anyone's ass today, Garfield?' club owner Ridge Clay said, his eyes still on the day's *Nice-Matin*.

'Not today, Ridge.' Darac replied, as ritual demanded. 'Good house in?'

'For Julia Hülsmann?' Palms were slapped in greeting. 'Of course.' Although Ridge was the master of the unreadable expression, Darac's long apprenticeship told him the man was happy about something. 'And speaking of sold-out gigs,' Ridge went on. 'Cambridge. Just heard. That makes two out of the four for the tour. So far. Five will get you ten both London gigs will come through for us, too.'

The Didier Musso Quintet's tenor player Dave Blackstock hailed from Canterbury, venue for the opening leg of the DMQ's annual tour, and that gig had been sold out for some weeks. Cambridge, though? This was news.

'We've no personal connection there, have we? Or would now be a good moment to mention you'd majored in Hard Bop Studies at one of the colleges?'

'At NYU, I did just that, more or less. No, this is all on the music, Garfield. All on the music. The two main guys at the club there are fans. One of them in particular. Name of Steve… Randall.'

With touching delicacy, Ridge aimed an *hors catégorie*-sized index finger at his mobile and handed it over. 'There.'

The email made interesting reading.

'Aah, he saw us the last time we played in England…

The Marsden Jazz Festival.' Darac pictured the scene: grey October day; polite but slightly wary welcome from the crowd; DMQ bang on it from beat one; rapturous applause at the end. 'Monsieur Randall has good taste. It was a great gig, that. Best of the tour.'

An all too familiar face appeared behind Darac, jowly, moustachioed, and irritated to be there.

'And as I recall,' Ridge said, exchanging nods with the interloper, 'No one showed up to drag you off to no crime scene. No offence, brother.'

'None taken,' Lieutenant Roland Granot said. 'Shall we?'

'If we must, Granot.'

'According to Public Prosecutor Jules Frènes we must.'

Darac handed back Ridge's mobile and the pair headed for the door.

'Say hi to Julia for me.'

'You can do it yourself when you get back.'

Darac and Granot shared a look. Back in less than two hours? It could happen. Somewhere over the rainbow.

On their way up the steps, Darac touched the club's talismanic poster for luck and on gaining street level, kisses of parting with doorman Pascal were exchanged before it was safe to ask Granot the time-honoured question.

'So what have we got?'

'A strangling. Port Lympia. Woman by the name of Dubreuil.'

ELEVEN

A t Port Lympia, lights were flashing from vehicles clustered around the entrance to a short flight of steps indirectly linking the quayside to the broad Boulevard Stalingrad beyond.

'There's our beacon, Granot,' Darac said. 'One that isn't attracting many rubberneckers by the look of it.'

'Good. Not in the mood for them tonight.'

Granot's radio crackled into life.

'Perand here, Lieutenant. Been at the scene about ten minutes or so.'

'Who've we got from Path?'

One thing was certain, it wouldn't be Chief Pathologist Professor Deanna Bianchi. The woman wasn't due back from leave for another week.

'The Prince of Darkness, sadly.'

Darac and Granot shared a look. Assistant Chief Pathologist Carl Barrau had many nicknames, none of which was flattering.

'We're just passing Notre Dame. What sort of gaff is it?'

'It's an odd little shoe box of a place tucked away on the *ruelle* behind that flight of steps. Three studio apartments. Two on the ground floor, one of the parties at home. Our Mademoiselle Dubreuil had the one on top. I can't get into it just now. It's about the size of the stationery cupboard next to your desk and Barrau and co are squeezed into it already. I'm going to question the retired gentleman who's at home downstairs, a Monsieur Maurice Thomas or Thomas Maurice, depending. He is the landlord of the other two and he was the one who sounded the alarm. He knew the mademoiselle was at home and went up to see her about some minor repair she had requested. Knocked on her door. No answer. Knocked louder, called out, banged on it – still no answer. Being a socially minded little fellow, he popped round to the Police Municipale station around the corner and eventually convinced one of the boys in blue to go back with him and take a look. Much to that officer's amazement – bingo! A body. Monsieur Thomas or Maurice was right to have been worried.'

'OK, question him formally. And Perand? Make sure you nail the man's name.'

'Yes sir. Got you, sir.'

'That's it.'

The radio crackled off.

'Still can't resist playing the smart arse, can he?'

It was with no great enthusiasm that they made the turn on to the Quai des Deux Emmanuels. Acting as a sort of prophylactic to what was to come, a couple of memorable passages from the Julia Hülsmann Quartet's previous performance at the Blue Devil came into Darac's head – drifts of notes and chords in which images formed and faded like figures in a mist. He wondered if they had begun their set and whether he might after all be in a time to catch a little of it later.

Noting that senior forensic analyst Raul Ormans's van was yet to arrive, Granot added his Renault to the cluster of marked and unmarked vehicles on the *quai* and the pair stepped out into the salt-tang of the evening air. It didn't take Granot long to find something that irritated him.

'Look at that little lot,' he said, indicating a row of "superyachts" moored on the opposite side of the port. 'If "little lot" is what you call an assemblage of floating gin palaces.'

'The collective noun for superyachts… How about "a vulgarity"?

Granot performed his impression of an irked walrus. 'If it

isn't, it should be. I tell you, it gets more like Monte Bloody Carlo every year down here.'

Darac knew what was coming next.

'How much do you reckon each one of those baubles fetches? Eh?'

'They don't call it Millionaires' Row for nothing, Granot. Actually, millionaires are ten a penny, aren't they? They're all *billion*aires these days.'

Granot had a concluding thought on the matter as they headed up the steps. 'As you may have noticed, I'm a middle of the road kind of guy, politically.'

'I've noticed.' Darac put his arm around the big man's shoulder. 'But I'm convinced you'll come to your senses one of these days.'

'As the youngsters say, "Good luck with that." But when I come face to face with a show of wealth like that back there? No. It sticks in my craw. And it gets *this* going.' He tapped his nose. 'I'd like to follow some of *that* money, I can tell you.'

'You see? There's hope for you yet but before we start the new revolution, let's suit up and sign in.'

A person for whom all hope was gone was one Denise Dubreuil. Play bills on the wall of her studio apartment revealed that in the late 1990s, Mademoiselle Dubreuil had been a member of the Lyon-based Fly By Night Players, a low-budget travelling theatre company specialising in comedy. On stage, her roles had included Antoinette in Feydeau's *A Flea In Her Ear,* and Dorine in Molière's *Tartuffe.* Her two final appearances on this earth had been as the victim of a brutal murder and as the subject of a preliminary post-mortem examination by Nice's deputy chief pathologist, Dr Carl Barrau.

A cluttered, airless space, the apartment was in the shabby state that property ads were apt to describe as "in need of some updating." One glance at Barrau was sufficient to convince Granot that more profitable lines of enquiry could be pursued elsewhere.

'I'll leave you to it, chief. Back in a bit.'

'OK, Granot.'

Dressed in a clean but worn-looking skirt and blouse with a newer cardigan on top, the body was lying on a rust-coloured rug at the foot of the bed. Her legs were slightly apart, one knee raised. Rising from a crouching position over the corpse, the skeletal form of Barrau put Darac in mind of a blood-sucking insect, the sort that prays on its victims at night.

'Captain Darac,' he said, his tone more of an accusation than a greeting. 'You took your time.'

For years, Barrau had offered few thoughts on the why, how and when of things at the scene of even the most clear-cut murder, an unhelpful attitude which had eventually landed him in hot water. Darac had been the instigator of a complaint that had led to Barrau's official reprimand and relations between them had never recovered.

'Manual asphyxiation, obviously. I'll know more later. My assistant will return shortly to answer any other questions. Good evening.'

'Just a moment, Doctor. Your thoughts on a time of death? Roughly.'

Barrau sighed. 'Between one and seven hours ago. Roughly.'

'Thank you and goodnight.'

Deciding to wait for the reappearance of said assistant before turning his full attention to the corpse, Darac confined himself to a glance at the ravaged mask that had been her face. Protruding tongue? Present. Petechial haemorrhaging in her wide-open eyes? Present. Ligature marks around her swollen neck? Absent. Yes, the poor woman had been manually asphyxiated, alright.

Darac tried to look beyond the horror. Denise Dubreuil had been an impressively bright-looking woman in her day, he assessed. Bright enough to have played the sage servant Dorine in *Tartuffe*, indeed. He imagined that for actors involved in repertory theatre, the trajectory from playbills to penury was not uncommon. But the life stories of few could have ended as horribly as this. He felt nauseous suddenly and although he knew it would soon subside, he recognised it was a feeling that was happening increasingly. He also recognised that his resolve to bring killers to justice was as strong as ever. That was one feeling he suspected would never subside.

Downstairs, Granot found Crime scene co-ordinator Jean-Jacques Lartigue.

'Evening Lartou. Any goodies for us?'

Lartigue bent to retrieve a couple of bags from an evidence case marked P. O. BRIGADE CRIMINELLE, CASERNE AUVARE. 'In this one, I have the victim's passport, identity card, driving licence etc. And in this second one, her address book, a notebook, and a small collection of personal papers. If you sign for them, you can take them now.'

Granot examined the contents of the first bag and signed. 'No mobile?'

'Afraid not and we've looked everywhere. And there are no phone bills or other docs relating to one. Same goes for a car if she owned one.'

'Not everyone who can drive owns a car, but no mobile? In this day and age?'

'It's a tick in the suspicious box.'

'Quite. Where did she work?'

'Wherever it was, it was a cash in hand job, by the look of it. And we know what that could mean.'

'Hmm.' Granot took a glance around the corridor.

'Perand's in with the landlord, a Monsieur Maurice, I gather?'

'It's a Monsieur Thomas, but yes he is.' Lartigue indicated a door on which a plastic figure 1 was hanging at a diagonal. 'Apartment two next door, I've discovered, has been rented for the past nine months by a Gérard...' He consulted his phone. 'Ploine.' He spelled it. 'Funny name. I'm just about to run the usual checks.'

'Keep us posted. Lami around?'

Lartigue directed Granot to the yard at the back of the property where he found fresh-faced young path lab technician Lami Toto. Armed with a phone, tablet and laptop, he was nevertheless filling out a paper form.

'How's it going, Lami?'

'Fine, Lieutenant,' he said, smiling. 'Yourself?'

'Ask me after I've sunk a few boats.'

'Boats? I thought you were going to say beers.'

'That too. What are you doing out here? Apart from inhaling cat pee and a melange of foodstuffs on the turn?'

'It's pretty cramped upstairs.'

'I know you're far too polite a young man to agree out loud, but for a thin bugger, Barrau fills any space he's in, doesn't he? Like gas.'

Lami grinned. 'I wanted to check out these bins, anyway.'

Carrying out such a task strictly belonged to Raul Ormans's forensic team but there was good co-operation between the two units and in any case, R.O's outfit was yet to show. 'Anything of interest?'

Lami held out a poly evidence bag.

'Ah, I see.'

Behind them, Barrau flew silently away into the night, a departure that would have gone unnoticed but for red zone gatekeeper Patricia Lebrun sounding the all clear with a loud and hearty 'Goodnight, Doctor Barrau.'

'We can go back in now, Lami.'

As they approached, Patricia was chatting with what some of the less enlightened wags in the unit referred to as the "trolley dollies."

'Good work, that woman.' Granot said.

'All part of the service.'

Voices drifted up from the quayside.

'Ooh, I'm wanted.' She had a final thought for Granot. 'You still using that step counter?'

He grunted. 'Bust. Through overuse.'

'I know the feeling,' she said, beginning the descent once more.

'Evening, boys.'

'Lieutenant.' With a practised flick of the wrists, the men from the morgue raised the trolley's undercarriage. 'Now?'

'Be a little while yet.'

They reversed the move with equal panache. 'Just give us a shout as and when.'

Darac was looking through the contents of the victim's fridge when he heard familiar voices out on the landing.

Granot was quick off the mark with her personal details. 'As those wall posters indicate, the deceased is one Denise Ernestine Dubreuil. Never married. No next of kin. Born in the Pipet quarter of Vienne on August 29th 1968.'

Darac was surprised. 'She was only… 46? I know being strangled is likely to age a person but she looks about 20 years older.'

'She was 45, Captain,' Lami said, respectfully correcting him.

'Ah, yes.' Darac felt just the slightest pang of guilt. 'You'd never know my mother taught maths. Any more on the woman, Granot?'

Granot repeated what he had learned from Lartigue and then Lami took over the briefing.

'Here's the reason for that ageing effect, Captain. I retrieved them from the mademoiselle's bin in the yard.' Lami held up the poly bag. 'Needles. We'll determine later if it was she and not one of the two other residents who actually used them but…' Kneeling, he gently pulled back the sleeve of her cardigan. The track marks on her forearm resembled a schematised metro map. 'That tells its own story, I think.'

It was a story that drug squad Captain Jean-Pierre "Armani" Tardelli may have known something about and if he didn't, he would welcome being put in the picture. Darac put in a call for him and was advised he was out on a case of his own but would ring back within the hour. In the meantime, Granot had already found Denise's rap sheet on the database and read aloud from it as he scrolled.

'Cautions, rehab courses, community service, more cautions… And a couple of short terms. The first was three months for failing to show up for a court appearance.'

'That's harsh,' Darac said.

'See it from their point of view. After everything they'd tried, I suppose they'd had enough and were upping the ante. However, it didn't seem to work. The second term was six months… for soliciting. Not a pro, by the look of it. Did it just for a fix. Familiar pattern, isn't it? She was living in Lyon throughout most of this period, by the way.'

'That's where the theatre group she belonged to was based,' Darac said. 'Folded years ago.'

Granot's shaggy brows lowered. 'This is interesting. She was released after four months of the six in that second term but that was two and a half years ago now. Nothing since. Cleaned up her act?'

Darac took another look at the track marks. 'Lami?'

'Again, we'll determine it more precisely, Captain, but I'd say she was still using regularly. And there's something else.' He referred to his notes. 'She moved to Nice only six weeks ago. Before then, she was living in Marseille.' He opened his laptop. 'It was a rue de Rouet address. Quite a varied street scape. It is pretty swish in places.' He brought up an image of a high-end block. 'But she didn't go from there to here. This is the stretch she lived on.'

'Hardly Avenue du Maréchal-Lyautey,' Darac said. 'But pleasant enough. Well done, Lami, this is all useful stuff.'

The young man smiled. 'And this is the actual building. As for her apartment itself, who knows?'

Granot grinned. 'My grandfather used to say, "many a tattered shirt hides a proud breast." '

It took a moment but Lami caught the meaning. 'I see, yes. The Marseille address may have been quite luxurious inside. I've seen many apartments like that.'

'In which case,' Granot went on, 'this place would represent a definite downturn in Mademoiselle Dubreuil's fortunes and that could prove significant. On the other hand, it could have been quite similar to this.'

'If it proves necessary, we can check it out,' Darac said, and then a less than cheery thought struck him. 'Do you recall our esteemed former colleague Lieutenant Intern Christian Malraux, Lami? You can be rude, it's OK.'

The young man let his expression answer for him.

'He's over in Marseille these days. Full Lieutenant. If we were feeling neighbourly, we could ask him to check out the rue de Rouet address in person.'

Granot shook his grizzled chops. 'Don't think so.'

'You're right. It is a ghastly thought.'

'Not what I meant. When would it have been? Last August? Well, sometime in the Summer, anyway.'

'Last Summer?' A smile was never far from Darac's lips. 'Frankie and I had another little matter on our minds back then.'

'Ah yes, of course. But Malraux? Left the force. Went back

to Paris, I think.'

'Really?' Darac said. 'Well, I can't pretend I'm sorry he's no longer a police officer.'

'Quite.'

The pressure marks on either side of the victim's throat took Darac's eye.

'Thumbs made those deep, wide and obvious marks, didn't they, Lami?'

The young man appeared uncomfortable. 'Captain, I…'

'We understand your opinion isn't an official one so anything you say will go no further. We trust you – trust us. OK?'

'I do, Captain. Thank you.'

'So this was a frontal assault by someone with big hands. In his prelim, Barrau had to have moved the body to some extent but did he move it out of the position it's in now?'

'No, it's lying exactly where it was and in the same attitude as when we entered the apartment. Hardly a centimetre different.'

'Coupled with the marks around the throat, that suggests?'

'That the assault was brutal, frontal and began with both perp and victim standing. It may also have continued after she fell back on the floor.'

'Right.' Darac peered at the rug. 'See that small, slightly darker area next to her arm?'

'Yes, but there's a stain on it,' Granot said.

'It's not a stain. I think it's a shade effect caused by the overhead light hitting the pile at a different angle. The fibres are laying back slightly, more so in the middle.'

Granot leaned in closer. 'So they are. It's a depression, effectively, isn't it?'

'I think so and when R.O. gets here, he'll tell us if a knee was likely to have made it.' Darac turned to Lami. 'That would back up your thought that the perp had continued to strangle this poor woman once she was lying helpless on her back.'

'Yes it would, Captain.'

'She's clothed, obviously. Fully?'

'Yes and indications are that there was no sexual aspect to the assault whatsoever. But to sound like Doctor Barrau for a moment, we will know more when the post mortem proper has been completed.'

'Anything else to add, Lami?'

'Ye-es, but it's speculation and it doesn't add materially to what we already know. And once again, the PM will confirm it without any doubt.'

'Go on, nevertheless.'

Tracing a line from the chin, Lami hovered a gloved finger over the victim's throat. 'Behind this point lies the hyoid bone. With all the swelling and discolouration, it's difficult to tell but if I were to press here, which I should not and will not do, I am almost certain that I would find it broken. That is how brutal this assault was. That's all that occurs to me, Captain. Lieutenant.'

'Excellent, Lami. Thanks'

The actorish voice of senior forensic analyst Raul Ormans boomed around the landing.

'Sorry, sorry, sorry, everyone. Wretched van!'

For the next hour, officers and technicians hived off into various parts of the building. A two-man slog squad was also dispatched to nearby bars and eateries. Predictably, no one reported having seen Ploine today but by the end of the hour, the picture was considerably clearer. Ormans was on the point of breaking camp upstairs when Darac joined him. He had one final question on the strangling itself.

'I guess it won't really add anything, R.O, but do you think it was the perp's knee that made that slight depression in the rug?'

'Full marks, my friend. The pile fibres are more flattened in the middle of the depression which gradually become more upright the further they radiate out in a forward direction. Thus, it was something weighty and more or less rounded that made it. Also, there's a slight stub mark on the parquet about fifty-five centimetres behind and in line with the centre of the depression. I'm sure it was made by the toe of a rubber-soled shoe, probably a trainer, worn by the kneeling man in the act of completing his atrocity; a man therefore, who would be of above average height.'

'Which a certain Monsieur Gerard Ploine *is*, according to the signally diminutive owner of this building, Monsieur Thomas.'

'No previous for Ploine, then?' Ormans performed a double-take. 'There's a sentence I hadn't planned on uttering today. Or there'd be a record of how tall he is.'

'In fact, Lartou discovered there's no record of any kind about him because no Gerard Ploine is known to exist. It's an alias.'

'Ah.'

'That and Ploine's height aren't the only things implicating him.'

Following Perand's questioning of the timorous yet chatty Monsieur Thomas, Granot had succeeded in extracting far more from him, including a retraction of his original statement. The landlord hadn't ventured upstairs to discuss a minor repair with Mademoiselle Dubreuil, as he'd originally stated. He'd been alerted by the sounds of an altercation and shortly afterwards, footsteps hurrying downstairs. "Ploine" had been in situ before this sequence of events, absent immediately thereafter. A search of his room indicated he had flown the coop so hastily, he had left ample evidence of his stock in trade.

'He was the slain former artiste's pusher?'

'It seems likely, R.O. Thomas denies ever suspecting that such a thing was going on but Granot's going to grill him on that point back at the Caserne. If he does know more, he'll spill straight away, we think.'

'I would, if I ever found myself in that unfortunate position. A point about the killing, though. Pushers tend not to murder their clients. Not intentionally, anyhow.'

'But who knows what else there may have been between them?'

'True.'

As they reached the ground floor, the Brigade's sketch artist, Astrid Pireque, was making a characteristic entrance.

'Mwa, mwa. That's all the kisses *you're* getting, Darac – I was just going out on the town when Charvet called.'

Actual kisses of greeting were exchanged with Ormans and the man flashed a triumphant grin in Darac's direction as he went to liaise with his team.

There was still a little meat to chew on Astrid's funny bone. ' "The Captain says he urgently needs your talent," Charvet said. Serve you right if I'd gone all cubist, wouldn't it?' She riffled pages in her sketch book. 'This was courtesy of Amal, barman at *L'Etoile d'Argent* just along the *quai*. He says I've caught "Géri" perfectly and a couple of regulars agreed.' She displayed her work. 'Whether I did or not and they were all lying is another matter. I've photographed and filed it.'

Astrid had depicted a white, shaven-headed man aged about thirty. The face was taut, dark eyed and somewhat rodent-like. Two rings in the left ear, one in the right. The sketch credibly matched the verbal description Thomas had given but working with the man himself would enable Astrid to produce a still sharper portrait.

Darac essayed a winning smile. 'I am very sorry to have dragged you out but we've no photo of the likely perp to circulate and the guy made a run for it a good couple of hours ago now.'

'Hmm, reasonably grovelling so I'll leave it there. And where's this Monsieur Thomas on whom I'm to further squander my talent?'

'Here.' Darac opened the door to apartment one. 'Perand's in with him.'

'Perand? Shit — *so* blessed. *So*… Evening, gentlemen!'

Darac's mobile rang as he closed the door behind her, and before he answered it, Granot appeared. The caller was Armani and, putting him on speaker, he passed on what they had learned so far. Armani knew nothing of Mademoiselle Denise Dubreuil and he hadn't found her rap sheet of much interest. But he did have one nugget for Darac and Granot.

'We've watched Monsieur Maurice Thomas's address before,' he said. 'And last year, I even sent a guy in — Jéro Quentin — posing as a tenant.'

'Why? Despite appearances to the exact contrary, did it turn out Thomas owns one of the swankier yachts in the port?'

'That would've been a bit of a tell. No, it was just the activity round and about his spot on the quayside.'

'And at the end of his tenancy, Quentin's conclusion was?'

'That Thomas's place may not have been a miniature Villa Rose but it wasn't any kind of trap house. And Thomas himself? Chatty busybody of a guy not overly concerned with formalities. But clean as a Baggio strike on the ball. From our point of view, at least.'

'That's pretty clean, I take it.'

'The cleanest, my friend.'

'OK. Does the alias of the other tenant, Gérard Ploine, mean anything to you?' Darac spelled it. 'He is very much in the frame for the murder and, although Thomas denies any knowledge of it, it seems he was supplying Denise. Astrid's just filed a likeness of him.'

'Hang on, I'll bring it up. *Pazzo* alias for a pusher to use. You're better off calling yourself Bernard or Dupont. Here we go... No, don't know him.'

'I know you've got a lot on but have you had time to go through the report and the photos of the various things he left behind in the apartment?'

'Hey, you're talking to Armani. I do everything on fast forward. And I've got the stuff itself in front of me. I'd bet my *Juve* life membership that it had *not* been planted by someone trying to incriminate him. He was dealing, alright. Semi-pro. New to the area.'

'Who was supplying *him,* I wonder?'

'We'll run tests on the gear but unless there's a clear batch match, we'll never know, probably.'

'Right.'

'Who was Astrid working with to get the ID image?'

'Guy in a bar Ploine frequented. She's in with Thomas himself at the moment. If the sketches don't match, I'll let you know but I don't expect it.'

'OK, Papa. My love to the ladies. Ciao.'

Darac couldn't resist a smile. 'And to you, man.'

The call ended, he turned to Granot. 'Any further developments?'

'None. We're still yet to discover where Denise worked, if she indeed did conventional work, nor does her address book reveal anything obviously promising.'

'Overall, we're making good progress though, and a further chat with Monsieur Thomas at the Caserne might give us more still.'

'Absolutely.' Whiskers bristling, Granot performed his impression of a sea lion scenting a wounded flounder. 'If he's hiding anything, we'll get it out of him, alright.'

TWELVE

At Maison Laborde, mother and daughter had wasted no time indulging in what some locals were now referring to as *le catch-up*.

'You know Sue just read a recent article of yours.'

'Did she, bless her? I thought she wasn't tech-minded. Except where there's a music-making connection. But I've never written on digital recording or anything.'

'It was in *Tek Mek Online*, I think? The English translation version, naturally. Something to do with sockets and messaging?'

'Oh, "From SSL To TLS." That's Secure Socket Layer to Traffic Layer Security. Dull? It wasn't *Around The World In Eighty Days*, put it that way. Why on earth did she read that?'

'She couldn't follow it, naturally. I think it just tickled her that the mother of a... close friend could write such a techie piece.'

'There must be far cleverer women than me in IT at Cambridge. Women who actually invent such things, not just write about them and work out how to fix them when they go wrong. There'll be many in the wider community, too, won't there? Cambridge *is* the Silicon Valley of England after all'.

'Silicon *Fen* they call it. But don't undersell yourself. I use loads of hacks and gizmos that you've come up with.'

'Not quite the same level, darling. *But,* if Sue wants to read something of mine she will completely understand, the thing I'm writing at the moment will fit the bill. It's not technical in itself.' Zoë paused meaningfully. 'I've been asked to contribute a chapter to a book entitled *Boss Women* that's coming out next year. It's a collection of accounts by women who, against the odds in a lot of cases, have set up and run their own businesses. I have been *dying* to tell you about it.'

Inès's smile was full and wide. 'Maman, I love this! And Sue will love it, too, I'm sure. How wonderful! How far on are you with it?'

'The submission deadline is in a couple of days, actually but that's not as scary as it sounds. To give a spontaneous feel to everyone's accounts, the publisher suggested we first record them as spoken-word pieces. I've already made the recording so all that's left for me to do is type it up and email it to them.'

'This is fantastic. Who's the publisher?'

'*Eumenides*. A feminist outfit, as you might imagine. And there's some *Libé* money behind it as well, I gather.'

'And *Libé* in the mix, too?' What does papa make of all this? Inès wondered. 'Wow!'

'Yes. It was International Women's Day last Saturday and they've been running articles on it and related issues. I imagine IWD didn't pass unnoticed in Cambridge?'

'Hardly – the celebration went on all week.' And what a climax yesterday had been. Inès pictured the landmark *Guardian* headline, Bobby's Tea Rooms, Choral Evensong at King's, Green's Restaurant, The Arts Picture House, and, finally and gloriously, bed. 'But back to this book, you dark horse, you. Will there be an English-language version?'

Zoë shook her head. 'Just French to begin with.'

'Never mind. I'll translate it for Sue.'

'And you'll be able to do it at reading speed, I'm sure. Your English has been word-perfect for years she told me when we were over.'

'Better than my French now at times, I think.'

'Don't tell your father that.'

'This calls for more wine. Shall we?'

As bedtime approached, both felt reasonably au fait with how things were going in the life of the other but neither had told the whole truth. With their glasses returned to the cupboard and the empty bottles buried safely in the recycling, they were sitting together on the sofa, Inès stretched out with one foot on the floor, her head on Zoë's shoulder. If ever there were a time for either or both of them to open up, this was surely it.

'You must be tired,' Zoë said, stroking the back of Inès's hand. 'Bed?'

'I thought I'd wait up until father came in from training.'

'That's nice, he'll love that. Shouldn't be long, now.'

'How about bed for you? You'd been working all day before I got here. All I've done is sit down on various forms of transport.'

'I'm not really tired, besides, your father will have a couple of laptops with him. One of his students, a nice girl called Samira Something-Or-Other was going to bring them in to training.'

'You're not going set to work at this time of night, are you?'

'Hardly call it work. It's basically a data transfer job. I just need to start them going and they will do their thing overnight. Be ready in the morning, touch wood.'

'Oh, well. That doesn't sound too onerous.'

The word "onerous" resonated in Inès's head. The phrase "an onerous task" joined it. And there was one onerous task above all, wasn't there? For the past quarter of an hour, she had felt the loving touch of her mother's hand, the rise and fall of her chest against her cheek and, most redolent of all, breathed in her perfume. But it was only now that the sense of security this all provided began to give Inès second thoughts. She could unburden herself right now, couldn't she? Spill everything. Wouldn't it make the eventual showdown with her father easier?

She righted herself. 'Sorry, Maman. Getting a bit of a stiff neck. And my head must have felt like a tonne weight on your chest, anyway.'

'Far from it, darling. Listen? Your father's home.'

If the perfect moment to segue into what Inès needed to say had come, it had disappeared just as quickly.

Gilles swept in at the same speed at which he'd left earlier. 'Good evening?' he said.

Zoë smiled at Inès. 'Oh, Marvellous. And you?'

'Excellent. But more later. Desperate for a shower.'

'Uh… Jackie waited up for you,' Zoë called out in the direction of his retreating back.

'Good girl! Down in a minute.'

Inès sighed heavily. 'I do feel tired now, actually, Maman. I'm off to bed.'

Zoë embraced her. 'I'm sorry, darling. He… I'm sorry.'

'He's the one who should be sorry, Maman.'

They released one another.

'I do love him, you know, Inès. Very much.'

'I know you do.'

After the women had said their good nights, Zoë went in search of Gilles's kitbag. Not finding it just inside the front door where he usually left it, she went upstairs. No luck on the landing, either. She finally came across it in the bedroom.

'Just picking up Samira's laptops,' she called through the open door into their en suite bathroom but the sound of the shower masked it. She unzipped the bag and under an assortment of damp sports gear, there they were, a note bearing the name Samira Padar attached to the new one. *Padar*, that's it, Zoë murmured but then her eye was taken by something else, something not usually found among Gilles's sports things. It was a small bag. A gift bag, indeed, one bearing the name of the upmarket jewellers *Bijouterie Daumier.* Nestled in it was a blue presentation box.

Zoë's heart thumped but sank a little, too. Her anniversary present for Gilles was a newly published collection of pieces by a favourite sports writer of his. The box was not locked or sealed. She glanced over her shoulder. The coast was still clear but for how long? Feeling a transgressive thrill alongside pure old-fashioned guilt, Zoë opened the box and a moment later, her heart shot back to the surface and kept rising. Bearing the maker's name Michel Vignot, the watch was delicate, elegant, beautiful. She turned it over in her hand and then she saw it. An engraved line of verse.

Had we but world enough and time...

Time didn't so much stand still for Zoë as fly backwards. On the eve of their wedding thirty years ago, Gilles had inscribed the flyleaf of a book of love poems with the same quote and given it to her as a present. It was her most treasured possession. And now, after all she had been worrying about, look at what he had... But she had to act quickly. Clumsy-fingered with the joy of it, Zoë took three attempts at returning the watch to the box. She closed it, put it back where it had been lying in the kitbag, and then, in a moment of sudden clarity, put the laptops and note back where they had come from. She stole out of the bedroom, padded lightly down the stairs and lingered at their foot.

A towel around his waist, Gilles soon appeared on the landing and, opening the airing cupboard door, caught sight of Zoë below, apparently heading to the front door.

'Ah, good, you're finished,' she called up the stairs. 'Did Samira What's-Her-Name hand over her laptops?'

'She did but my bag's up here. I'll bring it down in a minute.'

'OK,' she said, holding the look.

'Are you alright?'

Oh, yes, Zoë had not felt this good in some time. Everything that she feared was happening was clearly not. She had been a fool and never had she felt so glad about it.

'Perfectly. It's lovely being all together again, isn't it? That's all.'

'Isn't it,' Gilles said, and disappeared into the bedroom.

THIRTEEN

Darac had always felt enriched by living and thinking on the cusp, the points at which different, even opposing, spaces and ideas cohered or crashed into one another. He had moved into his apartment in Place Saint-Sépulcre ten years ago and had felt at home immediately. A roof-top eyrie hovering between the spice-toned knot of the old town – the Babazouk – and the modern tree-lined Nice of the boulevards suited him right down to the ground.

While all that went with leading a double life held no particular fascination for Frankie, she too loved the apartment's Janus-like setting. At some stage in the future, the pair might have to consider a move but, sitting out on their roof terrace on this starry night in Spring, it was difficult to imagine ever saying goodbye to the place. Just for a change, they had arranged their loungers top to toe.

'I haven't asked about Port Lympia,' Frankie said, taking a last sip of her rosé. 'How did it go?'

'It was grisly, as every strangling is. But the lines of enquiry are well defined. Drugs involved.'

A car horn blared below.

'There's a likely perp?'

'Another tenant, a pusher, looks nailed on for it but he's using an alias and he's skipped. We have an APB out using a couple of sketches Astrid produced: one via the victim's landlord who we believe isn't implicated in either the murder or the drugs part of it; the other via a barman from just along the quayside.'

'Playing Find The Pusher can take a while but it *is* usually just a matter of time.'

'Absolutely.' Darac drained his Leffe and the pair settled back.

'So did you make it back to the club afterwards?'

'I think I could have just about made the encores.' Frankie's left foot was just too close for his guitarist's right-hand fingernails to ignore. 'But I had another date, anyway.'

'Ah, ah… Not the sole!' Frankie pulled her foot away but she slid it back immediately. 'Paul, do you think we'll ever tire of flirting, et cetera?'

'Me? No – the *et cetera* part, especially. You? I think the rot's already set in.'

'Think so, huh?'

Her kohl-black hair spilling over his face, she rose and broke over him like a wave on a midnight shore. Not for the first time, the absence of any sight line to the terrace was soon proving a blessing.

Looking in on Lily before they finally went to bed, Darac was reminded of a lyric from a number he hadn't heard in years.

'What?' Frankie whispered, reading him.

'I was thinking of a song. By Jacques Brel.'

'Brel?' Frankie eyebrows lowered in disbelief. 'Really?'

'Not one of the fiercely melodramatic ones. It's about the love he feels for his daughter, Isabelle. There's a verse about watching her asleep in her cot.' He recited it. 'Sweet?'

'Very.'

It was only when they finally climbed into bed that Darac realised he had forgotten to ask Frankie about her get-together with Chantal the previous day.

'It was lovely. Something odd happened, too, which interesting.'

'Tell me.'

She recounted the story of their most entertaining shopping expedition and the visit to Noëmi and little Fabien at home in Place Wilson.

'Chantal must have enjoyed meeting Noëmi at last.'

'I'm sure she would have but there was no meeting. Some sort of issue with an elderly neighbour came up en route – nothing too serious I gather – but Chantal went off home to sort it out. Despite young Monsieur Fabien Tardelli's initially tired and emotional mood – picture a young Genghis Khan in a strop – we proceeded to have a lovely time. Noëmi is such a fabulous cook and lunch was wonderful. Lily was on her most charming form. Eventually Fabi followed suit and the pair of us left in high good humour.'

'If he's anything like his father, the tantrum probably had sartorial origins. A smudge on a loafer has been known to push Armani over the edge.'

'Fabi doesn't wear loafers. Yet. But the strange thing had nothing to do with him. We set off down Gubernatis, crossed Postes, and it was only then I remembered I'd intended to call in at that *chocolatier* on the corner. Mariette had been *so* brilliant dealing with all our rearrangements and things last week that I wanted to get something for her. So we did a quick about face and set off back. That is the moment the strange thing happened.'

Building the suspense, Frankie's eyebrows lifted expressively but she went no further.

'Go on. I'm riveted.'

'Correct response. I bumped almost literally into… Noëmi's twin sister.'

'What?'

'Yes. Those cheekbones, the Sally Bowles-style bob, the eyes, figure – everything. Apart from wearing earphones, which I've never seen Noëmi do, she was even dressed like her. As twins sometimes are.'

It was well over a decade ago that Darac and Armani had first run into each other at the Brigade Criminelle's HQ, the Caserne Auvare. Sharing just one overnight stake-out with the man had been sufficient to learn a great deal about him, and the pair had shared many such nights in the intervening years. If Noëmi had a twin sister, Darac would most certainly have heard about it.

'No, Frankie.'

'No, of course not. I'm being figurative. But I tell you the woman was so like Noëmi, I actually spoke to her.'

'What did you say?'

'Something along the lines of, "Oh, uh, hello? Aren't you… No, sorry. You're obviously not.' At that, the poor woman scuttled off. And one could hardly blame her.'

'There's that old saw about everyone having a dead ringer somewhere, isn't there? A doppelganger.'

'True. You remember from the wedding that one of my many times removed Greek cousins looks very like me – Selene.'

'She one of the doctors?'

'The one who kept calling you Pavlos.'

'Ah, yes. She *does* resemble you but it's inadmissible. She's a relative, however distant.' Taking her hand, Darac looked into Frankie's eyes. '*And* she is nowhere near as beautiful.'

'Uh… *Again*, Paul?'

Whether Frankie was impressed by his ardour, amused at his pretension, or gently cautioning him against further activity, Darac couldn't quite tell. Feeling utterly spent, he hoped it was the last.

'I was just saying.'

'That's a relief.'

'Isn't it?' He blindly patted the bedside table. 'Of course, *I* have, or rather had, a doppelganger.' He found his mobile. 'On your rare visits to The Blue Devil, have you ever wondered why Ridge calls me Garfield? Usually after he's asked if I've kicked anybody's ass that day?'

'Oh, *that's* what it is. I can't always follow what he's saying.'

'It's French à la Bronx. You need to get your ear in. Anyway, here look.'

On the screen, the broad-boned face of 50s Hollywood star John Garfield looked back at the pair with a decided twinkle in his eye.

'Good Lord,' Frankie said. 'You really do have a look of him...' She yawned. 'Scroll down. Yes, that same tough but amused by everything look... Oh, *really* brooding in that one. That's you, too.'

'Seen enough?'

She sank back on to the pillow and closed her eyes. 'Uh-huh.'

'That looks like a good idea.'

A goodnight kiss and the pair settled down. Or rather, Frankie did. After no more than a moment, Darac found himself staring at the ceiling. Of all the times to air a potentially concerning thought, moments before drifting off to sleep ranked among the worst. Save it for the breakfast table, he told himself. You and Frankie could use a good night's sleep, too. And yet...

Agnès had long contended that when investigating a murder case, or any sequence of events, one seldom encountered the phenomenon known as a complete coincidence. What appeared to be the accidental or uncanny conjunction of apparently disparate entities almost always involved some logic that explained it. And on occasion, for logic, read meticulous planning.

Still, "seldom" didn't mean "never." A case in point was Darac's connection to an actor from the other side of the Atlantic long dead before he was even born. No planning involved there. Aside from the striking resemblance, nothing linked the two men in any way. So to which category did Frankie's encounter with Noëmi Two belong? Frankie, a senior police officer, visiting the wife of another senior police officer, and then bumping into a woman who could have been that woman's twin more or less directly outside her apartment house? He couldn't help it. 'There's quite a difference between our two doppelganger stories, you know,' he whispered.

'Hmm?'

'Nothing. Go to sleep, darling.'

The couple may have been leaving it for the night but the matter definitely required further discussion. If the appearance – in both senses – of Noëmi Two was not an accident, then what was it? Tomorrow, he decided, they should at least call the Tardellis. Or if they were at home, call *on* them on their way to work.

Sunday, March 16th

FOURTEEN

G ood morning, darling. Happy anniversary!'
Emboldened by the discovery of her gift, Zoë's hand
began to explore Gilles's chest. And then his stomach. Those
tightly packed muscles had always aroused her. The waistband
of his boxers was next. Alright, he had been too tired the
night before. Understandable. But this was a new day, a new
dawn, a new life.

'Happy anniversary, angel.' Gently removing her hand,
he swung his legs out of bed and stood. 'But my morning
breath, it's really not…'

'Brush your teeth and come back to bed. I want you.'

'Sweetheart, you know we have so much to get through
before the party. Plus we've both got places to go and people
to meet this morning.'

Zoë knew Gilles had a point and she could see he was
slightly unsettled by her show of naked desire but she sensed
he was turned on by it also.

'And besides…' He cast an anxious glance at the wall and
when he continued, his voice was barely above a whisper.
'Jackie might hear us.'

'When she was small, we used to say we were play fighting.
Do you remember?'

'Really, I do think we need to …'

'Rain check? For tonight?'

'Sure. Now let's…'

'Coming.'

FIFTEEN

Having left Lily in the more than capable hands of *nounou* Mariette, Darac and Frankie did something they had hardly ever done before. They drove off to work together.

'You know....'

In the adjacent lane, the front wheel of a bicycle suddenly emerged in the narrow gap between two stationary vehicles.

'Bike left, Paul. Watch him!'

A raised fist was Darac's reward for avoiding flattening the man. He lowered his window but by the time he'd advised the cyclist that slaloming blindly across the road could lead to his arrest or death whichever came first, the lycra-clad lemming was continuing his run on the opposite carriageway.

'Nothing like issuing a rhetorical threat to change minds,' Darac said.

'*I* nearly totalled Death Wish On A Bike there, last week. I think it was him, anyway.'

'At least he wasn't a dead ringer for Noëmi.'

The discussion resumed.

'OK, let's recap who Noëmi Two might be if turning up where she did *wasn't* a coincidence. It's not all that convincing but I think our best benign explanation is that she's a relative from a side of the family Noëmi knew nothing about – and possibly vice-versa - until say, a spot of family history research brought Noëmi One into Two's orbit. She then finds an up-to-date photo of One on the internet, is immediately struck by the resemblance and decides it would be fun to contact her. A surprise visit.'

'Unless Two happens to be a police officer or other official of the State, she would need to have been pretty resourceful to discover the Tardellis' home address.'

'Two might *be* such an official. And if she isn't, there are ways for amateurs.'

'It's *possible*, Paul, though I still don't buy it. And don't forget, Noëmi Two hasn't actually contacted her long lost whatever she is.'

'True and another thing against this particular interpretation is why a woman seeking to introduce herself to a newly discovered relative might dress in just the manner that person does? Even in Benign Land, that would be an odd thing to do, wouldn't it?'

Frankie made a moue. 'I was struck by it, yes. But now I've stopped exaggerating my story for effect, the clothing part of it wasn't *that* odd a coincidence, really. Our Noëmi may not dress as conventionally as I do but it's not as if she goes around got up as a Hawaiian hula dancer or anything.'

'White trainers and a dress? That's pretty unusual and Noëmi Two was wearing the same, you said.'

'Check out Vogue – it's the new thing. More and more women are doing it.'

He smiled. 'OK, I concede that one, as well. So let's turn to our *less* benign interpretations of the appearance of Noëmi Two.'

Frankie shrugged. 'Don't think it's really necessary. And neither, significantly, did Noëmi or Armani.'

'Nevertheless, they gave their blessing to my running the story past Agnès this morning.'

'True.'

'*And* I wouldn't be surprised if Armani didn't ask folk they know around the Place to keep an eye open for anything suspicious. On the QT, so as not to worry Noëmi.'

Frankie gave a conceding nod. 'That would be like him. Al-right. Malign Land, it is. First, although the concept rather appealed to you, I think we can overlook the realms of Sci-Fi and Fantasy for a motive, don't you?'

'Sadly.'

'Hmm. So that leaves us with the possibility that Noëmi Two, or someone controlling her, is planning a crime in which a convincing impersonation of our Noëmi is essential to its success.'

'Right.'

'According to Noëmi herself, the archival work she's doing at the moment is so... what was her phrase?'

'Teeth grindingly unimportant, I think it was.'

'Yes – to the extent that installing a dead ringer in her place would yield to the impostor nothing of any commercial, intellectual or political value.'

'So we can probably rule out the world of work. Or, rather Noëmi's work. Although Armani himself pooh-poohed the idea, what if a con bearing a grudge against *him* is planning to stage some sort of felony which eyewitnesses will testify with absolute certainty was committed by Madame Noëmi Tardelli? Providing the con had ensured that the real Noëmi had no alibi and preferably some sort of motive to commit the crime, the Tardellis would be in for an anxious time of it, at the least. If the crime happened to be *murder...*' He let a raised eyebrow complete the thought.

'You're right *in theory*, of course,' Frankie said. 'Hate and revenge crimes are expressly designed to deliver the maximum amount of pain to the victims. And this *could* God forbid, turn out to be a prime example of it.' She shook her head. 'It's *so* outlandish, though.'

The radio crackled on. Charvet with a report. A young dog walker had called in from Villefranche. Scenting something of interest, his multiple charges had pulled the lad into a back alley, ruelle Moncet, which houses a pair of dumpsters. A clothed body had been crammed into one of them. Sight unseen, Public Prosecutor Frènes had already assigned the case to the Brigade. Granot and Bonbon were en route to lead the investigation on the ground.

'If ruelle Moncet is the alley I'm thinking of, there's no CCTV anywhere around there.'

'Which is why the dumper chose that particular dumpster, presumably.'

Turning into Avenue des Diables Bleus, Darac's eye was drawn to his second home, the Blue Devil Jazz Club, where a trio of seagulls was engaged in a turf war over the *terra infirma* that was the club's temperamental neon sign. He blared his horn and, still spatting, they took off as one.

'Gulls – what's the point of them?' he said.

Frankie gave him a reproving look. 'Paul, seagulls are an essential part of the urbano-marine eco system. Though I hope the one who made off with my lunch in Jardin Albert three years ago is rotting in hell.'

'The Prosecution rests.'

Ahead, a double-parked van was making life difficult for a queue of buses attempting to pull out of the new *gare routière* at Vauban. Darac pulled on the handbrake.

'Logjam,' he said, stating the obvious. 'As if I needed reminding. For just about the first time ever, there's a sizeable example of the phenomenon on my desk. Glad Granot and Bonbon are on today. A trip out for me would not have been ideal.'

SIXTEEN

Since there had never been occasion to celebrate an international call-up for members of a Gilles Laborde athletics squad, no one was quite sure what form the party should take. Although the logic was unclear, it was with an eye to its "potential publicity value" that Dilip Padar had offered to host the event. A quiet word from Samira to team captain Emil Arcot was all it had taken to quash the proposal: 'He's under orders to keep a tight rein on me, Emil. He'd bind and gag me if he could.' Shot putter Emil had replied that if Samira ever required it, his 105 kilos of solid muscle were at her disposal. The prospect excited her. Emil, she suspected, was one member of Gilles's squad who definitely wouldn't suffer from TLS.

In the end, Emil had booked a small performance space adjacent to a bar in the Department of Letters and Human Sciences building for the occasion. Now that the morning before the night to come had arrived, all that remained was a meeting to recap a few points and "the job," in the words of farmer's son Emil, would be "a good 'un." The team met in the refectory.

Star steeplechaser Julien was usually the last to arrive at any form of gathering. After all that had happened between them, Samira wondered if the wounded little warrior might not show at all. But he did and although he returned her words of greeting with a cool nod, he didn't appear nearly as suicidal as Samira had suspected he might. It was an act, she assumed. No one could get over the loss of a beauty like her as easily as that.

Uniquely, Emil was the last to arrive but only because a crucial delivery had been late turning up.

'Morning, all,' he said, dumping a stack of T-shirts on the table in front of him. 'Unisex. Four sizes. *Petit* to *Fucking Huge*. A word to the fashionistas among you.' He gave Samira and long jumper Ade Okoko meaningful looks. 'There's no obligation to wear these but we're all going to wear them so get over it, OK?'

'Yessir,' Samira said, saluting, a move which Ade copied only half-ironically.

'Good. And here's the message.' Emil held up a *petit* against the vast acreage of his torso to reveal the legend: *Nahili et Baille, Le Jour de Gloire Est Arrivé*! 'And on the reverse, we have...' Finding his inner fan dancer, Emil threw a few shapes while flipping the garment seductively around: *Laborde pour Président*!

There were cheers and even the woebegone Julien seemed to find something to enjoy in the moment. 'OK, let's divvy 'em up,' Emil announced. '*Petits* first. Samira? Catch.'

'That's the furthest you've thrown all season,' Grace Nahili said, bringing laughs to which Emil added more by launching the next garment in a parody of his shot-putting technique. Shouting 'Go-oooo!' he watched hawk-eyed as the cloth orb floffled down hopelessly short of its target, 'Another PB,' he said. 'And Mademoiselle Nahili? Come the *moyennes*, you'll be lucky to get one at all.'

New items of business came and went in quick succession. Music? Emil had engaged Ade Okoko's DJ sister Lisa for the evening. Drinks? Gilles had already set up a generous tab with the bar. But everyone agreed that the highlight of the evening would be the live exchange of greetings and congratulations with the Laborde's own party over in La Ginestière. And when the man in question arrived as the meeting was drawing to a close, it was to a warm round of applause followed by a chaser of quips and inappropriate suggestions.

'I'd be careful if I were you,' he said, smiling. 'Remember you'll all be at training tomorrow evening. Stade Walter

Vallain 7 o'clock. No absentees.'

Groans and further challenging suggestions.

'Loving the T-shirts,' Gilles went on. 'But me for president? I've already got a better job.' Gravity now. 'And I mean that. Tonight, when the announcement is made that Grace and Julien have been selected for our national squad?' His hand went to his heart. 'That will quite simply be the happiest moment of my professional life. Look forward to seeing you all later.'

More applause and, led by Captain Emil, three cheers for the three heroes of the hour.

It was a good moment on which to end and with one exception, the team dispersed in an upbeat mood. But Gilles had a couple of tasks still to perform and when Samira approached him wearing an enquiring expression, he set about the first of them. 'Your new laptop? It's in my office.'

'Madame Zoë has had time to transfer all the files from the old one and so on?'

'She had.'

'Excellent!'

'Let's go.'

In the office, Gilles opened his kitbag, took out both machines and speed read an accompanying note. 'So… there were no problems. Bill to follow at some stage. I *think* that's all…' He looked up. 'Can you manage both of them?'

'Yes. I'll send her a thank-you text.'

'She'll like that. Here we are' He handed them over. 'I have something I'd like to run by you.'

'Uh-huh.'

'Although we didn't take him up on it, I think it only right and proper the team formally thanks your brother for his generous offer of hosting this evening's party. Don't you?'

'No,' she said.

'Oh.' Gilles was taken aback. 'I didn't mean thank him in

any material way. As head coach, I just thought I'd write him a letter or something.'

Samira could look and sound cloyingly sweet if it pleased her to do so. She could do sour just as easily. 'No, Gilles. And that, as you often say, is the end of the matter.'

SEVENTEEN

Darac was preparing to set off for Agnès's office when the crown of an ash-blonde bob appeared over the stack of paperwork piled up on his desk.

'Anyone there?' she asked.

He stood. 'Fair point, Agnès.' He glanced at his watch. 'But I thought I was coming over to you?'

They exchanged kisses of greeting.

'Sit, sit,' she said. 'The exercise is good for my back. As is standing.'

'If you insist. And by this time tomorrow, I swear that Mont Papier here will have been levelled. At least a thousand of these pages is assorted guff from on high. Even Granot would give most of it a swerve.'

'And the other five thousand?'

'Just… things. Nothing crucial. Everything that's supposed to have been actioned, has. Including stuff for Frènes. Altar boy's honour.'

'You were an altar boy?' she said. 'This is my sceptical look in case you've never seen it before.'

'Me an altar boy? Not as such. But we established some time ago that "*guitarist's* honour" doesn't quite work somehow.'

'Quite.'

Agnès had understood from the beginning that, so long as it wasn't overdone, banter, asides and gags were useful tools in maintaining the morale of any police unit. That it came as naturally to her as it did to her second-in-command was one of the reasons Nice's Brigade Criminelle was the harmonious outfit it was.

'You caught the flash about the Villefranche dumpster incident, Paul?'

'Uh-huh. The victim isn't someone who happens to bear a marked resemblance to Armani's wife, by any chance?'

'Noëmi? No, the body is male. That's all we know so far. Why might it resemble her?'

'This is why I wanted a word.' Leaving nothing out, Darac recounted Frankie's story. 'So,' he said at the end of it. 'What's your assessment, Agnès? Coincidence or crime?'

'What would be *your* response to that question?' she said, her tone neutral, her eyes locked on his. 'If you were commissaire?'

Agnès had been on the point of retiring for some time but a date had finally been set.

From January, 2015, roughly nine months away, Nice's Brigade Criminelle would have to function without the leadership of the most admired commissaire in its history. It was a prospect almost no one at the Caserne wanted to entertain. And as to the appointment of her successor? Agnès herself had no doubt who should succeed her and had already made a powerful case on their behalf both in writing and informally to anyone she knew had a say in the decision-making process. Her choice was an officer who, for the time being at least, had no idea of her advocacy.

Agnès's counter question and the way she had posed it made Darac come out in goose bumps. 'My first thought is that I already know your answer to *my* question.'

Agnès's eyebrows rose, reforming the fine lines on her forehead into deeper creases. 'I'm waiting, Monsieur Le Commissaire.'

'Lord. Alright, I don't necessarily believe that there is a potential crime here but it's better to err on the side of caution, isn't it?'

'As a rule. What should we do practically?'

'Frankie can't work with Astrid to produce a likeness of Noëmi Two and have it circulated, obviously. Every time

Noëmi herself steps out, she's liable to be recognised as the impostor. Besides, on its own, it's too passive.'

'Quite. So?'

'We'd need to detail a squad of undercover watchdogs to patrol Place Wilson and environs. A squad commanded by the Invisible Man himself, Alain Terrevaste from Foch.'

'Agreed – Tee-Vee would be ideal. How big a squad for a covert operation like that?'

'As big as staffing rotas and the budget allow. Five? More, ideally, some walking through, some installed in spots commanding views of the scene.'

'And for how long should this undercover operation go on?'

'As long as it takes? Bit of a fudge there but, again, I guess staffing and budget are key.' The goose bumps returned with a vengeance. 'Agnès, this role play. You're not testing the water, are you? About me, I mean.'

'I don't think I follow you.'

'You don't?' He gave her a look. 'Agnès, you may remember that we Daracs descend from a long line of sheep farmers.'

'From Creuse way back, as I recall. So?'

'So I know when the wool is being pulled over my eyes. You follow everything. Always.'

'If that is the case, it's something we share, isn't it?'

'Thank you, but if you're looking at the possibility that I, of all people, might make a reasonable stab at succeeding you, of all people, as the next commissaire of our beloved Brigade, I have to declare I wouldn't. I would be worse than useless.'

'As acting commissaire, you've stood in for me on numerous occasions. And made a good job of it.'

'Thank you but the keyword there is "acting". Yes? It's not the same at all as doing the job full time.'

'Paul, have I ever lied to you? And don't answer glibly. Think about it.'

'Alright.' He ran a hand into his hair and kept it there. 'I… don't know.'

'Correct answer,' she said, producing an enigmatic smile that would have given the Mona Lisa a run for her money. 'Right, I'm away to set up that watch on the Tardellis home patch.' She turned on her heel and, disappearing behind Mont Papier, called out. 'Let Armani know, will you?'

'Yes,' he replied, so in a daze, his voice scarcely reached the lower slopes of the mountain. *Commissaire Darac?* No. It was an idiotic concept. Well, perhaps not *idiotic*. But it was plain wrong. And Agnès knew that. Surely. Didn't she?

EIGHTEEN

'At last you answer,' Cassie said, thinking aloud. Dangerous. 'At last you ring, Carmen. What do you want?'

She breathed again. The signal was threadbare. Perhaps he hadn't heard.

'I've got something to report.'

'Important?'

'I think so.'

'You *think* so? I told you never to ring unless it *was* important.'

'It's Dédé.'

'No names!'

'Sorry but she didn't make our rendezvous yesterday.'

'I know and you should've rung *yesterday* to report it. Do not deviate from the plan. Ever again. Hear me?'

'Yes.' If Cassie hadn't been so scared of her boss, she would have laughed. If what they were doing qualified as a plan, it was the foolhardiest ever devised. But it wasn't only exasperation at the chance of it succeeding that distressed her. It made her sick to her stomach to think of what it involved. If only she were in a position to extricate herself, she would. But how? The odds on that were longer still.

'When will she—?'

'Not for a while. She's taking a break.'

'Taking a break?' How had she managed to pull *that* off? 'What does that mean for me?'

'I'll tell you at the place. Usual time.'

'Don't forget—'

He rang off.

'… To go fuck yourself.'

As the light began to go down on Place Garibaldi, Cassie

abandoned her post and walked slowly away. She knew Dédé was renting a first-floor studio flat somewhere on the quayside at Port Lympia. She'd whispered something about steps. Perhaps she ought to try and see if she was there. It was risky, though. The pair had never been allowed to meet outside the job. If he caught her, Cassie would regret it, she knew. But somehow, Dédé had got herself a break. It might be worth the risk to find out how. Yes. Cassie was going to see her. First thing tomorrow. Before the Briefing.

NINETEEN

At Maison Laborde, Gilles's and Zoë's three surviving parents had been first to arrive and by late afternoon, the house was either buzzing with family (Zoë's perspective) or crawling with them (Gilles's take). The man's social skills were such that, Inès aside, no one would have guessed they weren't truly welcome. If necessary, it was a performance he could have kept up all day.

'Maman, you look gorgeous.'

Zoë only half-guiltily showed off her dress. 'It's Chanel. Off the peg, of course, but still *wildly* expensive for me. I hardly know I'm wearing it. It *is* wonderful, isn't it?'

'It is but I meant *you* look gorgeous, not just what you're wearing.'

'I don't look like a cross-dressing construction worker in it?'

She didn't, Inès assessed, though if she had – so what? 'No!'

'Aah, darling. You mean that, I can see.'

Inès did indeed mean the compliment and it struck her that despite the many stresses incurred in planning such a party, now the day itself had arrived, her mother appeared more relaxed than she had seen her in years. Relaxed, happy and so obviously in love with her obviously fabulous husband.

'Look who's just arrived,' Fabulous said, sweeping past. 'I'll settle her in.'

'I'll come too.' Zoë turned to Inès. 'Better wait here a moment. Remember?'

Inès had never known the great aunt after whom she had been middle-named, but Odette, the sister who had survived her sibling by some 30 years and counting, had done her best to make up for the loss. Eclipsing her grandparents on both sides of the family, Great Aunt Odette had been Inès's favourite since childhood. A conventionally minded but kind-hearted soul, it seemed that Odette had latterly been given to voicing thoughts uncensored by the constraints of decorum, a development that endeared her to Inès all the more. Other developments, Zoë had warned, were less cheerful. While the robust eighty-nine year-old's long-term memory was as reliable and rich as ever, its everyday counterpart had become a pale shadow of its former self.

'Maman, she will recognise me?'

'I hope so.'

When the moment came, the outcome was not as either had anticipated.

'Inès!' the old lady said, setting down her champagne glass. 'Give your sister a kiss! It's been so long. How lovely to see you, darling!'

'No, Auntie,' Zoë said. 'This is *my* Inès, your great-niece.'

Perhaps it was out of habit, Inès reflected, that her mother checked Fabulous was not in earshot before using Inès's preferred forename.

'Of course!' Odette shook her head. 'I'm sorry, Inès. What was I thinking? Let me look at you, sweetheart.'

"Let me look at you, sweetheart." Accompanied by a beaming smile, Odette had greeted Inès with these words for as long as she could remember. As a child, she never once had to work at securing her great-aunt's love; it had been given freely and it pleased her to recognise that whatever dislocations were confusing the old lady's perceptions in the here and now, seeing her great-niece once more was still a happy moment for them both.

Quite unselfconsciously, Inès stood back, performed a pirouette and then curtsied. 'There. See? It's me.'

'Yes! But I'm not surprised I mistook you for her. Zoë, isn't she like your auntie?'

'In some ways.' Zoë smiled. 'Her eyes, definitely.'

'But my, what a fine bosom you have, darling.'

Inès grinned. 'Bless you.'

'My Inès was flat-chested, wasn't she, Zoë? Like two fried eggs! And so was our mother. And so, come to that, are—'

'Yes, that will do, I think,' Zoë said, her eye drawn to the kitchen, suddenly. 'Coming! Annette needs me.' Muttering "fried eggs", she took her leave.

Inès took her great-aunt's arm and for the first time since her father had met her at the airport, she wished Sue had come along, after all. 'Do you know what FaceTime is, Auntie?'

'Of course!'

'You do?'

'It's how long it takes to put your make-up on.'

'You adorable old thing. Let's go into the garden. I want you to meet someone who isn't actually here.'

'Oh, that would be nice.'

As the day wore on, the three principals experienced the party in different ways. For Gilles, things picked up considerably when friends and selected neighbours began to arrive and, with the day's two major set-pieces still to come, he began to enjoy himself thoroughly. Glass in hand, Zoë felt a sense of deep contentment as she circulated around the groups, sometimes like a bee gathering pollen, sometimes feeling as if she were scudding high above them on her own personal cloud nine. Inès had taken an existential position on Odette mistaking her for her long-dead sister on two further occasions, but when Gilles's former distance-running star Dr Muhammad Al Zeriya had arrived, Inès's existentialism failed to come to the rescue when the old lady cheerfully enquired: "Who's that handsome little darkie with your father?"

'My glorious great-aunt, I love you to bits but just so you know, the word you used beginning with D? Not acceptable.'

'What – darkie? It's better than—'

'Let's leave it there.'

Phase Four was due off at 6.30 and, never late on the start line, Muhammad wheeled in the anniversary cake with some ceremony. To a second round of applause, he then invited the happy couple to cut it into "32 exactly equal segments or risk a ban from the French Pâtisserie Association."

A voice rose from a thicket of cousins. 'But there are 31 of us.'

Inès half expected her father to suggest all was well since his daughter would happily volunteer to scoff two pieces. *I was joking!* But he refrained and it was soon time for Phase Five – the exchange of gifts.

'Have you all got a glass of something fizzy?' Gilles asked.

The feeling of the meeting was that everyone had.

'Excellent!'

Their gifts safely concealed, he and Zoë took up places with their backs to the open patio doors and as a breeze ruffled the bunting and bumped the balloons, the pair grinned at one another so charmingly, it brought tears to some. The exchange itself though, would have to wait. At the moment, dry or damp, all eyes were on Inès's own gift to her parents sitting beautifully wrapped on the antique *poseur* table set between them.

Zoë's voice faltered slightly as she read aloud the accompanying card, words Inès had intended for her parents only. The paper was peeled carefully away and the gem of the ceramicist's art that was a Moorcroft vase made Zoë gasp.

'It's beautiful, darling. Gorgeous! Is it English?'

'It is, yes.'

Zoë examined the base and recited the maker's name in such Gallicised tones, it made Inès smile.

'I'll treasure it, always. *We'll* treasure it.'

Inès blew her a kiss.

'If we had known, we would have ordered a few flowers to put in it,' Gilles quipped, drawing laughs. 'No, seriously, Jackie has always had an eye for beautiful things. Thank you, indeed, darling. And for your loving words.'

Great Aunt Odette's short-term memory may have been threadbare; her voice was not. 'Who's this Jackie?'

'And now,' Gilles said, moving swiftly on. 'Our turn. Ladies first.' He treated the audience to his best speech smile. 'Sorry if that offends anyone.'

A chorus countering the notion went up and as Inès sank into her shoes, Zoë handed over her gift, the last-minute substitute for the set of sports books she had originally bought.

'Just what I always wanted,' Gilles said, grinning as he opened it. 'An envelope!' It contained two enclosures. The first was a card written in Zoë's hand which he read to himself. 'No one's *that* wonderful a husband,' he declared drawing more laughs and earning a mock ticking-off from Zoë. The other was also a personal message, one written on paper headed *Gianluigi Vera,* Nice's premier tailor. Gilles appeared genuinely astonished as he began to read aloud : ' "*A Gianluigi Vera suit is not simply tailoring at its finest, it is a work of...*" '

A *Vera* suit, no less? Inès thought to herself. Maman has really... She recalled Sue's expression... *pushed the boat out.* Pushed it out big style.

'That is what I call a gift!' one of the cousins called out, and it was a view shared by most.

'I know you've always wanted a Vera suit,' Zoë said, just loud enough for Inès to hear as Gilles took his wife's hand. 'And because your measurements haven't changed a millimetre in the whole time we've been married, you can pick up the suit itself tomorrow. It's ready and waiting for you.'

Inès couldn't hear her father's response but it was clearly not the kind of easy one-liner he had been favouring all day. The way the couple embraced gave Inès an unfamiliar thought. Maybe he really does love her.

Someone bellowed *shhh!* and the room quietened. The moment for the inevitable Gilles speech had arrived.

'As you all know, indeed many of you were present at the time, Zoë and I married 30 years ago to the day. And because there's nothing more important to me than the promise of sharing the next 30 with the woman I loved then and love more now…' He turned to her. 'I thought this little trinket might mean something.'

Odette had a thought on the matter which struck a chord with many. 'I thought he'd go on a lot longer than that.'

And so it was against a backdrop of laughter as well as expressions of sentiment both heartfelt and mawkish that Gilles produced a small, be-ribboned, box-shaped item from his pocket. Before he handed it over, Zoë reached for her left wrist, Inès noticed. She had strained it recently, she knew. Untying the bow with one pull, Zoë was aglow with anticipation as she removed the paper, flipped open the box and there it was… A watch! The light in her eyes dimmed. Yes, it was a watch but it was not *the* watch. It was nothing like it. She turned it over. Where was the inscription – the poet's reflection on the world and time and their life together?

'Make sure your glasses are brimming, everyone!' As the partygoers did the needful, Gilles turned anxiously to Zoë. 'Do you like it?'

'Yes, yes.' She essayed a smile as he hugged her. 'It looks expensive. All these dials and so on.'

'You've mentioned needing to get fitter. This gizmo has numerous functions that will help. And that will help safeguard our future together, darling.'

'Yes. I see.'

He'd changed his mind about the gift, she realised. As she herself had. Yes, the watch she had found in his kitbag was far prettier and while its inscription was doubly meaningful, this one went beyond *meaning*, addressing issues practically that were only reflected upon in the other. What with her degrees in computer science and her years of hands-on experience, she was usually all for such an approach. So – as with her gift to Gilles – the replacement was actually superior to the original, wasn't it?

'I… love it,' she said.

'I'm so glad. I wasn't quite sure if it was the right thing.'

Gilles poured champagne for them both and, in the absence of their best man from 30 years ago, he asked Inès to lead the toasts.

'Jackie? Would you?'

'Oh, I think our beloved Odette should have that honour. Auntie?'

'What?'

Laughter.

Inès whispered a few words in her ear and she nodded.

'That's right. To the happy couple! Zoë and… her husband. The happy couple!'

With the toast safely, if uniquely, negotiated, Gilles Laborde ticked off another box in his head and the party rumbled on. From Phase One – Meet and Greet – the party had been a resounding success, he thought. Now, only one set piece remained, and *that*, he knew, would be the greatest success of all.

TWENTY

Beyond the door, the muffled thuds of a high b.p.m dance track were as nothing compared to Julien Baille's own pulse rate. But that detail alone didn't concern him. In his burgeoning career as an athlete, he had learned that the more important the event, the harder it was to calm his nerves beforehand. On a mission to secure the greatest prize of all, it was hardly surprising he was so wound up. Shaking out his muscles, he took several deep breaths and rang the bell.

Borne on the flood tide that was Donna Summer's 'I Feel Love', Dilip Padar was still moving to the music as he opened the door. The feeling didn't last.

'You bastard! You show up at my apartment? This is not your party.' He moved to close the door. 'Fuck off!'

Julien surprised him, and himself, by shoving the door so hard, Dilip was left grasping at thin air.

'I know this is not my or Samira's party, Monsieur Padar. I'm going there immediately after I tell you that if you threaten her again...' He darted glances in both directions along the corridor – still empty – and then in a quiet voice, said: 'I will kill you. Do you understand? I will kill you.'

Dilip was a good 25 kilos heavier than Julien but nothing softened the sinews quicker than laughter and as he threw back his head, he took a kick in the crotch which dropped him to his knees.

'Now you can close the door,' Julien said, turning on his heel.

'You don't know,' Dilip moaned, clutching his groin. 'You don't know who you're dealing with! *You* will die!' he screamed down the corridor, the commotion opening a couple of neighbours' doors. *You*! Do you hear me? I'll see to it! *You* will die!'

Hips swinging in time with Donna's love, a woman emerged from the party. 'Dilip!' She bent to tend him. 'What happened?'

Heads appeared along the corridor. Mugging fear, Julien caught their eyes as he hurried past.

'You're dead, Baille! Hear me? Dead!'

It wasn't until no one could see him that Julien finally cracked a smile.

TWENTY-ONE

There was no sign of Donna Summer at Maison Laborde but Françoise Hardy was casting a spell in its way every bit as potent.

'Cut the music, Jackie,' Gilles said, glancing at his watch as he finished a slow dance with Zoë. 'It's almost time.'

No clarification was needed. The link to the announcement party at the Department of Letters and Human Sciences building had already been set up and routed to the lounge TV.

'Everyone got a drink?' Gilles asked, brandishing a fizzing champagne flute. 'Gather round, gather round.'

Inès had never seen her father wielding such an assortment of glasses as he had today. It was a subterfuge, of course. On several occasions, she had seen him take a couple of small sips then surreptitiously jettison the rest.

Several cousins had maintained a different approach. One, a ruddy-faced man wearing a natty shirt and cravat combo, invited Inès into his boozy orbit with a discreet gesture and a loud 'Psst!'

She joined him. 'Michel?'

'Jackie, Jackie – listen. Supposing, right? Supposing Gilles's progétées, No! Pro-té-gées – that's it – didn't get picked for France? Eh? Could happen. Be a damp uh… thing, wouldn't it?'

'No need to worry,' she said, backing away. 'You'll see.'

The announcement itself had been leaked several hours before and there had been no unfortunate surprises. Her glass refilled, Zoë nestled against Gilles' chest and both were beaming at the TV as it fizzed into life. On the screen, Captain Emil Arcot had already assembled the team around him, each member wearing their celebration T-shirt and raising a glass in mute expectation. Faces lit up at the moment of connection and as toasts were made and cheers went up and died away, a slightly out of synch exchange of congratulations and thanks began.

It was then Zoë saw something that made her look harder. It couldn't be…

But it was. Her blood ran cold and with it, the cocoon of warmth and happiness and promise and hope in which she had wrapped herself during the past 24 hours froze around her.

In the bedroom later, Gilles begged off fulfilling the commission Zoë had encouraged him to accept that morning.

'I'm sorry, my darling,' he said, en route to the shower. 'I've had far too much to drink. Not used to it. Another time, eh?'

She was going to claim a headache as an excuse but his reneging on the agreement obviated the lie. She closed her eyes, feigning sleep. But she could still see it clearly; the gift she had assumed had been intended for her; the token of love that bore their special inscription, a sexual *carpe diem*; the gift adorning the wrist of another woman right there in plain sight on the screen.

Questions began to pile in: almost clichés of the situation in which she now found herself. She felt their barb and sting, nevertheless. It was clear how the lovers had met. But how did they fit having sex into Gilles's full-on work schedule? There had been world enough and time for that, it seemed. Where did they go to do it? How long had it been going on? Had there been others before her? Would it be better or worse if there had?

Hearing Gilles step into the shower, Zoë opened her eyes but found no respite from her dark thoughts. It occurred to her that if this were a scene from one of those Technicolor Hollywood melodramas she used to enjoy watching with her grandmother, the camera would have dollied slowly in to her dressing table until the gift she *had* been given filled the frame; the watch that was less a timepiece than a performance-recording and target-setting device; a symbol of her failure to keep properly fit; a lifestyle *mea culpa*. But this wasn't a movie and the so-called gift had been left downstairs.

The key question for Zoë was what to do about the situation. She could have it out with him there and then but with Inès, yes *Inès*, Gilles, you arsehole, in the adjoining bedroom, it would not be a good idea. Tomorrow was a normal workday. He would leave early and wouldn't be home until after the training session he was leading in the evening. Inès was returning to Cambridge on Friday. That would be the obvious time. If, that was, Zoë could wait that long. And a bigger doubt: if she could muster the courage.

Monday, March 17

TWENTY-TWO

Joining her mother for breakfast in the garden was one of Inès's favourite things about being back home, especially as it was always just the two of them. Her father made a point of being up and running at his desk by 7.30 every morning, an example his loyal PA Monique followed unquestioningly. This morning, he had left a note by the juicer. Would Zoë be a darling and pick up his new suit from Gianluigi Vera? *Ciao, bella.*

It was a blazing morning and both women were wearing shades, a double boon to Zoë who was turning in quite a performance as the contented wife when in her heart and mind she felt betrayed, ridiculed, lost.

'There are more peaches, darling.'

'Could but shouldn't, Maman.'

'Are you sure?'

'They are wonderful but two for breakfast is quite enough.' Feeling the breeze freshen a little, Inès turned to the Alpes Maritimes, a bulky-shouldered massif flattened into overlapping planes by the low morning sun. 'Architecturally, Cambridge is of course glorious. On the whole, anyway. And the way the river winds its way through the heart of the city *is* beautiful.'

'Between the colleges and so on. Yes, it's lovely.'

'And not just for us college types. There are acres of green space in the city accessible to the public. There are some particularly wonderful avenues of trees. All quite special.'

'I didn't realise. There wasn't really time when we… for your ceremony.'

'But the landscape beyond?' She swept a hand across the

panorama. 'It's not this, put it that way. *This*, I love.'

'I'm glad,' Zoë said, her words flat as Inès's forsaken fens. 'I never tire of it.'

'I'll tell you what *I* tired of by the end of last evening.' Shaking her head but smiling despite herself, Inès turned back to Zoë. 'My beloved Great Aunt Odette. She is fabulous but her position on any number of things is so way off...' It was only then that Inès caught the mood her mother was trying so hard to conceal. 'Something is the matter, Maman.'

'No, no.'

'Yes, *yes*. Tell me.'

'It's just... you know, the party. The build-up went on for so long and now it's...'

Inès reached for Zoë's hand. 'You're not wearing your new watch.'

Tears came and when Zoë took off her shades, Inès could see just how exhausted she was. As tears gave way to sobs, Inès rose and took Zoë in her arms, daughter cradling mother, a reverse Madonna and Child moment that moved them both. Nothing was said until the outpouring was over.

'Maman, there's clearly more to this than post-party comedown and a sleepless night. For God's sake, what's wrong?'

'I wasn't... I wasn't going to say anything.'

From the beginning, Inès had prepared herself for an emotional scene with her mother but this was not how it was meant to begin. 'Whatever it is,' she said, 'we're going to discuss it.' From Madonna to confidante, Inès drew her chair alongside. 'Fully. Alright?'

'Alright.'

As she told the story of her evening, Zoë stared at the tablecloth in front of her, drawing an index finger backwards and forwards between the squares of its gingham pattern like a blind person struggling to read a line of Braille. At the conclusion of her account, there were more tears at first but talking things through with her seething but sharply focussed daughter helped provide a different perspective. And as their conversation drew to a close, that perspective opened up new directions, possibilities that Zoë hadn't previously considered. A plan of action, sketchy but a plan nevertheless, was put together. Or that was how it seemed to Inès.

'I'm so glad you came.'

'Hey, what are genius daughters for?' Inès squeezed her mother's hand. 'You know I have to be back in Cambridge on Friday. And not just because of the ticket hassles it would involve if I wasn't.'

'Of course. It's ironic, you know. I've been aware for quite some time that things haven't been right between Gilles and me. Yet, I still couldn't quite believe what has happened. I feel so much more positive about it now. Thank you, darling.'

'I'm so glad.' With all the drama of the past hour, Inès had put one of the principal reasons for her trip so far to the back of her mind, she had all but forgotten it. But it came to her now. Should she? In a way, it was the perfect time and she no longer cared what her father's reaction to the news would be.

'Maman, there's something I need to tell you.'

TWENTY-THREE

A pair of folders under his arm, Granot sidled huffily into Darac's office, plonked himself down and stared meaningfully at the espresso machine.

'Need I say more?'

Darac set his Gaggia to work. 'Two doubles coming up.'

'I should never have lost all that weight, you know.'

'You had to lose it. If you hadn't, it would have been bye-bye Brigade. It might even have been bye-bye life.' He left unsaid that as successful as it had been, Granot's enforced weight loss programme hadn't exactly reduced him to a sylph.

Granot raised a conceding hand. 'Yes, you are right. At the start, it was essential.'

'But now?'

'It's Odile. Ever since I slimmed down, she's gone all… Bio Nazi on me. Look at my breakfasts these days. Croissants? Forget it. Pains au chocolat? Forget it.' A very dark place now. 'Have you ever heard of…?' Granot's moustachioed chops drooped disdainfully.

'… Muesli?'

'Measly?'

'Myooosli.'

'Ah, muesli – yes. I think I may have.'

'It's like eating sawdust. And try getting a decent coffee at my place in the morning.'

Darac knew that allowing Granot to air a grievance fully was the quickest way of exhausting it. Their espressos had been downed for some time before the moment came.

'Anyway,' the still big man said, fully recovered. 'Couple of things.' He opened the folder. 'The ruelle Moncet dumpster murder. No papers or other personal effects to ID the victim and his face is unrecognisable as a face let alone a particular individual's.' He passed over the file. 'I'll warn you now it's hideous. A sledgehammer, R.O thinks.' He winced at the thought. 'Worse still, additional work with a claw hammer on the eye sockets.'

Flattened violently, what had been a human face was a whorled mass of umbers, crimsons, ochres, purples and greens.

'Lord… If you'd said these were shots of an artist's palette after a long day in the studio, I wouldn't disbelieve you.' Having seen all he needed to, Darac was grateful to slip the photo back into the file. 'Who was on from Path? Not Barrau again?'

'No, Map, thankfully. He's specified the T.O.D as between 9 o'clock and 11 on Saturday night, the body dumped between 1 o'clock and 4 yesterday morning. Despite all the devastation to the head and neck, he determined the cause as a severed jugular. Butcher's type knife, unrecovered, blade about 25 cms long. The battering was all carried out post.'

'Clubbing a corpse?' Darac stared at the floor. 'It was an attempt to mask the ID of the victim, wasn't it?'

'It's the conclusion Bonbon and I came to.'

'Which suggests something about the killer.'

'No pro hoping to conceal the ID of a victim leaves him practically swimming in his own blood and gore, does he? It's a DNA treasure trove, practically. Swabs have already gone off for sequencing. Including some interesting thumbnail scrapings that could well be the perp's.'

'Let's hope there's a match on file. I suppose the killer might have known there wouldn't be one. But he would have had to have known the victim pretty well to be sure. Odds definitely favour a non-pro killer.'

'I was saving this for a big finish but we've got there sooner than I thought. We do have one potential steer on the victim's identity and it suggests the killer didn't know him well, or at least not intimately. Go on to the morgue shots.'

The steer proved to be a rapper-style name tattooed in stencilled lettering on the man's lower abdomen.

' "MC Ride Boy" huh?' Sometimes, it was the obvious question that no one thinks to ask. 'I take it someone checked the victim wasn't the man himself?'

As if honouring the question, Granot nodded thoughtfully. 'One of the brighter young ones came up with the idea eventually.'

Darac raised his hands palms outwards. 'Guilty as charged.'

'Of course we checked! He wasn't the man, for several reasons including the fact that he's on tour in the US as we speak. Has been for the past three weeks. Credit where it's due – showing good initiative, Perand contacted Ride Boy's manager to enquire if any members of his entourage were unaccounted for, or had failed to make the trip, and so on. No one had but he wasn't finished yet.'

Darac's habitual expression, a sort of quizzical amusement, morphed into a moue of surprised appreciation. 'And?'

'He asked the manager if he would release the email addresses of all his client's followers on social media. He couldn't, of course, but then he discovered young Monsieur Ride writes a squad-blog, the terms and conditions of which state that all who join agree to share their details. How did he put it? Something like: "Apart, you're just subscribers. Together, we're all homies." '

Darac's expression morphed once more, this time into one of astonishment. 'Mate, not for the first time, I think the real Granot has been abducted and replaced by a poorly briefed replica. Squad-blog? Homies?'

'You jazzers are *so* yesterday with your "hep cats" and your… other sayings like that. If you have to get down with the bros, you've got to learn the lingo.'

Darac grinned. 'And who did *you* learn it from – Perand?'

'Bullseye. Anyway, the manager surprisingly agreed to his suggestion and has already emailed the list. He thought "The Ride", as he calls him might be inspired to write a new song about "this murder thing". If song is the word.'

'That sounds like the morals of your average manager in the music business. You've trusted Perand to check the list?'

'Good Lord, no. Bonbon and Adèle from Archive are doing it. It's a few thousand names but it's an easy check in itself.'

'And if the victim *wasn't* a member of said rapper's fan club?'

'We've got a couple of uniforms pounding pavements in Villefranche and Flak is combing tattoo parlours both there and here in the city. It seems "The Ride" is a popular performer, as is the design of the tattoo honouring him, unfortunately. But its position on the victim's body might just jog the memory of whoever did it. If it was done locally, that is.'

'No properties directly overlook ruelle Moncet and there's no CCTV in the vicinity, I gather?'

'None. We've got Lartou's lot looking at footage from further afield but unless the perp was dragging the body in an open tumbril along Avenue Albert, he isn't optimistic.'

'Not for the first time. So the DNA result looks like our best hope with this one.'

'Agreed.'

Darac closed the file and handed it back.

'I've just seen Armani,' Granot said, taking it. 'He recounted Frankie's Noëmi look-alike story. Agnès's surveillance team haven't come up with anything as yet.'

'Good. What do you think about this operation, Granot? Sensible? A bit over the top?'

Granot shook his grizzled chops. 'No brainer. The former.

Although Armani himself favours the latter, he did tell me he'd already asked several shopkeepers and so on that he's matey with in the Place to keep an eye open – which is just about all of them, of course.'

'That's Armani, alright,' Darac said, smiling, but then the goose bumps from his earlier conversation with Agnès made a comeback. 'Out of interest, how many watchdogs did Agnès put on in the end?'

'Three. Alain Terrevaste on the street; two posing as *Télécom* engineers, one of them up a pole.'

'Only three?' Darac let out a long breath. 'Sounds as if I flunked the exam, then.'

'What?'

'Oh, nothing. The second thing you had?'

Granot turned to a file bearing the name of one Denise Ernestine Dubreuil.

As the officer nominally in charge of the case, Darac was au fait with all current developments. Or thought he was. 'Something new in?'

'No, we had it from the start but I've only been able to look at it in detail just now.' Granot produced a coverless pocket-sized notebook that Lartigue had logged in at the scene. Tucked inside its mangled pages was a till receipt. He held it up. 'At 11.48 on Friday morning, Mademoiselle Dubreuil checked out of some shop or other – can't tell which one, the top of the receipt is torn off – having bought two tins of Portuguese sardines, a half-baguette, a jar of strawberry conserve, and a four-pack of cola. All mainstream brands. Could have come from anywhere.'

'For what it's worth, I saw just such a four-pack in her fridge on Saturday evening. Minus one can.'

'Right.' Granot handed over the notebook. 'It's all shopping lists. Only the jam and cola were on Friday's list. There's no reminder for the half-baguette on that or any previous day because she presumably bought one every morning. The sardines must have been an impulse buy. But the main interest is in what she wrote *under* the list. The pen she was using was on its last legs but you can make it out.'

Joining up the intermittent script, Darac read: *SM with MT? No.*

'MT? Suggests Maurice Thomas, obviously. Who's this SM, I wonder?'

'Thomas reports that the man calling himself Ploine did have a "friend" who visited him on a few occasions. He refuses to believe the young man had any connection with the drug dealing Ploine, it turns out, was involved with. But considering Thomas said he had no suspicions about Ploine himself, what faith we can have in his assurances about said friend?'

'None, I would say.'

'Indeed.' Granot referred to his notes. 'Ah yes, Thomas heard Ploine use the friend's name once or twice, he said. For what it's worth, it was Ludo.'

'Ludo? No S or M there. But as you imply, when we're dealing with aliases…' He shrugged. 'Another question is what did the note Denise made actually mean?'

'Just hold you there a moment. SM could be Ploine's true initials.'

Darac's brows lowered. 'If so, it's interesting that Denise knew Ploine's real name when their landlord didn't – if Thomas was telling the truth about that. If SM *is* Ploine, why would his being with or *not* with Thomas matter enough for Denise to make a note about it? And on a shopping list, of all things?' He looked back through the notebook. 'As you say, that's all she used it for.'

'There's another curious thing. My Odile tends to put the date on her shopping lists. Makes sense – a lot of people do, I imagine. But I've never known anyone…' He pointed to the top of the page. '… do *that*.'

Under the date and in the same erratic hand, Mademoiselle Dubreuil had written: 11.25.

'The time she went into the shop? It does fit with the check-out time on the receipt.' Darac stared at the floor. 'But why note the time at all?'

'Absolutely.'

'Whatever it means,' Darac said, 'We need another chat with Monsieur Thomas. And we need Astrid's services again.'

'Ludo?'

'Ludo.'

TWENTY-FOUR

The minute Cassie saw the tape cordoning off the steps, she suspected the worst. But she had to know for certain.

'What's all that about, then?' she asked a man waiting for his dog to relieve itself on the quayside. 'Something happened?'

'Woman got herself killed,' he said, angling his head towards the first floor of the building. 'Lived up there, I think.'

A shiver ran down Cassie's spine and for a moment the pavement felt like sponge under her feet. 'Oh dear. Do you know what—'

'Don't know nothing about it but I suppose she was one of the usual sort.'

'I suppose. Anyway, good morning.'

Her stomach in knots, Cassie walked away. "Taking a break" the bastard had called it. A break! What had Dédé done? Tried to run away? Questioned an order? No, she had probably just ceased to be of use to the operation, hadn't she? She had served her purpose so that was the end of her.

Even though Cassie knew she was far more valuable to him than Dédé had been, she realised as never before just how very careful she was going to have to be. No more talking out of turn. No thinking aloud. She glanced at her watch. He wouldn't tolerate lateness but Cassie would be on time for the morning briefing if she hurried. And boy, was she ever going to hurry now.

TWENTY-FIVE

Julien Baille's love for the English Metaphysical Poets he had first encountered at undergraduate level had only grown since concentrating exclusively on the work of John Donne and Andrew Marvell in his postgraduate studies. He had been lucky indeed to have been tutored and now supervised by one of the country's leading experts in the field, a woman every bit as important to his academic development as Gilles Laborde was to his burgeoning athletics career. The latter, though, would typically peak and then peter out within ten years. Three Olympic Games at best. The former would go on developing into late maturity. He intended to rise to the top in both arenas.

The latest chapter in his thesis well ahead of schedule, Julien was going through what was his fifth set of stretches for the day, a necessary counter to the hours spent sitting still at his desk. Legs wide, he was sitting with his torso flat to the floor when the doorbell rang. He ignored it. Accompanied by a gentle couple of knocks, the bell rang again. Curbing an urge to shout "Go away!" it made his heart quicken to realise that against the odds, his visitor might be Samira. He certainly hadn't given up on her and after laying down the law to the miserable excuse for a human being that was her brother, Julien believed he could only have improved his chances.

He sprang to his feet, padded barefoot to the door and checked the spyhole.

Shit. A man. Far Eastern ethnicity. Thick-set running to fat. Battered face. Dead eyes. Julien's heart quickened once more. The man ducked down, his face out of sight. After a long moment, the leading edge of a postcard bearing an image of the Hotel Negresco's pink cupola appeared at the foot of the door and the man reappeared at the spyhole, looking down. Realising the visitor wanted Julien to give his presence away, he left the postcard where it was. After a longer moment, the whole thing shot through. Julien kept his eyes on the man as he turned and headed away.

On the reverse of the card, clumsily-formed but legible capitals read:

LITTLE BOYS SHOULDN'T KICK THINGS. THEY MIGHT BREAK THEIR LEGS.

JUST FOR STARTERS.

Julien's blood ran cold but he didn't panic. Yes, he had been threatened but he was as certain as he could be that the message was aimed solely at scaring him. But this encounter, complete with its fingerprint-bearing calling card was going to backfire on Dilip and his pal. After tonight's team training session at Stade Walter Vallain, there would be ample time to seek law student Samira's opinion on what to do about the postcard. And that too, Julien resolved, would be just for starters.

TWENTY-SIX

With the last of Darac's paperwork logjam cleared, he was free to lead Granot and Bonbon's second Caserne interview with Monsieur Maurice Thomas, although to him, they referred to it as a chat which would be neither filmed nor recorded. They failed to mention that this assurance would only be honoured if he continued to convince them he had nothing to hide.

Opting for the comparative informality of Darac's office rather than the interview room, the trio positioned themselves in a tried and tested formation: the captain himself perched on the front edge of his desk, his two trusted lieutenants sitting apart door-side of the interviewee.

'Thanks for coming in again, Monsieur,' Darac said, motioning Thomas into a chair by a radiator to which many a suspect under questioning had been handcuffed over the years. No need for such draconian tactics today: conviviality was the name of the game. 'Our paths didn't really cross at your place but I'm Captain Paul Darac, and I'm in charge of the investigation. Not that you would convince these two of that.'

Bonbon caught Thomas's eye and winked. 'Best go along with him, Maurice.'

Already relaxing, Thomas grinned. 'You're a caution, you are, mate.'

'That'll come later.' Bonbon grinned. 'Just kidding.' He indicated the cooler. 'Some water?'

'Yes please.'

'Watch the cup. They make them out of recycled fluff or something and they're liable to spill.'

'Same with everything these days.' His face contorting,

Thomas produced a damp-looking handkerchief but the urge to sneeze disappeared and he returned it to his jacket. 'Sorry about my nose, by the way. I haven't got a cold. Allergies. Prone to them.'

As Bonbon did the needful at the cooler, Darac took the opportunity to study the mien and body language of Maurice Thomas, the man Denise Dubreuil may have referred to on her shopping list as MT, the person apparently denied union with one SM.

While Darac knew that pure physiognomy gave little clue as to a person's character and none whatsoever where likely culpability for a crime was concerned, he couldn't help employing a sort of reverse anthropomorphism to distinguish facial and corporal types. His closest colleagues were cases in point. With his tawny colouring, mischievously twinkling eyes and light, agile gait, Bonbon's physical mien was irresistibly fox-like. Granot conjured images of bewhiskered sea creatures, spectacular in water, cumbersome on dry land. And facially at least, their boss Agnès Dantier personified the adjective "feline". Round, timid-looking and prone to snuffling, Maurice Thomas put Darac in mind of nothing so much as a hedgehog. It remained to be seen if he would roll into a ball at the first signs of trouble but the way he talked gave no indication of any such frailty. A garrulous hedgehog? There was a first for everything.

'Bumped into one of my old tenants downstairs,' Thomas said, giving Bonbon a nod as he gingerly took the water cup. 'From a couple of years ago. Jacques Derain or Gerain... Lerain! Wasn't with me long. Nice chap. Talk the hind leg of a donkey, mind you. And nosey? They talk about women. Nothing on him, I'll tell you. Always asking about this and that.' He took a sip of water and winced. 'Ow, that tooth! Must get it sorted out.' He carefully set down the cup. 'Anyway, Lerain has just started working in the canteen here, he was telling me. Tall, rangy, fair-haired fellow. Freckly. Come across him?'

Darac shared a look with Granot. The description of "Lerain" fitted Jérome Quentin, the undercover narco officer Armani had sent in to Thomas's place in 2012 and come up empty. The canteen job story had been quick thinking on Quentin's part and Darac made a mental note to pass that on to Armani as and when.

'He works in the canteen?' Granot said, feigning disdain, 'Between us, we've barely set foot in the place since they contracted out the catering. No offence to your old tenant.'

Darac always felt a buzz when his band or his police team were on song. He felt that way now. 'So, Monsieur – are you bearing up?'

'I'm a cheerful chap by nature, Captain. Ask anyone down the quayside. But to be honest with you, hold it…' Another contortion; another false alarm. 'Sorry about that. Where was I? Yes – I'm devastated at what's happened. At the start of the week, there I was sailing along quite happily with my two tenants. Now I haven't got one.' He shook his head at the degree of his misfortune. 'And why? Because one of them murdered the other and then scarpered! By the look of it, anyway. I know it's what you're all thinking.'

'Let's say it is a strong possibility. I'm sure you'll have gone over some of this before, but just for my benefit, let's start with Mademoiselle Dubreuil. What was your take on her?'

'She was the nervy type, God rest her soul. Not always very talkative but she was nice. No bother. She used to be an actress, you know? Fifteen years a landlord, I've been. Never had a theatrical in all that time and my mother before me, neither, so far as I know.'

'Did she have any regular visitors?'

Thomas shook his head. 'None, and I know what you're wondering. How did she earn a living? Well, I can tell you that whatever it was, I doubt it was *that*. But if it was, as I told your mates here, I wouldn't allow such a thing in my house.' He raised a finger and wagged it emphatically. 'Except on the day she died, as far as I know, she never had nobody in her room for any purpose whatsoever. Of course, I'm not in all the time and I'm not on the *qui vive* all the time I *am* in. But you heard how creaky them stairs are. You hear if someone goes up them. Prostitution? Quickest way to rack and ruin for the landlord. Well, that and...' A study in regret, he closed his eyes and took a deep breath. 'That and yes, turning a blind eye to drugs. I've always said if you allow them on the premises, the next thing, you're overrun with the bastards and you've had it. That's why I was so shocked to learn what had been going on with her and Ploine.'

'You mentioned that you found the mademoiselle nervy. It never occurred to you she might be a regular user?'

'It didn't. I swear. I suppose I thought "these theatricals," you know. They're all like that, aren't they? Highly strung.'

'On the day she was murdered, you heard someone mounting the stairs? Is that what alerted you?'

'No, I was out when he must've gone up. I only heard it on his way down *after* the row. Feet bang bang banging down, then slamming the door and he was off.'

'The row itself. The male voice was definitely Ploine's?'

'It sounded like it.'

'And you definitely didn't see who it was?'

'Nnnn-no.' Another contortion and it was third time lucky for the subsequent sneeze. 'Good – that'll be it for a while. Uh, yes, the footsteps. It seems obvious now that it was young Ploine, as he called himself, but I couldn't swear to it and that's the truth.' The hedgehog turned sheepish. 'Look, I know I fibbed at the start about why I'd gone up to Mademoiselle Dubreuil's apartment. I shouldn't have done that and I'm sorry. But all that shouting and me just sitting there, below?' He lowered his head. 'It only went on for about a minute but I was scared. I daren't go up until it had finished. Daren't.' He stared away. 'I was ashamed, if you want the truth. Ashamed I hadn't done anything to help her. Ashamed I didn't know what Ploine was, the bastard.' Another shake of the head. 'A drug dealer on the premises... My mother's turning in her grave, God rest her.'

Granot and Bonbon made sympathetic sounds and the interview continued.

'The man known as Gérard Ploine,' Darac said. 'The fact that he was a drug dealer using an alias tells us a great deal, obviously, but how did he strike you?'

'You get to know your tenants over time, I always say. To begin with, they all come across as pleasant, dependable, honest. Twelve months later, things can be very different.'

'Until yesterday, you hadn't known him long enough to have formed a truer opinion. Is that what you're saying?'

'He was never late with the rent or anything but as I say, they tend not to be any trouble at first. And now look what's happened. Skipped off owing two weeks, as well. Won't see that now, will I?'

'I see you've agreed to assist our sketch artist once more.' Astrid had already trawled the quayside bars on what was her second commission of the case. 'This time to depict a visitor you say called round for Ploine a few times.'

'Definitely. Anything to help.'

Darac glanced at the file. 'A tall, dark-complexioned, slim white male whom you heard Ploine call "Ludo." Nothing passed between them that you saw indicated anything suspicious?'

'No, Captain. They just seemed to be mates off out for a drink. Joshing about football, that sort of stuff. Seems Ploine was a PSG fan. Don't know who Ludo supported but he hated PSG.'

'Paris Saint-Germain,' Bonbon said, interpreting the sport-speak for Darac.

'Paris? I see.' Darac set down the file. 'Well, once again, you've been a great help, Monsieur.'

'Don't know if I have.'

'Oh, one last thing. You know someone with the initials SM, I believe. Or perhaps just know *of* them.'

Thomas looked blank, then wary, but for the moment, he eschewed rolling himself into a ball.

'SM, Monsieur? Didn't you meet him or her recently? Or were due to?'

'I can't think of anyone with those initials. What's this about?'

'Think again, mate,' Bonbon said. 'Last Friday morning, we're talking. More water?'

'No, no. Uh… SM?' He shook his head. 'I know an S*N*.'

Darac realised that if Denise Dubreuil had only heard Thomas or someone else say that he hadn't been with SN, she could easily have misheard it as SM. And she might have misheard it in a supermarket from which, according to her till receipt, she checked out at 11.48 on the day before she was murdered. In their earlier conversation, Darac and Granot had noted that Denise had written 11.25 next to the date on her shopping list, the implication being that it was the time she had entered the store but neither could fathom why she had bothered to do so. Now what ifs? began to collide and connect in Darac's head and he saw a possible purpose. It was a practice every police officer working on a case or journalist working on a story employed every day. She hadn't pointlessly *noted* the time, had she? She had *logged* it as a significant detail. Just as Narco officer Jérome Quentin had worked undercover at the Port Lympia house two years ago, perhaps Officer Denise Dubreuil had been watching Maurice Thomas – or MT – over the past weeks. The first problem officers faced when investigating an individual whom they hadn't realised was a fellow officer working undercover was that the more important the operation, the more watertight was the cover story. Darac had spoken to two people connected with the theatre company in which Denise had supposedly been employed years before. Both had said that they knew her and were able to identify her from recent-ish photos. But were they telling the truth? Who knew?' Darac made a second mental note: to ask Agnès to make a series of calls to the GIGN, DGSI and other elite units of the nation's security forces. It wouldn't have been the first time an operation had been undertaken without the knowledge or consent of a local force. If Thomas was worthy of such high-level attention, though, his garrulous hedgehog routine was one hell of a performance.

At the scene, path assistant Lami Toto had drawn their attention to the track marks on Denise's arms and although other factors appeared to corroborate it, this was not proof positive she was a user. In his role of Head of Narco, Armani's full undercover disguise included fake needle marks that appeared identical to the real thing. Until Barrau came through with his full post-mortem report, the team could not be certain whether she had used such drugs. And even if she had, class A drug-dependent cops were far from unknown.

But clean or not, if Denise Dubreuil had been some sort of undercover operative of the state, it was far more likely that the activities of a drug dealer carrying false papers would have been her focus. Darac had earlier wondered if SM might have been Ploine's true initials. What if MT didn't refer to Thomas at all? *They* could have been Ploine's initials.

Riffing on these ideas had taken no more than a couple of seconds and a number of further thoughts were already taking shape in Darac's head. But first things first.

'Going back to last Friday again, Monsieur. Did you go

shopping in the morning by any chance?'

'Friday, Friday... I did as it happened. There's quite a big *U* just around the corner from me. In Boulevard Stali...Stali... Wait for it...' Another sneeze. '... Grad.'

'What time would that be?'

'Ooh... Just after nine. I was getting low on bog rolls.'

Bonbon gave him a look. 'Best way when you think about it.'

Thomas chuckled. 'You should do stand-up, mate, I'm telling you.'

'You're sure about the time?'

'Yeah, it's when I usually go.'

It was still worth asking the question. 'You didn't happen to see Mademoiselle Dubreuil in the shop?'

'No. But that doesn't mean she wasn't there. Biggish shop, as I say.'

'Uh-huh. On to this person you know with the initials SN. Who would that be?'

'My niece. Well, step-niece. Step-niece in-law, to be accurate. Sometimes see her at L'Archet where I go about this.' He indicated his nose. 'She's a nurse there. Used to be just up the road at St Roch which was handy but she moved and I decided to move with her, as it were. L'Archet's further but it's a lot nicer.'

'And her name, Monsieur?'

'Oh, sorry. Suzanne. Suzanne Nairault. Lovely girl. Well, woman now.'

If Thomas's entire performance had been an act, it had come time for his audience to put in a performance of its own – pretending Suzanne was a stranger when she had played an important role in several cases for the Brigade. She had also been Darac's close friend and neighbour since he had moved into his Place Saint-Sépulcre apartment. He would trust Suzanne with his life; indeed, he already owed it to her. And further, he and Frankie trusted Suzanne to the extent that hers had been the first name to spring to mind as a back-up carer for Lily. Suzanne was on point in every conceivable way. If Thomas was not what he pretended to be, she would know. Wouldn't she?

'And did you have a clinic appointment at L'Archet on Friday at which you expected or hoped to see this Nurse Suzanne Nairault?'

'No. Next one's October. You still haven't told me what this is all about?"

Deciding they had gone as far as they could for the moment, Darac drew the interview to a close and the trio dispersed to make calls. First, Darac rang Agnès and asked her to contact what Frankie always referred to as "The Acronyms in Paris".

'Sorry to land this on you but you've got the clout and the contacts. They'll listen to you.'

'Whether they'll respond fully is another matter but either way, we'll get our answer.'

'How?'

'If it transpires Ms Dubreuil was indeed an undercover agent, they won't comment but will immediately take us off the case, tacitly confirming it. If she wasn't, they will probably tell me outright. I'll get back to you soonest, Paul.'

God, we're going to miss you, Agnès… Next, Darac tried Suzanne's number and he pictured the phone ringing in the apartment directly beneath his and Frankie's.

'Hello?'

'Good, you're off duty.'

'Paul, hi. I am until this evening, anyway. Am I free to have Lily, is that what you're after?'

'No, no.'

'Shame. Just in the mood for a cuddle.'

'I'll send Bonbon round.'

'That'll do.'

'Listen, I have a name to put to you. Maurice Thomas. Maurice Baudouin Thomas, to be exact. Ring any bells?'

'Nothing's happened to him?'

'To him, no. So he is known to you?'

'Since I was a kid, yes. Uncle Atchoo, we used to call him. I got my comeuppance for that later. I always seem to be on in S and S whenever he has an appointment.'

'S and S?'

'Snot and Spit.'

'Ah – he said he often sees you in clinics. I was hoping he'd made it up.'

'Why is old Uncle Atchoo on your radar?'

'Yesterday, one of his two tenants, a drug user, was murdered at the Port Lympia house; the probable culprit is the second tenant, a drug dealer using a fake ID who skipped immediately afterwards.'

'No-o. What a terrible thing to happen.'

'MT has a clean record but on the quiet, you've never suspected him of say, being a drug dealer's bagman?'

Suzanne's laugh was the sort people were apt to call "infectious" and Darac went down with a mild case even over the phone.

'So that's a no, I guess.'

'No flies on you, Paul.'

As the call ended, Darac reflected that if a typical murder investigation were written out as a musical score, the instruction *Da Capo* – go back to the beginning – would be the most frequently cited instruction to the player.

A couple of hours later, Agnès walked into Darac's office and, taking the chair drawn up next to his, set down a trio of files. 'Ooh, you do have a desk, after all.'

'Told you it would be cleared.' *Idiot!* 'Not that deskwork is my forte, of course. The streets. That's where I belong.'

'Paul, you're so transparent, I can see right through you.'

'That's another thing I'm terrible at.'

'Let's get on, shall we? First, I bring word from Paris.'

'The security agencies on Denise Dubreuil? That was quick.'

'Yes, wasn't it?' She handed over the printed-off replies. 'The first one in was from GIGN.' Darac speed-read it. 'They all say the same thing, Paul.'

Darac handed them back. 'Straight denial but we're still on the case? So, she wasn't working undercover. Or at least not for any recognised department of the State.'

'Next, Operation Place Wilson.' The file was thin. 'Happily, Terrevaste reports no suspicious activity whatsoever but it's early days.'

Darac's habitual half-smile widened a little. 'I hear I was well out on my estimate of the numbers required for the operation.'

'Not at all. You recommended deploying as many as budget and staffing levels allowed. That was precisely the principle I applied.'

'Oh.' Darac's face fell. 'Agnès, I can't tell you how touched and flattered I am at the faith you seem to have in me. But…'

'Faith has nothing to do with it. But in any case, if I were you, I wouldn't worry. For once, you appear to have overlooked a rather significant point. *I* shall not be appointing my successor. The Board will.'

'But a recommendation from you would carry enormous weight.'

'Enormous?' The idea amused her. 'I doubt it. They're strangers to me, most of them.' She gave his hand a squeeze. 'So just relax about it, Paul. Alright?'

He brightened a little. 'Does that mean…?'

'It means… relax. Let's continue.' She turned over the next

file. 'This is Barrau's PM report on Denise Dubreuil, just in.' She passed it over. 'Routed just to me. He should have copied you in too of course, the worm.'

'That's an insult to worms, I think.' Darac took the report and turned first to the cause of death entry. 'C.O.D is... as we thought. And the hyoid bone was broken as young Lami Toto suspected. He's a good lad, that. A lab assistant but he's worth ten of the dep chief pathologist. T.O.D estimate... Between 4.45 and 6.15 pm. That's quite a bit more focussed than Barrau eventually proffered at the scene. What else...? Ah – those track marks on Denise's arms were quite genuine. She *was* using.'

'Conclusion?'

'She was who she said she was. A row with a pusher using the alias Ploine appears to have led to her murder. What the cryptic note she made means, we have no idea and possibly never will.'

One of the desk phones rang.

'Darac? It's Map.'

'Good to hear from you. Agnès is with me and you're on speaker. Go ahead.'

'I'm emailing you a splay of photographs on the dumpster murder, some familiar, some new; and an updated dossier on the victim.'

'Updated already? Sounds promising.'

'The times of death and the dumping of the body remain the same as my initial estimate – respectively between 9 o'clock and 11 on Saturday evening, 1 o'clock and 4 the following morning. On the question of finding our prime suspect for the Denise Dubreuil murder, the white male using the alias, Ploine, we need look no further. We had him already. We just didn't know it.'

Darac and Agnès's shared a look. 'Ploine is the man in the dumpster?'

'There's no doubt about it. His true name was Hugo André Cragnat, age 31, born in Tours. Listen, I have to go but the material I'm sending is all you'll need to take things further.'

'Great work as always, Map.'

Darac rang off. 'So, the question now is whether Ploine, real name, what was it...?' He checked the scribbled note he'd made. 'Hugo André Cragnat, murdered Denise as we believed, was then *himself* murdered and his body dumped by person or persons unknown. Or whether Cragnat's murderer *also* murdered Denise. Thomas couldn't swear it was his raised voice he heard rowing with her, remember. Nor that it was his retreating back he glimpsed momentarily as he hurriedly made his exit.'

'That person might just prove to be Cragnat's chum, Ludo.'

'Indeed. So first, I'll update the whole team which will release Flak from her tattoo parlour crawl and then... what? Detail Perand to help her put Cragnat's bio together?'

Agnès nodded. 'At this stage, yes. Granot's already building up a head of steam on the search for Ludo and the news will supercharge his efforts all the more.'

'Yes, it will.' A thought struck him. 'We were speculating earlier that Denise's notebook entry "SM" might have been Cragnat's true initials. It seems they weren't.'

'Absolutely. And you're also wondering if MT might not refer to Maurice Thomas?'

'It might not but anyway, there's no indication of any wrongdoing on his part.'

'Unless, Paul,' Agnès said. 'He is a very clever man indeed.'

TWENTY-SEVEN

How many training sessions had Gilles Laborde led since his appointment as head coach to the university's athletics team? Thousands. But to each one, he brought the same energy and drive, ever-increasing knowledge, and a redoubled commitment to excellence. And it wasn't just on the technical side. His people management skills, he believed, were second to none. To perform at their best, some athletes required an occasional kick up the backside. Others responded to an arm around the shoulder. And to get the most out of some, you had to get into bed with them, metaphorically speaking. But with young women as beautiful as Samira Padar, there had been nothing metaphorical about it.

A stats man, Gilles had noted that Samira had been the 13th athlete under his care he had bedded. Ever since playing at centre three-quarter in his college rugby team, 13 had always been his lucky number. But attachment to the number had had nothing to do with his decision to leave the tally where it stood and not just for the foreseeable future. There would be no 14th young woman for him to bed because he knew he had found his ideal. It was true that Samira's athletic potential was not great. Training to be the best athlete she could be was all he asked of her, or of anyone. That was all he had ever asked of his own daughter but she had never understood it. Samira would never become a second Grace Nahili but in every other respect, she was unsurpassable, indeed perfect, and most importantly, she was his.

Zoë? He should never have gone with her in the first place. The marriage was a sham and she knew it. Look at how she had behaved once the anniversary party had reached its climax. Pathetic. Getting rid of her wouldn't be easy.

But it was going to happen. Quite simply, Zoë's days were numbered.

Gilles had predicted that the more gifted members of his squad would not overindulge at the announcement party and as the session had ended on a positive note for most of them, he had once again been proved right. If Gilles had allowed it, Julien Baille might even have run a PB for his event but wanton disregard of the meticulously prepared schedule for any athlete could not be tolerated. No one ever won a medal for peaking in training.

'What was Julien up to?' assistant coach Kevin Macdonald had asked Gilles as, casting weak shadows from the Stade's antique floodlights, the squad trooped off to the changing rooms at the end of the session. 'He was running like a kid with a wasp up his arse until you stepped in. What do you reckon? Gaining his international vest gone to his head?'

'He knows better,' Gilles said. 'I'll have a quiet word with him before our debrief.'

'Maybe calling him out in front of the others would work better. Temperamental bastard.'

'Mac, I'll have a word with him and that's an end to the matter.'

But the matter did not end there. Julien had ridden away into the night before Gilles got the chance to say anything at all. On any other occasion, a display of such wilful disrespect would have greatly angered him. Tonight, he barely registered it.

Gilles had arranged to meet Samira by her car. Most members of the squad preferred to take the team bus to and from the stadium's grandly named Players and Officials Only car park, a poorly lit and bumpy strip of overgrown wasteland laid out in the shape of a hockey stick. Some, though, opted to drive or ride themselves. Spaces at the top, handle-end of the stick were the favoured ones and not only because they were closest to the changing rooms. Those further out were darker and bumpier and furthest of all, the few spaces hidden among trees around the blade end of the stick were seldom used at night. Except, that was, by anyone wishing not to be seen.

Samira wound down her window.

'Sam, I've only got a second – I'm already late for the post-session with Mac and Franck but I've got something I must tell you.'

'That's a coincidence.'

'Even in this light, you look beautiful. And you didn't have a shower. You know how that turns me on... But that wasn't what I wanted to say. Aren't you going to get out of the car?'

'Actually, Coach Laborde, no. I'm not.'

Gilles's smile faded but he was not disheartened. This was some sort of game, wasn't it? The pair liked to play games. Especially in bed. He made a remark of the sort Alain Delon, Michel Piccoli or Jean-Paul Belmondo might have made in a movie. Cool. Hip. Sexy.

Samira relented, but she left her driver's door open as she joined him.

'I'm here because I agreed to meet you,' she said. 'I was going to wait a little but I may as well say it now. It was fun while it lasted, Gilles, but no more. It's over.'

'Yeah – right.' He aimed a hand at her groin. She took a pace back. '*Really* playing hard to get? Love it!'

'I'm not playing games. I mean it.'

'No, no. Come on, now.'

The minutes ticked by with Gilles continuing to cling to the belief that Samira was teasing or testing him, but as her message finally began to sink in, he began to sink into hopeless denial. 'But we're so good together.'

'Gilles – we were only "together" for a few weeks.'

'It was a whole month.'

'Was it? Well it was a whole month I deeply regret.'

He was stunned but words continued to come. 'Regret the sex? No, no. You can't pretend all that moaning meant you didn't love it.'

She shrugged. 'I enjoyed it. I did. But that's all.'

'And now…what? There's someone else? Someone better? Than me?"

'There might or might not be. But that's not your concern.'

'Our ages? Is that it?' His eyes bored into her. 'I know I'm thirty years older than you but…'

Samira had once before witnessed Laborde losing his temper. But she was not going to be cowed. 'But what?'

'Look, there's something you don't know. This is not just a fling for me. Our time together is… I've made up my mind.'

'Oh, you have?' She waggled her head. 'So have I.'

'But you… You don't know what plans I'm making.'

'Plans?' She made to get into her car. 'Save them for poor, poor Madame Zoë. Who in case you've forgotten, is the wife you so despise and laugh at behind her back. Samira glanced at her watch. 'I must go. And so must you or Franck and Mac will coming looking for you. And find you *here*. With *me,* right? You'll be blown, Coach Laborde. Blown!'

'Yes, yes, it's still too early for that – you're right.' He jumped back into his car. 'Look, we can't leave it like this. After you've driven out, wait for me around the corner, will you? In that spot I showed you, once. By the builders' yard. No one will see us there. I'll be no more than twenty minutes. *Be* there, Sam.'

As he hurried away to the session debrief with his assistants, Samira was already thinking beyond the next twenty minutes. She was thinking about her plans for the following morning.

TWENTY-EIGHT

For as long as he had been playing guitar, Darac had begun most days with his "morning detox" – jamming along with a favourite track or two, improvising all the way. Priorities had inevitably shifted with Lily's arrival but if one source of inspiration had become a little more difficult to tap into, another had come on stream and it was magical. Lily was going to grow up around music and both he and Frankie believed her life would be all the richer for it. Might the cot-side lullabies he was playing to her help engender a love of melody, harmony and rhythm? Perhaps; perhaps not. Of one thing, they were sure. Alongside the shared bedtime stories to come, papa's bedtime busking could only have reinforced Lily's sense of security and of being loved.

On this particular evening, Darac *père* had treated Darac *fille* to an arrangement of Grant Green's 'Idle Moments' so liltingly serene, he had been in danger of nodding off at the fingerboard half-way through the number. Had Frankie caught a few bars, she might well have followed suit but the Manzano case was keeping her at the Caserne and would continue to do so for some hours. At least the couple were off-duty tomorrow.

It was well past eleven when Darac's mobile groaned in his pocket. Bandleader Didier Musso began as if the conversation had been going on for some minutes.

'Still can't find those Mingus scores and I'd love to do the whole of *Black Saint* on tour.'

'Evening, Didi.'

'And to you. The Mingus scores?'

'What's the problem? It wouldn't take long to download

them for everyone. Besides, we've performed most of it before.'

'Yes, and that's when I made the extensive notes and revisions I want to go over tomorrow.'

'Ah.' Darac took a sip of his beer. 'We're a jazz group, I seem to recall. You know, making stuff up as we go along?'

'Exactly. I want to work through what we did before so I can cast it from my mind.'

It made a sort of sense. 'Can't you just… Never mind. I bet Luc has them.'

'It's not impossible. It being Mingus and all.'

Frankie appeared, set down her bag and, miming that she was going to look in on Lily, blew Darac a kiss en-route.

'Listen, Frankie's just home after a really challenging day. Call me in the morning, alright?'

'Roger. Or is it over and out?'

'Night, Didi.'

Tuesday, March 18th

TWENTY-NINE

Darac had never subscribed to the view that continual
exposure to beauty eventually bred indifference toward
it – indeed he felt quite the opposite – and as he turned by a
Colonne Morris on to the Promenade des Anglais's westbound
carriageway, the glitter-and-be-gay dance of light and colour
that was the Baie des Anges did its best to compensate for
losing his day off with Frankie and Lily. It was a reaction that
led him to reflect more deeply on how things had changed
for him over the past year. Leading a double life as a police
detective and a jazz musician, albeit a part-time one, had long
suited his instincts and temperament. But now he was a family
man too, would leading a triple life give him more satisfaction
still? Could such a way of living even be sustainable in the
long term? Might something have to give, eventually? And
what might that something be? Realistically, there was only
one candidate. All would become clear, he supposed.

With Bonbon in the passenger seat and young officer
Yvonne Flaco scrolling her laptop in the back, the trio had
been en-route to the city's *zone sportif* for a good five minutes
before the conversation turned to the matter in hand.

'Right, that's enough fun for one day, what do we know so
far, Bonbon?'

'O-K… At just after seven o'clock this morning, the Stade
Walter Vallain's night-security-cum-gateman, an old-timer by
the name of Eric Cauvin, found a body half-submerged face-
down in the track's water jump. It was definitely no accident.'

'A water jump on an athletics track?'

Flaco looked up from her screen. 'They use it in the 3,000
metres steeplechase, Captain. There are barriers on each lap

which the athletes hurdle but behind one of them is a pit filled with water that slopes up. The runners hop on to the barrier and jump off as far as they can so they land in the shallow end of the pit and then keep running. Some hardly break stride doing it.'

'Each to their own, Flak. Anything on the victim, Bonbon?'

'Not as yet. Understandably distressed at the discovery, night-man Eric was pretty incoherent on the phone, apparently. The stadium's just down the road from Commissariat Joinel and so under the command of one… Just a sec.' Bonbon consulted his phone. 'Sous-Brigadier Bernard Sorbissone, uniforms from there were dispatched to guard the scene and act… Oh-oh.' Bonbon's bad news face had been known to make hardened criminals weep. 'Act as crowd control.'

Darac shared the sentiment. 'Give me Foch's site-security-cum-crowd-control unit any day. But into every life and all that. Path there yet?'

'On their way and they'll probably beat us to it but no-one had turned up as of five minutes ago. Oh, and Agnès has dispatched a mobile incident truck to the site, as well.'

'With Joinel just up the road? Interesting. Flak, you're checking what?'

'Whether there were any events or matches at the Stade last evening. It seems there weren't but it's used for other things, too. Still looking.'

'Good work.'

'Here's one for you while we await news from the rear,' Bonbon said. 'Now you're a husband and father, you need to know these things. Including the Allianz Riviera, how many full-size football pitches do you reckon there are within the *zone sportif?*'

'You're asking *me* a sports question? I've just been telling Frankie how brilliant you are. I take it all back.'

Flaco's habitual scowl softened into a grin as she continued her search.

'A: what happened to Agnès's "No knowledge is valueless"?' And B: why were you discussing my brilliance with Frankie? Do B first.'

'It's March 18th.'

'Uh-huh?' Bonbon's elastic band of a mouth formed an upside-down U while he weighed the point. 'Thanks but I can't really take credit for that.'

'It's the first anniversary of your finest hour, you idiot.'

Bonbon still looked blank.

'The Saint-André poisoning case, Lieutenant?' Flaco said, ever respectful of a senior officer's rank. 'The plea change in court?'

'Ah, the Saint-André.' As if fondly recalling his part in what had been a hideous business, Bonbon's foxy features took on an extra twinkle. But he had a concerning sidebar to add. 'Flak – do you remember a couple of years ago, I cordially invited you to drop the stiff formality and just for once, call me Bonbon?'

'And I did, Lieutenant.'

'Just that once, yes.'

'With respect, that was all you asked for.'

'Well, and this is the last time I'm going to say this, anytime you feel like relaxing the rules permanently, feel free.'

'Thank you.'

'But back to my question. *Zone sportif.* Football pitches. Captain Sportphobe here has no idea. Flak?'

'Oh… Four. Five, maybe?'

'Try twelve. Twelve plus four rugby pitches.'

'It's just come to me,' Darac said. 'Twelve plus four rugby pitches. How's that?'

'Sufficient to earn a yellow card but I'll waive it – with an i – this time. Of those sixteen pitches, only two are surrounded by athletics tracks. One is the new, smallish but beautifully formed Stade Charles Ehrmann; the other is the really small, wood-wormy old wreck that is the…'

'Stade Walter Vallain?'

'Exactly. I've never actually been there but I gather it hasn't changed in years.'

'As someone once said, all will become clear. Especially to you, Bonbon. You always seem to be on fire at this time of year. Ask Saint-André poisoner Alain Daillier.'

On cue, palm-piercing shards of sunlight caught the spool of copper wire that was Bonbon's hair and appeared to ignite it.

'Too kind but just between the three of us, my part in it was sheer luck. It turned out Daillier was from Le Boulou near the Spanish border, 20 kilometres from where I grew up. A link, right? I just carried on adding others. As is well known, I sport a head of beautiful auburn hair…'

'Coveted by jobbing electricians everywhere,' Darac said.

'*Phht*! But I decided to refer to it to Daillier as ginger and, suspecting that, in combination with other factors, his out-and-out ginger locks may have made him a bit of an outcast as a child, I said that mine had, too. But that wasn't all we shared in the looks department. There's my skinny yet powerful physique…'

At that, the seriously powerful Flaco couldn't help emitting her signature laugh, an incongruous lawn sprinkler *tst-tst-tst*.

'Thank you, Flak,' Bonbon continued unabashed. 'The skinnier Daillier is a life-time supporter of Barca as is every right-thinking Catalan including myself. The list goes on, most of it from that point – such as our mothers sharing the same forename and a cousin working at his favourite pâtisserie *etc* – I fabricated for effect. In the end, I suspected the boundary between our separate identities had somehow blurred for him. Pathetic, really. In fact, if he hadn't murdered his wife, I might have felt sorry for the man. But he had and

I didn't.'

'You were brilliant, Bonbon. In fact, the whole team effort was exemplary. And that very much includes you, Flak.'

'Thank you.'

The radio buzzed.

'Charvet, Captain.'

'Go ahead.'

'Doctor Mpensa's team has just arrived at the scene. Patricia is already taping it off.'

'Excellent.'

'Finding the way into the Stade is straightforward enough but I take it you won't be familiar with the lay-out of the place once you're there?'

'You take it correctly.'

'Bonbon or Flak know it?'

The pair shook their heads.

'That's a no, Charvet, but even my old Peugeot has satnav. And we've got all the usual portables onboard.'

'The lay-out doesn't appear on satnav and although the satellite view on a mapping app shows the pitch and seating areas clearly, the various ways and paths around the site are not clear at all. Fortunately, I've known the place since childhood. I'll talk you through it.'

Darac shared a grin with Bonbon. Charvet didn't often get the opportunity to play *eminence grise* and although the pair suspected his info was going to prove entirely superfluous, raining on the man's parade was not an option. 'Local knowledge, Charvet? Hit it.'

'Saint-Augustin's first team used to play their home matches at the Walter Vallain and the first open-ish space you'll come to is what's left of the spectators' car park. The far end funnels down to railings, a couple of old-fashioned turnstiles and a wide gate behind which is a static caravan jacked up on bricks. If he's stopped vomiting, that's where you'll find night watchman Eric Cauvin who'll probably have been joined by his daytime counterpart by now. The turnstiles give access to the football pitch and the athletics track directly behind Eric's caravan. The gate opens on to an unmade track signed: PRIVATE: PLAYERS AND OFFICIALS ONLY and this is what can't make out on aerial photo. Once through the gate, you need to turn immediately sharp right. The track winds through a lot of greenery to the opposite end of the site where there are changing rooms and a second car park exclusively for the use of the above. That's where I directed Ops to earlier.'

'Excellent.'

'Oh, and I had a sneaky word with Patricia who'd had a quick glance at the corpse when they arrived. Don't quote her or me, Captain, but a blunt force injury to the back of the skull, it's looking like. Nasty blow with something heavy and not therefore caused by the football that was also found in the water. One last thing. It looked to Patricia that the body had been lying there all night. Nothing on the victim's age or gender as yet.'

'Thanks – that's all really useful, Charvet. Out.'

'Got something here, Captain,' Flaco said, settling on a new screen.

'Go for it.'

'The University's sports team schedules. Most use the pitches and various indoor facilities at *STAPS*, but both the football and athletics teams also use stadia for training – the new Charles Ehrmann, which the athletics team also use for competition, and the old Walter Vallain. That's where the athletics squad met last evening.'

'We'll need to talk to everyone who was there. Especially as Patricia reckons the body had been in the water jump all night.'

Bonbon nodded. 'With any luck, gateman Eric will have a list of attendees. FYI, there's some decent talent in that athletics squad at the moment. Two of them have just been selected for the French national team. I mean literally, within the last day or two.' Bonbon's tawny eyebrows went in search of his hairline. 'That's a coincidence, now I think.'

Darac waited for a conclusion but none came. 'Coincidence?'

'Yes. One of those selected is a steeplechase specialist. Julien Somebody. Future world beater, they reckon, a lad that in less aware times would have referred to as "The Great White Hope" in the national press.'

'A white boy called Julien beating the world in the steeplechase?' Flaco said, ever the straight talker but not usually tart with her mentors. 'A couple of hundred African boys would be interested to hear that.'

'Go, Flak!' Darac said, slowing for a red at the Gambetta intersection.

The young woman from Guadeloupe needed no second invitation. 'And is the national press really more aware than it was? Such terms as *Great White Hope* may have disappeared but the thinking behind them is right there in plain sight.'

'Fair point,' Bonbon conceded. '*Libé* excepted. Plus Charlie, and the other satirical mags.'

Darac didn't usually talk politics on the job but being held at the lights somehow encouraged him to push the topic further. 'If that thinking isn't exposed for what it is, the return of racist terms may only be the start. And it wouldn't be for the first time in our history, would it? If any more middle-ground minds are poisoned by the Far Right's lies, where will that leave us after the next election? French society could rupture irreparably. I fear it already has in some places.'

'Hear, hear,' Bonbon said. 'Le Pen and co are hugely dangerous. There's no doubt about it.'

In what was for her an unprecedented display of intimacy, Flaco reached forward and just for the briefest moment, gripped Darac's and Bonbon's shoulders. In both senses touched, the pair opted for words of solidarity rather than the usual throwaway quips. The lights changed, the conversation returned to the case. 'These training sessions, Flak,' Darac said. 'Got anything else on them?'

'Yes... It states that all sessions are led by the head coach, one Gilles Laborde.' She looked up, meeting Darac's eyes in his mirror. 'His work number's here.'

'Good – should gateman Eric not have a list of attendees, this Laborde will. And that will be useful even if the victim turns out to have no connection with the team or the university. He won't be at work yet though, will he?'

'Laborde? I'll bet you anything he is,' Bonbon said. 'The man's as driven as they come.'

THIRTY

This was the third time that Cassie had had to go through the morning briefing without Dédé. She missed her. Not that they had been allowed to sit together, and with their arrival and departure times staggered, they had never had the opportunity to establish any real rapport. Handovers on the street had been the only time they had managed to exchange a few words. But even then, they had to rely on Dédé's rare ability to whisper things to her partner – her partner in crime as they had become – without moving her lips. He was watching. They knew he was. He who saw and heard everything. And now she was dead.

'Where was Chantal Darac born?'

Here we go... 'Uh... Agen.'

'Speed up. What was her maiden name?'

'Chantal Lantosque.'

'What are her daughters called?'

Dédé was usually asked the Chantal daughter questions. Cassie began to sweat. 'Sophie and...

'Come on!'

'Jeanne. No, Jeannine.'

'Ages?'

'Sophie is 33. Jeannine 31.'

'Work?'

'Sophie is an editor in a publishing house.'

'Which one?'

'Éditions... Gallimard.'

'Where?'

'Paris.'

'Jeannine?'

'She...' What the hell does she do? It's financial. Lucky

cow. 'She's an investment analyst for a bank – a private one.'

'Which?'

'Darsey.'

'In Paris?'

'No.'

'Where?'

'Strasbourg.'

'Are they married?'

'Jeannine. Only Jeannine.'

'How long?'

'Three years.'

'To?'

'Uh… Mark? No Marcel. Marcel Bourges.'

'So she's Jeannine Bourges?'

'No. She kept her maiden name.'

'Children?'

'No.'

'Why?'

Don't get it wrong, Cassie… But don't guess. Ever. Has he even told you this?

'Well?'

'I… don't know.'

'You don't know? Why?'

'Because you haven't told us. Me, I mean.'

'Correct. Where was Noëmi Tardelli born?'

Cassie began to breathe more easily. She knew Noëmi backwards. 'Antibes.'

'What was her maiden name?'

'Noëmi Aubert.'

'What's her daughter called?'

'Emma.'

'Age?'

'Seven.'

'Son?'

The sound of scuttling somewhere behind her made Cassie jump.

'Answer!'

'Fabien. 18 months.'

'Did I ask you how old the little bastard was? Eh?'

Cassie shook her head.

'Speak!'

'No, you didn't.'

'Don't anticipate what I'm going to ask or say to you. Just do as I tell you. Right?'

'Sorry.'

'How old did you say Jeannine Bourges was?'

'I didn't. Her name is Jeannine Lantosque.'

'Better. Now listen, Carmen. We went over the old plan countless times so you'd get it in your head. Since Debreuil has left us, the plan has had to change. Yesterday, I told you something about it. Now I'm going to tell you the rest. The first thing is that that the operation is much simpler now. And it will be over far quicker than before.'

Cassie almost smiled.

'But it's going to be harder to pull off.'

Cassie almost cried.

THIRTY-ONE

By the time Darac's Peugeot was bumping and bouncing its way through the dust towards stadium gateman Eric Cauvin's caravan, Bonbon had twice called Head Coach Gilles Laborde's office. On the first occasion, he had reassured PA Monique Azzani that he was calling on a routine matter and she had put him through to Laborde's phone only to discover he was not yet at his desk. Delayed by traffic, she imagined, although he invariably called her if that were the case. However, she was confident he would arrive at any moment. The second call found her perplexed and more than a little concerned. Since, she had claimed, Laborde "had never having a day off for sickness in his life," perhaps he'd suffered an injury while out exercising or jogging before leaving for work. Trying his mobile first – no answer – Monique had then called his home but fared no better, wife Zoë confirming that he had left for work at the usual time and counselling Monique not to worry.

A decrepit 2CV was parked alongside the caravan and in the shaded area behind it, a tired-looking Vespa sat double-chained to the railings. Stubbing a fag end into the dashboard, a man got out from behind the wheel of the 2CV and, replicating the sound of a tin shed collapsing, slammed the driver's door.

'All that's missing is a snatch of 'Duelling Banjos,' Bonbon said.

Darac nodded. 'Does have a *Deliverance* feel about it. Know the movie, Flak?'

'Seen it, Captain. One viewing was enough.'

Wearing a short-sleeved polo shirt, knee-length cargoes and a lanyard ID, the man was a stocky individual with better things to do.

'This isn't Cauvin, clearly,' Darac said, rolling his window as he slowed. 'And where's the uniform Sous-Brigadier Saucisson should have assigned him?'

Bonbon grinned. 'I think the name was Sorbissone but your version may turn out to be closer to the truth.'

The man stepped forward and in a vaguely border guard-like manner, peered into the car.

'Morning Monsieur..?' Darac canted his head. 'Reixe.' He showed his own ID. 'Where's the uniformed officer who should be controlling this entrance?'

'Assisting me, you mean. He had to nip down the other end. Be back in a minute. If his Yammie 900 copes with the potholes, that is.'

Darac made a mental note to have a word with the officer. 'I see. Monsieur Eric Cauvin around?'

'How many more of you are there?'

'Monsieur Cauvin?'

'I see. Like that, is it? He's probably home by now.'

'What hours does he work?'

'Comes at 6 in the evening, goes off at 8 in the morning. Friday to Monday.'

Darac was astonished, 'He works 14-hour shifts?'

'When he's awake. And if you can call it work. Like I said, he gets off at 8 when I come on but he usually sticks around for a natter. And he would've done today for sure but once the local *flics* turned up, he came back here and started throwing up.' He indicated the caravan with a back header. 'It stinks in there.'

'So the 2CV's not his?'

'Site vehicle. We use it to shuttle between here and the players' car park.'

'Really? How far is it?'

'If you straightened it out, it'd be a couple of hundred

metres, maybe. It all adds up, you know.'

'OK. And the scooter?'

'Mine.' Reixe confirmed the cut of his masculinity by spitting into the dust. 'I've got a 750 Kwaker at home but if I come on that, it'd be gone by lunchtime.'

'A 750 quacker, eh?' Darac said, deadpan. 'Sounds impressive.' He turned to Flaco. 'We've got an address for Eric?' A couple of taps on her phone found it and he recited it to Reixe. 'Apartment 7, *La Bella Vista*. That correct?'

'Yeah.'

'Where is that?'

'Off Montel, up that way.' He nodded towards a cluster of high-rise buildings in the distance. 'He uses the 2CV here on-site but he walks to and from his apartment. Takes him half an hour with his leg. Does him good, he says.'

Darac nodded. 'It would take us a few minutes to get a mobile number for him but if you could speed that up for us, we'd be grateful.'

Reixe hesitated before reaching into the thigh pocket of his cargoes. 'We've got all this data protection crap now but I suppose it's alright.'

'While you're finding it, do you and Eric routinely make a complete list of everyone you admit through this gate? Athletes and coaches heading for the far car park, in other words?'

'*I* don't. No point, is there?' He displayed Eric's phone numbers and the trio shared them immediately. 'Alright?'

'CCTV on site?'

'Oh, yeah, we're living the dream here, mate. Lasers, drones, force-fields, the lot.'

'We'll go again with the question. Do you—'

'No. No CCTV.'

'Alarms?'

'Only the changing rooms. Keypad's in the caravan here,

would you believe.'

'That's a bit inconvenient, isn't it?'

'Tell me about it.'

'Finally, and we'll ask him this ourselves, I take it Eric is responsible for locking up the site each night he's here?'

'When he remembers.' More spittle bit the dust. 'So you ready to go and join the others, then?'

'If you please.'

'I reckon it's a vagrant, the stiff,' he said, producing a bunch of keys. 'Vagrant or a druggie or both. And that's what Yammie Boy reckons as well. There's various ways you can get in here if you know how. And they know how, these people. Especially the muzzies. Shouldn't be here, most of them. Once we get Le Pen in, it'll be a different story.'

'You're right there,' Darac said. The gate opened with a grudging whine and Darac pulled slowly away. 'All too right, Monsieur Reixe.'

'You surprise me. I thought you'd have a different idea about it with her in the back.'

Darac hit the brakes. Reixe hit the panic button.

'No, chief!' Bonbon said, laying a skinny arm across Darac's torso. 'Not now. Not here.'

'It's alright, man,' he said casually and turned to Reixe. 'I've just been stupid. Irony is not much of a weapon where people like you are concerned, is it? And I suspect reasoned argument is not your thing, either. So I'll just say that if next time you don't keep your racist crap where it belongs, i.e. up your arse, we'll be looking at you in more detail, Monsieur.'

'Well, look at that,' Bonbon said. 'The white man just turned whiter. Scared, are we?'

'Y…you lot don't scare me… And what about the… the… It's supposed to be a free country…'

Reixe's puerile protestations drifted away as Darac drove on. In the rear-view mirror, Flaco's face was a picture of dignified forbearance. Inside, Darac knew, she was seething.

'I think you both realised what we spoke about earlier meant to me,' she said. 'I don't need either of you to speak *for* me but now, at the first opportunity, you've just called out a racist bigot, Captain. Thank you.'

'No, I didn't, Flak. I threatened him, effectively, which isn't the way forward. Quite the opposite, in fact.'

'You threatened the bastard effectively, alright,' Bonbon said, smiling his foxy smile. 'And that may have just cowed him sufficiently to make him think twice the next time.'

'I doubt it, man, but thanks for the thought.'

The trio soon discovered that Charvet's route to the players' car park was all of the twisty, ill-defined affair he had described and when Reixe's "assistant" suddenly buzzed around a corner on his return trip to the caravan gate, he was already out of sight before Darac could flash his lights to stop him.

'At least the guy was in a hurry to get back to his post,' Bonbon said. 'That's something.'

'I'll have a word on our way out.'

A flotilla of familiar vehicles was waiting for them in the players' car park, a group in which chief forensic analyst Raul Ormans's flagship van was once more absent.

'R.O's late again,' Bonbon observed rhetorically, his mobile producing a mournful but insistent moan as they docked alongside the morgue van.

'Is that Coach Laborde for you, by any chance?'

Bonbon brought up the text. ' "*Sweetie, don't forget to pick up Elisa's flowers from Philippe Graves's stall on Cours Saleya. Nikki's put them aside. Kiss, kiss.*" No, on balance, I don't think it was.'

Darac gave Bonbon's knee a squeeze. 'Right. Here we go.'

The trio slipped on their armbands and got out of the car.

'Those calls I made trying to locate Laborde,' Bonbon said,

shaking his head. 'Haven't encountered a character like the good and faithful PA Monique in some time. Her boss is late for work and she's practically got him dead and buried. If I'd told her *why* we were calling, she'd have had a fit.'

'Maybe it *is* his body in the water jump,' Flaco said, grazing the boot for what Perand always referred to as the "usual shit" needed at a scene. 'But that's dependent on Patricia being wrong about the corpse being there all night.'

Darac shook his head. 'Patricia wrong? I doubt it. And of course, there are other possibilities.'

Holding an imaginary microphone, Bonbon essayed his best piece-to-camera face. ' "Opined chief advocate to the devil, Captain Paul Darac." '

'That's me, Bonbon. What if Laborde's wife made a mistake about the timing of her husband's movements last evening and this morning? What if she was asleep when he came in late, was still asleep when he left early and she just assumed he had come and gone as usual? Or what if she deliberately misled the dotingly anxious Monique to mollify her as we just did? Or even misled her for more nefarious reasons?'

'There we go,' Bonbon said. 'Neglected wife kills workaholic husband, dumps the body at his workplace to show him why, drives happily away and starts lying her head off the following morning. Case solved. Let's go home.'

'If only it were that simple.'

'Would you still want to do this job if it were?'

Darac's initial reaction was to say yes, he would – its object was to bring killers to justice, after all. But Bonbon may have touched on something.

'Have to wait for another time for that one, I think.'

The Peugeot's locks chirruped shut and the trio set off towards the cordon tape.

'Quite apart from this rickety old stadium,' Darac said, taking in the wider scene. 'It's a curious area this, isn't it?

Considering how developed it all is, you wouldn't think there were still odd parcels of wasteland, thorny thickets of greenery, and fenced-off… nothingnesses dotted between all the corporate glitz.'

Bonbon nodded. 'Give it ten years and none of this will be here. That disused builder's yard back there, for instance? That could be gone by next week.'

Darac scanned the skyline. 'Plenty of medium to high rise buildings out there. None close enough to command a bird's eye view of the Stade, unfortunately.'

Away to their left, a bird of a different feather rose nose-up above the treeline and almost immediately began carving a perfect slow-motion arc over the Baie des Anges: a flash of white fading into infinite azure.

'I wonder if anyone taking off or landing has ever witnessed a crime on the ground somewhere?' Bonbon said. 'Other than the traffic queues outside the airport, that is.'

Darac's mobile rang, suppressing any further comments on the question.

'Granot? Go ahead, you're on speaker.'

'We've found Ludo.'

'Excellent. He know anything?'

'Not anymore. He's dead. No cover-up mutilation this time and there's no ID on him but thanks to Astrid's work, there's no question it's him. He was stabbed in the neck possibly with the same knife that did for his mate Cragnat. Naturally, Barrau is mute on that point so far.'

'Naturally. T.O.D, roughly?'

'I'll quote the man: "Between 8 o'clock last night and six o'clock this morning." Usual terms and conditions, in other words.'

'Taking the piss is another way of putting it. OK, when this is all over, I'm making another formal complaint against him. It's clear he hasn't learned anything from last time.'

'With you all the way.'

'Moving on – where did you find Ludo's body?'

'Among shrubs the other side of a fence flanking Boulevard Blanqui. One of the wilder spots. Nothing overlooking it. Body looks to have been chucked over from the road.'

'How are you doing for forensics up there? R.O and co are their way here and we'll definitely need them.'

'Hold on to your hat. Acting decisively and imaginatively, Frènes has got a top-notch Gendarmerie unit to pitch in with us and they're doing their stuff already.'

The trio shared looks.

'Top-notch?'

'Well, for the Gendarmerie. Decent bunch, actually.'

'Glad to hear it. And it shows Frènes can do it when he wants to,' Darac said, speaking for them all. 'That it, Granot?'

'For the time being.'

'Thanks for the update, man.'

'Will you need Perand, by the way? He's here with me at the moment but I could spare him.'

'Not sure yet – I'll let you know. Right, we're almost on.'

They ended the call.

'First, Denise Dubreuil,' Bonbon said. 'Then Cragnat, and now this Ludo all murdered with nothing much to go on apart from the obvious connection between them. Let's hope we can wrap *this* one up quickly, chief.'

'Absolutely. While we still have her, we do have one priceless asset in all this, though, don't we? When it comes to directing overstretched forces, there's no one to touch Agnès. Although, I'd rather not drag her away from the conveyor belt that doubles as her desk if we could avoid it.'

The trio arrived at the inner cordon tape denoting the red zone, the hot spot at the centre of the investigation.

Completing the required suiting-up and signing-in formalities with a warm, vibrant soul like gatekeeper Patricia

Lebrun could make it a surprisingly cheerful experience at times. This morning was not one of them.

'Later, Patricia.'

'*Courage.*'

Ahead, a young uniform was standing point outside a wooden pavilion-like structure set at forty-five degrees to the walkway. Doors bearing signs reading HOME, AWAY, and MATCH OFFICIALS indicated to even the sports-averse Darac that the building served as changing rooms, and had presumably been put to use by Laborde's athletics squad the previous evening. Darac introduced himself and the others to the young man and enquired as to the whereabouts of his commanding officer.

'Sous-Brigadier Sorbissone? I think he's back at the Commissariat, Captain.'

'So who is in charge of your people on the ground here?'

'Uh…He is.'

'Right. And you have your instructions?'

'Oh, yes Captain. He briefed us all thoroughly.'

'You're a good man, Officer..?'

'Angers. Thank you, sir.'

Wishing the young man good luck, the trio took its leave and made its way into the arena proper. Thanks to Flaco's precise description of the water jump earlier, Darac had no difficulty picturing the thing itself but he couldn't quite visualise how it was incorporated into the overall layout. One glance was sufficient to complete his education. Demarcated into six lanes, the athletics track was laid in some sort of synthetic material coloured shale red. The football pitch contained within it naturally offered sizeable semi-circular areas at either end and it was close to where the inside lane gave on to the home straight that the exam tent was set up. Singly and in groups, personnel were already going about their business in and around it.

'Alright, the stadium's small and it's seen better days,' Bonbon said. 'But you can see why the university football team still play some of their games here. The pitch is beautiful.'

'And the running track, too,' Flaco said. 'Six lanes instead of the usual eight but it looks a quality surface.'

Darac's pulse rate quickened a couple of beats as they headed for the action. 'OK. Mask time. Shall we?'

Nods and muted words of greeting were exchanged as they entered the tent to the intermittent firing of the photographer's flashgun. Picking their way carefully around various items of kit, the trio moved closer to the water jump. They found pathologist Djibril Mpensa standing up to his booted shins in its deeper end, the prone form of the victim lying semi-submerged in front of him. The situation made even a superficial examination difficult but regulations demanded that until Darac as chief investigating officer had had the opportunity to view the corpse in situ, it was to remain in the position in which it had been found. The image of a clubbed seal irresistibly sharing the moment with him, Darac fulfilled the brief, and turned to Mpensa.

'Map? Talk us through this unholy mess.'

Before he could, a commotion outside the tent stopped him. Raised voices and then anguished screams rent the air, shouted entreaties to the screamer to go no further, more screams and shouts.

'Just need to deal with that, Map.' Darac turned to Bonbon and Flaco. A look was all it took. 'Whoever it is, they'll get them back a safe distance. Right. Take two.'

'Obviously, I'll have more once the body is out of the water, and much more when we can examine it back in the lab but what we've basically got is the second destruction of a human being's cranial bone structure, cartilages and brain tissue we've been confronted with over the past couple of days. As far as I can tell at the moment, the difference this time is that it's all this visible blunt force damage that caused the death, a sudden, devastating blow administered from immediately behind. The murder weapon is nowhere to be seen.'

The eye of the storm outside was already shifting away.

'So it's not a cover-up job.'

'No, but don't read too much into that. Although the m.o. is different, it doesn't mean the perp couldn't have committed the ruelle Moncet murder. A different point: wherever this attack occurred, I doubt it happened exactly where I'm standing.'

The water eddying gently around his legs, Mpensa stepped cautiously backwards out of the pit. 'Lami? Benjamin? We'll lift now. Morgue team? Assist them, please.'

A study in concentration, the quartet edged down the slope into the water.

'Very carefully now.'

'Map, under the circumstances, this is an impudent question…'

'We have no name and only a few personal details to give you at the moment, I'm afraid.'

'That's fine.'

'All we have is the gender, approximate age and ethnicity.'

'Which are?'

'Female. Aged in her teens or 20s. Asian ethnicity.'

Accompanied by a fusillade of flashes, the body, small and slender as a child's, was laid still prone on to a stretcher. Darac took in what he could see of the victim's apparently uninjured face and he noted the fine gold chain around her neck; the gold ring clamped tightly around the flesh of the little finger on her right hand; her expensive-looking running shoes, tracksuit bottoms and short-sleeved top. And something else caught his eye. In such a unique crime scene, it stood out as a cliché of the genre: on the victim's wrist was a stopped watch. And true to form, there was surely something anomalous about it, a detail that already ruled out robbery as a motive in Darac's mind.

'I have another impudent question for you, Map.'

'From the pathology *alone*,' Mpensa said, indicating the watch to emphasise the point. 'I estimate a T.O.D. between 9 o'clock last evening and 1 o'clock this morning.'

His implication was clear. The time shown on the stopped watch – 10.30 – had played no part in his initial estimate of the time of death.

'Got you. Two more quick questions and I'll get out of your hair. Any sign of a mobile in her pockets or in the water?'

'Hear that, Lami?'

'Yes, Doctor. Nothing in her pockets. And no mobile in the water. Sorry, Captain.'

'Pity. Anything *else* in the water?'

'When we arrived, a football. Lartou has logged it in already.'

'We know about the football. Thanks, Lami.' He turned back to Mpensa.

'That anguished outpouring outside? I don't know how but someone close to the victim must have got wind of what had happened here. Might ID-ing her formally be any kind of possibility later?'

'Will we be able to hide the horror? Because of the anterior nature of the damage, the judicious addition of cloths to the sheet is all we would need to prepare her for the video viewing room. Once we have her back in the lab, it wouldn't take long at all.'

'Now you've got her out of the water, and providing whoever was outside is in a fit state, could we say about a couple of hours from now?'

'An hour and a half should do it. The PM itself? It depends on what we find, of course, but I'll have a lot more for you, including a smaller window on the T.O.D, probably by late afternoon.' Another sequence of flashes. 'Oh, and all the photos will be shared to Lartou before we head back.'

'That's excellent, Map. One final point. The gold ring on the victim's little finger? It's before your time but Geeta who worked with Adèle in Archive used to wear a ring just like it and on the same finger. I asked her about it once. It had had been given to her at birth – a naming ceremony gift from someone in the family. She didn't wear it as a baby, of course. Her mother kept it until her 12th birthday, I think it was.'

'And you think the victim's ring might bear a similar named inscription?'

'It might. Will you be removing it here for releasing to Lartou?'

'Back in a second.'

Mpsensa's estimate proved optimistic; it took him all of thirty seconds. 'Your hunch was right, Paul'. He placed the ring on Darac's gloved hand. 'It's easier to read with this.' He handed over a magnifying loupe.

It took Darac a few moments to focus but then he was able to read on the ring's inner surface: the name Samira Naidu Padar; the date June 16, 1990; and a sequence of characters in some sort of exotic script.

'The age and ethnicity appear to match,' Mpensa said. 'But we're not exactly talking a photo ID here, are we?'

'No, and as noises off suggest we won't be waiting long for an official identification, we shouldn't get ahead of ourselves. Nevertheless, it gives us a definite steer.' He handed back the loupe. 'I'll pass the ring on to Lartou. Thanks, Map.'

'You're welcome. Now you'll have to excuse me.'

As was his wont, Darac gave Mpensa's shoulder a parting squeeze and, picking his way back through the tent, went looking for crime scene co-ordinator Jean-Jacques Lartigue.

'Lartou? An inscribed naming ring for you. Victim's little

finger, right hand.'

Lartigue took it and made the entry on his sheet.

'When you receive the scene photos, share them just with me, Bonbon, Flak and R.O for the time being, alright?'

'Right, chief.'

'And if he hasn't got here by the time Map releases the victim's effects, log them in as usual but then...'

The arrival of Ormans himself obviated further clarification.

'Gentlemen, once again, I apologise for the tardiness of my entrance. I am however assured that my long-promised replacement vehicle is being delivered this afternoon.' His gaze fell on the stretcher. 'Good Lord. The dumpster murderer's work again?'

'Map isn't ruling it out but listen, R.O. I'm interested in the victim's wristwatch. Once Lartou's logged it in, he's going to hand it over to you straight away. Do your usual stuff and then try to work out why it's in the state it is, will you?'

'Certainly.'

Lartigue's bald head was a blank canvas on which even the slightest deviations from neutrality were readable. At Darac's question, frank puzzlement registered vividly. 'Sorry, chief, but it got smashed, didn't it? In the attack. And that's presumably why the attacker didn't take it in the end.'

'*If* it got smashed in the attack, Lartou, the question is how and why.'

Darac had no sooner left the tent than his mobile rang.

'Bonbon?'

'Can Map hear this? We may have something useful for him as well as us.'

'No, I'm en route to you, now. Go for it, anyway.'

'OK, the source of the anguished outpouring is a 34 year-old local businessman by the name of Dilip Padar.' He spelled it. 'He's a cloth importer hailing originally from Bengaluru in southern India which is home to the family's silk production business. He is saying that the murder victim is his 23 year-old sister Samira who was studying for a post-graduate degree in law at the university, and who was a member of Gilles Laborde's elite athletics squad. Flak's checking what she can of that as we speak.'

'That potentially fits what Map and I have just learned but how does this Dilip character know *who* the victim is?'

'Hold on to your hat, chief. Before he hobbled off to his apartment for a restorative lie down, nauseous gateman Monsieur Eric Cauvin called him on his mobile with the news.'

'He did what?' Darac looked to the heavens, momentarily. 'Do you know what an oxymoron is, Bonbon?'

'Sounds like a good name for a Real Madrid fan.'

'Possibly, but I was just about to tell you in plain language that I was speechless. *That* is an oxymoron.'

'Got you.'

'So Eric recognised the victim and rather than telling us about it or keeping it to himself – which some might well have done – he calls the victim's brother to tell *him*.'

'That's about the size of it, chief.'

'The man sounded hysterical just a few minutes ago. He said all this coherently?'

'In between tears and vows to get the killer.'

'Will he be calm enough to go through a video viewing in the lab, do you reckon? In about an hour and a half, Map estimates.'

'I think he'll want to try, anyway. He was desperate to see what we were trying to prevent him seeing in the tent, after all.'

Darac had another uncomfortable thought about Eric Cauvin. 'Let's hope misguided compassion was his motive and he left it at just that one call. If Annie Provin from Télé-Sud turns up at any moment, we'll know it wasn't.'

'Head Coach Gilles Laborde's another possibility and let's hope Dilip didn't call anyone else.'

'Indeed. Cauvin must have been sure, mustn't he? Of who had been killed, I mean. I don't know how, though.'

'He sees these people regularly, mind you. Maybe only one of the women wore those particular trainers or whatever.'

'I guess so although a killer could easily swap something like that around. Other items wouldn't prove so easy, mind you.' He referred to the naming ring. 'Although it doesn't make sense to have gone to the trouble of doing any of that and then leave the body.'

'You mean if there was a point in making us believe the victim was someone else for what would obviously be a very short time, you can't think of one?'

'Exactly.'

'Me neither. But as someone once said, all will become clear.'

'I should have copyrighted that line. Where are you exactly?'

'Next to a squad van parked outside the changing rooms. We left Dilip in the back of it – the van, not the rooms –with a trio of Joinel's most *sympa* uniforms.'

'OK. This looks the sort of case in which things happen thick and fast, Bonbon, so let's put a quick plan of action together.'

Raising Eric Cauvin on one of the numbers Reixe had given them was their first priority. Darac resolved to do this, and conduct the consequent interview himself. Unless other developments intervened, Bonbon and Flaco were to continue with Dilip for the time being.

Staffing wasn't usually a problem for the Brigade but with Granot now leading the Port Lympia/dumpster murder investigation, the trio would have to progress matters on the ground without the invaluable contribution he would certainly have made. Functioning without the erratic assistance of young Max Perand was of lesser importance but he too would be missed.

'Does he live nearby, this Dilip?'

'Saint-Philippe. Hang on… *Les Appartements Mimosas*, Avenue Primerose, to be exact.'

'About fifteen minutes away, then. How did he get here?'

'Drove. Parked in clear sight of the caravan gate where – get this – there was no sign of *anyone* on guard. What say Reixe hadn't nipped home for his quack-quack and he and Yammie Boy had gone for a burn-up on the A8? So Dilip just climbed in, got straight on to the pitch and, dragging a couple of uniforms behind him, made it as far as the tent.'

'Until he ran into the rock that is Flak. Oh, and the hard place that is your good self.'

'The strongarm department was all Flak, don't worry.'

'I can believe there was no one on the gate but we can't have this, Bonbon. I'm calling Saucisson *now*.' He hesitated. 'No, wait. There's a better way. I didn't really want to do this but… Putting you on hold a second.'

He tapped key number one. 'Agnès? With all you have on your plate, I thought twice about asking but we need tighter security at the Stade. It's open house here, practically. Could you do something?' Agnès promised that she would get on to Commissariat Foch immediately and that their preferred site security unit would be dispatched within minutes. She would then call Sorbissone at Joinel to explain matters.

'I'm back, Bonbon.' He updated him. 'So Agnès to the rescue again, basically.'

'Whoever said "no one is irreplaceable" didn't know her.'

'Absolutely. Anything else from said Dilip?'

'A good few things, potentially. He wanted to know where

Samira's Renault was. Did you notice the parking area kinks sharply round to the right at the end?'

'I saw the way the surface deteriorated the further it went but I didn't notice the kink.'

'We haven't explored it yet but I asked Patricia to tape that area off, too. With the tree and shrub cover, it's hidden from the end everyone uses, as you've just proved.'

'Interesting. Obviously, the Renault wasn't there or we'd already have been made aware of it.'

'True but perhaps she didn't use it last evening. Got a lift with one of the other athletes? Maybe she often does that.'

'Maybe so. Ah, I see you, now.'

'Ditto. And Flak's just rejoining me. I'll update her and we'll wait for you before going any further.'

The trio came together and Flaco was given the floor.

'Everything Dilip Padar said about his sister checks out.' The natural gravity of Flaco's mien perfectly matched the moment. 'Here's a photo of her.' She held out her phone and the image of a self-assured, beautiful young woman smiled back at them. It was a look of infinite promise and Darac let the moment make its mark before he went on. 'We all observed the damage to the back of the victim's skull but I saw more of her face after you left the tent. If she does prove to be our Samira here, I wouldn't be at all surprised.' A new thought emerged from the crossfire of possibilities ricocheting around in his head. 'When Dilip received Eric's call, he presumably didn't believe his story right away, did he?'

'We didn't ask him that directly,' Bonbon said. 'But once he'd rung Samira's mobile and got no response, he implied that he did give credence to the story, more or less. Flak?'

'That's my impression, too.'

Darac's brows lowered. 'He didn't have to be convinced? Odd, isn't it? I would take a hell of a lot of convincing if a member of the public called me out of the blue with such news.'

'Now you say it, I suppose it is.' Bonbon produced a bag of wrapped sweets from his pocket. 'Goo-goo Jube, either of you? No? We'll need to question Dilip properly in time, obviously, but considering how he was, we weren't in full-on probing mode.'

'Yes, I see that. Of course, it could all have been an act and the easy-to-convince Dilip might himself be the murderer, one who spent the intervening time after he climbed into the site eradicating clues from his work the night before.'

'Not impossible, chief.'

'And I'll answer my own question, throwing in a couple of what ifs? for good measure. You *are* inclined to believe things that people *you know well* tell you. What if Dilip and Eric are not the strangers we assume them to be? Secondly, what if Samira was not murdered out of the blue? Perhaps her life had been threatened before.' Darac's next question scarcely needed asking – harvesting potentially useful contact details was second nature to police detectives working on a murder case. 'You offered to try Samira's number yourselves?'

'Yes, and got voicemail.'

'And you also offered to send someone off to her address?'

'On that, the first info to come in on Samira stated she has been resident in the country since last July and the address given was Dilip's own apartment in the *Mimosas* building on Avenue Primerose.'

'That changes things.'

'Yes, for a moment, we were excited.'

'But?'

'*But* Dilip says that was a temporary arrangement until she got settled in and she moved out within a couple of weeks. He wouldn't divulge where to, interestingly. We wondered if he planned on going there himself once we thought it safe to release him.'

'If he does, we'll send someone with him. Or depending on developments, tail him.'

'I've approached the student records office for Samira's current address. No one in the office at the moment but it shouldn't be long.'

'Good. As we have Samira's number, I'm going to ask someone in IT to chase up her call and text log. Bonbon?'

'Why not ask Erica, herself?'

'I thought she and Serge were on leave?'

'Back today, chief. They *are* rostered.'

'Are they?' Darac could have kicked himself – it was part of his remit to be on top of such routine matters. 'With one thing and another, I missed it. But anyway, one of us is awake. Well done, Bonbon.'

'Anything else we can help you with today? Your call *is* important to us.'

'Yes – try Samira's number again, Flak.'

'I'll share it to the case file as well.' She tapped it in. 'Should have done that as soon as I was out of Dilip's sight. Sorry.'

'A few minutes delay on making a note when you're flying around? *Don't* be sorry.'

Giving the slightest of smiles, she nodded and listened. 'No, it's going to voicemail again.'

'If it's Samira's own voice, put it on speaker, will you?'

'It's the provider's generic message.'

'Don't worry, then.' He tapped a number on his own phone. 'Morning, Erica.'

'Morning to you, Paul. I sense I've been missed. My bottom has literally just hit my seat here in the lab.'

'Of course you've been missed. Welcome back. Hope you and Serge both had a lovely time in...' He gave Bonbon an enquiring look.

'Their apartment.'

'… in… instead of going off somewhere.'

'Nicely finessed but the words "cut" and "chase" come to mind?'

Darac filled her in on what they needed and, concluding with the thought that if they were able to find Samira's phone itself, Erica would be able to work real miracles, he rang off just as Bonbon's mobile rang. The caller's number looked unfamiliar.

'Lieutenant Busquet?'

'Speaking.' He answered the others' enquiring looks with an uncomprehending shrug.

'It's Monique Azzani here. You rang me earlier?'

'Oh yes, yes.'

'I have Coach Laborde. Putting you through.'

A click and the line muted momentarily.

'Just delay a fraction on the news,' Darac said, hurriedly. 'It'll give us a steer on his mood.'

'Good idea. Unless Eric Cauvin or Dilip Padar called him, he shouldn't be aware of anything sinister, should he? Ah, Monsieur Laborde. Thanks for ringing back.'

Negotiating an initial exchange of pleasantries partly on sporting matters may not have been the severest test, but if Laborde knew anything of the grim events at the Stade Walter Vallain, he gave no sign of it.

'Before we continue, may I just say what big fans of your coaching methods we all are here at the Caserne?'

Big nod from Darac.

'You are? Well, that's really gratifying.'

Laborde's wheels well and truly oiled, he agreed without demur to Bonbon's request for a list of all those who had attended the previous evening's training session.

'Hold a moment, Lieutenant Busquet, would you? Monique has your number so I'll ask her to text you a copy immediately because if I don't, the moment we finish, I'll be on to the next thing and forget.' The line went dead and it was presumably done. 'There. Now, why exactly are you calling?'

Giving no specifics as to the identity or gender of the victim, Bonbon gently broke the news.

THIRTY-TWO

Inès wiped a tear from her cheek and blew her fiancée a kiss. 'This is so much better than a phone call, isn't it?' she said, in English. 'Despite the occasional interruption by the… what do you call them? Grumbles?'

'Gremlins,' Sue said.

'Gremlins – yes. Don't usually have problems with the signal out here in the garden.'

'The real thing is so much better still, Innie. Can't wait for Friday. Bring Zoë with you, if you like. Sounds as if she could use a break, the poor woman. Just for a day or two. And then I want you all to myself.'

Inès wiped her eyes once more. 'Maman was so sweet about us, Sue.' She gave a sad little laugh. 'Already looking forward to the wedding. Impressive, considering her own marriage has just gone into the toilet.'

'Tell me she *is* going to fully break with him. Formally, I mean.'

'Divorce?'

'Yes, divorce. Citing the fact that he is a complete and utter shit.'

'I can almost see your… What is it you say rises when you get mad?'

'Hackles. And yes, mine are well and truly up. *Is* she going to?'

'Hackles… I can't tell you how un-French that sounds.'

'You're stalling. Divorce, Innie.'

Inès produced a very un-English pout while she thought about it. 'I'm not sure but if I change the subject quickly, you'll know she's joined me out here.'

'Why the need for that? I don't suppose she would *relish* the three of us discussing the matter on screen but there's nothing clandestine going on now, is there? Not one cat left in the bag. They're all out in the open.'

'That's true, I suppose. Not used to it. Yes, I think she will go for a formal split with him. Although the context is different, she's good at striking out by herself. In fact, she's just contributed a chapter to a book that's coming out next year on the subject.'

'Not to do with sprockets again, is it?'

'*Sockets*, it was. No – this is only tangentially about IT.' Inès summarised the book's raison d'être. 'It's entitled *Boss Women*. How good is that?'

'It sounds great.'

'Went off to the publisher just last night. You heard it here first, Sue.'

'Oh, I came across something yesterday, too. With one thing and another, I hadn't really looked at the latest flyer from the jazz club but guess what?' She held it up 'See who's going to be playing at The Vault shortly?' She adjusted the focus. 'The Didier Musso Quintet. They're from Nice!'

'Musso? That's a local name, alright. But quintet? There's... nine of them in the photo. I hope they can play better than they can count.'

'Just their joke, by the look of it. But can they play? Caught a couple of things online. Put it this way – I was wearing socks when I started. Two women in the band as well, notice, and neither's a singer. Anyway, May 1st they're playing. I've checked the diary – zilch at the mo. Why not come along?'

'Because however brilliant they are, I'd be bored... hard?'

'Stiff.'

'Stiff – yes.'

'Innie, Innie, Innie.' Sue shook her head. 'Why do I love you?'

For the first time in hours, Inès felt warm inside. 'Let me count the ways?' she said.

'Better still, let *me* count the ways.'

'Only if you make a better job of it than Monsieur Musso.'

THIRTY-THREE

The car radio beeped. Police comms.

'Listen.'

It was a superfluous instruction. Cassie had been doing nothing but listen for the past ten minutes.

'Mobile control. Lacquet, come on? Over.'

'Lacquet here. Over'

'Location and ETA? Over.'

'Crossing the Var on the 6098. One moment, I'll ask Garlet… Ten minutes, he says. Over.'

'Pathology already in attendance. Victim still at the scene. Captain Paul Darac leading the operation on the ground. Clear on where you're heading on arrival at the Stade? Over.'

'The players' and officials' car park? Over.'

'That's the one. Over and out.'

'Ah, what a shame,' the man said as the radio beeped off. 'Somebody got themself killed.' He handed her a folded piece of paper. 'Know where to go?'

'Yes.'

'Then why are you still here?'

Cassie got out of the car and, glad to be breathing fresh air, was soon toying with the idea of keeping on walking. But then a voice called out from behind.

'Noëmi?'

Her blood ran cold. What to do? Steeling herself, she turned. The man wound his window back up and nodded. It had been his voice. She had passed the test. This time.

THIRTY-FOUR

The immediate upshot of Bonbon's call with Coach Gilles Laborde was that the Brigade now had to contend with a second inconsolable man bent on vengeance. At least Dilip Padar had agreed to be taken home where the two uniforms assigned to him would continue to keep close tabs. Requesting that Laborde remain in his office until Bonbon arrived to continue their conversation in person had not taken. He was setting off to the stadium immediately and nothing was going to stop him.

It was an arrival Darac was set to miss but it couldn't be helped. Interviewing the man who had discovered the body remained his first priority and besides, he had complete confidence in Bonbon's and Flaco's abilities to handle any tricky situation.

In his time with the Brigade Criminelle, Darac had interviewed far too many Eric Cauvins – ordinary people who in the course of a perfectly ordinary day had chanced upon the entirely extraordinary. For homicide detectives, coming face to face with the brutalised remains of what had once been a human being was an everyday occurrence. In every sense, they were prepared for these moments and for what came next. For a civilian, dealing with the trauma of discovering a murder victim might only be the start of their ordeal. There was no telling how those thrust unwittingly into the foreground of a murder investigation would cope with this second challenge. Whatever the cost to their own wellbeing, many saw it as their bounden duty to offer every assistance they could to the authorities. On the opposite end of the scale, some positively welcomed the celebrity that making a grisly discovery had conferred upon them and relished talking about it. Some would dine out on such a story for years.

With Bill Evans's *Sunday Night At The Village Vanguard* along for the ride, it took Darac just over five minutes to drive from the Stade to Eric Cauvin's address, a venerable four-storey apartment block named *La Bella Vista*. Circling the building in search of its main entrance, Darac concluded that the beautiful view in question was long gone. Or perhaps there were people who found it pleasing to be hemmed in by the efforts of architects engaged in what Frankie referred to as corporate willy-waving.

To the unlikely accompaniment of the Scott LeFaro tune 'Gloria's Step', a police motorcyclist made a sudden appearance in Darac's rear-view mirror as he parked. Gathering his things, Darac stopped the track and got out of the car.

'I have a document for you, Captain.' He opened his nearside pannier. 'From Lieutenant Busquet.'

'Your timing is perfect, Officer..?'

'Nmante. Based at Joinel.'

'Yes, I was just about to disappear into the building. What is the document?'

'All I know is the Lieutenant emailed the incident room asking for it be printed and passed on to you here. I was in there at the time so came immediately. I believe he emailed it to you also, Captain.'

The LaFaro tune Darac had been listening to was a quiet, lyrical piece yet Darac hadn't heard the message alert. The reason, he discovered, was not that the email was yet to come in: he had left his phone on silent. This was not best practice and it was his second screw-up of the morning. So far. Telling himself that a fitful night's sleep was no excuse for sloppiness, he took a deep breath and turned to Bonbon's accompanying message: *Laborde's attendees list attached. Joinel agreed to deliver paper copy just in case.*

Nmante handed over an old-school cardboard file labelled: *Fantasy Football 12/13.*

'Bit rough and ready, sir. Sorry.'

'It does the job. Thanks, man.'

As Nmante rode away, Darac opened the file and grimaced. There was a lot of work here and with the Brigade's forces stretched, the need to strengthen them was clear. For a moment, his finger hovered over Agnès's designated number. She had given him carte blanche to call her again if needed, after all. He tapped Bonbon's number instead and with the phone to his ear, set off up a short flight of steps to the building's front door.

'Chief?'

'Good work on sending Laborde's list, Bonbon.'

'Quite a tome, isn't it?'

'I guess I had some sort of personal trainer scenario in mind – four or five athletes at most. There must be what… 25, 26 names here? Added to that, although three are sub-headed *Coaches,* there are no other details or contact info.'

'Flak has already been on to the university's central HR for the coaches' details. As for the athletes, the student records office has returned her call and she's now talking to them.'

'Excellent. We'll need statements from all of these people, obviously. Granot offered Perand's services earlier. Get hold of him and say yes to that, OK? Of course, if the bodies were available, what we really need is a decent-sized slog squad. If I were acting commissaire at the moment, I could authorise it but I'm not and I'm loath to ask Agnès.'

'What do you think she would rather do? Keep ploughing through all that crap for the Palais and for Powers That Be in Paris or engage in a spot of proper policing?'

'You're right, I suppose.'

'Plus, she'll do anything for her golden boy, won't she?

That's you, in case you didn't know.'

'If I am, that's something else that won't continue when the new commissaire takes over. I'll call her after I've interviewed the human radio station that is Monsieur Eric Cauvin.'

'Whatever happens with Agnès, we will have at least one more on the strength, chief. Beat Officer of The Year, one Serge Paulin has managed to swap shifts and he's joining us.'

'Perfect. OK, I've arrived. One last thing before I go in. Laborde won't have had time to get to you yet. Anyone else shown?'

'No, but hang on, do I hear..? Yes, I do. The mobile incident truck is just trundling in. Adam Garlet at the wheel... and praise be, it looks as if we've got Bé Lacquet aboard as well. Just give them a wave... Alright, guys? Yeah, so we should have no problems with comms. That'll make life easier for us.'

'Excellent. *Courage,* Bonbon.'

Darac pressed the appropriate number on the Bella Vista's entry panel and waited. A background check had revealed that Eric Lionel Cauvin had a clean record and had worked for 30 years in the postal service before ill health forced him to take early retirement. It occurred to Darac that someone used to the hustle and bustle of the streets might find working night shifts at the Stade Walter Vallain a somewhat empty experience, particularly after the athletes or the footballers had all gone home. But now the old man with a gammy leg was at the centre of things, wasn't he? Now he had something unique and important to circulate. Delivering mail? Small fry. This was big news and although it seemed he had been appalled rather than cheaply thrilled by the scene at the water jump, he had already spoken out of turn to at least one party about it.

Tempted though he was, Darac told himself to resist kicking off the interview with a dressing down. It would likely prove counterproductive anyway.

'Yes?'

'Captain Paul Darac from the Brigade Criminelle. We rang earlier.'

Buzzed in to the building, Darac looked to the far end of the lobby where a worn-out looking man was standing in an open doorway.

'Here, Captain.'

Darac reached for his ID but Eric was already hobbling back into his apartment and Darac followed him into a tidy, if fussily decorated space. Every wall in the room doubled as a picture gallery for works on sporting themes.

'We won't have long, Monsieur, so forgive me if we get straight into it.'

'That's fine with me.' Motioning Darac towards the sofa, Eric eased himself into a straight-backed armchair to which a crocheted blanket had been attached with ties. 'But first I must apologise. You'll know by now I rang Mademoiselle Padar's brother with the news of the… what had happened. I thought it important he knew straight away but I didn't think he would set off to the Stade there and then. I urged him not to but I couldn't stop him and that will have made life difficult for you, I know.'

'It has and yes you shouldn't have but it's done and we're dealing with it. I've got a lot of questions to get through and the first one is, did you call anyone else?'

Eric reacted as if the idea were preposterous. 'No, of course not. Just Dilip Padar, the brother. And I'm sorry, as I say.'

Encouraged that Eric may not have been the irresponsible blabbermouth he had feared, Darac pressed on. 'When the uniformed officers arrived following your call, you told them about a couple of young boys who had sneaked into the stadium for an illicit kick around. Their football found its way into the water jump and it was in retrieving it that they literally fell on the body. They took fright and ran off. You saw all this from your caravan and that's what alerted you to go over there. That right?'

'Yes. Don't ask me if I know who the kids are. I don't. They must live around here somewhere but you know, they're just kids. I wouldn't recognise them close to.'

'I doubt that identifying them will prove necessary. From a purely forensic perspective, that is.'

'Good. They're mad about football, that's all. They don't mean any harm.'

Darac liked Eric's protective attitude toward the boys but there were other considerations here. 'However, they may themselves have been harmed by the encounter, so efforts *will* be made to find them, Monsieur.' He raised his eyebrows enquiringly. 'You have no clue at all as to their identity?'

'I understand it's for their own wellbeing but I just can't help you.'

'Alright. So they sneaked into the stadium unseen. How?'

'There are various paths off the old builders'yard and if you know which one to take you end up end up at a spot where the spectator entrance fence alongside my caravan doesn't mesh together properly. If you push and pull it in a particular way at one of the posts, you can squeeze through if you're keen enough. Then it's a case of dodging behind the stand for the length of the pitch and you get the far goal to yourself for a bit.'

'You witnessed that?'

'Not the first part but it's what kids do.'

And perhaps not just kids. 'Could an adult gain entry to the site like that?'

'Not impossible, I suppose. No one ever has, to my knowledge.'

And overnight, there would be far easier ways, Darac reflected. Especially if day man Reixe's remark about Eric's habit of sleeping on the job could be believed.

'The victim, now. We don't know for certain yet that she was Mademoiselle Samira Padar. Her face was almost completely submerged and the water in the pit was far from clear. Did you enter it to get a better look? Did you touch any part of the body?'

'No, no. It was all I could do to look from the side.'

'With so few visual clues to go on, how could you be certain of who it was?'

'I wasn't sure at first. But I remembered she used to wear studs in her ears. Three either side. Stones of some sort. Tiny little things. And then she stopped wearing them and I joked it would save weight so she would run faster. She laughed, bless her.' He teared up at the memory. 'I noticed the three pin-prick holes in her right ear. The one that hadn't been... damaged.'

It was a telling detail. 'You knew her well, clearly.'

'I know them all. The ones who can be bothered talking to you, especially.'

'When you found her body, did you notice her watch?'

'You couldn't see it. Both her hands were under the water. Shows you what state that water was in, doesn't it? But you've seen it, so you know.' He shook his head. 'That watch, I tell you.'

'Something occurs to you about it?'

'Big chunky old thing. That's why my quip about her ear studs being heavy made her laugh, you see. Partly.'

What was this? 'It was chunky, you say?'

'It was one of those sports watches. Proper athlete's one with loads of dials and things, not just for fitness. It looked all wrong...' Once again, Eric was having a tough time keeping it together. 'Yes, it looked too big for her skinny little wrist.'

'She never wore a *dress* watch to training? Smaller, more elegant, just the one conventional dial?'

'Not that I remember but that doesn't mean she didn't

have one. She was wearing the usual chunky one on Friday, I noticed. But you don't always take things in, do you?'

In Darac's many years of questioning witnesses, the majority reported seeing nothing at all. But there was a type who would swear blind they always noticed everything. That Eric fell into neither camp inclined Darac to give credence to those things he had reported seeing. 'That's true, Monsieur. And you definitely didn't notice what kind of watch she was wearing last night?'

'No, I didn't. Was it a smaller one, then? Perhaps she had just got it or something.'

'Perhaps she had. The call you made to Dilip Padar earlier. You knew how to get hold of him? Or did you just—'

'I know him. He slipped me 30 euros at the start of each term to keep an eye on his car, not because he was worried it would get nicked but he *was* concerned the team bus might give it a good old scrape one day and a witness might come in handy.'

'Sorry, *his* car, you say?'

'Yes, the one Samira used, a Renault Mégane. She had it on a free loan basis but it was his.'

'And why the need for a witness? Does the team bus often scrape people's cars?'

'The thing is, most of the athletes use the bus to come to training and it's about the size of a regular *Lignes d'Azur* single-decker. To be fair, it does take a bit of to and fro-ing to get it into the players' car park. Never has scraped anything, mind you.'

'Right. And was Samira driving the Mégane last evening?'

'Oh yes.'

'There's no vehicle of any sort in the car park now.'

'No, I checked them all out.'

'By what time?'

'Last one left just after 10.30. Bit later than normal. We

aim for 10.15 as a rule.'

Whether it would prove to be of the utmost significance or entirely misleading, the hour and minute hands on Samira's possibly brand-new dress watch were stopped at 10.30, Darac recalled. 'You saw her leave?'

Eric took a couple of deep breaths. 'Yes, I did.'

'We'll get to everyone's movements in due course but what time would that have been?'

'Didn't really notice. Wasn't before ten. Maybe five past? Something like that.'

'Was she with someone else or was she in her own car?'

'No, she was in the Mégane. Alone.'

'Colour of the car?'

'Grey. About five years old. Never really noticed the number plate.'

'That's fine.'

If, as seemed the case, the Mégane was registered to Dilip, finding its number would be a routine matter. As finding the vehicle itself was something of a priority, that process just got a whole lot easier.

'And was there anything out of the ordinary about Samira's departure? Did she seem distressed or anxious to get away?'

'The team bus was parked alongside the changing rooms with its lights on and I was looking into them as she passed, so I didn't see her clear enough to tell what mood she was in. Just her silhouette. She waved, though.'

'She did?' Or someone did, Darac thought to himself. 'Uh-huh.'

'Her whole life ahead of her, Captain.' Eric's eyes welled with tears. 'Beautiful young woman, too. Shouldn't make it worse but it does, somehow.'

'How did she get on with the other athletes and the coaches? Do you know?'

Eric blew his nose and set himself to answer what he

clearly recognised was a key question. 'I don't speak ill of the dead even if they're bastards. And she wasn't.'

'Samira isn't just dead though, Monsieur Cauvin, is she? She was murdered. We need to know everything.'

Eric considered the point. 'Alright. She could be a bit… uppity with people, though never with me. You'll have encountered Brice Reixe, I suppose?'

'Yes.'

'She cut him well and truly down to size. Deserved it, though. He's OK really but he doesn't half fancy himself, does Brice.'

One of the first lessons Darac had learned from Agnès was that the defensive male ego was a fragile thing. And many a male had expressed his fragility by brutally murdering a woman. And, come to that, so had seemingly harmless old men with spotless records like Eric Cauvin.

'Fancies himself?'

'Yeah, even when he turns up for work on his wife's scooter.'

'Rather than his motorbike?'

'He hasn't got a motorbike.'

'My mistake,' Darac said, scribbling "bullshitter?" next to Reixe's name in his notebook. 'Have you ever witnessed a heated exchange between Samira and anyone else here?'

'Oh, it wasn't an *exchange* between Samira and Brice. She just told him where to get off and he did. Her loss, he said to me afterwards. Her loss! Load of crap.'

'Quite. Heated exchanges?'

'Sorry.' Once again, Eric settled himself before answering. 'Yes… It wasn't *really* heated but a couple of weeks ago, she and one of the athletes had a bit of contretemps outside the changing rooms.'

Long experience told Darac that Eric was more likely to answer the "who with?" question if he asked it later. 'What was it about, this contretemps?'

'She was tired and wanted to go home. The other athlete wanted to go with her. And more besides, if you follow me.'

In lieu of a red flag to hoist, Darac's eyebrows rose. 'For sex, you mean? He wanted it and she didn't?'

'Well, that was my impression. Though I could be wrong.'

'Was this first-time sex, do you think? Or were they in a relationship?'

'I never saw them holding hands or anything but I'd sensed they were an item a few times before. Just little things, you know? Until that exchange of words, that is. There was nothing really nasty in it. It was a... lovers' spat, I suppose you would call it.' His eyebrows knotted, Eric appeared to be considering the accuracy of the term he'd used. 'Yes, that's about the size of it.'

Darac produced the lightest, matiest smile he could. 'And *did* they leave together?'

'Did his bleating wear her down, you mean?' Despite the anguish he was clearly feeling, Eric managed a smile in return. 'No, it did *not*.'

Now Darac needed to know if there had been any witnesses to the encounter, a leading question which required a little disguising. 'They must have felt pretty relaxed about things to air their views on the subject in public.'

'Oh, there was no one else there at the time and they didn't notice me, either.'

'That was a couple of weeks ago, you said. Fast forward to yesterday's session. Had they patched things up? Did you see them together at any point?'

'No, I didn't but that doesn't mean they hadn't. With people coming and going at different times and so on – I often miss things.'

Opting to park the question for the moment, Darac took Laborde's list out of his bag and handed it to Eric.

'On the issue of comings and goings, Monsieur, we've been in touch with Coach Gilles Laborde and his PA has supplied a list of everyone who took part in last night's session. I gather you don't have a list?'

'Not as such. I only make a note of how many vehicles have come in. Otherwise I wouldn't know when they'd all gone at the end. So I know when I can lock up.'

'It would be a great help if you could give us a steer on who was doing what and when, both before and especially after the session.'

The request appeared to discomfit Eric.

'I'll do my best, Captain, but…'

'Yes?'

'Monsieur Laborde – he knows what's happened, then?'

'Not in any detail. Why does that concern you, particularly?'

Eric hesitated. 'It doesn't,' he said, turning distractedly to the list of names. 'Except they're his life, these athletes. It'd be a terrible shock to him, all this.'

'I'm sure.' He brought up Bonbon's emailed list. 'You've said that most of the athletes use the team bus. How does that work?'

'You mean where do they catch it to get here and where does it go on the way back?'

'To start with, yes.'

'Do you know that line of bus stops at the bottom end of Boulevard de la Madeleine in Magnan? On the bay side of the rail bridge?'

'Yes.'

'The bus starts and finishes there and then calls at various campuses and other spots en route. On the way back, Roger – Roger Lauvette, the driver – he's been known to drop people more or less at their doors if they don't live too far off the beaten.'

'He must work to a passenger list, I imagine?'

Catching the implication, Eric nodded, 'I see what you mean – he does, yes. Ticks the names on and off at the various stops and everything. Be worth talking to him.'

'Indeed. Got his number there?' Darac said, realising that Eric's mobility issues probably meant he'd keep a lot of things to hand.

'On my phone, yes. I've got it here.'

Darac entered the number in his case contacts list.

'For the time being, could you tell me roughly how many of the 26 names on the list you've got there used the bus last evening?'

'By looking at it the other way around, I could tell you how many should have used it and who they were. Process of elimination.'

Darac gave him an appreciative nod. 'Go for it.'

As Darac himself was wont to do while putting something together in his head, Eric stared at the floor. 'So, one, two… six… Seven *didn't* use the bus. And that means…' As an aid to the mental arithmetic, he closed one eye. 'Seven from 26… there were 19 on the bus. Of course, I don't know where they got on to get here or where they went eventually but you'll have Roger for that.'

'Good call. You've got a pen there, I see. Mark the bus users on the list, would you?'

While Eric added a letter *B* to every relevant name, Darac annotated the list on his phone accordingly and, adding that he hoped Perand was en route already, shared it with Flaco and Bonbon.

'So, that leaves the seven who didn't use the bus. Let's start with Mademoiselle Padar.'

'God rest her soul.' Eric took a couple of breaths. 'Yes, she came in her car, as I said.'

'And parked opposite the changing rooms.'

His forehead creasing, Eric didn't answer immediately.

'That's a funny thing now I think about it.'

'Go on.'

'She did park there when she arrived but when she left, she came up from the far end.'

'From the part tucked around the corner, you mean?'

'Yes. I'd been in the toilets a couple of minutes. She must've gone down that way while I was in there.'

'I see. The surface is poorer down that far end, isn't it?'

'A lot poorer. And it's further from the changing rooms, of course – two reasons why people don't usually use it.'

'Might there be more space there to turn, perhaps? Making it easier to get out?'

'That's true but the way things were last night, I think she could have just pulled out of her space, turned immediately left and gone. Like she usually did.'

'And like everyone else parked near her on the night did?'

For the second time in as many minutes, Eric hesitated before answering. A seasoned investigator, Darac understood that while such moments of indecision were not in themselves suspicious, less innocent explanations were equally possible.

'Let me think,' Eric said.

Whether Eric was intent on concealing an uncomfortable truth or not, Darac realised that a visual representation of the comings and goings in the car park would prove useful and for a moment, he considered calling in Astrid. But time was against them.

'Got a pencil handy, Monsieur?'

'Yes?'

Darac took a blank sheet of A4 out of his bag. 'The layout of the players' car park doesn't appear to be on any map so I think we need to make our own. Could you draw a rough diagram of it? And mark where people were parked, and so on?'

'Dunno. After a fashion I could, I suppose.'

'You'll make a better job of it than I could, I assure you.' He handed over the sheet. 'Something to rest on?'

Eric reached down and pulled a lap tray out from under his chair.

'I can still bend,' he said. 'Had a lot of practice picking the ball out of the net in my 20s.' He indicated a grouping of photos on the wall opposite. 'Keeping goal in front of a leaky defence will do that to you.'

'I guess so. I'm going to make a few notes so I'll look over your shoulder if I may.'

'Fine.'

'Just make it as clear as you can.'

Eric began promisingly, sketching in the site boundaries in what Darac thought a good approximation of the lay-out on the ground.

'Do you play, Captain? You look fit.'

'Football?' Darac could hear his police team, his jazz group, Frankie, and in time probably Lily, laughing in absentia. 'Afraid not.'

Under Eric's pencil, the changing rooms began to take shape and he seemed to be locating them in the right place on the page.

'The building isn't just changing rooms, by the way. It's an equipment store as well. Football goal nets, high jump poles, the lot.'

'A separate key for that, I imagine?'

'Oh yes. Well, keys plural. The groundsman has one. Each of the coaches do. So do the football and athletics team captains, as well. And they probably have spares if they've got any sense.'

'Quite. The groundsman – was he present at the session?'

It seemed Darac had posed a second preposterous question. 'Freddie Carlo? Works 10 'til 5 Tuesday to Sunday and boy, does he stick to those hours. He's the best turf man there is so he gets away with it.'

'We'll still need to talk to him.'

'Of course.'

'If he doesn't work in the evenings, who takes out and brings in the high jump poles and the other equipment you mentioned?'

'Freddie sets out all that stuff and after the session, the athletes bring in the smaller items like the runners' starting blocks and so on. Bigger things, like hurdles, they leave out for him to round up when he turns up in the morning. When there's a football match, the players take care of the nets, corner flags and so on.'

It raised a point Darac hadn't yet considered. 'If there's a match scheduled for later today, it will have to be postponed or played somewhere else.'

Eric shook his head. 'The next game is a week on Wednesday.'

'But the football nets are in place for a match, aren't they?'

'Ah, yes.' He gave a rueful smile. 'The team played in midweek. I asked the skipper to leave the nets up for the kids. It's a treat for them, you see.'

'The kids who sneaked in earlier?'

'Different ones come. I have to shoo them off after a few minutes. The ogre, you know. They think it's still worth it, bless them. The pair this morning? Doubt they'll ever come back.'

Darac felt it worth asking the question one last time.

'Are you still sticking by—'

'What I said about not being able to recognise them and so on? Yes. Absolutely.'

'Alright, back to the changing room-cum-equipment store. Who locks up the building at the end of the sessions? Coach Laborde? One of his assistants?'

'No one does. Or in a way, everyone. The door locks itself.

So if you've left something in there and you're the last one out, you're stuffed.'

'Unless you happen to be one of the keyholders.'

'That's right.'

Or there was one still on site whom you could approach, Darac reflected. 'Don't you and Reixe have keys, too?'

'No.' A vaguely self-pitying quality soured Eric's mien for the moment. 'Not trustworthy enough, Captain. Don't know what they think I might nick. Tend not to have much use for high jump poles and the like, myself.'

Eric may have been joking, but Darac had no problem doubting Reixe's untrustworthiness.

'To be fair,' Eric went on, 'we don't really need the changing room keys and it would only be something else to worry about.'

'No harm done then. Am I right in thinking you can't alarm the changing rooms until everyone is out of the players' car park, you've locked the gate and got back to your caravan?'

'You are, yes.'

'Uh-huh.' Another flag unfurled. 'And last night, no alarm was triggered at any point?'

'No. Never has since I've been here. Well, I tell a lie – once, it has. They reckon an insect of some sort got into the casing and triggered it. For the record, the insect wasn't interested in high jump poles, either.' He checked over his handiwork. 'That'll do for the changing rooms, I think.' He looked up. 'So you're not into football. You're more a rugby man, are you?'

'Don't play any sports at all, I'm afraid. Nor watch them, either.'

'Me, I'm *Le Gym* through and through but no use asking you who you support, then.'

'None. You're doing well, by the way.'

'Yes? I'll put the parking spots in. Apart from the bus bay next to the changing rooms, they're all on one side as you saw. Room for 30 or so cars theoretically but only the top ten have lines painted to demarcate the spaces.' He completed it in short order. 'That looks about right.'

'To me, too. Right, let's go through the sequence of events for last evening in as much detail as we can.'

'I ought to say I don't see *everything* that goes on, Captain. Especially if I get chatting with someone.'

'Sure, but you were on the scene when the first vehicle arrived to park?'

'Had to be or they wouldn't have been able to get in.'

'So when the first vehicle arrives, you unlock the outer gate where your caravan is and admit the vehicle in question. What happens then?'

'What's supposed to happen then isn't humanly possible and that's why it *doesn't* happen.'

'Explain.'

'The outer gate is meant to be locked at all times when the caravan is unmanned. The players' car park gate ditto when I'm down that end. So when I leave either gate, I'm required to lock them behind me.'

'Hang on. So you admit the first vehicle at the caravan, lock the outer gate behind you, nip down to the players' car park in the 2CV and unlock the inner gate. You let the vehicle in, lock *that* gate behind you and, shuttling backwards and forwards every time a vehicle arrives at the outer gate, repeat the process until everyone has arrived? Surely it would be a lot easier if—?'

Eric was ahead of him. 'There were two of us on nights? One at either end? Yes, and until last October, that's exactly how it worked. Streamlining they said. Cost-cutting exercise is what it really was. Been there 17 years, Mauro had.'

'Familiar story, alas. So what do you *actually* do each time, Monsieur?'

'Alright. I was going to ask you not to tell the Powers That Be but after today, I doubt I'll carry on there. How could I? Don't have to work, you know. I just do it for the… Anyway. This is what I do. The first one arrives at the caravan gate. I let it in and, leaving the gate open, escort it down to the players' car park, open that gate and stay there until they're *all* in. Only then do I head back to the caravan and lock the outer gate. What I do next is up to me until the match or the training session ends. What I usually do is go back and watch. It does my heart good to see young… Yeah well, you get the idea.'

'Indeed. And when the first vehicles are ready to leave the players' car park?'

'If I'm down that end at the time, and I usually am, I set off to the caravan gate, unlock it and what I'm supposed to do then is wait there until everybody's gone, lock up, head back to the players' gate, lock that, return to the caravan, turn on the alarm and that's me for the night. And sometimes I do just that even though it means I might miss the start of my programme.'

'Programme?'

'TV programme. I've got one in the caravan. It's a real boon to me. I like watching Annie Provin's 10.30 news round-up on Télé-Sud. Could do with more like her on the box, don't you think?'

'She has her place, certainly.' Darac omitted to specify quite where. 'Overnight, you make rounds of the site, presumably?'

'At midnight, 2.30 and 5 o'clock. But I don't shine a light into *every* corner. I wouldn't go down to the arse end of the players' car park for instance unless I saw or heard something.'

'And last night?'

'Nothing, Captain. The whole site was as quiet as the…' He shuddered and it took several deep breaths for him to continue. 'It was quiet.'

'When vehicles are arriving before a session or a match and leaving afterwards, do you roam about or stand more or less in one place?'

'Bit of both. I never stray very far from the gate, though. Quite often, I stand by the spaces nearest the gate facing the changing rooms. That way, you interact with everyone. Theoretically.'

'Mark that spot, will you? And put your initials next to it.'

Eric did so.

'Excellent. So, can you remember the order in which the vehicles arrived last evening?'

'The bus was first as it nearly always is. And it was all students on board. Again, that's the norm.'

'And when did it arrive?'

'About 6.35. The sessions are underway by seven.'

Under the heading *Cauvin Car Park Diagram*, Darac wrote *1 = Bus* in his notebook and added Eric's estimate of the arrival time. 'Will you mark on the diagram where the bus parked?'

Eric drew an appropriately sized rectangle parallel to the changing rooms' right-hand side elevation. 'Five-point turn Roger does to get it in there. Ends up facing out.'

'We'll be interviewing each one of those students, as I say, but from your perspective, did anything strike you in the way they disembarked? Were there any serious arguments going on or anything else out of the ordinary?'

'It was the same as always. Some wander in quietly; some have earpieces in listening to music. The rest? A lot of joshing and banter, Captain. It can get quite rowdy at times. Arguments? Of course – they're students. But there's never anything nasty in it.'

'OK. So the student athletes disembarked from the bus as normal. Did they disappear into the changing rooms right away?'

'Exactly so.'

'Who arrived next?'

'Monsieur Laborde, two or three minutes after the bus which again is usually the case.' Eric drew another roughly to-scale rectangle, this one occupying the car space nearest the gate. 'He backed in so it was facing the changing rooms. Always comes alone.'

'Put a figure 2 in it, will you?' Darac wrote *2 = Laborde* in his notebook, adding *arrived c. 6.40.*

'About another five minutes after that, a couple of the assistant coaches arrived together and parked right next to Coach Laborde. Again, they usually do that. Franck Chambron, whose car it is; and a tight-lipped Australian bugger called Kevin Mac-Something.' He checked the list. 'Macdonald.'

'And these two are his assistants, you say?'

'Chambron coaches the field events.' He looked up. 'You know, jumping, throwing things, and stuff. Macdonald does a bit of everything.'

Darac made the note. 'Thanks. Put a number—'

'Three in it? I'm with you, Captain. In case you were wondering, we don't do any of the long-throw stuff down there. The javelin, discus and hammer all go on at the Charles-Ehrmann. We've got the football pitch to think of, you see. Best in the area bar none.'

'Even I noticed how perfect it looked.' Darac made the note. 'And the next arrival?'

'I think it would be... Yves? Yes, it was. Got here just before 6.50. Don't know his surname but he's a distance runner.' He checked the list once more. 'Yves... Siagne. Fair enough. Timid lad. Sometimes he gets the bus, sometimes he comes on his bike. There's a line of concreted-in stanchions on the left of the changing rooms – the opposite side to where the bus parks.' Taking care with the orientation, he added a row of dots. 'He locks it to them and that's what he did yesterday.

Which one it was, I didn't really notice.'

'Doesn't matter – just put 4 next to the row and add the word "bikes." '

It was done.

'Then, and this was unusual, while Yves was locking up his bike, Koko turned up by car. Didn't even know he could drive. He'd always come by bus before.'

An anomaly. And one that had occurred on an evening that had led to a brutal murder.

'Koko?' Darac said, blandly.

'Adebayo Okoko is his full name.' Eric's smile was part amusement, part paternalistic fondness. 'He's a good lad is Koko. Long jumper.'

Eric clearly didn't share his colleague Reixe's racist views, Darac reflected, as he double-underlined the young man's name.

'Did you have a chance to exchange a few words with him?'

'Just to ask him where he'd nicked the car.'

Darac grinned, going with the flow. 'And where had he?'

'Nah, it was his sister's. She had DJ'd at a celebration party the team had put on the night before. He'd gone back with her and she'd let him borrow it.'

'A celebration in aid of?'

'Couple of the team had been picked for France.'

'Ah, yes, a colleague mentioned it to me,' Darac said, recalling Bonbon's earlier comments. 'Quite an honour.'

'Yes. We're all made up about it. Especially for Grace. Grace Nahili. Does the heptathlon. Lovely girl. Always got a word for you. She's one of the bus people.'

'Back to Koko. Where did he park?'

'A couple of spaces down from Chambron.'

A figure 5 went into the appropriate slot.

'Two more names,' Darac said, recognising that the light

lifting Eric's mien was already fading back. 'One of whom must be Samira.'

'Yes…' Eric steadied himself. 'But it was Baille who came next.' He gave Darac an enquiring look. 'Julien Baille? He's the other new international. The better known of the two.'

'The brilliant runner. Yes, my colleague named him specifically.'

'Be just after 6.50 when he showed.'

'By car?'

'Hasn't got one as far as I know. Almost always comes on his bike and he did again last night. Locked it up next to Yves's.' He pictured the scene. 'The stanchion furthest back from where I was, now I think.' Eric scribbled a figure 6 in the selected spot. 'Yes. There.'

'And finally?'

Eric took a deep breath but went no further.

'I know this isn't easy, Monsieur, but if we are to apprehend whoever was responsible—'

'Yes, yes. Absolutely. It was late for her to arrive – just a few minutes before 7. All the other athletes were out on the track.'

'Was there time to speak to her in passing?'

'No, our eyes didn't even meet. She dashed straight off to the rooms. I waited a good fifteen minutes in case there were any stragglers, then headed off to lock up at the other end.'

Darac went back to the sofa. 'We'll come on to how the departures went in a minute so hang on to that sheet for the time being.'

'OK.'

'Thanks for your efforts so far, though, Monsieur Cauvin. Providing such a detailed picture will be a real help to us.'

'I'd do anything to help you nail the bastard, Captain. Anything.'

'That's good to know. So may we return to the contretemps

between Samira and one of the athletes you mentioned earlier? Who was the athlete in question, Monsieur?'

'It wasn't someone who would murder anyone, let me tell you that.'

'I'm sure,' Darac lied. 'Just trying to get an even more complete picture of things.'

Eric thought about it. 'Yes, alright. It was Julien Baille.'

So it was Baille who was in a relationship with Samira. And all was perhaps not well between them. Darac circled his name. Eric seemed to feel some antipathy toward the man, too, Darac noticed. 'He runs the steeplechase, I gather.'

Eric shook his head. 'If you're implying there's some sort of connection to where the body... No. He couldn't. I'd stake my own life on it.'

'I'm not implying anything, Monsieur.'

Eric's body language required no translation but he gave one anyway. 'I know. I'm just ... jumpy, I guess. Carry on, please, Captain.'

'Well, tell me more about Julien. What do you make of him?'

'A brilliant runner, as you said, but he is temperamental – like a lot of champion types are. Single-minded. Been known to go off on one...' He caught himself. 'But not in a violent way. More like a spoiled child, he is. Most of the time he doesn't say anything. Brow always knotted. Lost in thought and it never seems a happy one. Weight of the world, and all that.'

With the remote possibility that Eric may himself have murdered Samira notwithstanding, Darac was beginning to realise just how valuable the observations of such a watchful night watchman were proving.

'And how are *you* feeling now, Monsieur?'

'So Brice told you about the... earlier.'

'He did and it isn't surprising. It was a ghastly sight for

us professionals and we see this kind of thing practically every day. And the most important difference – we weren't acquainted with the victim.'

'There's no use saying I wish I hadn't known her but…'

'It's alright. Take a moment.'

He stared at the window. 'I was on the post most of my working life, Captain. Before my leg, you know. One morning I came across a dog in a gutter. Run over. For weeks, I couldn't pass the spot without seeing that poor thing lying there. And now *this*?' He grasped the diagram sheet more tightly. 'I'll *never* forget it.'

'If it helps you in any way, neither will any of my team.'

'I don't know how you do your job.'

On more than one occasion, Darac had wondered the same thing, himself. 'Monsieur, perhaps we'd better turn to how the evening broke up. I'll annotate the sheet.'

Eric was still in something of a daze as he handed it over. 'Don't know how you do your job at all.'

'Someone has to, I guess,' Darac said, resuming his seat. 'Alright to continue?'

'Uh, yes. It's important.'

'Before we get into the departure sequence, would you first tell me how Roger Lauvette spends his time at the stadium? Does he stay in the bus, watch the training, chat with you?'

'A combination of all of them. But he's always at the wheel to tick off the names for the return journey.'

'And he does that meticulously?'

'He's the stickler type. The idea of setting off without anyone? Never happen.'

'OK.' Darac brandished his pen. 'So talk me through how the departures went. Apart from Samira's unexplained detour to the dark end of the car park before she left, did anything else strike you as odd?'

'Odd?' Once again, Eric honoured the process by considering the question carefully. 'Not *odd* but I have to report I didn't see Julien ride away. He must have, though, because his bike wasn't still chained to the stanchion when I locked up for the night.'

Consulting the diagram, Darac could see a possible explanation. 'The bus was parked at the other side of the building. From where you were standing, might Julien's departure have been shielded by the bus? If they left at the same time, I mean?'

Eric replayed the scene in his head. 'It *could* have.'

'And what time did the bus leave?'

'About 10.15.'

'Anything else out of the ordinary?'

Eric made a moue. 'Monsieur Laborde's mood, perhaps?'

'Go on,' Darac said, wondering if it would account for one of Eric's hesitations earlier.

'Perhaps it's because he's always the last to leave that we often exchange a good few words. And quips, too – especially if *Le Gym* have just forked out a hundred million for some useless tosser of a centre forward, or whatever. But he seemed... I don't know, preoccupied.'

'When he arrived, also?'

'No. Just the opposite. Joys of Spring when he got here. What with the national selectors picking Grace and Baille. Plus I heard him joking with Emil about his wedding anniversary party which was on the same night as the announcement, funnily enough. Practically bankrupted him, he said. Just for the flowers, alone.'

'Emil?'

'Emil Arcot. Another lovely lad. Team Captain. Always comes by bus. Big mate of Koko's. Big in more ways than one, actually. He's a shot putter. Don't suppose you've ever lifted one?'

'No.'

'Take it from me, they're heavy. When he nails it, Emil can launch the things nearly 20 metres. I've seen him juggle *three* simultaneously. Like bean bags.' He raised a self-admonishing hand. 'But that's all beside the point. Sorry.'

Darac pictured Samira's smashed skull. 'Not at all. He's the Captain of the team, you say? Be useful to talk to him.'

'It would, I'm sure. He knows everyone and everything.'

'Perfect. But back to Coach Laborde. You normally get on well with him?'

'We're not exactly bosom buddies but we get on well enough, yeah. To be honest, I sometimes think it's more that he knows how to manage people to get the best out of them. Goes with the territory, I suppose. Being a coach and everything.'

'He's a very driven individual, I hear.'

'He works bloody hard, I'll tell you that. Could do with a few more like him around.'

'And you have no idea what might have extinguished his bonhomie during the course of last night's session? Think.'

Eric gave due consideration to the question. 'Tempers can fray during the sessions themselves, of course. It's normal. But once they're over, they're over. It all stays out on the track.'

'A thought. Was Laborde on the phone when he pulled away? And that's why he short-changed you on the chat front?'

'He wasn't holding one. Even if he had been, he would probably have waved it at me to show why he wasn't stopping. He's like that.'

'When did he leave?'

'As I say, he and the assistant coaches are always last to go – they get together after the sessions to discuss how it all went, you see. Franck's car left first. A minute or so behind him, Monsieur Laborde went. In fact, now that I think, I can tell you exactly when it was because all I got out of him was: "Sorry we're late, Eric. You'll be missing your programme." So I said, "Not to worry, it's only been on two minutes." "10.32,

already?" he said. "Better go." He went shooting off and that
was me for the night.'

'*Shooting* off?'

'Yes, like I said, he seemed in a bit of a hurry.'

Darac made the note, photographed the diagram and shared
it with his team. 'Monsieur Cauvin, I want to thank you for
your help.' He shook Eric's hand. 'We may need to speak to
you again.'

'Any time at all.' He grasped Darac's forearm. 'But get him,
Captain. Do you hear me? Get him.'

'I assure you we will do all we can.'

As Darac buzzed himself out of the building, his mobile
rang. 'Bonbon? I'm heading back to the car and was just going
to call you. Go ahead.'

'First, Agnès has come through for us again. Our "They
Shall Not Pass" chums from Foch have turned up and we're
tight as a drum now. Alas, before they got here, Laborde arrived
and he was scarcely less distraught than Dilip Padar was earlier.'

'Had Map's entourage left with the body at that point?'

'Yes, and fortunately they didn't pass Laborde on the lane.
Didn't miss him by much, actually. But the tent is still up, of
course.'

'It's often when people see such things that the reality of
murder hits home.'

'There were words also, unfortunately. In fact, "unfortunately"
hardly covers it. Struggling to prevent Laborde catching sight
of the tent, one of the Joinel uniforms accompanied his efforts
with: "This won't help Mademoiselle Padar, Monsieur". Idiot!'

'God, what next? We don't even know for certain the
victim *is* Samira.'

'I know. Anyway, Laborde left immediately afterwards. I
suggested he wait for a car but he drove himself. Home, I
think. Ah, just a second, chief.'

Darac heard Flaco's voice in the background.

'OK, Flak has just received the contact details we needed. She's pinging them over to you as we speak. She has more, hang on... OK, she asks us to note that Samira shares an apartment with fellow law student Carole Monteux. Boulevard Bischoffsheim address. No landline to the apartment but we do have Carole's mobile number. What do you reckon – too early in the investigation to contact her?'

'I'd prefer to be just that little surer of the victim's ID before we do. So Carole's a fellow law student? She isn't a fellow athlete, or at least I don't remember her name on the original list.'

'Let me look... No, she isn't. In other news, Perand is en route from La Trin' and he should be here any minute. For once, I'm looking forward to seeing him.'

'Let's hope he's on one of his more inspired days. As you've already gathered, I gleaned a lot from Eric Cauvin who's something of a sweetheart and not the risk we suspected at all. We'll reconvene fully when I get back which should be less than ten minutes. Anything else?'

'R.O's begun his preliminary examination of Samira's watch. It's a Michel Vignot, by the way. Beautiful thing or rather was. I've come across other Vignots on my antiques travels over the years but I've never seen a contemporary piece before.'

'Might its provenance be traceable?'

'If the serial number is intact, it might well be. *Should* be, in fact.'

'Fingers crossed, Bonbon,' Darac said, zapping his driver's door. 'Fingers crossed.'

THIRTY-FIVE

The queue had been moving slowly but steadily until a protracted enquiry about the effectiveness of suppositories for a particular malady stopped progress altogether. Unlike her snatched exchanges with Dédé, Cassie hadn't strained her ears to decrypt the whispered details. 'No thought for others, some people,' said the woman sitting alongside her. 'It's been my turn for nearly ten minutes.' Cassie gave her a vaguely affirming look and returned to her magazine. 'Hey! Haven't got all day,' the woman called out. If she was hoping Cassie would add her voice to the protest, she was on a loser. Sitting in a brightly lit, sweet-smelling pharmacy waiting to be served? Cassie would happily have sat here for the rest of her life. Number 87 was showing on the screen. She was 90. Two people ahead of her. Only two. And now a second window was opening. A bigger shame was the reason for her visit. Shampoo, bath bomb or lipstick for her? No. A prescription. For him.

The door opened and Cassie's heart put in an extra beat and then missed several in a row. The newcomer was a cop, one of the trio watching Place Wilson: the one who spent most of his time up a pole pretending to be a *Télécom* engineer. He scanned the waiting area as if deciding whether to stay or come back later. To Cassie's chagrin, number 88 came up on the screen and, declaring it was about time, the woman on her right vacated her place. The cop detached a ticket from the dispenser.

What to do? Cassie couldn't walk out of the pharmacy, leaving the prescription unfilled. She would have to brazen it out. It was an alarming thought but it was probably safer if the cop replaced the impatient woman who'd been sitting next to her. Unless he wanted to talk. That would be curtains. Cassie's stomach, never the strongest, began to turn over. The screen display changed to 89 and a man sitting at a right-angle way to her left got to his feet. The cop took his seat. There would be no conversation but now he would be able to study her profile at will. And he would get a good view of her standing and walking to the counter. Not for the first time, Cassie cursed her good looks.

But think. Was she in real danger here? She was dressed in her own clothes and not wearing any of the disguise. That was key. And she was wearing glasses. The cop was off-duty now and perhaps he'd switched off his surveillance head. And – a daily question for Cassie – what was *more* dangerous, anyway? Continuing with the job or giving herself up? She could. She could do it here and now.

The screen display changed to 90. Cassie took a deep breath.

THIRTY-SIX

Inès Laborde embraced her mother in a way she never quite had before. Having dreaded the thought of coming out to her, she now wished she had done so years before. And when she had announced her intention to marry – now quite legally – the love of her life, she was delighted that Zoë's only question concerned the identity of the lucky woman. "It had better be Susan," she had said, the gifted musician whom she regarded as a "perfect match" for her daughter.

Had the break-up of Zoë's own marriage enabled Inès to come to this new and glorious understanding with her? Whether it had or not, it was a gift that would go on giving. There was no longer any need for Inès to toe the line with her disgrace of a father. The rat was out of the bag.

Inès understood that the road ahead was not without its obstacles for her mother. At the moment, Zoë was full of resolve to strike out anew. And years before, doing precisely the same thing in her professional life had worked wonderfully. Why wouldn't making a similar move in her personal life work equally as well? It was a source of comfort to Inès that her mother was in a stronger position to achieve this than many women in her situation. She ran her own successful business. She had her own money. She had a half-share in the house that she was already referring to as "the property." Despite the positives, Inès was still worried that Zoë's resolve might wane once the controlling Gilles, confronted with the prospect of losing something he didn't even value, began to employ his considerable powers of persuasion to win her back.

'You won't let that happen, will you, Maman?'

Zoë pulled out of the embrace. 'No, darling,' she said,

squeezing Inès's hands as she looked her squarely in the eye. 'I will not.'

'Promise?'

'Promise. I'm a Boss Woman, remember?'

The door flew open and the women turned. Before them was a sight neither had ever seen before.

'What are you doing here, you pig?' Eyes wide and wild, Inès bore down on her father. 'Sobbing won't do it for you. You've failed. Do you understand, Coach Laborde? You're last. Relegated. Thrown out of the league. So fuck off back to your… whatever she is. And don't come back.'

The man hadn't heard a word.

'Samira's dead,' he said, half-shouting, half-whimpering. 'She's been… murdered.'

THIRTY-SEVEN

On the return journey to the Stade, Darac suffered the profound displeasure of having to swap the melodious explorations of pianist Bill Evans for the odious posturing of Public Prosecutor Jules Frènes. With their mutual disregard to the fore, the call went the way of virtually every other since their first coming together twelve years earlier and it ended on the same unspoken understanding. As long as Commissaire Agnès Dantier's homicide clearance rate remained the highest in the region and just about the speediest in the whole country, her chief investigating officer Darac would continue to be granted freedoms unheard of elsewhere. Were Agnès's squad ever to be knocked off that top spot, Frènes had made it clear that everything would change for them.

Darac well understood that a successful outcome to the current case was not Frènes's only requirement and when he joined Bonbon, Flaco, Lartigue and Raul Ormans outside the mobile incident truck, he wasted no time in making the point. 'Should this murder prove a hit at the box office, and less face it, it has all the hallmarks, our plucky public prosecutor has volunteered to position himself front and centre for the media.'

'Good,' Bonbon said, 'The longer he sticks himself in front of the cameras, the less he'll get in our way.'

'Agreed.' Darac indicated the truck. 'Comms up and running yet?'

Bonbon essayed his "what a dumb question" look. 'With Bé twiddling the knobs?'

Darac nodded. 'Of course they are. Shall we?'

The trio boarded and, after warmly greeting its crew of

three, Darac opened his notebook and got on with things.

'Alright, I'll summarise where I think we're at in a moment but R.O, you've been able to work your magic on the victim's watch?'

'A Vignot, no less. I have indeed. Lartou here has logged it back in for further examination but I have some photos.' He reached for his tablet. 'I'll just retrieve them.'

Through the truck's open rear doors, a skinny young man with a blue chin loped lopsidedly into Darac's eyeline. Gaining with every stride, a second figure appeared behind him, alert-looking and strongly built. It was as oddly matched a pair as had ever worked out of the Caserne Auvare.

'Hang fire a second, R.O,' Darac said. 'Perand and Serge Paulin are joining us.'

As greetings were exchanged, Darac felt a slight frisson of guilt at welcoming Serge back from leave. Forgetting that he and partner Erica had told him they were spending it home was one thing; not realising that the pair were back at work from today, quite another. 'I've already had to enlist Erica's help this morning,' Darac said. 'Child's play for her but I suspect her superior IT skills will be called upon later.'

'Superior to those even of her superior?' Ormans said, feigning outrage. 'Actually, I wholeheartedly endorse the assessment.'

'*And…* scene,' Darac said, gently sending up Ormans's theatricality. 'Now we're all here, I think we'll begin with my summary, then go on to your watch findings, R.O. Alright with you?'

Ormans graciously inclined his head.

'Alright, mindful that the victim's ID is still to be *officially* verified, here's how I think we stand at the moment. Bonbon? Flak? Chip in if I leave out anything.'

No interventions proved necessary and by the end of Darac's summary, everyone was au fait with what had been factually established or at least credibly posited so far. Four details from Eric Cauvin's account particularly exercised him and he stressed them to the team: the "lovers' spat" between Samira and the temperamental Julien Baille; her unexplained detour to the far end of the players' car park on the night she was killed; Baille's unseen departure on the same night; and the fact that anyone using the changing-cum-storeroom had access to instruments capable of delivering the ultimate blunt force injury. Darac voiced a further observation. Although there was as yet no justification for suspecting the man himself, he couldn't shake the thought that shot putter and keyholder Emil Arcot had ready access to, and great dexterity with, those blunt instruments. Against this, he reminded the team that until Eric arrived back in his caravan after locking up the players' car park, any keyholder could have gained access to the changing rooms without triggering the alarm.

'As we gather more evidence,' Darac went on, 'we'll be continuously reassessing all these concerns, obviously. I'm hoping Map will be able to firm up the victim's ID for us shortly but, until he does, I think we should delay paying a visit to Samira's address.' He turned to Ormans. 'OK, you're on, R.O.'

'First, a thought about the meaty Monsieur Arco's metier. We're working on a number of things but I could add testing the shots to the list. Even the minutest traces of blood, tissue fragments and so on would be easy enough to find. And providing there's an inventory, determining if one is missing would be easier still.'

'Add them – absolutely. For now, tell us about the stopped watch you've been examining.'

'Your own misgivings about it being?'

'That there were no contusions or other marks on the victim's wrists or forearms consistent with her attempting to fend off a violent attack. And, quoting Map, bear in mind that the fatal blow was sudden, devastating and administered from immediately behind her. Yet the watch itself, a delicate analogue piece, has clearly taken a bash. There are a number of possible interpretations but the most likely hinges on that quality of delicacy. What do you call the little capstan thing on the side of the watch that moves the hands?'

Ormans shook his head. 'I know how it works but I'm not sure I know its proper name.'

'The crown,' Bonbon said.

'The crown?' Darac repeated, giving Bonbon an acknowledging nod. 'Even on my full-sized wristwatch, turning it can be quite a fiddly operation. The crown on the victim's watch is tiny, so she would have taken it off to adjust the time, wouldn't she? Frankie wears a not dissimilar watch and that's what she does. I think the evidence shows that's what the killer did, too. The motive? Probably to support an alibi yet to be provided by said killer, and/or to implicate someone they knew *would* have been with the victim at the time selected. The killer then bashed the watch to stop it, wrecking the crown in the process, and not realising that the likes of us would notice such an anomaly, refastened the damaged watch on the quite *un*damaged wrist of his victim.'

'Bravo, Darac – my findings entirely support your analysis and I discovered another factor that both supports it and it gives further evidence of the killer's competency or lack of it.' Ormans gave it an actorish beat. 'There were no fingerprints on the watch or the strap.'

Perand scratched his chin. 'You mean there were too many prints to isolate just one?'

With imperious disdain, Ormans turned to the young man. 'I mean there were no prints, Max. Not one, including, therefore, the victim's *own* prints. Ergo, the watch has been wiped. Under my travelling 'scope, one can make out the characteristic smears. Wiped presumably by the killer who evidently hadn't been wearing gloves either to commit the murder or to handle the watch. Yes?'

Perand shrugged. 'Alright, R.O.'

'So that's two misjudgements by the killer,' Darac said.

Flaco was in full scowl of concentration mode. 'Suggesting, Captain, that the murder was unpremeditated?'

'And in trying to cover things up, he then made some poor decisions? It's happened before.'

Bonbon nodded. 'It's the percentage play.'

Other possibilities were already trading fours in Darac's head but he needed to move things on. 'The percentage play? Definitely.' He turned to Ormans. 'Got anything else on the watch, R.O ?'

'Indeed I have.' He brought up an image on his tablet and displayed it to the group. 'As you can see, this shows the watch's..?' He turned to Bonbon. 'Proper term?'

'Case back,' he said. 'Sorry it's not more esoteric but there it is.'

'And I am sorry that what is inscribed upon it is such a miniature testament to the engraver's art. However, all is not lost.' Ormans brought up a second shot. 'There.'

Peering at the enlarged image, Darac read the inscription aloud: ' "Had we but world enough and time." Hmm. Poetic language. Without revisiting Lit Crit 101, I think it's a safe bet that the watch was given as a love token of some kind, wasn't it?'

'An engagement gift, maybe?' Serge said. 'It is an ideal sentiment to have engraved on a watch.'

Ormans grinned, archly. 'Never come across the source before, but I discovered the words were extracted from a poem by an Englishman by the name of Marvell, of all things, and it's less classy than one might have first thought. Entitled "To His Coy Mistress", it's certainly earthier.' He brought up a page of text. 'Listen to the opening couplet: "Had we but

world enough and time, This coyness, lady, were no crime."
The message is clear, isn't it?'

Perand grinned. 'He's basically saying "we haven't got all
the time in the world darling so stop your nonsense and get
'em off." '

Flaco's cornrows appeared more acutely aligned than ever
as she nodded in agreement with Perand – a rarity, Darac
reflected.

'The language may be cleverer,' she said. 'But unless things
develop differently in the rest of the poem, it sounds like
coercive sexual harassment in disguise.'

Ormans scrolled to the end. 'It *doesn't* appear to veer off,
actually. Here's the final couplet: "Thus, though we cannot
make our sun stand still, yet we will make him run."'

Serge gave Flaco a look. 'I take it all back.'

'"Make him run?"' Bonbon said. 'Seems appropriate,
considering where we are.'

Darac saw a further connection. 'It's more appropriate still
when we remember the "lovers' spat" between Samira and
Julien Baille that Eric Cauvin reported witnessing a week
ago. The nature of that disagreement seems to chime perfectly
with the theme of Mister Marvell's poem. He wanted sex;
she didn't.'

'How much does a Michel Vignot watch retail for,
Bonbon?' Perand asked.

'For the quality, they're not unduly expensive, actually. The
Vignots are not part of a conglomerate or anything. They're
watchmakers exclusively and so we're talking... 500 euros
or so here? Nevertheless, it would make a very extravagant
gift – if gift is the word in this case – for one student to give
to another.'

'Baille may well come from money, Bonbon,' Serge said.

'Perhaps. Even so. Chief?'

'We need more on this, obviously. Interestingly, Eric

Cauvin recalls Samira wearing only a "chunky sports watch" to training. He never once saw her wearing a dress watch but as he pointed out himself, that doesn't mean she never did. Naturally, we'll need corroboration on anything of note that Eric came up with earlier, but he's an observant type not given to exaggeration and I sense that that corroboration will come.'

Serge nodded. 'Particularly observant of him to have recognised those little pin prick marks in the victim's ear and from them, identified her. Nothing we've learned since contradicts his conclusion.'

Perand appeared to be considering a darker interpretation. '*Too* observant, do you think? He wouldn't be the first old man to become totally obsessed with a young beauty. She rejects him, perhaps humiliatingly, and he kills her as a result. He was in Position A to do it, let's face it.'

Darac appreciated the suggestion but he had already dismissed it as a possibility. 'And left her body where he did? I have a number of other objections, too. Let's move on. We'll get official confirmation from Map in due course but it's certainly looking that the victim *was* Samira.' He glanced at his watch. 'I shouldn't think we'll have to wait long to hear from Erica. And now that telecom carriers yield so much data, she'll be pinging over far more than just a list of incoming and outgoing numbers from Samira's phone. Next – her car.' He turned to the personification of attentive diligence that was Béatrice Lacquet. 'Bé, you've got both Dilip and Samira Padar's personal details, there?'

'Yes, Captain.'

'Samira was driving Dilip's roughly five-year-old grey Renault Mégane last night. Find the registration and APB the full description, would you? We need to find it soonest.'

'Understood.'

Darac turned back to the team. 'We're still largely in

conjecture mode at the moment but I'm sure we all realise that once we start interviewing those who were here last night, and other interested parties, the situation will quickly become a lot clearer. So let's keep an open mind on things for the time being and I'm very much including myself in that. For instance, I keep referring to the killer as male. We don't know that. And look at the image I have in my head of shot putter Emil Arcot wielding one of the things to perform the deed. That doesn't cut the mustard even as conjecture. It's painting by numbers thinking driven by presupposition, prejudice and good old-fashioned ignorance, probably.'

Flaco raised a hand. 'Don't forget that Grace Nahili is a heptathlete, Captain. Shot putt is one of her disciplines, too.'

'Is it? Well, there's a case in point.'

Darac's mobile rang once more and as he went to answer it, Perand leaned in to Flaco. 'Good to see your championing of women's rights includes putting them in the frame for murder,' he whispered.

'A black woman, too,' she whispered back. 'You missed an opportunity there, Perand. I'll be happy to discuss these things more fully with you but after work, alright? *After.*'

Darac's call connected. 'Agnès?' He gave Perand a hard stare. 'We're all listening.'

'With resources as they are, it was more a question of who was available rather than whom to select but I've assembled a nine-strong squad to slog through the bulk of the less critical interviews.' The announcement was welcomed warmly. 'Have you had time to triage those out yet?'

'We're just about to start.'

'Armani has been able to spare Farid incidentally, so I've put him in charge of them.' More approbation from the team. 'I'll share their details with Bé in a minute.'

'Thanks so much for this, Agnès.'

'*Pah.* How would you like to brief Farid and his team?

In person at the Stade? Or would you rather I set up a conference call on video? They're all here at the Caserne at the moment.'

'I think it would be useful for them to check out the Stade site in person. And although the Caserne is more at the centre of things and we're a bit out on a limb here, the addresses Farid and co will be making for after the briefing are mainly halls of residence and most of those are nearer here.'

'That settles it. I'll detail them over to you now. Be there in about 20 minutes. And depending on how the day goes, I think we should schedule a full team meeting here at the Caserne this evening. Time TBA.'

'Agreed.'

The call ended, Darac picked up where he'd left off.

'Thanks to Agnès, we can breathe more easily so before we get into the triage, let's return to the watch for a moment. Whether its engraved message strikes you as heartfelt eroticism or sex-pest patter, the fact of it, coupled with Eric's report of Julien Baille's sexual entreaties to a resistant Samira make the watch's provenance all the more important, right? R.O, underneath all the damage, were you able to determine its age, roughly?'

'It was in new condition, I would say. Brand new, possibly.'

'Perfect. Any joy with finding a serial number?'

'There are two sets of numbers on it and one of them looks complete.' He referred to his notebook. 'B22X17. Sound right to you, Bonbon?'

'Alphanumerics tend to be used for model reference numbers, not serial numbers. Did you find that on the case side between the strap lugs?'

'Yes – at the 12 o'clock position. And there are four numbers above and to one side of what's left of the crown but it looks to me as if they would have continued on the other side as well. Sadly, there *is* no other side, practically. It's telling, don't you think, that the damage is greatest in that area? Irredeemably so, from our point of view.'

Perand treated Ormans to one of his sourest sideways grins. 'The rest of the serial number has been obliterated? I think you could say that's telling.'

'I *am* delighted you agree, Max.'

'Gentlemen?' Darac said, a reminder rather than a rebuke.

'I've had a thought about the provenance,' Bonbon said. 'I'm not sure how Michel Vignot's numbering system works but I know people who will certainly be au fait with it. And with any luck, the missing numbers may not have contained the info that would have been of most use to us, anyway. A combination of the model number, which we have intact, and those first four digits from the serial number might well be sufficient to track down the seller and eventually, therefore, the purchaser.'

'As soon as we've divvied up the interviews, will you start the ball rolling on that?'

'I will, yes. A couple of calls will do it.'

'Good. OK – triage time. Stick around, R.O. Your input will be welcomed, obviously.'

'Obviously, but immediately afterwards I must take my fine-toothed comb and a brace of my finer supporting players over to that place of interest that is the far end of the players' car park.'

'Sure.' Reflecting again that Raul Ormans's thespian speechifying seemed more pronounced than ever, Darac opted to keep what he had to say next plain and to the point. 'We all know that other persons of interest may ultimately come into the picture here. And if the killer *does* prove to be one of the 30 or so folk we and our nine slog-squad mates are going to start interviewing shortly, that killer might be someone we have no handle on at all as yet. But we have to start somewhere so, as we stand, who do we five interview first? And who goes to the back of the queue for Farid's guys? At this stage, we will be taking one interviewee each. Lartou? We need more cars.'

'I'm on it, chief.'

'Depending on developments, we'll aim to reconvene here afterwards, assess and go again. Right?'

In less time than it took Darac's band to agree on a set list for a night at The Blue Devil, the team came up with a running order for the interviews. No one disagreed about which of the 30 names stood alone at the head of the queue and when moments later, Lami Toto rang from the path lab confirming that Samira had now been formally identified as the murder victim, the way ahead seemed clear.

'Bé?'

'Yes, Captain?'

'We need to make some calls.'

THIRTY-EIGHT

It was a good hour later that having prepared the ground with the directors of study and departmental secretaries concerned, Darac, Serge Paulin and slog squad acting C.O. Farid drew up at the complex of *résidences étudiantes* overlooking the Faculty of Letters building and, synchronising their watches, dispersed to interview their quite unprepared interviewees. The same scenario was being enacted at various other campuses and private addresses across the city. But only Darac had the ultra-capable Serge standing by to assist with an arrest should everything go perfectly. Cloud Cuckoo Land was a real place wasn't it?

The *résidences* varied in size and orientation and though he knew it was idiotic, Darac couldn't resist ranking them for desirability as he followed a combination of slopes and steps to his objective, which, with its wide-open view over the Baie des Anges, proved to be his favourite. After entering the code he'd been given, he pushed through the glass outer doors and headed for the top floor.

The door to number 53 opened to reveal a lean young man of average height, wearing jogging bottoms and a plain white T-shirt. A remarkably alert if nervy expression animated what was an otherwise unremarkable face. Eric Cauvin had described him well, Darac reflected. The young man's eyes were dry and there was no puffiness around them. Whether they would remain that way remained to be seen.

'If you're media, my agent should have told your office I never give interviews during term time.'

'Not media, Monsieur Baille. I'm Captain Paul Darac of the Brigade Criminelle.' He showed his ID. 'May I come in?'

'Uh… what's this about? I was just about to go for a run.'

'It will have to wait. I'm afraid I bring bad news.'

A picture of disquiet, Julien stood slowly aside and Darac entered one of the tidiest student rooms he had ever encountered. The young man had won numerous trophies and prestigious medals in athletics but there was nothing on view to indicate that celebrity. A corner of his parents' home in Grenoble was festooned with such things, Darac presumed. Monsieur and Madame Baille, the team now knew, ran their own accountancy business. So had only child Julien "come from money" as they had speculated? It seemed likely. They had certainly produced a talented son, on and off the track. When laying the groundwork for the interview, Darac had learned from Julien's director of studies that his reading for a doctorate in European Literature came on the back of a bachelor's degree in which he'd achieved the joint second highest grade score in the country. "What is Julien working on, exactly?" Darac had asked the director. "Would you be any the wiser if I told you?" came the reply. "I might." And so it had proved. In spades.

There were two chairs in the room, one at a desk set beneath a window overlooking the bay, the other against the wall at the foot of the bed opposite. As it was door-side, Darac indicated the latter. 'May I sit?' Julien absently waved assent. 'And I suggest you do the same, Monsieur. I further suggest you permit me to film this interview on my official device here.' He took a small videocam out of his bag and set it on the desk. 'It's neither providing a live link, nor are the results it produces editable in any way. Again, this is for the benefit of us both. Alright with you?'

'*What* is this about?'

'That's a yes?'

'Yes, yes.'

While Darac tagged the recording, Julien moved to the

chair next to the bed and lowered himself on to it almost as if he were in a trance.

Darac gave it a couple of beats and in a neutral voice said: 'I have to tell you that this morning, the body of a fellow member of Coach Gilles Laborde's elite athletics squad was found dead at the Stade Walter Vallain. Murdered. I'm afraid the victim was Mademoiselle Samira Padar.'

Julien's jaw dropped and his whole body shook. Tears stained his eyes and ran down his cheeks. For some moments, all he could utter was a series of incoherent sounds but when words finally came, he said: 'And why are you telling *me* this, specifically?'

'Why? Because you were in a relationship with her, were you not? One that perhaps wasn't going as well as you would have liked.'

Julien stirred uncomfortably, the pulse in his neck throbbing visibly. 'Who told you that? Carole, that harridan of a flatmate of hers? She tried to poison Samira against me from the beginning.'

'We are yet to speak to Mademoiselle Carole Monteux, Monsieur.' Actually, Darac suspected that Flaco's interview with her was probably already underway. 'But rest assured, we will.'

'No, I can't believe this. For fuck's sake! Me *murder* Sam? It's… absurd! Totally! I couldn't have harmed a hair on her head. How did— No! Don't tell me. I don't want to know.'

More tears came and they persisted for some time. If you're not as innocent as you claim, Darac thought to himself, you are certainly turning in a compelling performance. As to informing Julien of how Samira had been killed and where her body had been discovered, Darac had decided not to provide such details at this stage, anyway. Over the years, many suspects had implicated themselves by offering alibis for times and locations unspecified by the officers questioning them.

'Are you in a fit state to continue, Monsieur?'

'I…' He couldn't seem to articulate the thought. 'I suppose so.'

'Alright. "Had we but world enough and time." Does that line of poetry mean anything to you?'

The question appeared to wrong-foot him. At first.

'I suspect, Captain… Darac, is it, that you know damn well it means more than just *anything* to me.'

'Because?'

'Because? It's from Marvell. And Marvell's work is at the centre of the doctoral thesis I'm writing.' In lieu of a harder surface, he brought his hand sharply down on his thigh. 'As you bloody well know, don't you!'

As yet, the team hadn't been able to trace the full provenance of the watch Samira had been wearing on the evening. But Julien couldn't know that.

'You bought a rather lovely wristwatch for Samira, didn't you?'

'I did no such thing.'

'And you had it engraved with just those words. Words from a poem that no one in my team has ever heard of, nor the poet himself, come to that.'

'*Flics?*' He gave a sour laugh. 'Why doesn't that surprise me?'

'But *you* could recite the poem backwards, probably, couldn't you, Monsieur? There's no crime in buying your lover an expensive watch and having a rather beautiful sentiment engraved upon it.' This was not the moment to offer alternative interpretations. 'Is there?' This was also not the moment to bring up issues foregrounded by the time-tampering and smashing episodes. 'Why not admit it?'

Julien jumped to his feet. 'You… you're trying to trap me.'

'Sit down.' Julien remained standing, eyeing the door. 'And don't think of trying to make a run for it. In the unlikely event that you got past me, I wouldn't be able to catch you, obviously. But there's a man outside who most certainly would.' As long as, Darac realised, the race was kept short. Gifted rugby player Serge Paulin was built for speed, not endurance. And there was the little matter that by "outside" Darac meant somewhere outside the building, not Julien's door. He kept both thoughts to himself. 'Sit down!'

Bristling and swearing under his breath, Julien didn't comply immediately but he finally did as he was told and for a moment, Darac could picture him as a "difficult" child, the sort that throws things if it doesn't get its way.

'That's better. You're surely not denying that you and Samira were in a relationship?'

Brow crumpling, Julien turned, stared out over the bay and just when it appeared that the outgoing tide of his grief or his regret or both had left him high and dry, an incoming wave swept him up. 'Deny it? I'm proud of it! Understand? We loved each other!' His head fell. 'Passionately, if you can comprehend such a phenomenon.'

Darac's mobile throbbed against his chest. A case file entry posted by Bonbon and headed "Vignot Provenance" was a timely intervention. He read it, opened the attached photo and with some gravity, turned the phone towards his chief suspect. 'Monsieur Baille, as I'm sure you recognise, this is the shop's copy of a receipt issued by the jewellers *Bijouterie Daumier* at 16.46 last Saturday afternoon on which you are named as the purchaser of a Michel Vignot wristwatch priced, with its custom engraving, at €578. What do you have to say?'

The import of the moment struck the young man with some force and with the colour draining from his face, he looked for all the world like his own ghost. 'Alright. Yes, I bought the watch. I did. And had it engraved. And gave it to Sam.'

'When did you give it to her?'

'On Sunday, before the celebration party.'

Tears came once more and Darac allowed Julien to shed them freely and fully before continuing. There was no hurry now, after all. Darac was within a gnat's eyelash of wrapping up the case before it had barely begun.

'Why did you lie before, Monsieur?'

'What?'

'It's a straightforward question. Why did you state you had not bought the watch? What had you to gain by lying about something that could so easily be disproved?'

'Well, I … I don't know.' A quick stick shift up through the gears and Julien was on the offensive once more. 'Has anyone ever broken into your day to inform you that the love of your life has been murdered? Eh? Have they? It's a shock, you… It's a shock! I didn't know what I was saying. Shit! Shit!'

'I'll make it easy. You loved and desired Samira far more than she did you and she wanted to break off your relationship. Perhaps for someone else. You don't like coming second, do you, Monsieur? Especially after you'd splashed so much cash in a last-ditch attempt to buy her love. Not very grateful of her, was it? "Thanks for this. Now get lost." '

'Nooooooo!' Julien wailed, clamping his hands over his ears. 'Stop it! Stop!' But with alarming speed, he began to gather himself. 'Listen. Listen. I am innocent. Innocent of *any* crime. But now I'm thinking rationally, I'm sure I *do* know who is responsible for Sam's… ' Closing his eyes, he took a couple of deep breaths. '… for her murder. I *know*, right? Would you allow me to go to the desk? There's something I need to show you. I was going to take it to the police at some point, anyway.'

'I'll be standing right next to you.'

Another flashpoint. 'Do you honestly think I might…?' Another fade back. 'Sorry. Alright, yes. On the face of it, it's not a particularly controversial object.'

As Darac took close order, Julien produced a postcard portraying the Promenade des Anglais in all its balmy palmy-ness. Holding it gently by its upper and lower edges, he turned it around to reveal a message sloppily handwritten in capital letters. Darac read it aloud:' " Little boys shouldn't kick things. They might break their legs. Just for starters." Explain, Monsieur?'

'A sub-moronic heavy from the Indian sub-continent employed by Sam's sub-everything brother Dilip penned that little warning shot outside this very door. He rang and knocked but one look through the peephole was enough to deter me from letting him in. Fortunately, I hadn't been playing music or anything and he didn't realise I was at home so he shoved the card underneath the door and left. I saw he wasn't wearing gloves so I was careful how I handled it.'

A warning shot? Whatever it was, it triggered a firefight of interesting possibilities in Darac's head. Taking a paper evidence bag from his rucksack, he asked Julien to drop the postcard into it and return to his seat.

'When did this happen?'

'Yesterday morning. About 11 o'clock.'

Another arrival for the CCTV cameras to verify.

'How did he gain entry to the building? There's a key code to input.'

I don't know but gain entry he did.'

'Uh-huh. The reference to kicking?'

'I gave Dilip a good one the day before. In the balls.' He looked proud of himself, suddenly. 'He was lucky that's all I did to him.'

If this was how Julien hoped to convince Darac of his peace-loving nature, the young man was not doing himself any favours. Displays of bravado were always pathetic but this one seemed particularly so to Darac.

'You decided to spare him? Fortunate for you both.'

'For him, especially.'

'Monsieur Baille, you have just admitted to assaulting Dilip Padar and were he to bring charges, there would be consequences for you.'

'When I explain why I did it, you'll understand, Captain.'

'I'm listening.'

Julien gave chapter and verse on the fiscally challenged Padar family's attempts to control the day-to-day life of its "self-willed" prize asset, the peerless Samira. 'What she does. Whom she sees. What she wears. Everything! They didn't see her as a human being, Captain. She was a bargaining chip. One to be given up in a brokered marriage deal with the shithead son of a rival family whose business was outstripping theirs. And I'm quoting Sam virtually word for word, there. But of course, for the sale to go ahead, it was essential that the…' He curled his lip. '… *goods* remained undamaged so when Dilip overheard us making glorious love – he owns the apartment Sam shared – she was in danger of crashing her market value and thus the deal.'

'This is appalling, obviously, but—'

'There's far more to it.'

Julien went on to describe the veiled and more explicit death threats Dilip Padar had made against his sister. 'It frightened her, Captain, and that's why she felt she had no alternative but to end our relationship. We argued. From emotional blackmail on up, they had been manipulating her for years so I was convinced they were bluffing.' Hanging his head, he addressed his next thought to the floor. 'Worst decision of my life. Of *anybody's* life.' He wiped his eyes and straightened. 'But believing that, I couldn't just stand by and let Samira, the most beautiful thing I've ever seen in my life slip…' He appeared to catch himself. "… slip away because they were trying, and succeeding, to scare her into obeisance.

That's why I went to have it out with Dilip.'

The Padar family revelation was potentially of huge significance to the case and for Darac to choose this moment to ponder what many would have deemed a side issue may have appeared a waste of time. Whether the excursion proved fruitful remained to be seen but, honed in countless hours of improvising with the DMQ, Darac's speed of thought was such that whole continents of possibility could be explored in no more than an instant.

It was gifted wordsmith Julien's use of language that required a moment's reflection. Of all the terms he could have used to describe Samira, he'd called her a "beautiful *thing*". Wasn't this objectification, impure and not so simple? And "slip *away*" he'd said. Darac guessed that before Julien thought better of it, he had been going to say "slip through my fingers" instead. What would *that* have implied about his concerns at losing this peerlessly perfect object, a prize not just to be held but held fast?

Was Darac reading too much into this? Perhaps, but his interpretation was consistent with earlier observations. From Eric Cauvin's reference to Julien's persistent pleading in the "lovers' spat" he'd witnessed, to the young man's use of the crypto-coercive Marvell poem, there were more than just connotations of manipulation here. As always, every line of enquiry would be rigorously pursued and it might soon become apparent that Julien's account of the antediluvian sexual mores, financial vulnerability and readiness to employ strong-arm tactics of the Padar family may hold the key to the whole case. For the time being, though, Julien himself was squarely in the frame for Samira's murder.

'And so it was in the role of Samira's champion that you went off to Avenue Primerose to have it out with Dilip?'

'If you're ridiculing me about it, I don't care. But note this, Captain. At least three of Dilip's neighbours came out of their apartments – I could tell you which ones – and they saw and heard him threaten me.'

'You had just assaulted the man, Monsieur. Painfully.'

'It's what he threatened me *with*. Something along the lines of "You're dead, Baille. Hear me? Dead!"' He indicated the evidence bag containing the postcard. 'And the following morning, that card-carrying goon turns up at my door.'

'The fact that a third party delivered the message is suggestive, I grant you. And yes, in its form and content, the message *is* threatening. But if the messenger had had orders to beat you up or worse, he wouldn't have turned up on the campus to do it. The intention, I suspect, was to intimidate you which it signally failed to do, didn't it? You went about your work normally, went off to training on your bike in the evening as normal, opened the door to me just now without having the faintest idea who I was, and so on.'

'You know my routines?'

'Do you own or have access to a car here?'

'No.'

'But you hold a current driving licence.'

'Yes. Look, who have you been speaking to about me?'

'We'll come to that but back to the message and the messenger. Did you recognise him? Was he a member of the Padar family, do you think?'

'I'd never seen him before and if he was a member of the family, he was a very distant one. Samira was drop... Samira was beautiful and although he's overweight, most would say Dilip is a pretty good-looking fellow. Although I only saw the goon through the fisheye distortion of the peephole, he was obviously an ugly piece of work. I would definitely recognise him again, incidentally.'

Darac reflected that while the Brigade would probably give at least some credence to such evidence, the courts would not. In a recent case, the testimony of just such a fish-eyewitness had been thrown out and the case lost. 'But rest assured, we will be following up this and other aspects of the story of Monsieur Dilip Padar.'

Astonishment now. 'Following it up? Considering he or his henchman killed my beloved, I should hope you would. Dilip warned her to stop seeing me or else, Captain. She was frightened. And now she is dead.'

'Let's look at last evening's training session in more detail. You arrived by bike, locked it to one of the stanchions close by the changing rooms as usual, took part in the session as did Samira who had arrived later than you in her car—'

'*Dilip's* car. Dilip's apartment. Dilip's everything. That's what he wanted. To own Sam's very being, Captain. And I can tell who you've been talking to. Eric. The creep.'

'Why creep?'

'His eyes are everywhere.'

'Appropriate for a night watchman, don't you think?'

'He's too… familiar. Sad little man.'

So according to Julien, Sam's flatmate was a "harridan," Eric, a "creep." A pattern was emerging here.

'And at the end of the session, did you and Samira leave the track together? Did you speak?'

'I run the 3,000 metres steeplechase, as you know. Sam, I'm sure you also know, was training for the 800 flat. Although there are overlaps, the regimes are different and we usually left the track at different times, then met up after showering.'

'And is that what happened yesterday?'

'Uh… We didn't meet afterwards. The last thing I saw her doing in this life was beginning a set of interval sprint reps.'

'That being?' No response. 'Monsieur?'

'What? Oh, does it matter?'

'The fuller the picture we're able to form, the better.'

'Alright. Interval sprint training varies but in Sam's case, it meant sprinting thirty metres, recovering, going again. Six reps make a set.'

'Was she doing this alone?'

'No. She was with Grace – Grace Nahili, the heptathlete – and Mac, one of the coaches. Kevin Macdonald.'

'I see. After you had showered, you didn't wait for her?'

'No. And I didn't shower until I got back here. To be honest, I'd been in a bit of a state all evening, I guess. The Padar family pressure thing finally getting to Sam had really got to me. She had even blanked me earlier in the evening. As good as. I just wanted to get away as quickly as I could.'

'And so, as far as Samira was concerned, your relationship was over?'

'So she had said but I was *convinced* I could make her see sense. What we had was too beautiful to lose.' He stared into space. 'Now, I'll never have the chance.'

'What time did you leave the car park last evening?'

'It was 9.02.'

'That's very exact.' And it was instantly recalled, too. A prepared answer? 'Isn't it?'

'You asked me when I left? That's when I left.'

'I understood sessions are scheduled to finish at 9.30?'

'I'd done all I needed to on the track and as I told you, I just wanted to get away.'

'Can anyone corroborate the time you left the Stade?'

'You mean, did anyone *witness* my leaving?'

'Answer the question.'

'The creepy Eric saw me, I imagine.'

'No. The man whose "eyes are everywhere" didn't see you leave.'

'Well, he must have been…' As if demeaned by having to give the question any further thought, Julien made a dismissive gesture with his hand. 'I don't know.' But then he had something. 'Yes! That clown Koko saw me – Ade Okoko, the so-called long jumper. He's usually the last into the rooms after the session but he was coming off early because he'd tweaked a hamstring.' He suddenly saw the value of the recollection. '*And*, Captain. He didn't just see me leave. We exchanged a few words.'

'Where did this exchange take place, exactly?'

'By the players' car park gate. I'd just got on my bike and a couple of pedal strokes later, he called out a parting comment about Emil – that's the ox in human form that is shot-putter Emil Arcot. It was some drivel about him being in a good mood this evening, which since he's always so sickeningly upbeat most of the time, I didn't understand. Anyway, I didn't answer and carried on. Incidentally, I heard a couple of other voices behind me heading for the rooms. I didn't see who they were but they may well have seen me.'

Assuming the story checked out, it appeared that Julien had at least cycled away from the immediate vicinity but what was to say he hadn't lain in wait for Samira somewhere along the lane or elsewhere?

Julien's relief at recalling his encounter with stricken long jumper Ade Okoko proved short-lived. 'Just a minute, Captain. Just a minute. Your trying to establish when I left the car park can only mean one thing, can't it? Please don't tell me *how*, alright? But surely, it means that Sam was murdered there or nearby? I... can't believe it.' He shook his head and, his words emerging on an exhausted breath, said: 'I can't believe anything about this.'

'Except that Dilip and/or his associate was responsible.'

'What? Oh. As it obviously did happen – yes. *That* I do believe.'

'Where did you go after you cycled away? Back here to the *Résidence*?'

'Where else?'

'When did you arrive?'

'9.20.'

Even for a top-class athlete, that was some going, wasn't it? 'It took you less than 20 minutes to ride from the Stade to here? In traffic?'

'It took 19 minutes, 25 seconds. A PB for the ride, despite, or perhaps because of everything.'

'PB?'

'Personal best.'

'I see.'

The fixation with exact timings fitted Julien's profile, Darac realised, and it potentially explained the speed with which he'd recalled the time he'd cycled away from the players' car park. Arriving at the *Résidence* half an hour before Samira had left the Stade went some way to putting him in the clear for her murder but to corroborate this, he would need at least one human or foolproof electronic witness to replicate Ade Okoko's role at the start of the ride.

'Be aware that we'll check if the onsite CCTV backs up your statement.' And there were potentially other ways of checking his story. 'Right?'

'Fine with me.'

Julien's nonchalance over this suggested he was telling the truth. But what if he knew the cameras were out of action? Or perhaps he knew how to bypass them in the same way that his postcard-wielding visitor had managed to sidestep the building's key code entry system that same morning. And what was to say he hadn't ridden back to the Stade?'

'On arriving here, what did you do first?'

'Locked up my bike in the rack store downstairs.'

'And then came straight up to your room?'

'Yes.'

'Did you talk with anyone en route?'

The question, it seemed, merited a considered answer. 'Talk? No. But someone was emerging from the lift as I headed for the stairs. A couple of people, actually. Didn't notice who it was but they may well have noticed me.'

Since it wasn't his forte, it was with a little unease that Darac decided it was time to bring IT to the table.

'Did you call Samira yesterday at any point? Or text her?'

'I don't mind admitting that I texted her and left voicemails many times during the day.'

A clever killer usually in regular phone contact with their victim will continue calling and messaging them after the event since not to do so would appear suspicious.

'After the session, too? Did you attempt to contact her then?'

'No.'

Darac managed to keep his expression neutral. 'Nor after you arrived home and felt more positive about things?'

'No.'

Doubly suspicious? Potentially.

'Why didn't you?'

'Sam hadn't answered anything all day so I made up my mind to try and see her in person. Today.' The word sticking in his throat, he coughed drily. 'I need water. Lob over that rucksack next to you, will you?' Another cough. 'Or just lob the bottle and then you can rummage through the rest of it for weaponry.'

'I'm most certainly going to check through it, Monsieur.' It was clean. 'Here.'

He took a couple of long pulls and set the bottle down beside him.

Had Julien called or messaged Samira from the *Résidence* just once at about the time she was killed, he would have taken the heat off himself. But Darac knew that the young man's phone or laptop GPS could still come to his rescue. 'Did you call, or send or receive a message to *anyone* after you arrived back here?'

He didn't appear to appreciate the significance of the

question. 'For what it's worth, I emailed my father.'

'At what time was that?'

'Not until I turned in. Just before midnight, it was.'

'I see.' Whether Julien realised it or not, the answer didn't help him. Darac had one last IT card to play, one that might prove decisive either way. 'Once you had arrived here, how did you spend your evening?'

'What does—'

'How did you spend it?'

'Talk about a police state… I showered, like I said. For some time, actually. I felt the need. Then, I read for well over an hour.' He indicated his bookshelves as if the provenance of the reading matter was at issue. 'Then I just sat thinking until I decided to go to bed.'

'Did you look up anything on a website at all?'

'Uh… no.'

'Not all evening?'

The light of comprehension dawned in his eyes. 'Ah. I see why you want to know these things. It's to locate where I was when… it happened. No. Unfortunately, I didn't even turn my laptop on. Not in the mood for work.'

'Pity, Monsieur. For you, that is.'

'Look, Captain. Don't you believe what I've been telling you about Dilip Padar and his whole rotten family set-up?'

'We've been through that already but I'll repeat myself. Our investigation will reveal everything pertinent to the case in due course. And I mean *everything*. If you are innocent of this appalling crime, and at this stage I am by no means certain you are, you have absolutely *nothing* to fear.'

Julien shook his head. 'You suspect me of murdering the thing I loved most in the world? This is a nightmare.' He jumped to his feet. 'A fucking nightmare!'

While Darac sat calmly observing him, the young man spent the next half-minute amply exposing the short fuse to which his explosive temperament was wired.

'Finished?' Darac said, as his mobile throbbed against his chest.

At last appearing to realise that he was undermining his own position, Julien took a couple of deep breaths and did as he was directed.

'Thank you. We'll continue in a second.'

The message was from Erica: *Paul, I've just added Samira Padar's call and text log to the case file and I read a few of the latter. Transcripts included. No deletions of any kind within the last 7 days. On the surface, it all looks routine. You'll notice that the last message in was a CC'd mail-shot to the athletics team sent at 11.37 yesterday, confirming details of the evening's training session. And the last message out was to one Zoë Laborde sent at 13.07 the day before in which, as you'll see, Samira thanks her profusely for the excellent and prompt work she did on setting up her new laptop. She concludes by promising to post a stellar review to that effect on Zoë's website. I checked it out. The poor young woman never got around to it. Kisses, Erica.*

Where, Darac wondered, were the texts and unanswered calls Julien had mentioned? There were two obvious possibilities.

'Monsieur Baille, we are having this conversation because, as you are all too painfully aware, you are a person of interest in a murder enquiry. At this stage, you are neither charged nor held for questioning and although I wouldn't advise it, you could end this conversation right now.'

'At which point, Captain,' Julien said, his mouth curling sourly, 'you would cart me off to the Caserne Auvare, no doubt.'

'You may be less aware that at this early stage of our conversation, should I deem it necessary to seize any of your property for examination, I would be required to obtain official clearance in the form of a warrant from the Palais de

Justice. Which, without question, I would be granted. However, wheels at the Palais can turn slowly at times. It could help you and me both if you simply showed me yesterday's call and message list on your mobile. Unless you deleted those entries in which case it *would* be necessary to take steps.'

Julien thought about it and Darac could see it was taking him to a place of desolation.

'I didn't delete the entries. I didn't delete the messages themselves. You can read them. I'm not ashamed of hating the thought of losing Sam.' He indicated his rucksack once more. 'My phone's in there as you no doubt saw. May I?'

'Go ahead.'

Julien rose, opened the phone and showed the relevant entries to Darac. A quick perusal was all it took to corroborate the young man's account of his call and message traffic from the previous day – including his email to one Jean-Claude Baille sent just before midnight. And it also established something of equal if not greater importance: Samira had had not one but two mobiles, and they had run on different networks.

'Give me a moment, Monsieur,' Darac said, adding Samira's second number to the case file and then forwarding it to Forensics at the Caserne with the note: *Sorry Erica, but I've just learned that Samira was using a second phone on a different network, a phone she used for more personal stuff and one I suspect her brother Dilip knew nothing about. The number's on the attached file. All you can, soonest, please! Paul.'*

For the first time, Darac began to feel that the balance was shifting in favour of Julien's innocence for this crime. But there was still a long way to go.

'Right, Monsieur Baille. Let's go on, shall we?'

THIRTY-NINE

After almost two hours of increasingly focussed questioning, Darac concluded that he didn't have nearly enough to hold Julien Baille on suspicion of murder. But the young man was far from being home free. With crucial contributions from pathology, forensics and various security systems still pending, and with only the first round of interviews undertaken, the investigation was still in its infancy.

'So is that it? Captain Strong Arm of The State? Are we finished?'

'Almost.'

'*Not* finished. I thought so.' Julien's eyes were burning. 'Listen, I want to say something. Alright?'

'Of course.'

'You people—'

'Are all individuals, Monsieur but continue, by all means.'

Darac heard him out and at the end of it, he concluded that if Julien was acting the role of a persecuted innocent, the young man was up there with one of Darac's favourite performances in cinema – Anthony Perkins's portrayal of Kafka's Josef K in *The Trial*.

'Now you listen. As things stand…'

Darac proceeded to advise Julien of his rights, a consideration the young man clearly hadn't been expecting. But there were directives for him to follow, too, chief among them the requirement that he not leave the city while the investigation was ongoing.

'And I hope it goes without saying that you should not pay any further calls on Monsieur Dilip Padar at his Avenue Primerose address or anywhere else.'

'What about him and his goon? Tell *them* to stay away from *me*!'

'I can assure you that Monsieur Dilip Padar has this morning been issued with a reciprocal warning. If he disregards it and contacts you directly or via an associate, report it to us immediately. Here's a card with the relevant numbers.'

It was not without a measure of sympathy that Darac left the young man alone with his grief or his remorse or both and headed back to the Stade. He also left him with a hidden watchdog summoned from Foch's site security unit.

With so many players involved, it was only a matter of time before news of the murder broke and that meant coping with varying degrees of interference from both the media and the Palais de Justice. Half expecting to find a pack of newshounds baying at the caravan gate, Darac was pleasantly surprised to find that only Foch's Finest were in situ. And since there was no sign of the likes of TV's Annie Provin and her crew camped outside, it was unlikely that camera-hungry Public Prosecutor Jules Frènes was ensconced somewhere inside.

Having negotiated Foch's reassuringly thorough but speedy ID control, Darac fell in behind a couple of unfamiliar pool cars bumping along the lane. He may not have recognised the vehicles but he had no such difficulty with their drivers, though their simultaneous arrival with his own gave him pause. Assigned to continue with Dilip Padar, Bonbon had left the mobile incident room a full fifteen minutes before Darac had; Flaco had set off five minutes earlier than that to talk to Samira's flatmate Carole Monteux. Thanks to the case file log, Darac knew their interviews had begun within a few minutes of his own with Julien. That the three of them were arriving back at the same moment told him that they, too, must have had quite a time of it.

FORTY

'Innie, Innie, Innie – slow down!' Sue Talbot said, her words sounding a demi-semi quaver ahead of her mouth movements. 'I didn't understand a word of that. And do you have to sit with your back to the window? I want to see you sweetie and you're all in shadow.'

The request triggering another avalanche of verbiage, at first in vernacular French, Inès grabbed the tablet, jumped to her feet and, segueing seamlessly into English, set up facing the light.

'The world's upside down here and you're worried about... picture quality? Shit! Sometimes, I...'

'Wow, you look terrible. Come on. Stop! Breathe! That's better. Now tell me. What... has... happened?'

'Happened? Oh, just that my father's lover – the gorgeous young Indian woman, Samira? She's been murdered. Last night. Sometime after the training session.'

On the screen, Sue's expressive face took on a whole other dimension of incredulity. 'You... did say *murdered*?'

'Yes.'

'I can't believe it. Murdered? Who..?'

'Killed her? Too early to say. So many things to come to terms with here, I don't know what to think or even where to start. One item is that my mother's hateful, lying, pitiful excuse of a husband says he wasn't madly in love with Samira, after all. She was the one who couldn't get enough of *him*.'

'Well he would say that, Innie.'

'Oh, I'm sure he's had numerous affairs. But this one? Hypochondriacs get ill sometimes, don't they? Liars sometimes tell the truth.'

'But what about the watch? The gift? The Marvell

inscription and all that?'

'We confronted him about it.'

'And?'

'Can't blame Maman at all but she jumped to the wrong conclusion. Yes, my father had brought the watch home in his kitbag but *he* hadn't bought it as a gift – his star athlete, one Julien Baille had. The pair were having a word after training when Samira unexpectedly appeared as Baille was taking the watch out of his locker. He didn't want her to see it so he passed it behind his back to my father who discreetly put it in his own bag, then took it in the next day.'

'It sounds made up.'

'Maman believed it.' She swallowed hard. 'She went white and almost fainted when he told us.'

'Perhaps because she wanted to believe it, Innie.'

'I called him just now – Julien. He's a star post-grad student, too, by the way. Writing a thesis on the English Metaphysical Poets.'

'Really? Well, that does fit the inscription part of it. Did he verify the story?'

'He did and before you say that he and my shit of a father could have cooked it up between them, I just don't believe that.'

As Sue struggled to digest the story so far, nothing was said for a few moments and then as if a dam had been breached, Inès began to cry.

'Innie. Sweetheart!'

'I can't help it,' she blurted, her words careering around helplessly in the flood. 'It's just such a horrible, horrible thing to have happened.'

FORTY-ONE

For the moment, the man was out of sight but she could hear him – the toilet door was missing. And she heard something else. Scuttling, scratching.

'Oh, Lord,' she cried out, holding her blouse to her throat as she scanned the debris-strewn space behind her.

'Bring the stuff.'

Her stomach turned over as she picked it up and unscrewed the cap.

'Did you hear me?'

She had to end this. She pictured his knife. Always to hand; sometimes sheathed in a shoulder holster; sometimes in a scabbard looped to his belt over the back pocket of his jeans. But even if she could lay her hands on it, or finesse it away from him, could she go through with it? There would be blood. A lot of blood.

'Get in here now!'

He was standing facing away from her as she entered. The sight of his naked back and buttocks made her gag. But what she saw next gave her a scintilla of hope. He hadn't taken off his jeans. He'd just lowered them down to his boots, lassoing his ankles in the process. For as long as it took him to bend and pull them up, he was immobilised. And there was the knife handle sticking up proud of the rumpled cloth. Available. One quick grab away, that's all it was. One quick grab...

FORTY-TWO

With Darac's team, Raul Ormans's forensics unit, and members of Farid's slog squad crammed into the mobile incident truck, it was standing room only inside. The remaining squaddies were clustered outside like stage door johnnies on an opening night at the theatre.

'Farid,' Darac said, having to raise his voice over the buzz. 'Considering the size of the task, it's going better than we could have hoped and a lot of that is down to you.'

'Thanks, chief.'

'Credit where it's due, man,' Darac continued, the words momentarily emerging in a gnomic monotone as he performed a rough head count. 'Don't think all your multiple interview people have made it back yet, have they?'

'No, not all. The assistant coaches are proving elusive. A couple of the athletes are in classes and one is sitting an exam for a good hour yet – team captain Emil Arcot. Mobiles aren't permitted so he won't know anything of what's happened. Big Charlie Presse was my pick to talk to him. For a couple of reasons, it seemed a good match.'

'We'd better make a start without Charlie and the others, I think. Quiet please!' As the buzz subsided, Darac looked towards the open door. 'Can everyone hear me outside?'

'Yes, Captain!'

'Good. I don't think there's any point pressing the whiteboard into service…'

'What whiteboard?' someone quipped.

'Quite.' He peered in the general direction of the comms desk. 'Bé?' A Red Sea of heads parted and the pair made eye contact. 'Be useful if you would record the meeting as well and add it to the file log? Especially for those still out there interviewing.'

'Certainly, Captain.'

The heads closed ranks and Darac turned his attention back to the whole group.

'OK, everyone, it's clear that in a very short space of time we've garnered a lot of really useful material and so by the end of this session, we should've been able to form a picture of more than just the whereabouts of the principal suspects and witnesses on the night Samira Padar was murdered. I think we've gained some real insights into the wider picture as well. I filmed the entirety of my interview with our prime suspect Julien Baille but as we haven't got two hours to spare just now, I'll summarise. Ready to record, Bé?'

'Ready, Captain.'

In lieu of counting himself in, Darac gave Bé the nod and the performance began in earnest. Using a three-stage approach derived from playing any number of jazz tunes with his band – start by laying out the themes, fully explore them, finish by returning to the now greatly enriched themes – Darac fully reprised his interview with Julien and added his own take on the young man himself. Thanks to Bé's efforts, those who were still out in the field would be able to catch up with his account later.

'Right, let's test as much of that as we can. Farid, one of your guys interviewed the livewire long jumper, Ade Okoko?'

Farid pointed to one of the faces gathered around the open door. 'Tana, there. She got a solid confirmation from him that Julien *did* cycle away from the players' car park at the time he stated. As to when he arrived at the *Résidence*, things are far less sure. So far, we only have his word for it that he made it in less than twenty minutes. Several of the students who might have seen Julien return were unavailable earlier. Tana left call-back cards and you never know, they may pay off. Requests to the security people for last evening's CCTV have gone in but nothing back yet.'

'Yes, that evidence will prove key, I think,' Darac said. 'And well done, Tana, by the way. Staying just on Julien for the moment, do we have anything else?'

'Here.'

'Go for it, Bonbon.'

But before Bonbon could say a word, Darac's mobile rang.

'It's Path, everyone,' he said, holding up a hand. The gesture had the desired effect – on the off chance that a dropped pin would have made it between the press of bodies to the floor, the landing would probably have been heard. 'Map, go ahead, you're on speaker.'

'I have a meaningful update. The massive dorsal cranial injuries Samira sustained were caused by a pitted and jagged lump of rock I estimate to have been about half the size of a regulation football. Fragments of both the rock and crumbs of embedded soil removed from the skull are being analysed now. Purely on the pathology, we can narrow the T.O.D. to between 9 o'clock and 11 o'clock on Monday evening. Further narrowing *may* be possible later. As we thought at the scene, the fatal blow was struck sometime before the body was immersed in the water jump. At the moment, I'm favouring at least fifteen minutes. And we have something else. Traces of motile sperm were found in the victim's vaginal canal.'

As an aid to concentration, most had been listening with their heads bowed until this moment. Now looks were exchanged all around.

'Are we talking rape here, Map?'

'There's no indication of that at all. Samira was a healthy, sexually mature young woman who had had sex at some point in the day. You're going to ask me at *what* point and although at this stage it isn't possible to determine that with any accuracy, it wasn't immediately prior to the T.O.D.

window I gave you. In any case, it's established she took a full part in the training session which I believe began at 7 pm?'

'That's right.'

'So we're talking some time in the afternoon. As to who her partner was, we should have a sequencing result within 24 hours and if there's a database match, we'll have a name soon afterwards. That's all I have at the moment.'

'Enormously helpful, Map. Thanks.'

'More later.'

Darac rang off and turned to the group. 'We'll just reflect on all that before we go on. Alright, Bonbon?'

'Sure.'

'R.O. Where are you?'

'Find Serge and look left.'

'Got you. So, the murder weapon was a rock and although that doesn't rule out shot putter Emil as the killer, it does rule out the shots as a weapon.'

'I'll cross testing them off my list.'

'One more less, as my Aunt Sophie would say – always a good thing. So Map's team is testing rock and soil fragments at their end. Looks like you could be reprising a variation on your privet-finding exploits from the St André case when Map knows more. Any thoughts on that at the moment?'

'It's a very mixed environment around here. Not much exposed soil, though.'

'And that's true of the far end of the players' car park?'

'To which dark place, Samira made her unexplained detour? Well, there's vegetation, certainly. Trees, several varieties of shrubs, but no rocks of the size our good doctor referred to either lying on the surface or half-embedded. I gather we're in for sunshine and showers tomorrow but our enemy here is how unusually dry the weather has been for mid-March. Thus we have no useful tyre tracks or footprints to go on. There's a broken lower branch and a slight degree of grass compaction where someone may have stood at some stage – and we have a frankly bonkers number of photos of it – but that's all.'

Darac ran a hand through his hair. 'Have you found *anything* that made your forensic radar beep even a little?'

'It's what we *haven't* found that's beeping loudest – Samira's car. Once we have located that, the picture will sharpen immensely.'

'We'll need you again shortly, R.O. but Bonbon? You're back on.'

'Couple of points. First – and this is only indirectly concerned with Julien – but Dilip has a strong if pat alibi for the night of the murder. One Candice Valle, a girlfriend was with him from about 8 pm to breakfast time the following day. Candice works in outpatients at St Roch and I rang one of our mates at Foch to nip across the road to interview her. With all the usual riders in such situations, she independently came up with an account that tallies.'

'OK,' Darac said. And second?'

'Yes, I can verify Julien's death-threat story. Not the implicit one made during the encounter with the postcard-wielding heavy outside his room, but the *explicit* threats Dilip made to him after being kicked in the bollocks.'

'Interesting.' Aside from committing an assault, one gone unreported by Dilip, Darac noted, Julien had just passed another test, hadn't he? 'You must have spread your net wide, Bonbon – to verify something I imagine you had no idea had happened until I mentioned it just now.'

'Ah, but I did know. After a largely fruitless session with the defensive-aggressive Dilip, I thought it worth having a word with his neighbours. I sensed immediately that a couple of them were concealing something and after a lot of not so idle chatter and buttering up, I got my new best friends to spill. That's what took me so long. Two nights ago, they heard a right ding-dong going on in the corridor, went to investigate and actually witnessed the threats. The young man on the receiving end fits Julien's description and Dilip used his surname a couple of times into the bargain. And here's something. Vis-à-vis the account you've just given us of the Indian heavy who showed up at Julien's door the day after, a significant part of Dilip's verbal threat – and both neighbours report hearing it – was that he used the words "I'll see to it." If that doesn't suggest Dilip is well used to employing a third party to do his dirty work for him, I don't know what does.'

'Slipping people a few euros to do this and that for him? Fits the picture. Although it was innocent work, think Eric Cauvin's car-watching role at the Stade, for instance. Of course, we don't know what would have happened had Julien opened his door to the heavy Dilip does appear to have sent. But that's good work, Bonbon.'

Perand shrugged. 'As to the verbal threats Dilip himself came out with, I might threaten to kill someone if they tried to rearrange my furniture.'

Expecting a counter-argument, Darac's eye was drawn to Flaco. No stranger to the phenomenon himself, he recognised adamantine resolve when he saw it in others. Darac saw it in her at that moment.

Stone-faced, monumentally still, she raised her hand to speak. 'Since interviewing Samira's flatmate Carole Monteux, I have much more on Padar,' she said. 'All of it bad. And all of it puts him or his associate at least as squarely in the frame as Julien Baille for Samira's murder.'

'You've obviously got something crucial there, Flak, but before we hear it, does anyone have anything further just on Julien?'

Only Flaco herself nodded. 'As part of what Carole told me, I do but none of it relates to his movements on the key days or anything.'

'You clearly feel Carole is a reliable witness.'

'And not just because, like Samira, she's a law student. Yes, Carole did repeat to me things she said had been told to her by Samira and she knows that makes it doubly inadmissible as evidence. But some of what she told me reinforces the concerns Julien Baille told you that *he* has about Dilip Padar. And, Captain, some of those things are checkable fact.'

'Go on, Flak.'

Displaying a gravity of mien that put Darac in mind of Blue Devil club owner Ridge Clay, Flaco relayed everything Carole had told her and her account was received in rapt silence.

'Thanks for that,' Darac said. 'Comments anyone? Perand, you're looking doubtful.'

'Not doubtful, chief. I have no problem believing Padar is a control freak by nature *and* nurture. And from other cases in the news over the years, we all know the sort of primitive practices that haven't completely died out in that culture.'

Flaco gave him a look. 'Patriarchal is another P-word you could have used there.'

'Yeah, absolutely. I just think we have to be careful here. As you say, the source of the stories that so alarmed Julien and Carole about Samira's powerlessness and vulnerability came from Samira herself, didn't they? It *could* be, and before you bite my head off, Flak, I stress I'm conjecturing, but it *could* be that it suited Samira to portray the Padar family as this oppressive machine which would stop at nothing, including murder, to further its interests. In reality though, Dilip *might* just be a typical big brother type– I'll rephrase that – an *elder* brother type, one caught in a difficult balancing act between the demands of a struggling family business on the one hand, and the welfare of his younger sister whose wilfully wayward tendencies, as he saw them, made it difficult.'

'And if she had been his younger *brother*?' Flaco said. 'Would an appetite for sex have played *any* part in that balancing act?'

'Dilip's a hypocrite. Without question. And arranged marriages and all that? Terrible. But being an arsehole doesn't make him a monster and so far, we really only have Samira's word for it that he is one. We know from your interview that while Samira herself didn't take seriously the threats she reported as having been made, she did use them as the pretext for breaking up with Julien when in reality, it was the fact that she found him a dud in bed.'

'You don't think it was out of respect for his fragile male ego that she kept that from him?'

Perand scratched his blue chin. 'It might have been, yes. But my point, unlike Julien's member it seems, still stands.'

Reflecting that the argument was among the most constructive and least acrimonious the pair had ever had in a case meeting, Darac had a point of his own to make.

'There's reason on both sides there, I think. We would certainly be closer to a more definitive interpretation of things if we could trace the Padar family's possible connection to the so-called "honour" killing Dilip told Samira about. Was he telling the truth there? Or just using the story to scare her into submission? He'd deny ever mentioning it, no doubt, so we really need the help of the Indian authorities. How best to go about that, I'm not entirely sure. Except that it will begin with a call to Agnès and I will make that call immediately after the session.' Another consideration occurred to Darac and it was a pressing one. 'So Carole knew that story as did Julien. I gave him a stern warning not to contact Dilip, let alone go anywhere near him and I'm sure you issued a similar warning to Carole, Flak.'

'A very stern warning, Captain.'

'Right, but I wonder how many other people know the story. It's concerning, isn't it?'

Bonbon nodded. 'We've seen how bent on avenging her

murder a number of our principals are. And there could be others. Without knowing whether the story was true or not, should one of them be convinced that the controlling shithead that definitely *is* Dilip Padar was behind the killing, they might be minded to make good on those threats of vengeance.'

'Exactly. We've got people watching Dilip but I'm minded to strengthen that watch. Lartou? I know resources are stretched, but would you try and get someone? Anyone big from Joinel would do.'

'I'll do my best, chief, but the way things are, it might be difficult.'

'I know.' Darac noticed Flaco's habitual scowl had deepened. 'I want to make clear that granting Dilip such protection doesn't imply any lessening of our probing into his possible guilt. Far from it.' He glanced at his watch. 'R.O – can we turn to the disposal of the body now?'

'We can.'

'Have you been able to complete your inspection of the area around the water jump?'

'Indeed so, and we've now ruled out the idea that a vehicle of some kind was used to transport the body from the murder site itself. The noise factor. Hoping they may have been electric-powered and therefore virtually silent, we were momentarily encouraged to discover groundsman Fred Carlo has two small tractor-like machines with trailers. He uses them to set out hurdles and such like and had one of them been used, it would have been a simple matter to examine it thoroughly. However, both proved to be diesels and made a hell of a racket. There are no hand carts or wheelbarrows on site, incidentally.'

'So the body was moved under the murderer's own steam?' Darac asked.

'Almost certainly it was.'

Darac pictured the difficulty of the task and it prompted a thought he felt he should have had earlier. 'I know Samira was both short and light in weight and I also know that adrenaline can supercharge a person's strength – think of the numerous instances of frail old folk shifting enormous weights out of the way of vulnerable children, for example. Nevertheless, I'm still exercised about the physical effort that transporting her body to the jump must have taken. With that in mind, it's hard to picture skinny Julien Baille, as super-fit, explosive and determined a character though he is, being capable of such an effort.' And this wasn't the only doubt he was entertaining about his likely guilt. 'But I digress. R.O?'

'*Whoever* transported the body to the jump, let's look first at the question of drag marks and abrasions. If I had been in the murderer's position, I would have stayed off the revealing surface that is grass. And since it's not necessary to set foot on the football pitch en route to the water jump, avoiding it would be easy. But whichever route the murderer took, he or she would have to have crossed six lanes of running track at some point. Our enemy here is the composition of the track surface itself. It's a phenomenally durable material highly resistant to the sort of marks that would have been left by dragging a body across it.

'We conducted some experiments at the opposite end of the stadium. Young Nathalie is closest in height and weight to our diminutive victim and we dragged the poor girl backwards and forwards over a section. The conclusion we came to was that the victim's trainers would not have left scuff marks on the surface. But marks and stains from blood? That is a different matter. There would have been a lot of it and the fact that we can find not one drop leading to the water jump suggests that the victim's body, whether dragged or carried, must have been enclosed in some way – sealed inside the type of leak-proof body bag path units and hospitals use, for instance. Any connections to our suspects there?'

Bonbon shook his head. 'None of our students is reading pathology or medicine. Whether any of them or the coaches know someone who works in a related field or has a part-time job in one of the hospitals, or an undertaker's or wherever – that will take further questioning.'

'Indeed,' Darac said. 'Concluding thoughts on this, R.O.?

'Your comments about Samira's size and the galvanising effect of adrenaline notwithstanding, whoever transported the body to the water jump was a very fit individual of not inconsiderable strength. However, considering almost all our suspects are athletes of one sort or another, that is hardly surprising.'

'All athletes with the exception of Dilip Padar,' Flaco said.

Perand raised a hand. 'Candice Valle's alibi for him?'

'Yet to be verified,' Flaco countered. 'But if it is, don't forget Padar's henchman. According to Baille's description, he sounds well capable of lifting dead weights.'

'The sooner I can make that call to Agnès, the better,' Darac said, referring back to the "honour" killing story but also implying the need to move things on. And then, as often seemed to happen, mention of a call was followed immediately by the sound of a ringing phone and Darac held up his hand to request quiet while he took it.

'Erica. You're on speaker.'

'Oh, I'm disappointed, Paul.'

'Samira's separate phone account not cough anything up?'

'No. I'm disappointed that you didn't begin with one of your "Now would be a good moment to mention you've unearthed X,Y or Z that will lead us the killer" lines.'

In and out of the room, anticipation levels rose exponentially. 'Take it as read.'

'Alright, having now analysed carrier data from Samira's

second phone, and also to have speed-read some remarkable incoming and outgoing messages sent over the past three days, I discovered where she went immediately after the training session, or at least where her phone did, and ladies and gentlemen, that phone is still at the location.'

Anticipation levels rose still higher and quite instinctively, Darac's gaze locked on to Bonbon for the reveal. 'And that location is?'

'First, I must tell you something else.'

FORTY-THREE

For the past two hours, final year students in engineering had been sitting the latest in a series of exams in their chosen subject. At its conclusion, one of their number would be facing an altogether tougher examination in a subject no one would have chosen.

Everything about narco cop "Big" Charlie Presse was outsize including his heart and from the first, Farid had considered him the ideal choice to break the news of Samira's murder to athletics team captain Emil Arcot. In the meantime, the stakes had become somewhat higher. Acting on Erica's new intel, Darac had dispatched two of the Caserne's brawnier beat officers to assist Charlie in bringing the young man in for questioning. Message transcripts from Samira's mobile revealed that it had been Emil with whom she had been having sex only hours before she was killed. At this stage, the decision to detain him was as much in the interests of protecting the person of Dilip Padar as it was in questioning Emil. Besides, thanks to what Erica had just told them, the team had a surer-looking suspect in their sights.

'Your reinforcements arrived yet, Charlie?' Farid asked.

'Just here now. The exam is due to finish in three-quarters of an hour and we've got a decent sightline on the door. Young Monsieur Arcot won't be going anywhere. Where are you?'

'I'm finally about to introduce myself to Grace Nahili as she comes out of her class. Her room's nearby, fortunately. Here they come. And here she is, I think... Yes, it's her and she's by herself. Good. Later, Charlie.'

FORTY-FOUR

Frankie poked her head around Granot's office door and raised a quizzical eyebrow. 'Are those almond croissants?' she said, venturing no further. 'Plural?'

Granot's reply was filtered through a miniature explosion of crumbs but she took from it that he thought it had come to something when an officer investigating a triple murder almost single-handedly couldn't take a couple of minutes off to ingest some much-needed fatty carbs without attracting facetious comments from his fellows.

'Swap you one for a double espresso?' she said, still half-hidden behind the door. 'From the fair nozzle of Paul's Gaggia.'

'Show me,' Granot said, as if suspecting some Odile-led Bio-Nazi trap was behind the offer.

'*Et voilà.*' Frankie produced a tray bearing two cups. 'Or you could go for the mint tea.'

'No, no.' His shaggy chops garlanded in smiles, Granot bade Frankie enter and with the gallery of ghastliness that was a murder case photo array serving as a backdrop, the pair sipped and munched and chatted on a range of topics which concluded with every Caserne diehard's favourite of the moment.

'And how's that gorgeous little darling of yours getting on?'

'Paul? He's alright if you like that sort of thing.'

'Ker-tish!'

'Sorry. No, Lily's doing wonderfully, thanks. Teething at last which is a relief. Did her best to delay it as long as possible for us, bless her.'

'And the childminding? It was a pain in our day *and* we

had a nursery practically next door, plus four grandparents within a couple of kilometres.'

'It's a bit of a juggling act, I suppose, but everyone we have on board is wonderful. You know Mariette?'

'Not personally but she's one of those people you hear nothing but good things about.'

'Indeed. Lily, the little gadabout, is overnighting with her paternal grandparents over in Vence tonight. Have you met Chantal yet, by the way?'

'No, but she's rather wonderful, I gather.'

'Yes, she's great.'

'You know, not that it was for the want of trying, but I thought Martin never would find the right woman.' He gave Frankie a curious look. 'And perhaps partly because of your husband's exacting standards in the matter. Fair?'

'Oh, you're right, absolutely. And Paul knows it. Fortunately, he's as fond of his stepmother as I am.'

Smiling bemusement was a rare expression for Granot but he pulled it off with aplomb. 'Paul's *stepmother*,' he said, emphasising the word. 'Sounds really strange, that.'

'Does, doesn't it? But we'll get used to it.' Frankie gathered the crockery and stood. 'Right, back to my case.'

Ever the gentleman, Granot got to his feet, too. 'You're nearly there by the sound of it.'

'The team is really on song. I'm hopeful.' She scanned Granot's photo wall. 'The Port Lympia will have slowed somewhat now, I imagine. Unsurprising, considering you're practically a one-man band.'

'Yes, but it's the kind of case that could break very quickly. The gendarmerie is helping me a lot on the third killing – the one up on Boulevard Blanqui.' He pointed to the relevant photos. 'Victim's a fellow we knew as Ludo but he's the second individual in this thing to have been using an alias. But, and it's a very promising but, Armani's got a feeling about him and he's chasing things up.'

'Armani's feelings nearly always pay off.'

'And as if that weren't enough, I'm waiting on significant subungual evidence from the second murder victim, Ploine, real name Hugo Cragnat, who's in the frame as the first victim's killer. Because of a match on the murder weapons used, Cragnat's killer looks certain to have also killed Ludo. If the DNA sequencing on Cragnat's thumbnail scrapings comes up trumps – and since drugs appear to be at the heart of the three murders, it's likely to do just that – we are well in with a shout of being able to ID the killer. As always, though, who's to say there aren't more links in the chain we don't know about yet? With the possibility of further killings?'

'Let's hope there aren't.' In a grouping of shots under the heading E AND E – Evidence and Effects – one particular image caught Frankie's eye. 'What's the *C'est Ici!* receipt about?'

Granot was taken aback. 'It's Denise Dubreuil's. From the last shopping trip she made.'

'She was the first victim?'

'Yes, but how do you know it's a *C'est Ici!* receipt, Frankie? With the store name and number torn off and everything, we hadn't the faintest idea which supermarket it came from. Considering where she lived, we wondered if it was the U on Stalingrad but it turned out not to have been.'

'A U receipt? No, they're not the same design at all. *How* do I know? The different fonts used, the grouping of the characters – everything about it. I shop at *C'est Ici!* all the time.'

'Remarkable. I don't suppose....?'

'I could identify which store? Well, there are only three to choose from and two are nowhere near Port Lympia.'

'So the one in Garibaldi is the most likely?'

'Yes, and I think I can go one better. If I'm not mistaken,

the till that printed that receipt is the extreme right-hand one at the Saint-Séb exit. See the rather blobby quality of the first character of each of the prices? Makes it difficult to read? Because it had the shortest queue, I was at that very till with Chantal last week and we commented that it was all very well being precise about the cents you were spending when you had little idea about the euros.'

'Did I say remarkable? I meant incredible.'

'No, not at all and does it give you anything? Thousands of people shop there every day.'

'I'm only interested in two of them, potentially.' He indicated another wall photo. 'A page from Denise's shopping list notebook. I don't suppose *you* know of anyone with the initials MT or SM, do you?'

'Isn't the landlord you're all interested in called Michel... Thomas?'

'It's Maurice Thomas but we've already discounted him.'

'Ah. Can't think of anyone else, off-hand. As for an SM...' She turned to the photo itself but before she could take it in detail, her mobile rang. 'A moment, Granot... Claudia, what's cooking?' She listened, her lowered brow rising with each passing moment and when she exchanged looks with Granot, it was to nod encouragingly, mouth "I'm needed" and edge towards the door. 'Excellent, but we mustn't do that *quite* yet. I'll be right there.' Ending the call as she had begun her conversation with Granot – half-out of the room – she blew him a kiss and hurried away.

'SM and MT, Frankie,' he called after her. 'There could be a cash reward!'

FORTY-FIVE

Darac had Bonbon and Flaco with him in the Peugeot. Serge Paulin and Ade Okoko's interviewer, Tana Balaya, were following discreetly behind in an unmarked white van driven by the Caserne's grand prix ace *manqué*, Wanda Korneliuk. All three were wearing decorator's overalls. Having finally taken delivery of his new vehicle, Raul Ormans and a couple of members of his team were already circling the area.

'How's the signal, Serge?'

'You're clear as a bell, Captain.'

'You too. Right, low key, remember. You're just tradespeople who've stopped for a break en route to your next job.'

'We've got coffees – the lot.'

'Excellent. Parking, Wanda?'

'There's a good spot to pull in just around the next corner from the address. According to *RueVue*, there's a sightline into the back of the place. Or there was a year ago.'

'I don't anticipate anyone making a run for it but better safe and all that. Stay tuned.'

'Understood.'

'R.O. All good with you and yours?'

'Perfect all the way.'

'And the new van?'

'Fabulous. I may move in permanently.'

'Al-right, we're just arriving. Eyes and ears everyone. Out.'

FORTY-SIX

Emil Arcot knew he was in trouble but he didn't care. Great optimist though he was, he had never once imagined that a big lummox like him could ever have been head over heels in love with an exquisite beauty who desired him just as much. Head over heels? Oh yes, and in every other position and attitude of which his muscle-bound frame was capable. Three times in one afternoon? It had been paradise.

As for missing today's exam? It was only an elective in a part of the course that was itself optional. Yes, he should have told them he wasn't going to sit it as planned but there would be no real bother about it. Missing time in bed with the divine Samira? No. That was not going to happen.

'We'll call this a pull-in place, shall we?' the cab driver said, squeezing up to a quartet of recycling bins set barely off the road. 'Mate?' He grinned into his rear-view mirror. 'We're there.' The pair had enjoyed a lively chat and now wasn't the moment for his fare to start reading emails. 'Listen, I'm blocking everything. Shouldn't have stopped here at all really.'

Emil hadn't heard a word. There had been nothing from Samira all morning but that hadn't concerned him. Their plan had been made. But now there was a message. From Ade.

Bro I can't talk right now so sorry man Listen I can't believe this alright but it's Sam She's dead. Murdered. Last night. Flics talking to everyone. Gotta go A x

It was then that the cabbie saw all the colour drain from the young man's face. 'What is it?'

Feeling disconnected from everything he knew or had known, Emil was too stunned to react. But then energy began to surge around his body, a charge of such overwhelming intensity that it shocked him back to life. But what did life hold for him now? When he opened his mouth to speak, only incoherent sounds emerged at first but words were finally possible. 'Saint-Philippe, now driver,' he said. '*Les Appartements Mimosas*, Avenue Primerose.'

Eschewing the rear-view mirror, the cabby turned around in his seat. 'Are you sure?'

Emil nodded. 'I need to call at a florist first.'

'Aah. Condolences, mate.' He turned around and slipping the cab into gear, reversed smartly on to the boulevard. 'I know one I can pull up right outside.'

'Perfect,' Emil said.

FORTY-SEVEN

'Two cars on the drive, look,' Bonbon said as Darac made the tight turn in off the *chemin*. 'One behind the other. That's a stroke of luck. Just pull up behind them and we've blocked both.'

Leaving their police armbands in their pockets, the trio got out of the Peugeot, sauntered to the door and rang the bell. 'Did you pick up the court order for the phone, Bonbon?'

'*I* did, Captain,' Flaco said.

'Good.'

Through the dimpled glass, a disintegrated shape came gradually together as it approached.

'Looks like Madame,' Bonbon said, ventriloquially.

The door opened to reveal a tall, square-shouldered, harassed-looking woman who was not best pleased to see them.

'We're not talking to newspapers,' she said, her eyes darting from one to the other. 'What's happened is a tragedy, not a story to titillate the general public. Good day to you.'

'That is our view, also, Madame Laborde.' Reflecting that had they indeed been newshounds, Madame had already given them a usable quote, Darac produced his ID and introduced the others. 'We spoke to your husband earlier this morning but we need another word now things have settled a little. Is he at home?'

'Yes he is. I suppose you'd better come in.' Standing aside, she indicated the room beyond the hall. 'Go through to the lounge. The doctor gave Gilles something and he's upstairs, resting. I'll go and get him.'

'He's not asleep?' Bonbon said, as solicitous as a fox enquiring about the wellbeing of chickens.

'No, no… Go through. I shouldn't be a moment.'

As she scurried upstairs, Bonbon called out in a stage whisper. 'Chief – sorry. Forgotten something. Keys?'

'Again?' Darac called back, playing along. He tossed the keys to Flaco who relayed them along the hall and Bonbon retired to the Peugeot to keep watch on the front door.

'A word, Flak,' Darac whispered, inhaling a world of floral scents as he pushed open the door to the lounge. Not expecting to find anyone else at home, he was intent on reassuring her that although Erica's findings had changed their priorities, Dilip Padar had not been let off the hook for Samira's murder. Having been granted access to channels no one else could, Agnès was already garnering potentially useful intel on the Padars of Bengaluru. She had been informed that it may take some hours but if any member of the family or an associate proved to be a person of interest in an ongoing murder enquiry, she would be advised of the fact immediately.

'I just wanted to let you know—'

'Captain?' Flaco's eyes slid meaningfully sideways. 'We have company.'

'I think *you're* the company *we* have, aren't you?' the young woman said in an interesting variation of the local Nissart-inflected accent. Aged, Darac assessed, in her mid-20s, she was a person of some bearing. Setting down a magazine – written in English, Darac further noticed – the young woman moved to get to her feet.

'No, please, Mademoiselle…?'

'Laborde. Inès. Daughter of Zoë who admitted you.'

'And daughter of Coach Gilles Laborde, presumably?'

Inès stiffened slightly. 'Presumably. Although to him I'm Laborde, Jackie. I mention it so you won't be confused later. Sit down, Officers…?'

'Flaco and Darac.' Showing his lanyard ID to make the

distinction, he indicated the chair next to the small sofa she was occupying. 'May I?'

'Please. I heard a third voice, I thought?'

'That was Lieutenant Busquet. He had to go back to the car to sort something out.'

'I see.'

Behind Inès, patio doors were open on to the rear garden but the floral scents perfuming the space had a different source.

'I don't think I've ever seen so many vases of flowers,' Darac said. 'Not in one room. And for mid-March? Remarkable.'

'It's all a bit overpowering, isn't it? A celebration, Captain. My parents' wedding anniversary.'

'Congratulations to them.' He looked into Inès's dark eyes, reddened with tiredness or tears or both. 'You're aware of why we're here, mademoiselle?'

'This horrible murder. Of course.' She looked across at Flaco. 'We had thought to lose all the flowers but then we realised they could serve a different purpose.'

'Indeed.'

'I thought you had spoken to my father earlier, though, Captain?'

'Yes, we did,' he replied, affably. 'But there have been developments.'

She nodded. 'It's good to know that the... Brigade Criminelle, is it?'

'It is.'

'Yes, good to know you're keeping father in the loop. And in person, too.'

Until the man himself showed, a change of subject was called for. Darac's eye fell on the magazine. Reciting its upside-down title in a passable English accent tacitly asked the question for him.

'*New Scientist* – that's right. I'm part of research project in England.'

'How interesting. Neither of us is much of a scientist. Are you researching anything we're likely to be familiar with?'

'Yes, actually. As police officers, I'm sure you're conversant with the principles of DNA sequencing?'

'On a need to know basis but not much beyond that.'

'Well, try this on for size. My team is studying specific repeating sequences of bases. Why? Because these appear more prone to expansion during the transcription process. With consequences for various diseases.'

'Well over my head, I'm afraid.' He gave Flaco a questioning look. 'Officer Flaco?'

'Mine, too.'

Inès pulled down the corners of her mouth. 'It is rather esoteric, I suppose.'

'Whereabouts are you doing this esoteric research, Mademoiselle? That might be a more fruitful area.'

'Cambridge. Due back on Friday.'

'Oh,' he said, pleasantly. 'Been working there long?'

'This is my eighth year.'

Cambridge... Was there any reason not to tell the truth here? It would likely loosen things up and that could be useful. 'I shall be in Cambridge myself in six weeks time.'

Inès didn't reply immediately. '*Will* you?'

'Yes, as unlikely as it may seem, I'm a member of a jazz group and we're playing a few dates in England. A mini tour kind of thing. One of them is at the Cambridge Modern Jazz Club. The Vault, I think the name of the venue is.'

Darac could see it was Inès's turn to gauge how much to reveal. 'Uh... it *is* called The Vault, you're right. My... fiancée sometimes plays there. Pianist.'

'No, really? There's such a lot of cross-fertilisation in European jazz, I may have heard of him. May even have *seen* him with it being so easy to get around. What's his name?'

'Or hers,' Flaco said, her habitual scowl lifting.

Inès returned her look. 'Yes, it's Sue,' she said simply. 'Susan Talbot, actually.'

'Forgive me,' Darac said. 'Also for not being au fait with Susan's music. Perhaps we could meet at our gig. You're a jazz fan yourself, Mademoiselle?'

'Sadly, no. In fact, I have what Sue calls a tin ear for music in general.'

'We all have our proclivities.'

'I can't use my left-sided brain as an excuse, Captain. Many of my fellow researchers, especially the mathematicians, adore music. I think Sue despairs of me, particularly as she's pretty much an expert on everything from plainsong to hip-hop.'

While Darac couldn't claim *such* broad expertise himself, he was familiar with the phenomenon of loving something that left one's partners, friends and colleagues cold. 'It clearly hasn't…'

'No.' Inès smiled, saving him the effort of finding the *mots justes.* 'It hasn't.'

Looking no less harassed than before, Zoë appeared and hovered in the doorway.

'My husband is just taking a shower to freshen up. He'll be down in ten minutes or so. Would you like some coffee or anything?'

'No, thank you,' Flaco said.

In the parlance of the DMQ's tenor saxophonist Dave Blackstock, Darac could have "murdered" a double espresso but he declined also.

'Or perhaps you would prefer to talk to Gilles in his office at the faculty building? He'll be going back there shortly.'

'No, no, Madame. We'll wait. Please sit down.' He paused while she did so.

'You're heading back to Cambridge on Friday, you said, Mademoiselle Laborde?'

'That's right.'

'Actually, my daughter is *Doctor* Laborde, Captain.' Zoë essayed a smile but didn't quite nail it. 'Her field is biochemistry.' She turned to Flaco. 'What's particularly remarkable about it all...'

'Maman?' Inès interjected. 'We've talked a little about it already.'

Zoë was far from finished. 'What is remarkable is that she did her undergraduate work, her PhD, and has written numerous papers all in English. Speaks it like a native. But even if she were English born and bred, it's quite a thing to have become a Fellow of King's College, don't you think?'

'I don't know what a Fellow is,' Flaco said. 'But a Cambridge doctorate? That's tip-top.'

'In fact,' Inès said, 'I'm what's known as a *Bye*-Fellow. Not nearly so grand.'

'But her project is hugely important. Isn't it, darling?'

Inès nodded, thoughtfully. 'I think so, yes.'

'And so do several global organisations and—'

Inès grinned. 'Bless you, Maman but I don't think our visitors need to hear a list of all my credits.'

'I suppose not.' Zoë managed a fuller smile and caught Darac's eye once more. 'King's is so beautiful. You know the famous chapel?'

'Seen photos, certainly.'

Inès's gaze locked on to her mother's. 'The Captain is visiting Cambridge in person soon, Maman.'

The news appeared to perturb her. 'Oh?'

'Yes, you'll be there in about six weeks, didn't you say, Captain?'

'Indeed, but only for one day. I doubt there will be time for sightseeing.'

'It's a work commitment?' Zoë asked.

'Quite the opposite. I play in a band and we have a gig at the jazz club.'

Zoë brightened a shade. 'How unusual. For a policeman to play in a jazz group, I mean.'

'Such things are not quite so unusual as you might imagine.'

'Really? You're obviously accomplished or you wouldn't be travelling so far.'

'We're on a week's tour.'

'Like Sue's sextet had that tour of Scandinavia and the Baltic countries last year, Maman.'

'Ah, yes.'

Darac judged that the moment had arrived. 'I'm sure you both realise that as investigating officers in this murder enquiry, it's our duty to ask a lot of routine questions of those even tangentially connected to the events of yesterday evening. For elimination purposes, mainly. Would it be alright if we asked you those questions now?'

The request seemed to offend Zoë. 'And if it's not convenient? You could have rung.'

'It would help us all, I think. It would save us having to send cars for you later on, for instance. And with respect to your return to the UK, Doctor, it would obviously make sense to get this out of the way now. Were we to fall behind, you might end up missing your flight.'

'Yes, of course. Let's do it now, Maman.'

'Oh. If you insist.'

'Thank you.' Darac smiled. 'As I'm sure you'll further appreciate, this case is something of a cast of thousands scenario. With so many to talk to, it greatly speeds up the collating process later if we've been able to record all our chats. That alright with you?'

Zoë turned to her daughter but before she could air any objections she may have had, Inès was already nodding assent. 'Sure.'

'Excellent. We use what is a small camcorder, effectively. Once Officer Flaco here has set it up, you'll forget it's there almost straight away. Particularly if you sit next to one another? Or we could talk to you separately. It is the normal practice, actually.'

'Together,' Zoë said without hesitation. 'Together is better.'

'Are you sure, Madame? You run your IT business from home, don't you? If you would like to go and check your work emails or whatever for five minutes, please feel free.'

'That's kind.' A steelier look now. 'But you don't seriously think I could put in even one minute's work today, Captain? Just carry on as if nothing had happened?'

'Together it is, then,' Darac said, maintaining the mood.

Inès shifted uneasily in her seat. 'Yes, join me on the sofa, Maman.'

As the women arranged themselves and Flaco went about setting up the recording, Darac had a further question.

'Madame, if I may, I'll just summon Lieutenant Busquet? We wouldn't want your husband walking in while we're recording and have to do it all again, would we?'

'*Definitely* not.'

'But is the front door...?'

'The Lieutenant can just push it open. I left it on the latch.'

Did you, indeed, Darac noted. 'Thank you.' He called Bonbon, explained he needed him to play studio security guard for a few minutes and it was as he went to ring off that a starred notification flashed up on his lock screen. A couple of taps later and Darac opened the case file log to find that Farid had caught up with heptathlete Grace Nahili and posted a short, bullet-pointed summary. Having heard nothing about Samira's murder until he had broken the news to her, it was the greatest difficulty that Grace coped with the interview that followed. However, her tears hadn't prevented her from making what looked set to be an important contribution to the investigation. At the end of last evening's training session, she reported actually seeing Coach Gilles

Laborde heading towards the dark end of the players' car park moments after Samira had driven off in that direction herself. That made Grace the first, and so far the only, eyewitness to such a manoeuvre. Erica's mobile phone findings were far more critical to the case but it was a significant sighting, nevertheless. Asked why Laborde and Samira might have done as they did, Grace replied that with space at a premium at the gate end, it wasn't unknown for drivers to set off home in what appeared to be the wrong direction. It was easier to turn around that way, she thought. Had she seen Samira and or Coach Laborde return? No, Coach Macdonald had buttonholed her for a word shortly afterwards and her attention was then elsewhere. The summary ended and when Darac looked up, he saw Flaco was reading it, also. No doubt Bonbon was following suit outside.

'So, Officer Flaco?' he said, sharing a charged look with her. 'Ready?'

'Ready, Captain.'

Flaco tagged the recording and they began.

'Madame Laborde, would you mind telling me where you were between 8 o'clock yesterday evening and the small hours of this morning?'

'Why?'

Darac smiled. 'Why? I thought I had already explained that we need to form a complete picture of where everyone —'

'Yes, yes, alright. I was here. All evening.'

Inès nodded. 'Yes. I can vouch for that, Captain.'

'Uh-huh. Do you mind me asking what you were doing during that time?'

Her cheeks colouring, Zoë's irritation level appeared to be rising exponentially. 'If you must know, I was having a lovely dinner with Inès for most of it. Is that alright? But then I had work to do at my desk. I had a deadline on a book to which I've been asked to contribute a chapter and I was fulfilling that obligation. Started at about 9.20. I could give you the name of the publisher, show you the contract, print it off, if need be. I could print off the chapter. Chapter and verse! Literally! Or better still, why not take my laptop away with you, Captain? I insist! I'm sure you have IT people who could use it to verify where and when I activated my fingerprint ID to log in; where and when I accessed the document in question; where and when I then worked on it, completed it, emailed it to the publisher and finally, logged out. How's that?'

'Maman.' Inès took Zoë's hand. 'There's no need to fly off the handle, is there? The Captain and Officer Flaco are simply doing their jobs.'

'Well, they should do them more sympathetically.'

'I apologise, Madame Laborde, but I also want to thank you for giving permission to impound your computer. It will, as you say, remove any doubt as to your whereabouts during the critical hours of yesterday.'

Now it was Inès's turn to show exasperation. 'Captain – really! That's going too far.'

Zoë stood. 'No, darling. I said I insist he take it and I meant it.'

'Rest assured that we *will* take it at the end of our session, Madame. Please sit down.'

'Fine! Next question, please. When did my husband return from the Stade? Is that what you'd like to know?'

'Yes, as a matter of fact.'

'I wasn't serious.'

'I was, however.'

She let out a long, exasperated breath. 'Al-right. It was later than usual. About 11.45.'

'Did he give a reason for that? Traffic, perhaps?'

'No, and I didn't ask him.'

'You were still writing your piece at that point?'

'No, no. I'd finished it just before 11 o'clock. As your IT people will discover.'

'How did your husband seem to you when he came in?'

'I don't know.'

'You don't know?'

'You won't be satisfied until you've got the whole picture, will you? Alright, I'd retired to bed at about 11.30. Perhaps you would like to impound my pyjamas, too?'

'Maman! Stop it!'

Darac gave Flaco a look.

'Please, take a moment, Madame,' she said, correctly reading his intention. 'We know this is stressful.'

Zoë thought about it. 'Yes, well I'm glad you realise that.' A quick smile for Inès. 'I'm sorry, darling. Where was I? Yes, I was almost asleep when I heard his car draw up on the drive. I heard him come in but I didn't see him thereafter. If I'm very late to bed, I sleep in the spare room. Gilles does the same if he's the late one.'

'So as not to wake the other.'

'Exactly.'

'And in the morning?'

'What about it?'

'You saw your husband then.'

'No, actually, I didn't see him. I was late up and he had already gone to work.'

Darac smiled. 'I think that completes our questions to you, Madame.' He glanced at his watch. 'Doctor, you now? I think we should just have time before Coach Laborde is ready to join us.'

'Yes, alright. I too was here all evening and when Maman went off to write up her piece, I retired to bed. My room is sandwiched between my parents' bedroom and her workshop and I could hear her tapping away. I had a couple of email exchanges with some colleagues back in Cambridge. Again, you can check in any way that works but please don't leave me without a phone for Friday. Then I ploughed through a few chapters of a book I brought with me. I'm afraid I neglected to take a real-time movie of the experience but I could produce the tome itself with its bookmark suggestively close to the endpapers.'

'I imagine the tome in question was some impenetrable scientific treatise?'

'Brilliant though it is, I don't think *Harry Potter and The Deathly Hallows* quite qualifies.'

Darac smiled, this time without artifice.

'I turned off my light at about 11.15.'

'Thank you. A final question, Doctor?'

'Did I see or hear my father come in? No. Did I see him over breakfast the following morning? No, he had already left for work. But I could see he had had breakfast, Captain.'

'Excellent. That's all very...'

Voices off. One of them Bonbon's. A moment later, the door opened and Coach Gilles François Laborde walked gravely into the room. A moment later, Darac arrested him on suspicion of the murder of Samira Naidu Padar and, to a chorus of protests from his wife and daughter, he was led away too stunned to add his own voice to them.

FORTY-EIGHT

When it came to blending seamlessly into the background, the slightly built, slightly balding Alain Terrevaste was the best there was and he knew it. Aside from a preternatural inconspicuousness of face, form and manner, "Tee-Vee" a.k.a "the Invisible Man" possessed two additional assets: limitless patience and razor-sharp eyesight. A mirthless individual not given to any kind of outward display, Terrevaste's inner life was a closed book even to those with whom he had worked for years. However, the Invisible Man was not without an Achilles heel. His ego was as fragile as it was huge and on the few occasions an undercover watchdog operation under his command had gone down, his credo that there were two ways of approaching any job – his way and the wrong way – had succeeded only in compounding the problem. Once or twice, it had even caused him to blow his cover.

He had seen little point in the Place Wilson operation from the off. So an officer thought a passer-by bore a resemblance to another officer's wife who lived nearby? What was the fuss about? And when it came to it, he suspected that the resemblance was nothing like as "concerningly exact" as had been reported. And who was the source of the report on this "doppelganger" anyway? Had it been the Brigade's sure-eyed sketch artist Astrid Pireque, for whom Terrevaste held a grudging regard, he would have given it more credence. But no. It had been Captain Francine Lejeune, a "superior" officer with whom he had had run-ins in the past and, as a new mother, was probably blurry-eyed after a sleepless night.

The afternoon shift in and around Place Wilson completed,

Terrevaste left the neighbourhood with the consoling thought that one more day on the job should be enough to convince the mercifully soon-to-be ex-Commissaire Agnès Dantier that putting the thing to bed was the way to go. There was real policing to be done somewhere in the city and he wanted to be able to get on with it.

But for the moment, his thoughts went no further than food. Unlike almost every other police officer in France, Terrevaste eschewed the concept of frequenting tried and trusted places for meals. Indeed, with the object of remaining a stranger everywhere he went, he made a point of never showing his unmemorable face at the same eatery twice within one calendar year. He was triaging likely spots along L'Avenue de la République when a woman emerging from a homewares shop near the Garibaldi tram stop caught his eye. He studied her more closely. Age: late 30s, early 40s? Height: allowing for her heeled black leather court shoes, about one metre sixty-five. Weight: fifty kilos or so. Hair: short, fair. Eyes: brown. Glasses: thin, wire-framed. Face: pretty, subtly made-up; prominent cheek bones; small chin. Clothing: multi-coloured chunky-knit cardigan with a wrap-around collar; navy-blue calf-length cloth trousers.

Was it possible? On the surface, the woman looked little like Madame Tardelli. But he knew she was the doppelganger. And he knew, therefore, that he had made an error of judgment in discounting the possibility earlier. The feeling was as unwelcome as it was unfamiliar but it didn't last long. He told himself that no other officer in the region was capable of putting such a photofit together in his head – subtracting the glasses, adding the appropriate wig, clothes and shoes. Not even Astrid Pireque.

But what was going on here? Suddenly interested in a set of coloured plastic beakers in a shop window, Terrevaste waited for the woman's reflection to shrink away towards the far side of the avenue before turning to follow her. He thought about sharing the development but he decided not to call it in just yet. First, he wanted to discover where this woman was heading.

FORTY-NINE

Gilles Laborde had regained both his voice and the strength in his arms well before Flaco and Serge Paulin delivered him into the custody cells at the Caserne. His rights carefully explained to him, Laborde had used his permitted phone call to engage one Sylvain Gremat, a lawyer who wasted no time in registering his dismay at the arrest with anyone in a position to make life more difficult for Darac and co. Balancing this – and it was an issue that despite recent EU-directed changes, continued to exercise Darac and his more liberal-minded colleagues – criminal cases initiated by the Public Prosecutor's office severely limited the capacity of lawyers to intercede on behalf of their clients during interrogations. More lawyer-friendly rules applied to cases green-lighted by the examining magistrate's wing of the judiciary but when Public Prosecutor Jules Frènes lazily waved through Agnès Dantier's Brigade to investigate the murder of Samira Padar, he *de facto* gagged whoever would go on to represent the accused-to-be during questioning. Only at the end of sessions would said lawyer be permitted to speak, and then only to ask questions.

With Laborde safely, if noisily, ensconced in the cells, Darac and Bonbon made for Erica's lab where they found her performing an autopsy on a burnt-out electrical device.

'Afternoon, gentlemen,' she said, her fine blonde hair losing the anchorage of her ears as she swivelled around on her chair. 'It's a junction box, before you ask. Or was. Cleverly sabotaged, Armani believes, by a 12 year-old child which is quite disturbing. But anyway, Monsieur Laborde?'

'Thanks to you, we nabbed the man,' Bonbon said, honouring her contribution by proffering a packet of something brown. 'Toffee belly button?'

'Ooh, I love these. I'll save it for later.'

'Take two. Chief?'

'Trying to give them up. Anyway, it was great work as always, Erica.'

'Great? I'm sure you've both seen the Hitchcock movie shot around here in the 50s – *To Catch A Thief*?'

Bonbon nodded. 'Only about 50 times.'

'It's wonderful,' Darac said. 'Although I'd like to think our squad bests that useless bunch tasked with catching, what was he called…?'

'The Cat,' Erica and Bonbon said in unison.

'That's it.'

'Well,' Erica went on, 'you remember the sequence on the *Moyenne Corniche* in which Cary Grant's character calls Grace Kelly's "a girl in a million?" and she replies "It's a routine compliment but I'll accept it?" Erica's wispy eyebrows rose to complete the thought.

Darac grinned. 'You'll get no argument from us.'

'On this occasion, there really was nothing to it.'

Donning gloves, Darac opened his shoulder bag. 'Couple of more things for you.'

'One of them wouldn't be Samira's phone, would it?'

'Our guiding light to La Ginistière? The same.'

'Excellent. Useful though the carrier data was, now we've got the thing itself, I'll be able to extract virtually everything that's ever passed in or out of it. Where did you find it, out of interest?'

'R.O fished it out of Laborde's car,' Bonbon said. 'Glove compartment.'

'Judging by recent messages to the poor girl, the underpants drawer in the marital bedroom would've been more appropriate. The lying, cheating bastard.'

'Quite.'

'And your other gift for the overworked?'

'Laptop.' Darac set it on the bench. 'Belongs to his wife, Zoë.'

Bonbon's foxy eyes twinkled. 'Yes, this is a first, Erica. Far from having to go through hoops to impound the thing, Madame wound up *insisting* we take it.'

'Her daughter had already corroborated her story that she had been in all evening but we got a bit at cross-purposes – Madame and me – and we proceeded to round up a couple of high horses which we wasted no time in mounting. Anyway, upshot – we have her laptop. It's fingerprint ID entry only, by the way.'

'*Quelle* drag. Oh, I'm all film quotes today.'

'*Breakfast at Tiffany's?*' Bonbon said. 'The divine Audrey?'

'In one.'

'Why a drag exactly?' Darac asked.

'It means taking things apart more than usual which takes time but never mind.'

Bonbon grinned, mischievously. 'Madame runs her own IT business, by the way. Something of an expert in the field, it seems.'

Erica feigned a look of regal indifference. 'Is she now?'

'Actually,' Darac said. 'She made reference to just how many of her actions "your IT people" would be able to check on the machine. Log on and off times being just for starters.'

'Of course. All computers log every single move a user makes on it. Anyway, what exactly do you want me to do with the laptop?'

'As you've just explained, use it to prove or *dis*-prove the when, where and what Madame Laborde got up to yesterday evening. You should find a text file of about 4,000 words she says she typed up between... Let me check.... 9.20 and just before 11 o'clock last night. It's her contribution to a book coming out next year about women who've set up successful businesses. She says she then emailed the file as an attachment to her publisher.'

'Nothing could be simpler. Once I've checked the location and timing data, I'll send you both the text file and the email. I'd be interested to read her piece, actually. The whole book, in fact.'

'You wouldn't ever consider leaving us, would you? Working for the State may have its drawbacks but for the time being at least, the compensations outweigh them.' He essayed a modest smile. 'Such as getting to work with such interesting and accomplished people.'

Erica adopted the expression of a parent delivering a difficult truth to a child. 'On that, Bonbon's already offered me a partnership in the antiques business he's going to set up when *he* leaves.'

'What? This isn't true, is it, Bonbon?'

'In a sense.'

'In what sense?'

'In the sense of it being… a wind-up. And you can stop looking so aggrieved. Scarcely a week goes by without you wondering about leaving, quote "all this" unquote, to become a full-time jazz musician. And you're *not* kidding.'

'That's different. Somehow. But it's not going to happen. I have responsibilities now.'

'And more to come,' Erica said. 'Once you take over from Agnès as commissaire.' She shared nods with Bonbon. 'Right?'

'Right.'

'Now you really are winding me up.' Their expressions didn't change. 'Aren't you?'

FIFTY

Since being escorted back to his Saint-Philippe apartment, Dilip Padar had spent the entire time in heated conversations with his male relatives back in Bengaluru. Finally called upon to add their thoughts, his mother and aunts had been too overcome with grief to set even one foot outside the kitchen.

The avalanche of sorrowful words, cautions and threats having run its course for the moment, Dilip sank on to the sofa to try and put everything together in his head. Before he could work out what to do first, his gaze fell on the silk cushion Sam had clung to on her last visit. Her last visit ever. Dilip began to sob. He'd told himself over and over that he hadn't meant to do it. It was the last thing he'd wanted. The Last! Last!! Last!!! It certainly hadn't been his fault. It was his family that was responsible. His fucking, fucking family!

As Samira had done, he grabbed the cushion and threw it as hard as he could into the corner of the room. It did no good. He jumped to his feet and grabbed the nearest breakable object – a half-empty bottle of Scotch – and hurled it at the wall. A table lamp went the same way. Then a nest of tables, all three at once slung at the TV screen. The doorbell rang. Knocks at the door. Shouts. Another crash. The doorbell ringing repeatedly now.

Outside, his two police escorts from the Stade shoulder-charged the door but the impact caused more damage to them than to it. And then, as if in answer to a prayer, a grave-faced giant of a man appeared, a well-wisher carrying a bouquet of flowers.

'Help us!'

Without hesitation, Emil tossed the bouquet aside and flew

at the door, crashing it open in one massive effort. In his rage, Dilip appeared not to see him or the two escorts limping gingerly in his wake. A burning smell and a hint of smoke rising thinly from a power outlet was enough to trigger an alarm and while the officers set about dealing with it, Emil stared hard into the eyes of the man he knew he was going to kill.

'No,' Dilip said, edging back towards the window. 'No, I—'

Emil was on him before he knew, his weight and momentum sandbagging him to the floor and pinning him. Winded, his opponent could do nothing and it was easy for Emil to clamp his hands either side of the man's head and lift it. He could have dashed his skull against the parquet there and then but as efforts went on behind him to prevent a full-scale fire, first there were truths he needed to impart.

FIFTY-ONE

Darac and Bonbon were on the point of heading off to question Gilles Laborde when Farid hurried into the office.

'Breaking. Emil Arcot didn't sit the exam. Went off to see Samira instead. Got all the way over to Bischoffsheim before learning what had happened to her. Meanwhile, Big Charlie and his two mates are twiddling their thumbs outside the exam room. By the time someone bothers to tell them Emil had bunked off the exam before it began, the young man's already on his way to confront Dilip at his place. Of course, Charlie had no way of knowing that but to be on the safe side, he set off with the others to *Les Mimosas* just in case.'

'There were a couple of guys watching Dilip already and Joinel were sending a couple more,' Darac said. 'And if it weren't for the look on your face, I wouldn't hate the way this story is shaping.'

'I'll cut to *beyond* the chase. Dilip has lost it by now, OK? Raving. And while his minders are busy putting out a fire he accidentally started, Charlie and the boys arrive hot on the heels of Emil who's already pinning Dilip to the floor and explaining to him why he's going to bash his brains out. Charlie dives on them, the other two join in and the three of them succeed in pulling Emil off. Outcome? A massively distraught Emil is charged with assault and is on his way to join Laborde in the cell block. Meanwhile, though physically only winded and bruised, Dilip is completely in pieces mentally and so is ambulanced off to L'Archet where, heavily sedated, he is put to bed under guard.'

Darac let out a long, contemplative breath. 'O-K.'

Bonbon shook his head. 'Well, you said you had breaking, Farid.'

'Telling you both as soon as I could trumped updating the case file log but I'll do that in a minute.'

'Good work,' Darac said. 'Thanks, man.'

'Charlie's kicking himself he didn't double check Emil was actually among the students sitting the exam. He just assumed the list of names posted on the room door was an accurate one.'

'These things happen,' Darac said. 'The scene at *Les Mimosas*, though? I don't know where to start. The fire?'

'Extinguished. Very little damage.'

'That's something.' He picked up the phone. 'Charvet? We've got a young man named Emil Arcot coming in under arrest for assault within the next few minutes. He's got a completely clean record up to now but for various reasons, he's in a state. Get the duty doctor over to the cells to check him over, will you?'

'Will do, Captain.'

'That's it.'

'What do you reckon we do now, chief?' Bonbon said. 'Let those sleeping dogs lie while we question Laborde?'

'It's all we can do, I think.' He turned to Farid. 'Charlie or his chums pick up anything from Emil on the way here? That would help us with Laborde, I mean.'

'Possibly but can I just say that I know your paths haven't crossed with Charlie's much but despite his earlier gaffe, he is someone to take notice of.'

'Once he *did* know Emil was absent, he certainly showed good judgement in shooting off to *Les Mimosas*. And when he got there, he acted decisively which may well have saved the life of one of the protagonists and prevented the other spending the rest of his formative years behind bars. Charlie will do for me, don't worry.'

'Thanks, Captain.'

'So Charlie does have something?'

'Oh, sorry, yes.' A serious young man with a ready smile, Farid could do sheepishness, too. 'But it's only a feeling. An intuition.'

Darac gave him a half-sympathetic, half-reproving look. 'Mate…'

'I know, Captain.' He shrugged. 'But there's an important detail attached to it I definitely do need to tell you about.'

Picking up his interrogation notes on Laborde, Darac got to his feet. 'We've got a minute.'

'Emil is clearly guilty of assault and I suppose an attempted murder charge is not out of the question, either. I reported that Dilip was raving when Emil arrived, but something I haven't mentioned yet is that he – Dilip – kept shouting over and over again, "I didn't mean to do it."'

'He said just "do *it*"? He didn't say: "I didn't mean to kill my sister" or "kill Samira" or "kill her"?'

'No. Just "it".'

Bonbon was already picturing a scene in court. 'The prosecution would make a lot of that "it".'

'Agreed,' Darac said, running a hand through his hair. 'We will need to press him on what he meant, obviously. That intuitive feeling you mentioned Charlie had. Was it to do with this?'

'Indirectly, and Captain if it were anyone else, I wouldn't bother passing it on. But I owe the guy a lot and his intuitions about things are usually spot-on.'

'Go for it.'

'It's just that having witnessed Emil's capacity for explosive violence first-hand *and* heard Dilip's loudly repeated protestations, Charlie still doesn't believe either of them killed Samira.' He shrugged. 'That's all.'

'Farid, if our interrogation of Gilles Laborde goes the way we hope, you can be the one to tell Charlie his intuition was once again pitch perfect.'

The young man pressed his palms together in thanks.

'Ready, Bonbon?'

'Ready.'

They hadn't taken a step before Darac's mobile rang. 'I hardly dare answer,' he said, slipping it out of his pocket. 'R.O – you're on speaker to Bonbon and Farid as well. What have you got? And I warn you, it had better be good. It's one excitement after another here at the moment.'

'How about the identity of Julien Baille's doorstep assassin – correction – *would-be* assassin? That fit the bill?'

Darac's ears pricked up. 'It certainly does.' Identifying Dilip's heavy was a significant breakthrough in itself and could link to the "honour" killing story Agnès was working on. And there was a second potential significance here. Were the ID to have originated in time-tagged CCTV footage from the *Résidence*, there should soon be similar footage of Julien's arrival back from the Stade on the night Samira was murdered; footage that would further corroborate the account he had given of his movements. 'Are we talking CCTV here, R.O?'

'No. We are talking finding a print match on our database from the postcard the master hit-man so helpfully shoved through Julien's door.'

Darac shared a doubly disappointed look with Bonbon. Quite apart from the wider picture, it was clear from Ormans's tone that the heavy was far from being any sort of pro.

'The man's name?'

'He is one Rajesh Anil Sharma. Comte de Falicon address. Second generation Niçois. Runs the family wholesale fruit and vegetable business which has occasionally failed to meet the rightfully exacting standards set by our nation's taxation authorities. He has also failed to keep his fists to himself in a series of tawdry disputes over gambling. Hence his prints being on file.'

Already scrolling the database, Bonbon's eyes were all a-twinkle as he displayed Sharma's photo. 'You wouldn't bet against him in a competition to find the most lived-in face in France.'

Darac grinned. 'Or most bashed-in. Funny, isn't it, that all those scars give the impression that here's a tough guy who can really handle himself, when it actually means he's taken a good many pastings.'

'Nice observation,' Ormans said. 'Anyway, that's all I have for the moment. Fare well with Coach Laborde, gentlemen.'

'Thanks, R.O.'

The call ended, Darac turned to Farid. 'Sharma's bang to rights on threatening to cause bodily injury, obviously. How are you fixed at the moment?'

'Clear as far as interviewing goes. Want me to pay the man a visit?'

'How can I put this? Yes.'

Farid grinned. 'I'll get right on it.'

'Better take a couple of guys with you. Sharma may have the reflexes of a punch-drunk gorilla but he's still a gorilla.'

'With you all the way, Captain. I'll just make a call. Won't be a second.'

'And Dilip Padar's part in this?' Bonbon said.

Darac drew down the corners of his mouth. 'Considering the state he's in, I think we'll leave arresting him on suspicion of conspiracy for the time being.'

'He may have charges of his own to bring in time. Assault charges against Julien we know definitely *did* happen.'

'He may and it could provide grounds for the courts taking a more lenient approach with Sharma and with Dilip himself if it turns he *was* behind the threats made. But as Granot is fond of saying, that's not for us to decide.'

Farid finished his call and took his leave.

'OK, Bonbon. It's take two for Head Coach Laborde. Ready?'

'Ready.'

FIFTY-TWO

On the whole, Darac preferred questioning suspects in his office but the more formal setting of the interview room had its uses. Thus far, Gilles Laborde had refused to be intimidated, aggressive outbursts and tearful desolation following one on the other in a repeating sequence. At the moment, arms resolutely folded, jaw set firm, gaze hard and penetrating, Laborde was a picture of indignant invulnerability. But if his portrayal of an innocent victim of circumstance carried conviction, the evidence building up against him appeared to be propelling him towards a conviction of an altogether different kind. Sitting next to him, lawyer Sylvain Gremat was doing only a so-so job of hiding his dismay at the way things were going; his expression betrayed nothing so clearly as the thought that had the law permitted him to have read the case dossier beforehand, he would not have taken the brief.

'Monsieur Laborde,' Darac said, indicating the stack of printed-out emails and texts sitting in mute accusation between them. 'I or my colleague Lieutenant Busquet here don't need to read out any more of these... shall we just call them *overheated* messages, do we? We've made our point. I think.'

'You've made the point that you've raided my phone for messages which were...'

'Deleted?'

'Private!' He sank back in his chair. 'Do as you like, I don't care.'

'Perhaps we should just recap where we've got to. You do not deny that you were madly in love with Mademoiselle Samira Padar.'

'I reject the word "madly." It suggests I had taken leave of my senses. Nothing could have been further from the truth. With her, I'd come to my senses, if anything.'

That's sunk one potentially mitigating factor for Gremat, Darac thought to himself. 'You were in complete control of your faculties throughout? I see.'

'I was. At *all* times.'

Gremat opened his mouth to speak but thought better of it.

'There was something you wished to say to your client, Monsieur?' Bonbon asked.

'No, no.'

'Oh. I thought you were about to commend Monsieur Laborde for his honesty there. But just to remind you—'

'Yes, thank you, Lieutenant. I do not need to be reminded of the relevant protocols.'

'You're a stats man, aren't you, Monsieur Laborde. My colleague Lieutenant Busquet and I are more into visuals. We like to picture things. So to help us, I'd like to put a little demonstration together.'

Giving a running commentary on what he was doing for the benefit of the recording, Darac picked up the stack of messages and, locating the page markers dividing them, set out five pairs of piles on the desk. 'These on my left are from you to Samira; on the right, she to you. Five piles, one for each of the past five days of message traffic between the two of you.'

If Laborde had any confidence in the demonstration, he gave every indication to the contrary. 'It's obvious that you've gathered together only those messages that puts me in a negative light.'

'On the contrary. I grant we don't have absolutely everything at the moment but it's fairly complete.'

'Just get on with it.'

Darac smiled. 'Thank you. Going back to last Thursday, and I'm sure you'll corroborate this as well, Monsieur Gremat, the piles are fairly even in height, aren't they?'

Gremat shrugged assent.

'You agree. Good. But as the days wear on, it's evident from the increasing disparity in those heights that there's a growing imbalance in the flow of messages between you and that would tend to suggest one thing, wouldn't it? Samira's interest in you had begun to dwindle well before the final training session at the Stade.'

'It's not as black and white as that. Not remotely.'

'Then let's return to the content itself. By Day Three, despite or perhaps because of the bombardment of written and spoken words to which you were subjecting her, she's finding excuses not to see you – hoping, I imagine, that you would read between the lines. She's perfectly polite about it, I must say. Like this one, for example.' Darac showed the message to Laborde but nothing coming back, he handed it to Bonbon instead.

' "I'm afraid I can't, Gilles," ' Bonbon read aloud. ' "I'm too busy now for a while." ' He replaced it on the pile. 'Seems you're just not a read-between-the-lines kind of guy, are you, Monsieur?'

'Think what you like.'

Darac turned to Day Four. 'Very threadbare from Samira now, isn't it? You, on the other hand. Inverse ratio. Isn't that the term? And your choice of words.' He read out a couple of random phrases. 'Complimenting her on her beauty is one thing, but some of this stuff goes way beyond that. We're in sexual harassment territory here, Monsieur. Repeated references to the lusciousness of her body – especially to her… what was it?' As Laborde stirred uncomfortably in his seat, Darac peered at the page. 'Yes, to her *yoni*, in particular.'

Part of Darac and Bonbon's strategy in questioning

Laborde was occasionally to rile him into exposing the sheer explosiveness of his temper. It had paid off earlier and it appeared to be about to do so again.

'And who do you think taught me that word?' he shouted, the veins in his reddening head and neck throbbing almost cartoon-like as he jumped to his feet. 'Who? Eh? It was Sam herself! She loved... Loved it!' Tears now. 'Loved me and loved *it*. Sex! Sex with me! We were lovers! Why can't you understand that, you bastards!'

'Sit down, Monsieur.'

The instruction was superfluous. Muttering further insults, Laborde dropped back onto his seat as if he'd been hit by a crossbow dart. Meanwhile, Gremat stared at the ceiling, finding a little solace there before glancing at his watch.

'He's certainly a hot one, your client, Monsieur Gremat,' Bonbon said, pleasantly, but then as if a more concerning thought had occurred to him, he raised his tawny eyebrows. 'Makes you think. Doesn't it? You may answer. I asked you a direct question.'

None came.

'We'll take a few moments here.' Darac exchanged a look with the guard and while Bonbon tagged off the session on the recorder, the officer went about replenishing Laborde's supply of tissues and water. Meanwhile, Darac reorganised the messages into a single stack and brought a second evidence case to the party. As Laborde gathered himself and Gremat looked warily on, Darac produced print-outs of further messages, a whole new stack, and set them out in separate piles on the desk.

'OK, I'm ready.' But he waited until the man sitting opposite folded his arms and set his jaw before asking Bonbon to restart the recording.

'Ready, Monsieur?'

'Yes.'

'Before the break, you asked us to understand that you and Samira were lovers and we fully appreciate that.' He indicated the original stack of messages. 'We also understand that while your obsessive need to possess her grew hideously out of control, her feelings towards you were evaporating very quickly and come the day of that final training session, they had disappeared entirely. You could not stand the stark truth that your relationship was over, could you? Indeed, you were in denial it was even happening. Your avalanche of messages shows that clearly.'

'I... thought she was playing hard to get.' He shook his head. 'As a game. That was all. A game.'

'A game?' Darac shared an incredulous look with Bonbon. 'Well, if it was, Monsieur, it was a game only she was playing, wasn't it? Because you were serious. Deadly serious, in fact.'

Laborde closed his eyes. 'I did not kill Samira.' He opened them. 'Whatever you fine gentlemen may think of me, I did not. I did not!'

'After the session, two witnesses report seeing you and Samira repairing to the hidden, far end of the players' car park.'

'Who were they? That obsequious cretin Cauvin was one of them, no doubt.'

'It doesn't matter who reported it. Why did you go there?'

Laborde took a breath in but no words emerged.

'Monsieur?'

'Uh... As you have so *ably* demonstrated, and for reasons you clearly do not believe, my messages to Samira were going largely unanswered. I thought her game had gone far enough, and as I had something crucially important to tell her, I wanted to do it in person. And in private. So during the session, I asked her to meet me there afterwards. She said she would and she did.'

'*What* did you want to say to her?'

Laborde steadied himself. 'I wanted her to understand unequivocally that I loved her, that I intended to leave my wife and build my future entirely around her.'

'To which her response was?'

'I… I think it frightened her. The enormity of it. And it had all along, I realised later. I saw that it hadn't been a game, her increasing remoteness over the previous days. It was cold feet.'

Darac didn't believe this for a second but among the ideas trading fours in his head was the possibility that Laborde *did* believe it. 'And she said as much?'

'No. As a head coach, one of my primary aims is to build mental as well as physical toughness in my athletes. I think, no, I *know* Samira was scared of how deeply meaningful our relationship had become and so quickly. But although I hated to hear it, I was also proud of her bravery in being able to declare, completely against the way she felt, and in quite a strong voice, that she wanted to end our relationship.'

Darac marvelled at the man's ego. 'And then?'

'Initially, I argued but of course, I hadn't anticipated any of this and there just wasn't time to make her see that what I was offering her would change everything for the better.'

'Why wasn't there time?'

'Before leaving the site, my coaches and I always spend at least fifteen minutes discussing how we and our athletes performed during the session. I was already late for it when I headed off to meet Samira.'

'So how did you leave it with her?'

'I couldn't let my assistants down so I asked her to wait for me at a spot we knew just outside the site where we could discuss things properly.'

'So you parted from her there and then.'

'Yes.' Tears stained his eyes once more. 'Parted, Captain. Got that? I did not…' He gulped. 'I did not brutally slay the love of my life in cold blood and drag her body across the track to dump it!' Sobs now. 'God, you people!'

Darac's whole team knew that after *this* encounter with Laborde, Samira had driven out of the car park in perfect health. She had been seen doing so by Eric Cauvin, albeit in silhouette; in the full glare of his lights by bus driver Roger Lauvette; and by a couple of his passengers. Immediately after exiting the players' car park gate, the picture of what happened to Samira next was a little more complicated.

'We'll take a moment there. Keep it rolling, Bonbon. Some water, Monsieur?'

Laborde shook his head and it was with impressive or suspicious speed of recovery that he readied himself to continue. 'Yes, we parted. But, Captain, I was right. Samira had been overwhelmed by everything and if you had a *complete* record of our text exchanges, you would... see that... she...'

Laborde's words trailed away as he watched Bonbon unzipping a plastic bag.

'Here, chief.' he said, handing the contents to Darac.

'Actually, we do have a complete record, Monsieur Laborde. This is Samira's phone.' Significantly, a phone wiped of all prints. 'As you can see.'

'Oh!' Relief seemingly ameliorating his distress, Laborde exhaled deeply. 'Thank God. There's evidence. Evidence!'

There was evidence, alright, Darac thought, sharing a look with Bonbon. 'Yes, at 10.51 pm, that's about 40 minutes after she was seen driving away from the Stade, Samira sent a text to your mobile and that message reads: "Gilles, forgive me. I've just arrived home. I waited as long as I could where you said but I had to drive away. You're right. Our relationship is a source of pain to me but it is real. If you come to the apartment straight away, we will talk this through. Love, ever, Samira."

'Captain, I'm sure you and your team are well practised in

losing evidence favourable to —'

'No!' Gremat said, unable to help himself. 'Apologies, gentlemen.'

When circumstances demanded it, Bonbon was capable of a stare of death ray-like intensity. 'We'll overlook it this time but no more, Monsieur. Alright?'

'Apologies again.'

'It is I who should apologise, Captain,' Laborde said. 'I felt sure you were being selective with these messages to the point of losing some that didn't support your theories.' He gave the incredulous Gremat a meaningful look. 'But I was mistaken.'

'Where were you when you received the message?'

'At the spot I'd asked her to meet me. It's an unnamed lane around the corner from the site. Gives on to a disused builders' yard.'

'Remind me when you left the Stade through the caravan gate?'

'Just after 10.30. As I'm sure Cauvin told you.'

As you knew he would, Darac thought to himself. 'And from there, it's a three or four-minute drive to the meeting place you describe. So let's say you arrived there at about 10.35 to find that Samira had apparently not waited for you after all. Your mobile logged the conciliatory text she sent to you from her apartment all the way over on Boulevard Bischoffsheim at 10.51. Now, it's about a 15-minute drive to your villa in La Ginistière from the meeting place so I imagine you were almost home when you received her message?'

'I was not.'

'Traffic even at that time, huh?'

'I… was still at the meeting place.'

'You saw she wasn't there the moment you arrived but you didn't drive away until, as luck or something else would have it, your message from Samira came in? Why?'

'I was upset! I shed tears, alright? For the first time, I thought it really must be over between us.'

'But thanks to her message, your hopes were rekindled. And from the time it was sent, you worked out that you had only just missed her at the meeting place. She *had* waited a good while for you.'

'Yes. She must have.'

'So what did you do then?'

'I sent her a quick reply—'

' "My darling, I'm so glad. I'll be with you as soon as I can." '

'Will you stop asking me questions to which you already know the answers!'

'That's half the fun, Monsieur,' Bonbon said.

In fact, with the aim of exposing anomalies and deviations from known facts, police detectives already knew the true answers to 90% of the questions they put to murder suspects during interrogation. From Flaco's interview with Samira's flatmate Carole Monteux earlier, Darac had learned that she had been volunteering at a shelter for homeless women overnight – Flaco had verified this – and hadn't returned to the apartment until the following morning. Darac had reasons for suspecting that Laborde would have no way of knowing Carole hadn't been home the previous evening.

'And so, Monsieur,' Darac went on, 'you set off on the roughly 20-minute drive to Samira's apartment. What did you find when you got there?'

Conveying the sense that he was re-running the scene in his head, Laborde stared blindly into space. 'When I arrived, I stopped where I always had but as I approached the building, I saw Samira's parking space was empty. For the most horrible imaginable reason, I now know. But of course, at the time, I didn't think anything of the sort.'

'What *did* you think?'

'I thought she had had second thoughts again and gone off somewhere to think things through by herself.'

'Her flatmate hadn't heard from her?'

'I don't know. As I said, once I saw Samira's car wasn't there, I knew she hadn't come back and I didn't check further.'

You may have cleared that hurdle, Darac thought to himself. But there are still whole ranks of them set out across the track ahead. And they're going to get higher. 'What did you do next?'

'I… And now I am ashamed of this… I lost my temper. Lost my temper with Samira, with myself, with… everything. If there had been a cat around, I would've kicked it to death.' At his client's latest indiscretion, Gremat sighed audibly.

'You didn't message her at that point? Or, more like you, send several?'

'You know I didn't.'

'Pity. It would have helped establish where you were.' Laborde seemed not to notice the implication. 'And then what did you do?'

'I drove home. Still angry, I suppose because I didn't text her again until the next morning. Samira was something of an early bird, too, and when I didn't get a reply, instead of driving off to work, I went to her apartment instead. With the same result as before, of course. Except this time, I rang the bell. No one answered.'

'Her flatmate was out?'

'I felt so. There was not a sound from within. She may have still been in bed, I suppose.'

'You didn't have a key, then?'

The point seemed to rankle. 'No.'

'I see,' Darac said, picking up a fresh stack of messages.

'And there are these too,' Bonbon said, handing over a further selection.

'Ah, yes.' Darac took them. 'Monsieur, you mentioned that when Samira hadn't been at home the previous evening, you wondered if she had gone elsewhere to think things out.'

'Ye-es?'

'Might that "elsewhere" have been the *Résidence Baie des Anges?*'

'Why there? Her very unsatisfactory relationship with Julien was over. Yes, she did have a lot of respect for Grace. Grace Nahili, my heptathlete, that is. I suppose they *might* have been close enough to confide in each other.'

'We are thinking neither of Julien Baille nor the excellent Mademoiselle Nahili. We are thinking of your team captain, Emil Arcot.'

'Emil? What are you talking about? He's a great lad but she was about as likely to seek advice from him as…'

'Yes, yes, I think it's time to stop this playacting, Monsieur Laborde. Bonbon, you have those messages?'

'Here, I think,' Bonbon said, picking up the smallest of the piles on the desk. 'Did you notice that Emil's performance in the shot putt circle was a little below par yesterday evening, Monsieur? Or perhaps markedly better than usual?'

'I delegate the field event sessions to one of my assistants. What is this about?'

Bonbon shook his head in admiration. It was mock admiration of course, but he too was a consummate actor. 'Bravo, Monsieur. When you turned your talents to coaching athletics, what a loss that was to the world of stage and screen. I'm sure you could recite this verbatim, but make a show of reading it anyway.'

He passed across a message sent by Samira to Emil late on the afternoon of the previous day. Beginning "Emil, my beautiful boy, the first thing this afternoon proved to me was that all men are definitely not created equal…" and going on to contrast the young man's impressive virility with the inadequacies of her previous lovers, the message was a paean not just to Emil's supremacy in bed but to his utterly steadfast qualities as a human being. The latter, Samira emphasised, was also something she had not encountered to the same degree previously. Laborde appeared to be going through a kind of bereavement as he read the message, anger following denial in quick succession; acceptance still some way off. If it was a performance, it was as convincing as Darac and Bonbon had seen given by a suspect in his position.

'We have Emil's response to the message and more from Samira, too,' Darac said. 'Including her invitation to "do it all over again tomorrow morning" unquote. Big young Emil was in the position you yearned to be in, wasn't he? You were no longer needed – if you ever were. To make it easier to get rid of you, we wonder if Samira thought that blunting your feelings for her would help. Accordingly, in the course of your break-up meeting, we put it to you that she told you about the new man in her life. Now of course, we don't know how this meeting went. Even though she so wanted to be shot of you, perhaps she tried to spare your feelings during it. Perhaps she didn't even name who had beaten you so resoundingly as her lover. Or, and a couple of our colleagues absolutely believe this, perhaps she taunted you about him.' Darac gave it a beat. 'Taunted. Was that it? Was that what pushed you over the edge?'

Laborde couldn't speak.

Sensing the pressure was finally beginning to break Laborde's resistance, Darac pushed on. 'But as we said a few minutes ago, we don't need to prolong your agony by going through every word of this humiliating new strand of the story, do we? Monsieur? I'll take your lack of response as a no.' Darac gave Bonbon a look. 'I think we can wrap this up quite quickly, can't we?'

'Should think so, chief.'

'Monsieur Laborde… Monsieur Laborde!'

'What?'

'Are you listening?'

Looking utterly defeated, Laborde gave the slightest of nods.

'You are a controlling man by nature, are you not? A controlling, obsessive, perfectionist. In your career, those traits must have been of great value to you in shaping the minds and bodies of your charges. And you get results. Your athletes win things. And that's important because in your business, only winning matters. If it all ended out there on the track or the field, it wouldn't be much of a problem, would it? But it doesn't end there. You run your personal life on the same lines and that's hard on those close to you. The standards you expect of *them* are high. Exacting. *So* exacting that falling short of them is an inevitable consequence for any normally adjusted person. But that doesn't stop your need to obsessively control them, does it? In one solitary visit to your home, just meeting your very talented daughter Inès—'

'My daughter *Jackie!*' he screamed. 'Jackie!'

Realising he'd made Darac's point for him, Laborde threw himself back in his seat and folded his arms so tightly, he looked in danger of squeezing himself into unconsciousness.

'But there's one inescapable flaw in all this controlling perfectionism, *Head Coach* Laborde. You may meet, even exceed, the exacting standards you impose on others in some areas of your life but when it comes to your personal morality, it's you who falls short, isn't it? In that league, you're way down at the bottom. Thanks to your phone logs, we know Samira was far from the first student athlete you'd bedded and kept very quiet about. But she was the one who got to you, wasn't she? Samira, your goddess, as you were wont to call her.'

'I told you she was. I loved her. And I wanted my future

and hers to, to…'

'We contend that your infantile fantasies about a future together disintegrated when she made the fatal mistake of telling you about Emil.'

Laborde shook his head. 'No. She didn't tell me.'

In his seat, Gremat was clearly anxious to make a point about this – as Darac and Bonbon would have if the tables had been reversed.

'After the interrogation, Monsieur Gremat,' Bonbon said, cheerily. 'You may ask as many questions as you like.'

'But in the meantime,' Darac went on, 'we'll hazard a guess at what is exercising you.

As we've already established, after what was in effect a break-up meeting, Samira was seen driving away from the Stade in perfectly good heart. And *also* established, forty minutes later, she had had apparently second thoughts about the break-up and sent you a text summoning you to her apartment for further talks.'

'Well then?' Laborde said. 'And we've said all this, already.'

'Having not shifted from the spot you were supposed to meet, you then headed off as Samira had requested. But to no avail. When you got there, she was not home. Concluding that she had changed her mind once more, you set off home in a temper.'

'And I regret that. Hugely. But we've said this. Said it!'

'All in all, your homecoming in La Ginistière would have been delayed by 45 minutes to an hour by hanging around outside the builder's yard for 15 minutes, then driving over to Boulevard Bischoffsheim and back. Your wife, by this time in bed, reports hearing you come in and retiring at about the time that fits your story.'

'Of course. Why wouldn't she?

'So you left the Stade just after 10.30 and got home at the earliest, three-quarters of an hour later. You can get a lot done in that time, Monsieur. Can't you?'

The way Laborde's expression changed as the thrust of
Darac's insinuation appeared to dawn slowly upon him was
little short of a tour de force. For some moments, no dialogue
accompanied the performance but finally, he said, 'No. No,
no, no. You're trying to… The facts support what happened.'

'Oh yes, Monsieur,' Darac said. 'They certainly do.' He
brandished Samira's mobile. 'Let's return to the message sent
to your mobile by a rueful Samira; a message summoning
you to her apartment for what we've described as a
rapprochement meeting. As we can see, the message was
indeed sent at 10.51, forty-five or so minutes after she had
parted from you. But, Monsieur, it was not sent from, or
from remotely near, Boulevard Bischoffsheim which, as the
crow flies, is all of six kilometres from the Stade. The GPS
on Samira's phone records that it was sent from within a
200-metre radius of the water jump in which her brutalised
body was later found dumped. It's clear to us, Monsieur, that
you had possession of her phone and using it, composed and
sent a message to your own phone. A message sent *from* you,
to you, with the clear intention of giving yourself an alibi
for the time of the murder and throwing the subsequent
investigation off the scent.'

'No! No! No! No!'

'Sit down.'

He remained standing.

'Officer?'

Stepping forward, the guard gave Laborde the opportunity
to comply under his own steam. He took it and the guard
returned to his post.

'Thank you. Samira *was* still waiting for you at the meeting
place when you arrived there, wasn't she?'

'No! She wasn't!'

'But not because she'd had second thoughts about

the break-up. I suspect she wanted you to understand unequivocally that your relationship with her was irredeemably over, a conclusion that was still hanging in the air from your conversation earlier. Poor Samira. If she had just driven straight home, she might still be alive now. Her mistake was not to realise what kind of a man you really are.'

'No! You've got this all wrong.'

Laborde had settled into a pattern, Darac realised. A two-pronged attack was needed. And a change of tempo. Catching Bonbon's eye, he drummed the index and middle fingers of his resting hand on the desk.

'Where did you find the rock you used to smash her head in?' Bonbon said.

Darac now. 'How did you get her body into the water jump?'

'What did you do with her car? Answer, damn you!'

'Where did you discard all the bloody clothes you must have been wearing? Eh? Eh?'

In quick succession, further point-blank blows landed but if the battery were intended to cause Laborde to throw in the towel, it didn't succeed. Another look signalled an end to the assault and Darac continued at a more considered pace.

'Once in possession of her phone, creating an apparently genuine message was an easy subterfuge to pull, wasn't it?'

'I didn't take her phone. I didn't see her.'

'We know from examining *your* phone that, like many a low-life experienced in conducting extra-marital affairs, you were in the habit of deleting your messages to and from your lovers immediately after sending or receiving one. Clever you. Among the many differences we've detected between the messages garnered from your phone and from Samira's is that she was not in the habit of doing that. The messages printed out from your device were all deleted by you in the manner I described. One at a time. Except this.' Darac brandished

"Samira's" summoning message. '*This* one, you didn't delete at all. Why? Because, naive in such matters, you wanted us to find it. Find the one you were relying on to save you.'

'This is all complete rubbish. Rubbish!'

'In a vain attempt to hide any incriminating messages on *Samira's* phone, you deleted them all at once. When it comes to IT, you are a complete also-ran, obviously, but at least you knew how to quickly delete entire message histories between contacts. Having read her passionate exchanges with Emil first, of course.'

'I didn't know anything about them until now. Nothing.'

'You started deleting them on Samira's phone at 10.52 last night. Just after you had sent yourself the rapprochement message.'

'No!'

'After you had finished all you needed to do, and rest assured, we are shortly to come on to the murder itself, you drove home to your property in La Ginistière, arriving between 11.30 and midnight. The following day, members of our forensics team discovered Samira's phone immediately following our visit. The phone was in your car. The glove compartment.'

'If it *was* there, they must have plan—'

'Monsieur Laborde!' Gremat shouted. His eyes darted shiftily between Darac and Bonbon. 'I am sorry gentlemen, but you see my position, here.'

'Surprised it took you this long to intervene again,' Bonbon said. 'But that's an end to it. And this time, I mean it.'

Darac picked up the reins once more. 'By the way, Monsieur Laborde, if at some time in the *very* distant future, you are minded to send a message in the guise of someone else, here's a style point to consider. See there?' He indicated the last few words of the self-summoning message. 'The valedictory. Samira never once signed off to you with "Love ever." That had become *your* signature sign-off to her.'

'Telling mistake, that one,' Bonbon said, mugging a sort of disappointed sympathy. Darac picked up an evidence case bearing the label PHOTOGRAPHS. 'The murder itself,' he said simply and accompanied by with a loud, percussive click, flicked open one of its two catches.

For the first time in the interrogation, Laborde appeared scared.

'No. Please no. I can't look at photos of—'

'Your handiwork in killing in cold blood a young woman you called your goddess?'

Laborde hung his head.

Silence.

His hand poised to trigger the case's second catch, Darac shared a look with Bonbon. They had arrived at this moment many times in the past; the moment when an apparently rational human being who had committed a murder in what the tabloids were fond of calling "a fit of jealous rage" was most likely to confess. And despite all the EU-driven changes to French legal procedures in recent years, securing a confession from a perpetrator was still the only sure-fire way of guaranteeing a conviction in court.

It was some moments before Laborde, his head still bowed, finally spoke.

'It wasn't my handiwork. I don't know who did it. Or sent messages or any of that. I just know it wasn't me.'

Darac flicked the second catch and set a photo on the desk between them.

Laborde looked away. 'No! Please, I don't want to see!'

Gremat had no such qualms. At first, he looked suitably sickened at the image of a smashed watch on the wrist of the young woman for whom time had stopped for ever. But then his brow lifted and for the first time in the interrogation, a smile lightened his expression. A look of triumph now. It had, it seemed, been worth taking the case after all.

Laborde still hadn't found the courage to look. With an exaggerated display of respect to his inquisitors, Gremat said: 'I appreciate I appear to be once again in breach here, gentlemen, but may I?'

'May you what, Monsieur?' Darac said.

'May I instruct my client properly to consider this evidence as you request?'

'On this occasion? By all means.'

Gremat patted the man's shoulder. 'Monsieur, I advise you to look. Carefully.'

For whatever reason, Laborde clearly hated the experience of having to focus on a close-up, high-definition image of the watch and Samira's so perfect skin. After some moments, he shook his head and looked away once more.

'On your behalf, Monsieur Gremat,' Darac said, 'I shall ask the question you are supposed to have waited until the end of our session to pose. Head Coach Laborde, in the image you have just examined, did you notice the time at which Samira's wristwatch was stopped?'

It appeared to be dawning on Gremat that all may not have turned around for his client after all.

'No.'

'I agree, it's not that easy to make out. I'll help you. It shows 10.30 and a few seconds.'

'I don't see what you're driving at but whatever it is, it's irrelevant. I *didn't* do it!'

'No? I'll help you again. We know you left the players' car park at the Stade at 10.32. How can we pinpoint that time so precisely? Because you made a seemingly spurious but memory-cementing remark to Eric Cauvin about the time. Cementing it in *his* memory, that is.'

'Remind me exactly what the remark was, chief?' Bonbon said, masking the disingenuousness of the question with almost as much aplomb as their suspect.

'Sure. Monsieur Laborde expressed concern that Eric was missing the start of Annie Provin's news programme on TV.'

'I see.'

'Good of him, considering he was in such a hurry to make his rendezvous with Samira.'

'I was,' Laborde said. 'I told you that. I don't understand what you're getting at.'

Gremat, for whom the penny had well and truly dropped, was once more gazing at the ceiling.

'I can see that your advocate understands that we've got an anomaly of monumental proportions on our hands here, Monsieur Laborde.'

'*What* anomaly?'

'In winding back the hands on Samira's watch to a time just before you had left Eric to his programme, you thought you were giving yourself a perfect alibi for the time of her murder.'

'No! I did not! I've no idea about any of this. But what if poor Sam's watch *does* give me an alibi? What's so wrong with that?'

'Your alibi is based on the time-honoured principle that it is beyond human capability to be physically present in two different places at once. Another infallible principle is that a dead human being isn't capable of doing anything, let alone composing and sending a message a whole twenty-one minutes after they had been brutally murdered.'

Laborde looked stunned. Undone. Done for.

'Sending that message to yourself after setting up the false alibi, Monsieur Laborde?' Bonbon shook his head. 'You'd already incriminated yourself over the location, then you add a timing blunder into the mix? These are what we call in the trade schoolboy errors, mate. Sorry – Monsieur Head Coach.'

'Stop all these lies,' Darac said, eyeballing the man. 'And confess. Confess now.'

Mugging disbelief, Laborde looked to Gremat for a lifeline. A shrug was all that was thrown back.

Darac gave it a couple of beats. 'Gilles Francois Laborde, do you confess to murdering Samira Naidu Padar on the evening of Monday, March 17th, 2014?'

Laborde slowly shook his head.

'The suspect indicates that he does not so confess,' Bonbon noted for the recording.

'You'll have all night to think about it, Monsieur.' Darac summoned the guard. 'Back to the cells.'

FIFTY-THREE

Outwardly, Alain Terrevaste appeared to have not a thought in his head as he waited for traffic to clear a crossing on rue Beaumont. He was actually re-evaluating the whole situation. So the woman Agnès Dantier had told him to think of as Noëmi Two existed after all. And there was now little doubt in his mind that Captain Francine Lejeune had bumped into her in that guise just as she had reported. Since he and two of his keenest-eyed subordinates had begun the surveillance operation, there had been no sign of Noëmi Two in Place Wilson or any of the adjoining streets. But now, in a completely different guise – her true look, he suspected – here she was a good kilometre from that initial sighting. What *had* she been doing that day? Where was she going now, as herself? What *was* this all about? In the lighting shop opposite, an assistant flicked a switch and every bulb in the place flared into life simultaneously. It failed to trigger a concomitant reaction in Terrevaste's brain and still in the dark, he crossed the street and continued up rue George Ville.

At least, he assumed, the question of where Noëmi Two was going would soon answer itself. Wherever it turned out to be, she appeared to be in something of a hurry and for a pavement artist as skilled as Terrevaste, it made tailing her as easy as it got. He wondered about calling in this new sighting. So many pedestrians used Bluetooth to make calls these days, it wouldn't have looked out of place if he had suddenly started talking. It did however present a problem. The more discreet the mike and earpiece used, such as his own barely visible combo, the more passers-by were inclined to think they were being spoken to and say something in return. But drawing even momentary attention to himself was anathema to the Invisible Man and so calling now was out. Besides, he wanted to have more to report before he did.

The pursuit continued routinely until his quarry turned into the narrow conduit that was rue de la Malonnière. Deserted but for Noëmi Two, the street posed an altogether tougher challenge but Terrevaste needn't have worried. Almost immediately, she turned at a gap between buildings into a *ruelle* that gave on to a blind yard in which, he knew, there was only one possible port of call — a near derelict two-storey building that in a former lifetime had been a workshop of some kind. Ghosting quickly alongside a wall top-dressed with glass shards, Terrevaste stopped at the corner and slipped a hand mirror out of his pocket. By the look of things, Noëmi Two was knocking at what had once been the building's side door; knocking in what just might have been a coded sequence — three, one, and then two knocks. But if it was a code, had he heard it from the beginning? Gaining covert entry to the building presented no problem — he had a variety of means at his disposal — but since he or his unit might have to replicate the code at some stage, it was essential to be sure. The concern soon evaporated — no one came to the door and to avoid being seen by her as she retraced her steps to the street, Terrevaste prepared to dart back along the *ruelle*. But then she produced a key from her bag and disappeared inside. On the floor above, a thin curtain was drawn across the one window that hadn't been bricked up. A minute later, a light went dimly on behind it.

Terrevaste slipped the mirror back into his pocket and, taking a moment to gather his thoughts, realised that the safe course of action was to call this in now. After all, he had no idea why the mysterious Noëmi Two had come to this out-of-the-way hole, let alone who she had fruitlessly tried to summon to the door with what may have been a secret knock; summoned when she had a key. Odd. But how much better would it look to the brass, he told himself, if he waited until he could haul her off to the Caserne under arrest. Charges? Suspicion would do to begin with. Yes, that would make them sit up and take notice. Everyone from the high and mighty Commissaire Agnès Dantier on down would have to recognise that he was the only officer in the region who could have found this woman in the first place and then brought her in.

Keeping well out of a possible line of sight from the window, Terrevaste stepped smartly towards the blind front face of the building. He knew she had gone upstairs but he listened anyway. Nothing. His shoulder brushing the brickwork, he stole silently around the corner to the side door. He put his ear against it. As he expected, still no sound from inside. Now the lock. A spring latch. Child's play. He slid a titanium shim into position – credit cards were for amateurs – and the door opened without a sound. He stepped inside, opening a fan of daylight on to a debris-strewn floor. Closing the door behind him, he waited for his eyes to adjust to the thin light spilling down the stairs before treading as silently as he could towards them. The gods were with him. A toilet flushed on the floor above, giving him the cover he needed to mount the stairs unheard. Quickly gaining the top step, it pleased him to think he might catch his quarry literally with her trousers down. It would make for the easiest arrest ever.

For a split second, he didn't recognise the face that suddenly appeared before him. But he saw the blade. Cold steel jagged at his throat and Alain Terrevaste dropped gasping and gulping and gushing to the floor. In the shock and the pain, a solitary thought flashed and faded in his head. He knew who had done this to him. And only he *could* have known. Only he. Only…

'Carmen!' the man shouted, grabbing the mobile out of his victim's pocket. 'Pull yourself together! I need to go and check the car radio comms immediately. We're getting out. Now! Right?'

Cassie couldn't speak but she nodded frantically.

'Say you understand!'

She whimpered an approximation.

'Good. Take all the stuff down, bin-bag it – you should only need one – and lose it. Use the dumpster on the corner of Beaumont and Auguste Gal. I'll meet you at the car in ten minutes. Got that? *Ten* minutes.'

'Hm.'

He bounded down the stairs. The front door slammed. The stabbed man was twitching, spluttering, the head nodding as if accepting he was bleeding his life away. Cassie scrambled to her feet and backed away. If she emitted one scream, she knew she would succumb to full-on hysteria. She had to fight it. And fight the urge to throw up, too. Think! She realised he would be back for her if she didn't get to the car when he'd said. If she was still here, she would spend *her* last moments bleeding to death in all this filth. If she managed to get away from the building, he might intercept her. She had to face it. He would catch her eventually whatever she did. Think, Cassie, think!

FIFTY-FOUR

Agnès had chaired some remarkable team meetings at the Caserne Auvare over the years but tonight's had promised to be something special and it hadn't disappointed so far. Paraphrasing the title of one of Darac's favourite Fats Waller tunes, the squad room was jumpin'. And with Agnès's reading glasses making regular trips from the top of her head to her nose; her discarded slingbacks parked next to her bare feet; Bonbon sitting in a particularly contorted *contraposto* in his seat – all was as it should be in the Brigade's world. Even the squad room's brand-new boon to displaying case material – a multi-slotted frame allowing whiteboards to be left dressed and slid into position as required – was behaving itself.

'Frankie,' Agnès said, as the last aftershocks of what had been an eruption of applause finally died down. 'You deserve every second of that accolade. Posterity will decide whether your handling of this latest appalling child sex-trafficking case will stand as a landmark but I must tell you that when I reviewed the earlier stages of it, I thought your chances of nailing the Manzanos themselves were slim. Whatever happens in court, they will not escape heavy sentences thanks to the evidence you've so brilliantly and painstakingly put together. It is a veritable triumph.'

'Thank you,' Frankie, said, pressing her palms together. 'But if it is a triumph, it's a triumph of teamwork. Without the inspired professionalism and courage shown throughout by Claudia, Kadi, Jean-Louis, Salvatore, Frizzi, Eloise and Moussa, we would not have got over the line.'

Agnès smiled. 'You have *all* proved me wrong, Frankie.

Bravo, again.'

As a second rumble rolled around the room, Agnès called for the Manzano case whiteboard to be slid aside.

'Agnès?' Erica called out. 'Just need a minute.'

'I do, too,' she replied as she turned to the next case file in her stack.

Darac leaned into Frankie's ear. 'You going to be unbearable now? Lady Landmark?'

'See my agent, buster.'

Actually, the day already represented something of a landmark in their lives together. Tonight would be the first that Mademoiselle Lily Darac would be spending away from home. *Nounou* Mariette had already delivered her to Martin and Chantal Darac's villa in nearby Vence and, endorsed by live *Cot-Cam* footage from the nursery, reports were encouraging.

As Frankie brought up the link once more, a few of the Caserne's soppier souls craned in for a closer look. The mood was upbeat.

'*Bellissima,*' Armani opined, blowing the little one a kiss.

'Yes – look at her,' Granot's said, his old dog-blanket face taking on some unfamiliar creases. 'A picture of contentment.'

'*Too* contented, I think,' Darac said. 'Wouldn't wish a full-scale tantrum on the grandparents, obviously, but an occasional mizzle wouldn't go amiss. Where's the girl's loyalty?'

Archivist Adèle peered in. 'Her first night away? My little granddaughter would be bawling the place down.' She turned to Darac. 'Do you mind me asking where your nursery is *at home*? There's a practical reason for my question.'

'It's off our bedroom. Why?'

'That's ideal, I think. My son and daughter-in-law have Mara's cot *in* their room. I keep telling them they're making a rod for their own back.'

'Not necessarily.'

Claudia was up next. 'I can't get over her hair, Frankie. There's such a shock of it and it is *so* black.'

Raul Ormans gave a wry nod. 'One could ID her parents from that alone. What colour are her eyes?'

Astrid had that one covered. 'Having seen her in the flesh just a couple of weeks ago, I would say she was Book Seven, page 16, shade 5, IR fleck pattern 17 or 18.'

Granot grinned. 'In other words, green, like her mother's.'

Frankie had a further observation on the question. 'And like Paul's mother's, too.'

Cooing over babies may not have been something the team would have associated with Wanda "Pedal To The Metal" Korneliuk but one glance corrected the assumption. 'Where can *I* get one of those?' she said. 'Seriously, Frankie – she's *so* cute, isn't she?'

'Ah, thank you.'

'When the time comes, would you like me to teach her to drive?'

'No!' Darac said.

'Yes!' Frankie countered.

Bonbon had the final word. 'Funny to think but in time to come, that little bundle of joy will do things like… take the pair of you out for dinner.'

'Sounds wonderful,' Frankie said. 'So yours take you and Julieta out for dinner?'

Bonbon made a moue. 'No. But it could happen.' He produced a sticky plug of striped paper from his pocket. 'In the meantime, fancy a *frou-frou*? Help yourselves.'

'They're so beautifully presented, how could I resist?' Darac said. 'And yet.'

Frankie was similarly unimpressed. 'What's that red stuff that's leached through the paper?'

'Raspberry. Or could be plum.'

'*Frou-frous* are real fruit?' Granot said.

Bonbon nodded. 'And even realer sugar.'

'Sounds perfect.' Granot tried one and immediately had second thoughts. 'How much for the whole bag?'

'They're yours.'

Children's Corner was over for the moment, and as Granot's depleted blood-sugar levels began to top up, Agnès was ready to lead off the next item on the agenda.

'On to what began as the Port Lympia strangling case. As you can see on our brand spanking new whiteboard set-up, we have a comprehensive array of photos, diagrams *etc* and as before, these will be supplemented by slides. Erica – reloaded?'

Erica's expertise went way beyond the rudimentary skills required to prep and operate the Caserne's arsenal of slide, ciné, video and data projectors but she had no qualms about pitching in when required.

'Cued-up and ready to go, Agnès.'

'Excellent. So, here's a brief summary of the major points for those who aren't au fait with this one. In the early evening of Saturday last, a drug-dependent 45 year-old former actress named Denise Dubreuil, recently moved to the area from Marseille and living in a studio flat at the port, was brutally strangled by 34 year-old also new-to-the-area fellow resident Gerard Ploine, real name Hugo Cragnat, following a dispute over the class A substances we initially assumed *he* was supplying to her. However, via a successful batch-matching exercise by Armani and his team, the involvement of a second pusher was identified. Everything pointed to this second pusher stabbing Cragnat in the throat that same night and later on disposing of his body in the dumpster you see on the board and on the screen. The investigation then learned of a third person of interest, one Ludo, tellingly another newcomer to the area, apparently a friend of Cragnat and seen on several occasions in his company by their landlord,

Monsieur Maurice Thomas, an innocent, indeed hopelessly clueless, party to the goings-on in his very modestly sized apartment house.

'Following some initially scanty-looking leads, Armani then discovered that Ludo was Cragnat's own supplier; that he was connected to a Toulouse-based ring; and that his real name was Antoine Medot. Any thought that Ludo/Medot had himself murdered Cragnat was expunged when he too was discovered murdered, stabbed using the same method and with the same weapon type as Cragnat. Granot, you have more.'

'There are a number of unanswered questions about Denise – or Dédé, as our colleagues in Marseille tell us she was known to many. These questions include A: How had she managed to avoid or evade arrest in Marseille while continuing to use for over two years? B: Why did she leave Marseille when she did? C: What brought her here? D: What made her choose the studio flat she did? E: How did she earn her living here which appeared to have been a cash-in-hand operation?

'The answers to these seem obvious. Question A, for instance. Someone in Marseille must have been looking after Dédé's interests, mustn't they? Someone who had an *in* with, or some other influence *over*, Armani's counterparts there. Question B – that influence dried up for some reason, or any number of personal issues may have caused her to flee. As to question C – although our city is, to my mind, superior in every conceivable respect to Marseille, it's not an altogether different milieu. Perhaps she felt she could safely lose herself here as she had over the previous couple of years. Question D – Monsieur Maurice Thomas's apartment house? The answer to this may also answer question E. The appeal of such a cheap room may have been enhanced by its proximity to the port. A transient maritime population offers obvious pay-and-lay possibilities, doesn't it? To a drug-dependent soul who had resorted to turning tricks in her time, at least.

'Whatever the truth of these answers, one thing we can say with some certainty is that Denise Dubreuil was being supplied by a man who proved to be very handy with a knife. As to the nature of the dispute that led to her strangling and the two stabbings, her possession of some of the same consignment of heroin Cragnat had stashed in his room suggests she'd helped herself to it at some point. He discovered the fact and that signalled the end both for her and only hours later, for him.

'There are one or two other aspects of Denise's story we've puzzled over to no avail but I've decided to let them go. Why? Because as we realised at the time of the stabbings, there was so much blood and tissue to work with that identifying the otherwise anonymous victims from their DNA was likely to be an easy matter. And so it has proved. Map found particles of what looks certain to be the perp's own DNA-bearing tissue under Cragnat's right-hand thumbnail. Minute scrapings. This tissue is itself interesting, Map reports, and immediately sent it off for sequencing. In short, ID-ing the stabber is just a matter of time and the news is due tomorrow.'

Perand grinned, sourly. 'All we have to do then is catch the man. Easy.'

'As to preserving our clearance rate numbers for Paris, if, as seems likely, the double murderer has returned to the Toulouse area, they will be credited with the arrest, but we will at least get a big tick in the assist column. That's something.'

'More than something,' Agnès said. 'Any more, Granot?'

'Yes, if I may. No one here should be unaware of what Class A drugs can do to a person over time but just in case you'd forgotten… Next slide, Erica, please.'

Five photos appeared on the screen. Charting Denise

Dubreuil's gradual decline into riven desperation, the display put Darac in mind of several of his jazz heroes, especially the once supremely cool trumpeter, Chet Baker.

'We should make a poster of this,' he said. 'Send it to every school in France. What do you say, Armani?'

The head of the Brigade's drug squad for some seven years, Armani, it seemed, had heard this one before. Many times. 'What do I say?' He gave an uncharacteristically low-key smile. 'I say that similar posters, fliers, info packs, films, in-person visits by the likes of me and my team, *and* by ex-addicts – you name it – have been going out to schools for years. In a more Armanian gesture, he made loose fists of his hands and shook them. 'So yes, there are organisations and individuals who have a real will to tackle the problem but there's not always money from the top. And where it's needed most – the banlieues, the cités and the HLMs? Tough. Very tough situation.'

Darac nodded, sadly. 'Yes. Of course. And sorry, I took us down a bit of a side-track there.'

'Not at all,' Agnès said. 'Final thoughts on Port Lympia and beyond?' None coming, she slipped her glasses on to her nose and opened the next file in the stack. 'So…The Place Wilson surveillance. Armani?'

'Yes, boss?'

'When Frankie told me that your Noëmi may have attracted the attentions of a nefarious look-alike, my first thought was that she must have been a very bonny felon indeed.'

Armani had two signature *miens*: being as pleased as Punch with himself and as proud as a peacock of his family. At Agnès's gracious observation, the two combined to create a monster of impropriety.

'Agnès, if I had known you 20 years ago, I would have *killed* to have married *you*!'

All around the room, thighs were slapped, half-swallowed drinks spluttered out, and heads shaken in amusement.

'And *I*, Armani...'

'Yes?'

'... would have had to arrest you. Still, it was a lovely thought and on we go.'

Agnès's deadpan delivery brought more laughs. That Armani clearly didn't understand the strength of the audience reaction made it all the funnier. As he saw it, he'd made a chivalrous remark to someone for whom everyone had the highest regard, hadn't he? What was all the fuss about?

Agnès called the meeting to order.

'Thank you, everyone... Seriously, Armani, have there been any developments on the doppelganger front?'

'None. I think we can call Terrevaste and his two buddies off. Especially as I have my own personal watchdogs on the *qui-vive* around the Place. No one has seen anything suspicious.' Smiling sympathetically, he turned to Frankie. 'You're the only one.'

'My angel,' Bonbon purred romantically, unable to resist and drawing further laughs – especially from Frankie herself – before raising his hand in apology.

Visitors entering the squad room at that moment might have been bemused by all this levity. But such people had probably never worked in homicide.

'All the better for it, let's press on,' Agnès said. 'I'm inclined to keep the Invisible Man and the boys on for one more day, Armani. Alright?'

'If you say so, sure.' Daring anyone to come up with a further quip, Armani theatrically cupped his ear. None came. 'Thank you.'

One file remained.

'And finally,' Agnès said. 'We arrive at The Stade Walter Vallain case. But first, I have an announcement to make.'

Oh-oh. Granot gave Darac a searching look and he caught the gist unequivocally. Was this the moment Agnès was going to reveal her choice as candidate to succeed her? Darac so hoped it wasn't. Unless she had chosen someone else, of course.

'Paul?'

'Ye-es?'

'Just before the meeting, a source at the Palais de Justice informed me that after failing to engage with events over in the *Zone Sportif* for many hours, our much unloved Public Prosecutor finally bothered to find out something about the case. It was only then he realised what you so perfectly describe as the "box-office" potential in it for him. Accordingly, with TV-Sud's Annie Provin front and centre, a press conference has been arranged for ten o'clock this evening. To be televised live.'

As much as he hated spending time with a man who revelled in such hollow exercises in cant and self-promotion, Darac felt relieved at Agnès's announcement. But then he remembered that tonight, for the first time in seven months, he and Frankie were to spend the evening alone together. The continuing Orson Welles season at the Mercury Cinema around the corner was just one delight on the menu.

'As you know, protocol demands that the officer in charge takes to the mikes alongside Monsieur Frènes. However, protocols also dictate that the rank of commissaire trumps that of captain and so I'm going to do it in your stead. If that's alright with you?'

'Thank you so much, Agnès. What can I say?'

'What can you say?' She produced one of her most feline smiles. 'Updating us on the Stade Walter Vallain case would be a start.'

As conversations were renewed, phones and other devices were scrolled to the appropriate pages and the fully-dressed whiteboards on the case were slid effortlessly into position at the head of the room. Darac left his seat and took up station to the side of them. The hum of voices subsided and all eyes turned to him.

'First, I want to thank everyone who was involved in the investigation today. It's been a monumental effort and I was proud to have been a part of it. Armani, thanks for loaning Farid to us. He led the sloggers superbly and his contribution in general has been invaluable.'

'If you want him for the rest of the season, we'll talk,' Armani said, throwing his arm around Farid's shoulder. 'But I warn you. He won't come cheap.'

'Worth it whatever the cost. Before I go on to detail where Bonbon and I have got to with our chief suspect Gilles Laborde, let's stay with man-of-the-moment Farid. Earlier, he went to interview one Rajesh Anil Sharma, the slow-witted fruiterer-cum-enforcer − I'm not making this up − employed by Dilip Padar to do a variety of heavy lifting jobs for him. Farid − over to you.'

'The first thing I have is hot off the press. Literally a couple of minutes ago, Tana texted me to say that we've had a result on the call-back cards she left at the *Résidence*. Recalling the two students Julien Baille said he'd seen getting out of the lift when he was about to head up the stairs? Two of them… Names, hang on.' He consulted his mobile. 'Leia Ferranti and Fela Yusuf are, and I'm quoting them, "99% certain" that they saw him arriving in the manner he said, just before 9.30. And we know that that really means they are 100% certain, doesn't it?'

'Usually, it does,' Darac said, boosted by the news. 'It's a significant break, this. Well done Tana, again. Back to Sharma, Farid?'

It didn't take him long to flesh out the case log entries. 'And once we'd got hold of him, it took a three-man effort but we got him into the cells alright. Since the forensic evidence against him is incontrovertible, I charged him with threatening behaviour against student athlete Julien Baille and made it clear that other charges are possible. I put it to him that Dilip Padar had ordered him to threaten Julien. Sharma denied it, saying that upset by Dilip's account of Julien's groin-kicking exploits, he had taken it on himself to put the frighteners on the young man.'

Darac had a couple of questions on this. 'We're still waiting for Monday evening's CCTV footage from the *Résidence* – which would have gone a long way to establishing Julien's innocence or guilt for Samira's murder earlier – but did you ask Sharma how he gained entry to Julien's building? He couldn't have known the entry code.'

'But he did have cabbages and that worked just as well.'

'What?'

'As a fruit and veg man, Sharma naturally has all sorts of produce on his van so he picked up a couple of crates of cabbages and, exaggerating what a cumbersome load he was carrying, headed for the door. There are plenty of students coming and going and of course, what does a person entering or leaving a building do if they see a tradesperson approaching carrying a load of stuff? They obligingly hold the door open for them, don't they?'

'Simple but effective,' Darac said, not the only one in the room to be rather impressed by Sharma's ploy. 'Go on, Farid.'

'He set the crates down, went up to Julien's room – I'll bet the all-seeing, all-controlling Dilip Padar knew it was number 53 – returned to the ground floor, picked up his crates and left. There hasn't been time to add any of this this to the log yet but now we come to the big question – Sharma's possible role in the murder of "Dilip-ji's bitch of a sister," as he referred to Samira. The man is in the clear. He has a cast-iron alibi.'

Agnès looked dubious. '*That* solid? A character like him?'

'I meant it literally, boss. Yesterday saw the last horse-racing meeting of the season at the Cagnes hippodrome, a special gala event called the *Grand Critérium de Vitesse*. Lots of razzmatazz, lots of bets going down and all that goes with it. Monsieur Sharma left the course with a bunch of cronies who promptly got a card school going back in the city. This went exactly as you might imagine it would and at just after 9 o'clock, officers from Foch arrived, Sharma and his mates were arrested and three of them, including him, went to the cells where they remained until 2.20 this afternoon. Foch hadn't had time to update Sharma's file on the database or we would have known this before we set off to bring him in, of course.'

'You're right, Farid,' Agnès said, doffing an imaginary cap. 'Sharma's is about as safe an alibi as one could wish.'

Granot was not alone in seeing some humour of the situation. 'How long had the fool been at liberty before you turned up with your lads?'

'All of two hours. And a quick final detail, if there's time?' Farid gave Agnès a look and she nodded assent. 'I couldn't help chuckling at Foch's arresting officer's final comment in his report of the fracas at the card school: "In the exchange of blows that followed, Monsieur Sharma came off worst. *Again.*" '

Laughter all round.

'Good work, the three of you,' Darac said.

Agnès retrieved a note from her briefcase. 'I'm jumping the gun a little here but as we've been dealing with Monsieur Sharma, I must mention that I've had more from the Indian authorities on a possible connection between the Padar family and an ongoing "honour killing" investigation in that country. It's a story reported in a number of Indian newspapers, including one to which Dilip Padar is a regular subscriber. It's not a fait accompli but police in Chennai report that they have three suspects in custody described as "almost certainly guilty," none of whom, and I quote…' She flipped her specs into position. '… "have any familial or other ostensible connection with the Padar family of Bengaluru cited in your enquiry." There we have it.' Looking over her specs, she met Flaco's gaze. 'It appears Dilip fabricated the family's connection with this story to keep Samira in line.'

'It fits his character, Madame. Absolutely.'

Agnès gave Darac the nod to continue.

'That's a significant development. Thanks, Agnès.' He indicated the board. 'OK, you'll see there's another soul residing in our cell block at the moment: one Emil Arcot, shot putter and captain of the elite athletics squad of which his fellow inmate Gilles Laborde is head coach – head coach and prime suspect, as we'll expand upon shortly. Charged at the scene with assault, Emil was in a terrible state when he came in but by the time the duty Doctor saw him, he'd calmed down sufficiently for Flak to talk to him. As you'll also hear later, Emil and Samira were full-on lovers at the time of her murder. Just recap the immediate backstory to begin with, will you, Flak?'

'Yes, Captain,' she said, her trademark scowl etched deeply in her face. 'Convinced that Samira's mediaeval misogynist of a brother Dilip Padar was responsible for her murder, Emil arrived at his apartment to exact revenge. As we might see in a minute, he freely admits that. But even if he hadn't, evidence that he attacked Padar is incontrovertible. In all, five officers witnessed it, though two were concentrating on putting out a fire started accidentally moments before by a raging Padar.' She gave Erica a look. 'The first one, please?'

A shot of a partially smoke-damaged room racked into focus on the screen.

'Not exactly *The Towering Inferno*, is it?' Perand observed.

'Thanks to Padar's two watchdogs, no,' Flaco said. 'Led by Charlie Presse of Captain Tardelli's narcotics squad, the other three officers involved arrived on the scene moments after Emil, and found him and Padar engaged in a struggle on the floor. Padar has Officer Presse to thank for what happened next.' She gave Big Charlie a respectful nod. 'The others report that only he could have restrained Emil long enough for them to join forces in pulling such a very powerful young athlete off Padar, thus preventing further injury to him.'

During Flaco's report, Darac shared looks with Agnès, Granot and Bonbon. All, he was sure, were thinking as he was. Almost from her first day as a junior officer, the young woman all but Agnès and Frankie referred to as "Flak" had impressed with her seriousness of purpose and when it was needed, sheer physical strength. Over time, other qualities had emerged but her ability to deliver thorough, lucid and, on the whole, concisely worded reports was something Flaco had mastered only recently. No one, Darac hoped, would mark her down for squeezing a couple of value judgments into her account. Describing Dilip Padar as a "mediaeval misogynist?" That was alright by him.

'Bravo, Flak,' Armani said. He gave Darac a look. 'I can do Farid and Charlie on a close-season double if you're interested.'

'Such loyalty, man.'

'Paul will take it under advisement,' Agnès said, moving the thing on. 'You have more, Yvonne, I think.'

'Yes, Commissaire.' She caught Erica's eye once more. 'Is the next slide the statement I took from him?'

Erica peered at her preview screen. 'Looks like it... Yes, it is. Now?'

'Please.'

Pages of typescript formed on the screen.

'Thank you. Like Farid, I haven't had time to upload this to the file log yet.' She gave Agnès an enquiring look. 'May we read it now?'

'Absolutely.'

Given assurances both that Dilip Padar had not been behind Samira's murder and that the Brigade had a strong suspect already in custody, Emil had poured out his heart in the statement and it made pitiful reading. Concluding with the regret that he hadn't had the opportunity to "take out" Samira's actual murderer, he expressed no remorse at having roughed up "that fucking worm" Dilip.

Before she had left the cell, Flaco informed Emil that in an uncontested hearing such as the one that almost certainly awaited him, a short custodial sentence or a heavy fine was the likely outcome. He replied that he didn't care.

'Thanks for that, Yvonne. It's very raw for him at the moment, isn't it?'

Perand nodded. 'Don't think much of the chances of Samira's killer if Muscles there does run into him at some point.'

'And with that, we come on to you, Perand,' Darac said.

'Yes, I had all the fun of going to see Dilip Padar in hospital. No slides or anything on this. Just the facts.'

'Hit it.'

'When I arrived, there was no sign of the rage that had led to him singeing a number of cushions back in his apartment. Instead, he was morose and tearful. To be fair to the love-sick Emil Arcot, Dilip's making a lot of it but he has nothing but minor injuries to show for the attack on his well-upholstered person. You'll be pleased to hear though, Flak, that his balls did become unpleasantly acquainted with Emil's meaty right knee during it, and to add to the swelling caused by Julien Baille's fleet right foot just a couple of days before, it wasn't funny. But apart from that, bruises, sprains – that was it. Of course, but for Big Charlie, another minute and he could have been flying back to India with his sister in the hold luggage.'

'So you observed the benighted Dilip's rage had gone,'
Agnès said, pointedly. 'And he was tearful. Did anything of
value emerge through those tears?'

'Yes. He kept repeating "I shouldn't have done it." '

Ears picked up around the room.

'That got me going. At first. But it soon became clear he
didn't mean "I shouldn't have killed Samira or had her killed."
He meant, "I shouldn't have insisted she break up with Julien
Baille." '

Darac was intrigued.'How did you come to that conclusion?'

'I kept firing alternative suggestions at him; he kept shaking
his head until I hit on the right one. When I asked *why* he
shouldn't have told her to break up with him, he said it was
because if he hadn't, the humiliated Baille wouldn't have
killed her as a consequence. He's convinced of it. Genuinely, I
believe.' Perand's trademark sneery smile hadn't put in much
of an appearance thus far. It did now. 'But don't assume his
blame-ridden grieving is all for the loss of his sister. He's
mainly grieving the loss of *his* life. His high life here on the
Côte d'Azur.'

'Explain?' Darac said.

'Dilip has been summoned back home by his father.
Permanently. We've already said that but for Big Charlie's
speed off the mark, Dilip would shortly have been flying off
to his own funeral. I can tell you that's exactly how he views
his father's edict.'

'Nice work, Perand, and let's look for a moment at how this
supports other things we know. I completely agree with you,
Flak – I imagine we all do – that Dilip's values are utterly shallow
and his sexual politics are from another age and they were shit
then. But his assessment of Julien isn't so far off-beam, is it? His
psychological profile *does* fit that of a spurned lover-type killer.
And that must-come-first-at-all-costs mentality can't handle
losing *anything*, can it? We thought that way ourselves about

Julien, initially. However, we know both from Flak's interview with Samira's flatmate Carole, and from recovered emails, that Samira's decision to ditch him had nothing to do with Dilip's ultimatum. She was totally bored with Julien and wanted to end the relationship anyway. It was perhaps to spare his feelings that she used the ultimatum as a sort of get-out-of-jail-free card with him. But of course, neither Julien, nor Dilip, it now seems, was aware of that.'

'This picture is filling in nicely, chief,' Bonbon said. 'Especially when you consider Tana's eyewitnesses to Julien's arrival at the *Résidence*.'

'Quite apart from our compelling case against Gilles Laborde, Dilip's contention that Julien murdered Samira is looking less and less likely, isn't it? So unless something changes, let's park Julien as the killer. Agnès?

Absolutely.'

'Bonbon?'

'Fine by me.'

'Flak?'

'Yes, Captain.'

He scanned the room. 'Anyone against? No? So on we go to Gilles Laborde.'

Darac scrolled his laptop to the appropriate page, opened his notebook and, setting out his cue sheets for Erica, he was ready to roll. 'Right, has everyone got the case file log set up and working on their phones, tablet, whatever? Raise a hand if you haven't.' None went up. 'Everyone? So you'll all be familiar with at least the bare bones of the case.' He indicated the whiteboards. 'There we have blow-ups of the diagrams illustrating who parked where at the Stade last night – diagrams drawn by our star witness – night watchman Eric Cauvin, during my interview with him this morning. Has everyone had the opportunity to study them? Hands again, please. Be brave, if you haven't. No one? Excellent. Finally, next to them, we have the lists I put together of the principals' corroborated arrival and departure times. Everyone au fait with them? One or two aren't, OK. All will become clear. Ready, Erica?'

'Ready.'

'First slides, then, please.'

A side-by-side comparison: Samira the student lawyer; Samira the bludgeoned corpse. Darac gave the images a few moments to take, before launching into a detailed summary of Laborde's interrogation thus far. Agnès then read out a report from Djibril Mpensa to which Raul Ormans and Erica added their own. Each new contribution endorsed the contention that Gilles Laborde had murdered the woman he so desperately wanted and couldn't have. When Darac asked for questions, Armani was first in.

'Don't understand why you haven't charged the guy already. His story's got more holes in it than *Le Gym's* back three and that's saying something.'

A football-based jibe was usually sure to trigger a fusillade of comebacks among the cognoscenti but minds were too focussed on the case to react.

'I'm not playing favourites here,' Frankie said. 'But I can see why you haven't, Paul.'

Agnès nodded. 'I can, too. Yes, you have exposed a number of anomalies in his account and, if not outright lies, then things that aren't whole truths, either. Perhaps that's not surprising. Laborde is a man who seems to have had a lot of practice at deceiving others. His wife, especially. But charging him at this stage? There's no real advantage. We still have all of tomorrow, and with Frènes's agreement – which, after I've dotingly played second fiddle to the man later, he will most definitely give me – we'll be granted an extra 48 hours.'

'Shameless,' Darac said, smiling. 'Granot, you're looking troubled.'

'Erica has done some terrific work here but the biggest

anomaly in Laborde's whole story for me is the number and scale of the mistakes he made. For a famously meticulous and methodical type like him, it seems out of character.'

'Your take on that, Bonbon?'

'Given sufficient prep time, I'm sure he would have been able to plan something better. But if he put it all together on the evening – which is what we're leaning towards – it was inevitable he'd make mistakes that would catch him out.'

'Flak?'

'Agreed, Captain.'

'That's where I am at the moment, too.'

When Brigade Criminelle team meetings have effectively run their course, some commissaires signalled the fact by standing up and walking out of the room. Others had the manners to first thank the participants. It was when Agnès slipped her feet into her slingbacks that everyone knew the Caserne's shop was about to shut for the night.

'A very profitable session, everyone, thank you,' she said, straightening. 'But now, it's almost time to head off for my close-up with our friend Frènes and the probing Provin. See you all tomorrow.'

Chairs scraped, conversations sprang up and a tide of tired men and women began to drain out of the room.

'Oh, Frankie?' Agnès called out. 'A very quick word with you in my office?'

'Certainly. I'll be right along.'

Darac gave her a knowing look. 'She's putting you up for a citation. For the Manzano case. What's the betting?'

The ability of dogs to sniff out a thimbleful of lemon juice dropped into a swimming pool filled with chlorinated water was as nothing compared to Armani's ability to hear the word "betting" in a buzz of voices.

'I'll lay you two to one,' he said spiriting up alongside them. 'And that's my final offer.'

'Do you actually know what the betting's about, Armani?'

'No, but you won't beat that price, Darac.'

'I'm laying five to one,' Bonbon said, equally clueless.

'*Bel broccolo!*'

'*Boig*! That's Catalan, by the way.'

Saving further mudslinging, Erica side-slipped in between them. 'Got a new file for you, Paul. My report on Zoë Laborde's laptop usage last night.'

'Thanks,' he said, taking it. 'I imagine you would have brought it up in the meeting if the where and when she logged in hadn't checked out.'

'*And* when she typed in every line, logged out momentarily a couple of times – one a coffee break possibly but not even the log notes that. Yes, the whole thing checks out. You know, apart from being married to a lying, cheating psychopath, she's had a lot to deal with, that woman. I admire her.'

'By the appearance of things, she's not scared of hard work, either,' Frankie said.

'It's what she was working *on* that most impresses me – a chapter for a book on women who manage to run successful companies – *Boss Women*. Partly because hers is an IT business, I read it and it's interesting. And *really* sobering.'

Frankie made a moue. 'Hmm. I'd like to read it, myself.'

'I've got it here.' Erica rummaged around for the file and handed it over. 'Keep it. I can print another one off.'

'No, no. I'll make sure it goes back in the case file. Besides, we're meant to be cutting back on paper usage now.'

'So Erica,' Bonbon said, grinning naughtily. 'Madame Laborde's piece has given you second thoughts, has it? Post-Caserne, you and I *are* going into the antiques business together after all.'

'Ten to one says you don't,' Armani said.

FIFTY-FIVE

'On to today's sport now,' the presenter said, and Inès turned off the TV. For some moments she and Zoë stared blankly at one another as if the shock of it all had turned them off, too. It was Inès who finally broke the silence.

'That seals his guilt, doesn't it, Maman? They didn't even put up a contact caption at the end. For anyone with information.'

'Didn't they? I didn't notice.'

'Can only mean one thing, can't it?'

'It does seem the police believe they've got their man.'

The pair sank back into the sofa thankful that, try as she might, Annie Provin hadn't been able to coax a name out of the twin representatives of the police and judiciary featured in the broadcast.

'It's all so… unreal,' Inès said. 'Your husband – my father – is a murderer. It's a movie. Not real life. All the clichés – *I think I'm dreaming and will wake up in a minute* – it's all here. Now. And we were wondering how to deal with the trauma of your break-up with him? That was nothing, was it? Not in comparison.'

'No, darling. It wasn't.'

'You know, when his identity *is* revealed…'

'Don't. I can't bear to think of it.'

Inès sat upright. 'Maman, you do have to prepare yourself for what it will be like.' She took her mother's hands. 'Don't you?'

'I suppose so.'

'Look, why not come to Cambridge for a while? It's only a two-hour flight to Stansted. Three-quarters of an hour in a cab and you're in the city.'

'And drag the press core and the media along with me?' Zoë looked fully switched on for the first time in hours. 'Bless you but no. When it's all over, *then* I'll come. Not before.'

'Sue's going to videocall me in about twenty minutes or so.'

'Give her my love.'

The women embraced, declared their love for one another, and drifted away to their beds.

A sound like a boxer punching a speedball served as Sue's walk-on music. 'I have never been so happy to see you, sweetie,' she said, for once her words and mouth movements in perfect synch. 'Oh God you look terrible.'

'*You* don't. You look beautiful.'

Tears once more, and not the kind that ended with both parties laughing at how silly and dramatic it all was.

'You in bed?'

'Yes, but let's forget this weird place. I need grounding. Show me our place. Maybe just the living room. Every little corner.'

On her screen, the image of Sue and the scene behind her swayed up and away and suddenly it was there – the four walls Inès had come to know and love more than any other. It wasn't until the tour was drawing to a close that she realised something precious was missing.

'Where's the photo? The one of you with your arm around your hero? Alan What's-His-Name?'

'Shearer? In the bedroom. You have to take what you can get in a crisis, pet.'

Inès smiled. It was small. But it was a smile. The world was still there, wasn't it? And her funny, gorgeous, talented lover was right there in the centre of it. The final reveal of the tour proved to be the highlight. Opened out on the piano was a score annotated in Sue's hand and although Inès herself hadn't the faintest interest in music, the sight moved her.

'What's the piece you're working on?'

If Sue was startled by the question, she hid it.

'It's Debussy. His *First Arabesque*. I'm arranging it for a small chamber group from Trinity. Early days but it sounds bangin' so far.'

'That's wonderful. And thank you for understanding me so well.'

'Innie, if not me, then who?'

'Turn it round – the tablet. I want you back.'

It was done but nothing was said immediately.

'Shall we talk about it?'

Inès nodded. 'So… I can't believe I'm saying this but it does look as if it was my father who murdered the young woman.' She set out the evidence as she saw it, concluding with a summary of both the form and content of the televised press conference.

'And is he *still* denying he was having an affair with her?'

'When the police came to arrest him, do you know what he shouted as they dragged him away?'

'Tell me.'

' "How could I have killed Samira? She was the love of my life! I worshipped her!" I can't recall the exact wording that one of the officers – a foxy individual with a shock of extraordinary red hair – came out with but it was something like: "Pity she wanted shot of you, then." And of course, that is what got her killed. My father couldn't have her. He is a man used to bending everything and everyone to his will. He couldn't handle the rejection.'

'But to murder someone over it? It's mad.'

'He *is* mad, Sue.'

'How is Zoë taking all this?'

'She feels destroyed by the whole thing. And of course, she's going to be pitied now on top of everything else, isn't she? The woman who couldn't keep her man interested to the extent that he did *that*.'

'Is she capable of telling people to fuck right off?'

'Oh, she can fly off the handle at times, and keep right on going. But over this? It's too tragic, I think.'

'You know we should invite her here. Soon. Straightaway, if you want.'

'Bless you. As and when, she says. Thinking of us, actually. The media, and so on.'

'That's sweet.' Sue looked as if she had something to add but couldn't quite voice it. But she *was* a Geordie, after all. 'Innie, in your mind, is there even the slightest doubt that your father is the one? The murderer, I mean?'

'I've thought about it, of course. It seems that Samira was a honeypot around which a lot of bees were swarming. With their stings well and truly up, to labour the analogy. But quite apart from my father's sick psyche, there's a lot of incontrovertible technical evidence against him, too, apparently.'

'I see.'

'Oh, I nearly forgot. In all this weirdness, there's a – what do you call it – a humdinger of a sidebar to this morning's arrest.'

'Really?'

'Yes, the officer in charge is named Paul Darac. That ring a jazzy bell?'

'Paul Darac? No!'

'Yes.'

'He's the guitarist in the band I'm looking forward to seeing at the club soon.'

'I said it was a humdinger.'

'That's crazy. Unbe–cocking–lievable.' Sue let the thought sink in a moment. 'Actually, I've become a quite a fan of Monsieur Darac's band. They're great listeners. To each other,

I mean. But it's the way they manage to be tight yet loose at the same time that's most interesting. I'd like to talk to the bandleader about it – Didier Musso, the pianist.'

'Well, you'll get your chance, Sue. I should think.'

FIFTY-SIX

'Picture the scene! Picture it exactly!'
But all Cassie could picture was a man writhing in his death throes. And blood. Blood dripping, pouring, spurting, soaking the stair carpet. Blood everywhere.

'Carmen! Pull yourself together and pay attention!'

She couldn't help it. She was still in shock. She had never seen a man killed before. Killed? Executed. Butchered. Is this how he had killed Dédé? Butchered *her*? At Port Lympia, Cassie had realised that when she was of no further use to him, he'd kill her, too. And now she had actually *witnessed* him kill the cop – one who wouldn't have appeared if she hadn't allowed herself to be followed to the meeting place – that was another reason to kill her. So she must still be essential to his plan, mustn't she? It made her feel a little better.

'I… I'm sorry. I'll do better.'

'Forget about that snoop, alright? Police radio was cold. Not a word to or about him. So they don't know what happened or even where he was. His phone was switched off, too. Now it's in a drain nowhere near the place. Got all that? We're in the clear. So pay attention!'

'Yes, right.'

'Good. Let's warm up again. What's your name? Come on!'

'Noëmi.'

'Noëmi What?'

'Noëmi Tardelli.'

'Husband's true name?'

'Jean-Pierre.'

'Known as?'

'Armani.'

'Why?'

'He likes fashion.'

'Where was he born?'

'Nice.'

'Which football team does he support?'

'Uh… The one from Turin.'

'There are two teams there. Which one?'

'Ju… Ventus. Juventus.'

'Why does he support them?'

'Because his father's family comes from Turin and he really hates the other team from there.'

'Back to the new plan now. And you'd really better pay attention now, Carmen. Because we go tomorrow. Got that? Tomorrow, we do it.'

Cassie shuddered at the thought of it.

'I said, have you got that?'

Wednesday, March 19th

FIFTY-SEVEN

'Yes indeed – Zoë Laborde's piece *is* interesting,' Frankie said, slipping a wad of A4 pages back into their folder. 'And I can certainly see what Erica meant by "sobering".'

'I'll have a look at it myself, later.' Darac joined Frankie at the breakfast table. 'Loved last night,' he said, setting down her mint tea. 'Obviously.'

'I'm glad to hear that, sweetie.'

'And now, having the time just to chat and do things without breaking off to change a nappy or whatever? It makes life *easier*, I suppose, in a sense. And it's... not *empty*, of course, but it *is* really strange not having Lily here with us this morning.'

'Isn't it? It's not just anxiety, either. We know she's being beautifully looked after by people who love her and know what they're doing. Well, Chantal does.'

Darac grinned. 'And it's not the lack of spending time with Lily, *per se*. If this were a normal working day for us both, we would be handing her over to the likes of the wonderful Mariette shortly and wouldn't be seeing her again until the early evening, probably.'

'That's true. I'm sure it's good for her, you know. Ideal, in fact – to be cared for by two loving parents and a coterie of loving surrogates stepping in when needed.'

'Studies do show that, I think. When are you hooking up with Chantal?'

'Noon.'

'Excellent.'

He picked up his work bag. 'OK, I'm off.'

'Good luck with Laborde this morning. You one hundred

percent sure he's guilty, by the way?'

'As Agnès says, "a hundred's a big number" isn't it? And along with Granot, I don't much like *one* aspect of the case against him. But I'd need a hell of a lot of convincing it wasn't him. The guilty evidence is just too strong. Anyway, see you both later.'

'Don't forget this.' Frankie handed over the folder. 'I promised Erica.'

The couple embraced and Darac had reached the apartment door when Frankie said: 'So, shall we have a few more?'

'A few more what?'

'Kids, of course.'

'There's a thought,' he said, as if it had never occurred to him that such a thing were possible. 'How can I put it best? You know Kenny Barron's duo album with Dave Holland, *The Art of Conversation?*'

'Don't be ridiculous.'

'Take it from me it's a glorious, perfectly formed thing. For Kenny and Dave, read Paul and Frankie – right? Now consider their *Without Deception* album. It's Kenny and Dave again but with the addition of Johnathan Blake, for whose rhythmical majesty, read Lily.'

'Ri-ight.'

'Now, did adding Johnathan's drums bring much to the Kenny-Dave party? Of course, but mainly, it just made the magic happen in a different way. Kenny and Dave were perfectly wonderful all by themselves. With Jonathan they were no more or less wonderful, but they *were* different.'

'That's rather lovely and it makes me realise I should have phrased the question differently. How do you fancy adding a few players to our band?'

'Hmm... What do you reckon? Make it a quintet eventually?'

'As long as it's not a quintet along the number-without-end lines of the DMQ, I think it could work out.'

'You're on. We'll allocate the instruments later.'

Darac's mobile was already buzzing in his pocket and with duty literally calling, he blew a gotta-go kiss and closed the door behind him. Frankie had set aside the morning to think seriously about the "quick word" Agnès had had with her following last evening's team meeting but as she returned to her tea, her mood of playful contentment was keeping things light. A moment later, the door opened and still clutching his mobile, Darac reappeared. 'I forgot to ask. Agnès – what did she want to see you about last night?'

Frankie mimed concern for Darac's call.

'It's just Didier.'

'Oh.' She pursed her lips. 'I'll tell you later.'

'Alright. Love to Chantal.'

Darac was gone for a second time and what looked set to be a momentous day was finally underway.

FIFTY-EIGHT

On the bandstand, Darac was such a daringly inventive improvisor that it frequently struck bandmates and friends alike that his propensity to follow set patterns in almost every other avenue of his life was, well... strange. His usual response was to say that if you wanted to fly, first you needed the ground, didn't you? He had no comparable explanation for a rather more mundane trait: his tendency to notice how long it took to accomplish repetitive, routine tasks. His daily commute to work was a case in point. Unless he ran into his neighbour Suzanne with time to talk – a rarity for them both in the mornings – or his wine merchant chum Denis Martini breakfasting al fresco somewhere en route – far more likely – it usually took Darac seven minutes to walk his preferred route from the apartment through the old town to his below-ground space in the Promenade des Arts car park. As queues for the exit were usually short at that time in the morning, he was invariably back up on the street within four minutes. Some flexibility in route selection was then required but depending on traffic conditions, the Caserne was typically a ten-minute drive away, a journey he almost always set to music.

This morning had proved an exception. As Darac reversed into his designated space, he hadn't listened to a note: he was still chatting to Didier on his mobile.

'Hang on, Didi – I've arrived at work. Just grab my bag.'

With the forecaster's prediction of sunshine *and* showers so far only half right, Darac kept his shades on as, exchanging greetings with those coming on and off shift, he made his way to the Brigade's Building D. 'So it *was* Luc who had the Mingus scores?'

'True to form.'

'There's a good piece focussing mainly on him in this month's *Jazz Beat*, by the way.'

'On Luc?'

'On Mingus, you chump. It questions whether bassists tend to favour compositional approaches that stress the harmonic over the melodic.'

'Interesting. Pass that on, would you?'

'If you're in the vicinity, I've got it in my bag now.'

'Tomorrow night's gig will be soon enough. And speaking of The Blue Devil…'

'Just a sec, Didi. And to you… Both on lovely form, thanks… Sorry, carry on.'

'Our gig. With the usual rider, how free are you likely to be?'

'Could be tricky.'

Darac found Granot ruminating grumpily at his desk.

'Before you ask, breakfast was once more not to my liking.'

'I sensed that.'

'I don't know which geniuses dreamed up the so-called foodstuff named Cranberry Crunch but I'd like to get them in the interview room.'

The question of "stunt cereals" was debated for a good five minutes.

'Before we put out an APB for those responsible, anything from Path overnight?

'No but Map's due to ring later. Once we've got the DNA match for Cragnat and Medot's killer, we'll be well underway.'

'Indeed.'

'Laborde?'

'What about him?'

'Overall, I agree with you that he probably is guilty of Samira's murder. He's proving impressively sticky despite everything you and Bonbon have got on him, though, isn't he? Typical of sporting types. I love the likes of say, Franck Ribéry, but can you imagine trying to break *him* down?'

'As I'm sure you realise, I'm not familiar with the work of Monsieur Ribéry but I'll take your word for it. Time will tell. Later, man.'

Bonbon was already in situ in Darac's office.

'Lieutenant Busquet? Paul Darac, Brigade Criminelle. Nice to meet you.'

'Morning, chief.'

'Any news?'

'Haven't heard anything from below so I don't think Laborde decided to save us all a lot of bother and confess, overnight.'

'Pity.' He indicated his trusty Gaggia machine. 'Let's have a couple of doubles while we review where we've got to and work out how we're going to crack the bastard.' He set down his bag by the desk. 'And I say that with all due disrespect.'

Coffees were made and consumed; key elements of Laborde's story were re-scrutinised; and new plans and ploys to spice up the interrogation were thrashed out. It was while Bonbon absented himself on an errand that Darac opened his bag and took out what was in some ways an unusual piece of evidence – a document written by the wife of a prime suspect in a murder enquiry which, by dint of the multifarious technical data generated by the process of its creation, established with absolute certainty the writer's own innocence. And although under the circumstances there seemed no need of it, the data also served to corroborate Inès Laborde's account of her mother's movements on the evening.

Encouraged by Frankie's and Erica's reactions to Zoë's piece, Darac had meant to read it himself but hadn't found the time. Now seemed the perfect moment to check out a page or two. No slouch when it came to naming his own compositions for the DMQ, Darac's first thought was to compliment whoever had come up with the punchy and resonant title *Boss Women* for a compendium work on its subject. Zoë's contribution began well…

Zoë Laborde
Founder and Managing Director of Zed-Elle Computer Services

My business card says it all. I'm female and I run my own company. Just to underline those two points, there's a clue in the phoneticized spelling of the initials which form my company's name. Crystal clear, isn't it? One would think so. But think again, everyone. New clients arranging a home call still occasionally ask me when *Monsieur* Laborde might be available to fix their problem. Considering my husband's greatest IT triumph remains mastering the steps necessary to send text messages, such requests have been known to make me LOL!

I have occasionally asked the doubters if they had noticed that mine is the sole name on the company's masthead. Most reply that they thought some sort of tax dodge was behind it. How telling is that? And if it strikes you as disappointing that anyone should make such a regressive assumption in this day and age, I agree. But I must also report witnessing at least *some* improvements in this area over time.

It's almost fifteen years since I decided to leave my position as the only female computer science-trained manager employed in one of Nice's most successful IT companies. Had I received a better offer elsewhere? No. Indeed, when I left the firm in question, I had no other job to go to. Married and with an 11 year-old child in school, I knew that if I could make it work, running my own business would provide the perfect solution to the problems I had been experiencing both in and away from the workplace. I had no illusions that going it alone wouldn't be a tough hill to climb. But tough hills had never beaten me in my *VTT* days. And I was determined they weren't going to beat me now.

But let's rewind a little. Why did I *so* want to strike out on my own? First and foremost, I needed to repair myself but I don't mean that in a physical sense. Working the long hours increasingly expected of technical managers in my field had not worn me down as it had some of my male colleagues. My problems fell into four categories: ethical, logistical, cultural, and last but by no means least, sexual.

Let's look at ethics first. From embracing turnover-driven methodologies that inevitably vitiated the quality of work I could produce, to recommending expensive and unnecessary upgrades to clients, I had over time perpetuated any number of sub-ethical working practices. In talking with my child one day, it hit me just what a corporate mule I had become and it sickened me. That was one turning point. As was discovering that although I was one of the higher-grade "techies" in the company, I was working for only a medium-grade salary.

As to logistics, any working woman with children will be familiar…

Darac's heart sank. He shook his head. Shit! Everything he and Bonbon had so carefully put together on the case so far had just gone out of the window. Flown out of it, in fact. Flown first class one-way and was almost certainly not coming back. He took a moment to compose himself, then picked up the phone.

'Morning, Erica. Have you got Zoë Laborde's laptop out on your bench?'

'No, but it's still here. Why?'

'I need to come over and check a couple of text files – the original of the piece you printed out being one of them.' He could picture Erica's raised right eyebrow. 'Not checking on your work, obviously.'

'Good to hear but I'm not infallible, you know. Can't believe I said that! Anyway, I'll get it ready for you. Five minutes?'

'Five it is.'

Darac ended the call and he was already finishing another when Bonbon walked back into the office.

'So, Laborde time, chief?'

'No. Erica time. I'll tell you why when we get there.'

FIFTY-NINE

Erica was on the phone when Darac and Bonbon strode into the lab. Mouthing "Agnès," the news didn't appear to be good. There were a number of devices undergoing investigation on the bench but only one laptop had its lid open. Erica's eyes swivelled to it and an exchange of looks confirmed it was Zoë Laborde's laptop. 'Yes, they're here now. Would you like a word?' She listened. 'OK, I'll pass that straight on. Uh-huh? Yes, I'll get back to you soonest.'

The call ended, Erica was already tapping in another number. 'Worrying news,' she said, cupping the phone's mouthpiece. 'Alain Terrevaste hasn't turned up for today's final shift on the Place Wilson surveillance. One of the guys he was supposed to be working with rang Terrevaste's wife. He hasn't been home since yesterday. She assumed he'd been on a night job and hadn't bothered to call. Not unusual, that, she reports.'

'When was he heard from last?'

'Late yesterday afternoon. As to where he was when his phone shut down, I'm just going to sort out a fix but there's a complication. For reasons best known to himself, he always had his GPS disabled, apparently.'

'Watchers always hate the thought of being watched themselves,' Bonbon said.

'So we'll be on triangulation,' Erica made a moue. 'Nowhere near as precise.' The Caserne's queen of all things digital gave her phone a very analogue shake. 'Come on, answer for God's sake!'

'The guys are continuing the surveillance without him?' Darac said.

'Yes. Armani's off today but Agnès has already let him

know. Noëmi's off too, by the way.'

'Both of those things are a comfort.' He indicated the laptop. 'Sorry – how do I get in?'

'I've neutered the ID. Press any of the number keys and the file you mentioned will appear. You'll find other text files in the documents folder.'

'Excellent.' As the *Boss Women* piece pinged into view on the screen, Erica's call was picked up and she left them to it.

'The Invisible Man, missing?' Bonbon said, looking concerned. 'It *could* be nothing, of course.'

Darac shook his head. 'I don't like it. Terrevaste not calling his wife may be his usual practice; not signing on for his shift is not like him at all.'

'Agreed.' Bonbon turned his attention to the laptop screen. 'What are we looking at here?'

SIXTY

Occupying a shady site on the banks of the Loup a few kilometres to the west of Vence, the perfume house of Maison Darac was very much a boutique operation. And if its weekly tour and taster sessions could not match the scale of those offered by the behemoth houses that had built the nearby city of Grasse, visitors invariably found the personal touch with which they were conducted made for a far richer experience.

For Martin Darac, no experience in his life could have felt richer than taking his granddaughter on a tour of the perfumery his remarkable talent as a "Nose" had created from nothing. If Lily was impressed by the Maison's state-of-the-art solvent extraction drums and *enfleurage* frames, she kept it to herself but being introduced to her grandfather's 12 full-time employees, many of whom had been with him from the beginning, proved a different story. In short, little Lily was a big hit with everyone and Martin sensed that in some inchoate way, she appeared to realise it.

As the visit drew to a close, Martin's Head of Sales and Marketing, Joséphine, spoke for them all. 'You're not taking her away already?' The follow-up was an invention of her own. 'She hasn't signed up for the newsletter yet, for one thing.'

'Sorry, Fifi. I need to whisk her back to Chantal. She's due to set off to Frankie's by 11 o'clock and before you say it's only 9.30, preparing to ferry babies around these days takes forever.'

'Just the Q.A. form, then.'

At various times in his life, Martin had been described as a true romantic, a starry-eyed dreamer, and as a boy who never really grew up. Perhaps the truth lay somewhere in between. Whether it did or not, he drove away from the perfumery entertaining the thought that one day, it might be granddaughter Lily who took over the business that had never interested his son. Who knew? It could happen.

Slanting sunshine after spring rain brought a particular magic to the wooded landscape flanking the Route de Vence: buds breaking on branches glimpsed through steamy mists; birdsong carried on warm currents of air up into its feathery canopy; tiny creatures parting leaves and cracking twigs as they scuttled unseen through the undergrowth. But as the greenery began to thin out and drifts of apartment blocks began to appear in the distance, the landscape opening up all around was no less inspiring. Ahead, its rocky summit the shape of a raised eyebrow, the Baou des Blancs was the first of three peaks standing as gatekeepers to the higher ground to the north. Away to the right, the walls of Vence formed a ligature of stone tight as a tourniquet around the medieval heart of the city. Vence had been home to Martin all his adult life. And what a life it was continuing to be.

Sandrine came into his mind at that moment. Lord, wouldn't she have loved her granddaughter? Loved her every bit as much as she had loved Paul. Martin felt overcome suddenly but he told himself to snap out of it. Sandrine had died 26 years ago. The here and now. And the future. They were what mattered most.

'Almost home, darling,' he announced, taking the fork signed to St Jeannet and La Gaude. He glanced at Lily in the rear-view mirror and what he saw jolted him with such force, he lost all connection with the here and now. It can't be happening. It can't! A car beeped behind. Providence intervened – a one-vehicle wide chevroned area for parking appeared on Martin's nearside. He braked hard and jinked into the rearmost space. Horn blaring, the car behind roared past. He looked again, not so much *at* but *into* the mirror and there was Sandrine sitting alongside Lily, smiling happily, stroking her foot, kissing her forehead. Martin turned quickly around. Lily gurgled, happy to see him. She was quite alone. He turned off the engine and, slumping on to the steering wheel, tried to make sense of what had just happened before he got out of the car and joined Lily on the back seat.

At the house, Chantal appeared to be well on schedule for Lily's return home. The baby herself was fast asleep.

'Ah, Martin.' She made an almost comically sympathetic moue. 'You're all overcome, aren't you? So did they coo over her? Of course, they did. Silly question.'

'Oh, yes. Lily was a huge hit.' He handed her over. 'There.'

'As you're heading straight back to the perfumery…'

'Uh, no, actually. Changed my mind. I'll go in later.'

'Oh, alright.' She looked him up and down. 'You know, you don't have much colour. Feeling alright, sweetheart?'

'Never better.'

Lily began to stir.

'If you say so.'

'I do.' He glanced at his watch. 'Still a good hour before you're off. But I may as well transfer the baby seat now. Then it's done.'

'We should put one in both our cars, you know. Make life easier.'

He kissed her cheek.

'It would. But in the meantime…'

He went back out on to the drive still coming to terms with the trick his imagination had played on him earlier. Resisting the temptation to jet sudden glances all around him, he opened the rear door of his car and got on with the job in hand.

SIXTY-ONE

He had seen this man before. Seen him on the day that had changed everything for him.

'You've been mainly useless Carmen,' he said, concentrating on keeping the rubber eyepiece hoods of the binoculars a cigarette paper's width away from his eye sockets. 'But at least you attached the magnetic trackers where I said.'

'I always do what you tell me.'

'And you did clear *everything* out of the place?'

'Yes.'

'Where did you take it?'

'Where you told me.'

'*Where*? I said.'

'The dumpster on Beaumont. Opposite the second-hand shop.'

'Good. You've earned a reward.'

Cassie didn't have the stomach to enquire what his idea of a reward might be. She had prayed this might be the last day she would have to rub ointment over the parts of his body he couldn't reach, a procedure that despite the pain the bastard was in frequently aroused him. Not having to go through all that again— now *that* would be a reward.

'Thank you,' she said, her voice pitched right up. And it sounded trembly. He hated weakness in any form. It scared him. It made him want to lash out. But he hated shows of defiance, too. You had to obey in just the right way, without making any kind of fuss; obey until an opportunity presented itself that you might just be able to exploit. She had blown one of those opportunities the previous day. All that blood? She just couldn't bring herself to stab him. Anyway, what were the chances of her getting away with his murder? But there wouldn't be many more chances. And there wouldn't be *any* more if she ceased to be needed.

Yesterday had been a near thing, Cassie reflected. At the time, she thanked God for the car radio he'd had adapted to listen in to the police mobile control unit. If he hadn't needed to check immediately if the police were in contact with the officer he'd killed, he wouldn't have shot off, leaving her to gather her thoughts alone. Now, every time the radio beeped, her heart missed a beat.

In the passenger seat, he winced and caught his breath. He was in pain. Good. Die, you bastard. But he would never die, would he? Never.

'In case you're wondering, I still need you. '*That* is your reward.'

SIXTY-TWO

Erica had pinpointed Terrevaste's last known location as precisely as she could and if it had been in open countryside, finding traces of the man would have been relatively easy. Approximately two square kilometres of four and five-storey city blocks presented an altogether more difficult challenge. The search team Agnès had put together under Granot was made up of experienced officers but for most of them, showing residents and passers-by a photo of a man dubbed "invisible" and asking if they had seen him was a thankless task.

Serge Paulin had a more positive take on things. 'You know, Tee-Vee is going to go nuts when he finds out we've been blowing his cover all over Riquier.'

'I love your optimism,' Farid said, as they turned the corner into rue Scallero. 'I guess that's what comes of playing on the wing, does it?'

'Hoping someone's going to pass to you, you mean? When did you last see a rugby match? We wingers have to go looking for the ball these days.'

'Sounds like hard work.'

'No, not really but I take your point about our man. Out-of-character behaviour for a bloke like him isn't exactly hopeful.'

They had arrived at the foot of a smart-looking four-storey block with a row of commercial properties underneath.

'Is this number…? Yes, it is. Alternate doors, then, Serge.'

Sweeping the parallel rue Smollet, Granot and his ad-hoc team had not had the slightest sniff of a lead so far. But each of them knew that just one observant, serendipitously placed, or just plain nosey person was all it might take to change things. And that person might be the very next one they approached. Failing that, the flyers they were posting through doors and attaching to lampposts and the like might yield something.

Across the street, Granot's eye was taken by the entrance to rue de la Malonnière. It was just the sort of glorified alleyway in which anyone could go missing. 'Kaz?'

'Yes, Lieutenant?'

'You carry on along here. I'm going to head up there. Let Bertrand know when he comes out of the building, will you?'

'Will do, Lieutenant.'

'I'll be in touch.'

SIXTY THREE

Three members of the Laborde family were now helping police with their enquiries at the Caserne. Following his Damascene moment earlier, Darac had decided to leave Gilles Laborde in the cells and re-open proceedings with daughter Inès. Meanwhile, back in La Ginistière, forensic teams were already subjecting the family's villa to a searching examination of their own.

'Doctor, you are certain you do not wish to have a lawyer present?'

'None is necessary. And do please get on with your questions. Neither my mother nor I have the vaguest idea why you have brought us here. You have my… You have the killer in custody already, after all.'

'You genuinely have no idea why you're here?'

'No. We have already made complete statements. You and Officer Flaco here took them. I can't think of anything to add to what we already told you.'

'One thing would be the truth about how you and your mother spent the evening of Monday, March 17th.'

Inès froze. 'I don't know what you mean. Quite apart from our statements, your IT people have tested everything fully and I'm sure it all checked out.'

Darac set down a document on the desk.

'I take it you recognise this? It's a photocopy of a prose piece which your mother told us she had spent a couple of hours typing up on the evening in question – a transcription of an audio recording she had made of her thoughts on the subject of women in business.'

Inès no more than glanced at the top page. 'Haven't actually read it but we've talked about it, certainly.'

'It's an interesting piece. Well written, too, we all think. Would you be kind enough to look at it more carefully? Just the first couple of paragraphs will do.'

Her brows lowering in puzzlement, Inès began reading:

Zoë Laborde
Founder and Managing Director of Zed-Elle Computer Services

My business card says it all. I'm female and I run my own company. Just to underline those two points, there's a clue in the phoneticized spelling of the initials which form my company's name. Crystal clear, isn't it? One would think so. But think again, everyone. New clients arranging a home call still occasionally ask me when *Monsieur* Laborde might be available to fix their problem. Considering my husband's greatest IT triumph remains mastering the steps necessary to send text messages, such requests have been known to make me LOL!

I have occasionally asked the doubters if they had noticed that mine is the sole name on the company's masthead. Most reply that they thought some sort of tax dodge was behind it. How telling is that? And if it strikes you as disappointing that anyone should make such a regressive assumption in this day and age, I agree. But I must also report witnessing at least *some* improvements in this area over time.

Inès sat back. 'As I said, I've never read it before but I recognise it as the way my mother writes. I don't understand what I'm supposed to have noticed.'

'We have the digital audio file available, too – the material from which this written transcript was made. If you would like to listen to it?'

'No. Not particularly.'

'What's remarkable is how spot-on the typed transcription is. Absolutely word for word and no typos, our IT expert tells us.'

'I'm not surprised. My mother is a very precise person.'

Flaco handed Darac a second document.

'You may not be aware of a couple of false starts she made typing out the piece previously. Only got as far as two or three paragraphs. Probably other work got in the way and knowing she still had time before her deadline, I think she was waiting until she could bang on with the whole thing.'

'I didn't know she had done that but probably so, yes.'

'We printed this out just now. It's dated February 23rd Two paragraphs. I'd like you to look at them, if you would.'

Inès let out an irritated breath but once again, she did as she was asked.

Zoë Laborde

Founder and Managing Director of Zed-Elle Computer Services

My business card says it all. I'm female and I run my own company. Just to underline those two points, there's a clue in the phoneticized spelling of the initials which form my company's name. Crystal clear, isn't it ? One would think so. But think again, everyone. New clients arranging a home call still occasionally ask me when *Monsieur* Laborde might be available to fix their problem. Considering my husband's greatest IT triumph remains mastering the steps necessary to send text messages, such requests have been known to make me LOL !

I have occasionally asked the doubters if they had noticed that mine is the sole name on the company's masthead. Most reply that they thought some sort of tax dodge was behind it. How telling is that ? And if it strikes you as disappointing that anyone should make such a regressive assumption in this day and age, I agree. But I must also report witnessing at least *some* improvements in this area over time.

'It's the same as the one she did on Monday evening, isn't it?' Inès looked from one to the other. 'Yes, it's identical.' She sat back. 'What does this prove?'

'How long did you say you had been studying and then teaching in the UK?'

'Eight years, all told.'

'You were obviously quite fluent in English before you went up to Cambridge but you are absolutely top-notch now, aren't you? As your mother proudly told us, all of the written work you have produced in that time has been in your adopted language. We have an example from August 2012 to show you.' He gave Flaco a look and, opening a laptop, she displayed a page from the *Science Today* website, a celebrated journal written in English. 'Neither of us understood a word of what you're writing about here but one aspect of the piece is clear, isn't it?' He looked deep into Inès's eyes. 'Isn't it, question mark? Now look at this next piece, one you presented as a paper at a symposium in Paris last November. I need hardly add that although you wrote this one in French, Officer Flaco and myself still barely understood a word of it. And why *space* question mark? There are two reasons *space* colon: it's simply impossible for any non-scientist to grasp such esoteric concepts *space* exclamation mark! Secondly, comma... Need I go on?'

Inès's cheeks flushed. 'I... I may have written those pieces but I was not responsible for typesetting them.'

'Nice try, Doctor Laborde, but your personal emails also show that in those eight years of Anglophone living and working and writing, you have become accustomed to using

English punctuation, a form which eschews the use of spaces before question marks, exclamation marks, semi and full colons and so on – the form we use here in France. More to the point, the French way is the form of punctuation your mother used in those two false starts and in every other document written by her that we have looked at. What this unequivocally suggests is that *you* typed up the chapter from *Boss Women* on your mother's laptop – a task you and your mother claimed *she* had undertaken. She was *not* at home during the hours you both stated, was she? She therefore has no alibi for the time of Samira Padar's brutal murder.'

'But how *could* I have used my mother's laptop in her place? You're forgetting that her fingerprint ID is the sole means of logging into the device – without taking it apart, that is. And the internal log will have shown that neither she nor I did that.'

'Yes, and because 99.99% of the time, fingerprint log-in *does* ID the user accurately, our IT department initially took it at face value. Of course, it *was* your mother's fingerprint which opened the laptop so you could begin your task and it reopened it after two brief intermissions during the session, as well. However, *she* wasn't there in person at the time, was she? We believe she inscribed her fingerprint on a sliver of some form of conductive rubber – probably silicone – which you then applied to the sensor at the agreed time. As a scientist, Doctor, you must realise that it is pointless to deny all this.'

Slewing forward on to her elbows, Inès dropped her head into her hands. A barely perceptible nod told Flaco that they were going to remain still and silent for as long as it took Inès to think the thing through. It was some moments before she righted herself.

'There wasn't an *agreed* time,' she said, finally.

'No?'

'No. It just fell out that way. But what you're clearly deducing from all this – that my mother could have...' Her face crumpled. '*That* is not what happened. No, no, no. I... Oh God... May I have some water, please?'

Flaco provided it and for a moment Inès looked as if for succour into the eyes of her silent inquisitress. None was given.

'Thank you.' She took a sip and, cradling the cup, appeared to be resetting herself for what was to come.

'We're listening, Doctor.'

'I... did do as you said with the typing. I was so careful to get the words down, I didn't think about the punctuation. I finished it, sent it off to the publisher, got an acknowledgement and all seemed well. Look, I know my assurances count for nothing, especially now that I lied to you both for which I'm truly sorry but the thought that my mother could have murdered *anyone*, let alone that lovely young woman, two-timer though she undoubtedly was – it's just not... Just not true or possible. You've both met my mother. Does she look or act like the sort of person who could do such a thing?'

'Was it your mother's plan? The business with the laptop?'

'It sounds so incriminating to put it like that. No, I offered to do it.'

Darac shared a look with Flaco. If it transpired that Zoë Laborde had killed Samira, daughter Inès had just put herself in the frame as an accessory to that murder. It was a thought that gave him pause.

'*Why* did you offer to do it?'

'Because she needed to go out to the Stade and that evening was the deadline for sending the piece.'

'Why did she need to go to the Stade?'

'May I come to that in a minute?'

'Al-right, *when* did she leave?'

'It was 9 o'clock on the dot.'

'Twenty minutes before you logged on to her laptop and started typing out the piece as her.'

'Yes and I know using Maman's silicon fingerprint looks suspicious but using such hacks is an everyday thing for us.'

'She took her car?' The BMW Estate that Raul Ormans and his team were now taking apart. 'The newly valeted one? The one with a folding bike in the boot?'

'I don't know what is in the boot but it is the BMW, yes.'

From Eric Cauvin's diagrams to a battery of corroborating witness statements, everyone attending Agnès's team meeting knew that wherever Zoë had then parked the BMW, it had not been at the Stade itself.

'And when did she return?'

'About 11.25. I'd finished the typing and had gone to bed, a bit worried actually because I hadn't heard from her since she left.'

'And how did she seem when she came in?'

'She was very upset and that leads me on to why she wanted to go out to the stadium in the first place.' Inès outlined the scenario of the dress watch they had seen Samira wearing on the video footage from the athletes' celebration party, a gift Zoë originally believed her husband had bought as an anniversary present for her.

'And that is how she came to suspect they were having an affair?'

'Yes. We learned eventually that the watch hadn't been purchased by my father after all but Maman didn't know that until yesterday morning. It's ironic because she hadn't wanted to believe what she saw on the video link. So the night before, she went off to see with her own eyes – my father and Samira together, I mean. Not to catch them having sex in the back of a car or the showers or wherever. She didn't need to go that far. She would know, she told me, just by watching how they were together – walking back to their cars, say – that they were definitely an item.'

'And did she? Watch them "walking back to their cars?" '

Inès let out a long, slow breath. 'No.'

'She was away from the house for over an hour and a half. What *did* she do, then?'

Inès gathered herself. 'She said she knew a way of getting into the stadium unseen. My father used to sneak in with his friends as a kid and he described the route to her once. Being him, in great detail. You can still do it apparently, even after all this time. But it's a convoluted path and she took a wrong turn somewhere. I hate to think of her scrambling around in the dark trying to find her way and getting more and more lost.' Tears came. 'If you appreciate a telling metaphor, Captain – how does that one work for you? She fell over a couple of times.' More tears. 'Like a child, she was – coming home all grubby with ripped trousers and a cut knee.'

Darac pictured Samira face-down in the water, the back of her head a bloody mess. 'Those trousers have already been binned, haven't they?'

Inès dabbed her eyes. 'Uh… Well, they couldn't really be worn anymore.'

'However, your mother washed them first.' But if she had assumed that would have taken care of the bloodstains, she was mistaken. As Professor Deanna Bianchi had once remarked to Darac: "There's clean and there's Luminol clean, isn't there?"

'Had they been washed?' Inès's brow lowered. 'Well, I suppose Maman wanted to see if it was worth repairing them. I don't know.'

'Doctor, why did you lie about your part in this?'

'I've already said I'm truly sorry about it and I mean that, Captain. When we learned what had happened to Samira, we realised just how suspicious it might look.'

It seemed to Darac that he had gone far enough with Inès

Laborde for now.

'It's been explained to you that you're being held for questioning in connection with a murder enquiry and as such I'm returning you to the cells for the time being.'

'May I see my mother?'

'Not at this time.'

Inès looked utterly forlorn but she nodded, stood, and as Darac formally tagged off the session on the recorder, she was led away.

'We've got quite a lot to digest here, Flak,' Darac said. 'I think we'll give it a good half an hour before bringing Madame Laborde up.'

'Right, Captain.'

Darac turned to the two-way mirror wall. 'Come on in, Bonbon, and we'll head off to my office in the interim.'

Once there, Darac parked his backside on the corner of his desk and got the discussion moving immediately. 'So what do you make of what we've just heard, Flak?'

'As to Madame Laborde's possible guilt and Inès's complicity in the murder?'

'Uh-huh.'

'I'm not sure about either. You, Captain?'

'Let's look at the second question first. OK, Inès fibbed to us about how the pair of them had spent their evening but I'm pretty sure she was an innocent dupe in the murder itself. Why? Partly because once Inès had admitted that she had typed up Zoë's piece, she made no attempt to hide the fact that she'd done so voluntarily. In fact, she stated that she'd *offered* to do it. I don't think she would have done that if she'd suspected for a moment what might have been its true purpose − i.e. providing her mother with an alibi for murder. Do you? For one thing, consider the charges it opens Inès up to.'

'I hadn't thought of it like that, Captain.'

'What's your take on this, Bonbon?'

'I agree. As for Zoë's possible culpability for the murder?' He drew down the corners of his elastic band of a mouth. 'I strongly suspect Inès is soon to become mightily disillusioned with her dear Maman.'

'The case against Coach Laborde *has* got a lot weaker.' Flaco said.

Darac nodded. 'Killed it altogether, in fact.'

'Another thing I would never have thought of, Captain – the French/English punctuation anomaly.'

She was in good company, Darac reflected – neither had Frankie and Erica. And they had both read the piece. 'Once again, jazz comes to the rescue, Flak.'

'Sorry? Don't understand.'

'My knowledge of English? Yes, I learned the language in school as we all did but I owe the more nuanced stuff mainly to *Jazz Beat* magazine. Every month since my teenage years I've waded through it, dictionary in hand.' Absent for some hours, the smile that habitually played around Darac's lips put in a return appearance. 'You could do worse than take out a subscription.'

Bonbon's brown eyes were all a-twinkle. 'He never stops, does he?'

Darac glanced at his watch. 'Moving on… Zoë's appalling plan was clever, I must say – exacting revenge on her husband by murdering "the love of his life" and implicating him into the bargain. And we may never have realised it but for her brilliant daughter's most uncharacteristic lapse typing out the *Boss Women* piece. And this is the key thing. Zoë will have had complete confidence in Inès's ability to accurately transcribe the audio file. Even if it contained mistakes, well, Zoë could've made them, couldn't she? What she could never have guessed is that the *nature* of the mistakes Inès made would tell us so clearly that Zoë had *not* made them.'

'Absolutely,' Bonbon said.

'Flak, any questions?'

'Yes. We know how Madame Laborde could have used her IT and *Télécom* expertise to implicate her husband before and after the murder. But how do you think she went about the murder itself?'

'We can really only speculate at the moment.'

Bonbon gave Darac a look. 'Mate – we know that behind that "we can only speculate" front, the What Ifs are going hard at it. Want to walk us through them?'

'OK. Where to begin?'

Bonbon took a small yellow tin from his pocket. 'With a lemon love drop?'

'What's the love made of? No – never mind. Pass.'

'Ditto,' Flaco said. 'But thank you.'

'You literally don't know what you're missing.' Bonbon took one. 'OK, let's hear it.'

A moment gazing at the floor was enough to focus Darac's thoughts. 'Zoë's folding bike is the key, isn't it? Considering all we know or strongly suspect so far, how's this? Feeling safe in the knowledge that Inès is giving her a perfect alibi, Zoë drives off and parks somewhere near the Stade. She takes the bike out of the boot and with her *VTT* skills to the fore, rides it along the secret path she knew about from her husband's childhood days – the same route, presumably, taken by the young footballers who discovered the body on Tuesday morning. She *doesn't* stumble around in the dark getting lost as she told Inès she had. Once in the Stade itself, she makes her way unseen to the players' car park and from there follows Samira to the hidden area at the end where she witnesses the clandestine encounter we know then took place between Samira and Gilles Laborde. What Zoë overhears appals her. Gilles then drives away leaving Samira alone for a moment or two. However humiliated and infuriated Zoë is feeling at that point, she doesn't show it as she makes herself known to Samira who must have wondered what on earth she was doing there and what she had overheard. We know Zoë doesn't kill her there and then because several witnesses report seeing Samira driving away from the site perfectly happily. I think we're alright with this so far?'

Flaco nodded. 'I think it must have been something like that, Captain.'

'Bonbon?'

'Agreed. I tell you one thing. I'm looking forward to discovering what Zoë said to Samira to account for her popping up like that in the dark. Whatever it was, it seems it convinced her all was well.'

'I wonder if the bike is key to that, too. There used to be a jogging enthusiast who lived downstairs from me in the Place. He went running at night. Preferred it that time, he said. We know Zoë won trophies for *VTT* when she was younger. I bet every member of Laborde's squad knows that, too. So although seeing her emerging from the trees on a bike would certainly have been a surprise, it may not in itself have been a shock. There was a ready-made context for such a happening in Samira's head.'

Having extracted all the lemony love his sweet had to offer, Bonbon crunched its dying embers between his teeth and nodded. 'I can picture that. All Zoë needed to say was "Ooh, sorry if I scared you. I love bombing round all these rutted tracks around here but I don't have time during the day." That would work fine, I think.'

'I think it would, too,' Darac said. 'An issue we have from this point on is that we don't know whether Zoë had planned everything that happened or whether she just came up with it on the hoof. A mixture of the two is most likely, I think. Flak?'

'If Madame Laborde *had* overheard her husband asking

Samira to wait for him at the place he'd once shown her – a secluded spot around the corner by the builders' yard – she would know where to find Samira, wouldn't she? And it was from around there that the message we originally thought Coach Laborde had sent to himself came from.'

'True, Flak, but there's one small and one huge potential problem here. If Gilles Laborde's account of the break-up conversation was accurate – and I think with what we now know, there's little reason to doubt it – when he left Samira to attend the meeting with his assistants, she hadn't given any indication that she *was* going to wait for him at the place he suggested. Granting that Zoë did park her BMW in or near the builder's yard, we know that she would have headed back there at some point. So she *could* have come across Samira sitting waiting there or thereabouts, engaged her in conversation once more, killed her, somehow retraced her initial route back into the Stade and disposed of the body in the water jump. But let's rewind to the surprise encounter between Zoë and Samira at the far end of the players' car park. Yes, it's a dark, out-of-the-way spot but the lane behind them is quite a crowd scene – athletes, coaches, and the ever-watchful Eric Cauvin, knocking around. It's not a very secure spot to murder someone. So how's this? Zoë is astride her bike chatting with Samira when she glances at her watch and says, "Goodness, is that the time?" Or perhaps she suddenly notices something is amiss with her bike: "Damn, I've got a flat." Or with her person: "Ouch, I've pulled my calf muscle, it feels like." All of these could lead to her asking Samira to give her a lift back to her car. "It's parked nearby. My bike folds, it'll easily go in your boot." "Certainly," Samira replies. However inconvenient it may have been, what else could the young woman say?'

'But, Captain, no one reported seeing a passenger in Samira's car when she left.'

'True. This is speculation and then some but the guy I was telling you about – the one from my apartment house who used to enjoy going for runs at night? His girlfriend *didn't* enjoy it. She was convinced he would come to no good doing it. So what if Zoë said something on the lines of, "It may sound silly, Samira, but Gilles doesn't like me going out training at night and as we'll have to go through the gate, he might see me or someone might tell him they saw me, so is it alright if I sit in the back, bob down, put my tracksuit top over me?" Or something to that effect.'

In need of more lemon love, Bonbon slipped the tin out of his pocket. 'It's possible. Perfectly possible. So what's the huge problem you mentioned?'

'Samira's car. Think it through: Zoë dumps the body, gets back to her BMW which is parked in the vicinity of Samira's Renault. What did she do then? She couldn't fold *that* up, stuff it in her boot and drive away. So what on earth became of it? She didn't have time to drive it anywhere, did she? Unless it's right there under our noses somewhere.'

Bonbon rose. 'Let's go and ask the woman, shall we?'

SIXTY-FOUR

Action at the villa. Grandmother carrying the baby to her car. Departure looking imminent. But something was missing. Something central to the success of the plan. Cassie saw his eyes dart back to the front door. It had been left open.

'Turn on the engine.'

The thought that Chantal had no concept of what was going to happen turned Cassie's head into a maelstrom of distress.

'I... I feel sick.'

'No, you don't.'

Feeling sick or not, everything in place or not, it was happening. They watched Chantal fuss over the baby as she strapped her in to the rear seat. Cassie knew that thinking aloud was the last thing she should be doing but she couldn't help herself.

'She loves that yellow bonnet.'

'What?'

'The bonnet. She loves it. The baby.'

'What are you talking about, you stupid bitch? That little mewling bag of shit doesn't *love* anything.'

Be careful, Cassie. 'No, I didn't mean that. I meant, they often put it on her. The family and the carers. We need to know things like that. *They're* the ones who love—'

'All *you* have to worry about is what *she* does or doesn't do next,' he said, spitting out the pronouns as if they were something foul in his mouth.

Chantal hurried back to the door.

Don't just close it, Cassie said to herself. Please, God.

Chantal disappeared for a moment and returned carrying

the buggy, folded for the journey.

'Good,' he said and Cassie breathed again.

'Shall I put my wig on now?'

'What part of "do the wig last" didn't you understand?'

'Sorry.'

'Sorry?' He tapped the knife blade against her thigh. 'You will be if when we start the tail, you try to warn her, or crash the car, or jump out, or do *anything* I've told you not to. Because if you do, Carmen, I'll stick this knife so far up you, you'll be able to taste it. Got that?'

A whimpering nod was all she could manage. He meant it, she knew.

'Say yes.'

'Yes.' Her voice was minute. 'Yes!'

On the drive, Chantal put the car in gear and pulled slowly out into Avenue Henri Matisse. In her rear-view mirror, the white walls of the Chapelle de Rosaire appeared to melt dreamily away into the haze.

SIXTY-FIVE

Front of house, the city's forensic pathology facility was a place of carpeted calm, harmoniously blended earth colours and surfaces that were warm to the touch and to the eye. Back stage, a complex of white-tiled spaces were as echoingly reverberant as the tomb, or as senior pathologist Professor Deanna Bianchi was wont to characterise it – a 50's rock 'n' roll record.

Djibril Mpensa had had such a busy couple of days, there had not been a moment to reflect on how unfortunately timed Deanna's U.S holiday had proved. Culminating in a ten-day stay with her sister Veronica, a fellow nicotine enthusiast and possibly the last living survivor of the species residing in California, the three-week trip had been long-planned, keenly anticipated and, mercifully for Mpensa and his colleagues, due to end today. In short, Map couldn't wait for Deanna's return on Monday morning and there would be no mistaking when that moment had arrived. The sound of her signature cough reverberating around the corridors would sound to him sweeter than any dawn chorus.

Out in the field, lab technician Patricia's principal role was to maintain the integrity of a crime scene, controlling the flow of personnel in and out of the red zone with a cheery smile and an iron grip. In the lab, mid-morning was her time for replenishing, replacing and ordering supplies of everything from crime scene tents and overalls to the smallest paper and plastic specimen bags. It was a process after which coffee time followed as naturally as night follows day. The skill and care Patricia brought to every task she performed had not gone unnoticed. Only she was allowed to operate Deanna's beloved La Marzocco espresso machine in her absence. It was a privilege she took both seriously and selectively. Of the coffee drinkers, Djibril Mpensa was her favourite and she found him hard at work at his desk.

'Map? Join me in one?'

'You wonderful woman. Cappuccino, please.'

'Biscotto?'

'Feeling reckless. Make it two.'

'Cappuccino and biscotti for the young gentleman coming up.'

When Patricia returned with the order, she found Mpensa staring incredulously at his screen.

'What is it? If you can tell me, that is.'

'We've got a DNA sequencing match on Cragnat's killer.'

'From the fingernail evidence?'

'Yes. Look at that name, Patricia.' He sat back, questions already lurching around in his head like a storm-tossed raft.

Patricia gasped. 'And look at that face,' she said. 'My God. I can't believe it.'

SIXTY-SIX

Granot's hunch that rue de la Malonnière might provide a clue to the whereabouts of Alain Terrevaste had so far yielded nothing of any value.

His mobile rang. Perhaps that would change his luck.

'Map, good to hear from you.'

'Listen, we've got a DNA ID back on the killer of Ludo/ Medot and Cragnat. The man in question is none other than retired ex-CRS beat officer Christian Malraux…'

'What?'

'… Latterly *Lieutenant* Malraux of Marseille and, two or three Brigade postings before that, Lieutenant *Intern* Malraux with us. As I'm sure I need hardly remind you.'

'Malraux? Malraux killed those people?'

'It's incontrovertible.'

Malraux a killer? Yes, Granot could imagine such a thing without difficulty. But try as he might, he found it hard to insert the man he'd known into the scenario that had begun with Cragnat's killing of Denise Dubreuil.

'Be prepared for a second shock. I've sent you a recent-ish photo.'

The image came in.

'Sweet Mary, mother of Jesus. His face looks as if it's been flayed.'

'I said he'd retired from the force. He was actually invalided out. He has toxic epidermal necrosis which usually proves fatal to the sufferer. And that's a well-chosen word. It's a desperate condition.'

'As is the thought of Malraux being at large. But there's no time to debate such things now, Map. In fact, there's no time for anything much at all - we're stretched all over the place.'

'Listen, I know you're leading the effort on the ground to find Terrevaste, so would you like me to call Agnès with this?'

'If you would. She will get straight on to Marseille, I'm sure. And do a hundred other appropriate things. Including drafting Frankie and Armani in, possibly. Both of them are off today.'

'And Darac, Granot?'

'With Bonbon and Flaco, he's interrogating the Labordes. Mother and daughter.'

'For a second time? Why?'

'Don't know. I guess it'll be on the Stade W.V. case file log but I haven't had time to look. Speaking of which, this Malraux ID flash needs adding to the Port Lympia. I'll do that in a second.

'I'll get on to Agnès now.'

'Map, you're a brick.'

'If I'm a brick, the whole wonderful edifice that is Professor Deanna Bianchi will be back with us on Monday. Think of that!'

'You've held things together brilliantly in the meantime, my friend. Out.'

SIXTY-SEVEN

'Take the next right at the roundabout,' Malraux said.
'But she's going straight ahead.' Before recrimination
came, Cassie was quick with an explanation. 'I don't want to
lose them for you.'

Malraux took a deep breath but decided to let it go. And
then he realised it would probably be better if the bitch knew
more, anyway. Might cut out mistakes later.

'Just this once, I'll give you a reason. Now we know she
is going straight ahead, we know where she's going in the
end, don't we? She's taking the kid back. So we don't need
to follow right behind her. That way we might be seen.
And it doesn't matter who she's handing it over to in Nice.
Whichever one of them it is, the Promenade des Arts car
park is where she's heading. When she comes back up on to
the street with the buggy, that's when you do your thing. And
I do my thing. And then the fun really begins. Now shut up
and just drive to the city. We'll get in position well before she
gets there.'

'Thank you. Yes.'

A beep heralded a police message coming in on the radio.
'Quiet!'

It seemed routine – two vehicles had had a shunt on the D
2085 at La Fumade – but the man listened carefully, anyway.
As if it granted her a sort of amnesty from his scrutiny, Cassie
began to think. Whatever happens, she couldn't bear the
thought that the baby... No, she couldn't bear it. As to the
parents... And that Mariette, their main nanny... But people
got over things, didn't they? Eventually.

The police message ended and another came in. A burglary.
In somewhere called Lauvas. More time for reflection. Cassie

had stopped asking herself how she had got herself into this situation. She knew how. Weakness. She had been two years into her role as assistant payroll supervisor for a group of Marseille hotels when an idea to earn some extra money occurred to her. Appreciating that she probably hadn't been the first person in her position to realise how easy it would be to invent and pay a fake employee, she wondered if the internet would be littered with stories of those who had tried and failed to operate the scheme undetected. She found that it wasn't. She did however come across one case in which the "payroll purloiner" in question had been caught and sent to prison. How had he come unstuck? It seemed to her that there were three principal reasons: he had made his fake a full-time employee; he had put him on too high a grade; and he had paid him monthly by cheque. Resolving not to make the same blunders, Cassie's Monsieur Durand was a low-grade part-timer paid by the week in cash. Nevertheless, his earnings built-up over the years and Cassie would probably still be drawing his wage now but for a terrible stroke of luck: the murder of her immediate boss by another employee in the office. But for that completely unrelated act, she would not be in the situation she was in now. Everything had been fine when the investigation began and had she left modest Monsieur Durand in plain sight on the system, no one would have discovered his non-existence. But she panicked and decided to lose him.

She had never thought of police officers as pigs but if they were, it was the runt of the litter who noticed the discrepancy and, keeping it to himself, worked out how much Cassie had stolen from the company over the years. She had been in Malraux's pocket ever since.

It made her sick to think how easily he'd manipulated her from the off. Dédé had been easier still. She would do anything for a fix. But Cassie? A thousand times, she had tried to work out how to free herself. But even if she could, what could she do then? He had all her documents and money. She couldn't go anywhere. It was as if she was tethered to him by an invisible chain. When she had fallen under his "protection," it had been the threat of prison that had stopped her from trying to slip that chain. He knew she couldn't stand the thought of it. That was his first hold on her. 'Alright, but what do you want me to do in return?' she had asked him. He didn't know then. He just knew she might be useful to him at some stage. 'Wait and see,' he'd replied, and kept her in limbo for almost a year before the opportunity he had been waiting for presented itself. He outlined his plan, with it putting a second hold on her and Cassie's fate was sealed. 'There's no going back now,' he'd said to her. 'We're not just talking prison. I'm warning you on pain of death not to even think of crossing me. And that death, I promise you, would be very, very painful, Carmen.'

But supposing she *hadn't* agreed to go along with his initial offer? What would her sentence have been as a first offender? The "payroll purloiner" had been given three years and, as a model prisoner, had been released after two. For her own more modest felony, she might have served no more than a year and a half, yet she'd still baulked at the thought of it. To avoid eighteen piddling months inside, you've got yourself up to your neck in this living hell? Cassie, you shithead! Over the past days, she had chickened out of many opportunities to give herself up. There was the cop in the pharmacy, for instance. Or she could have walked into Commissariat Foch, the Caserne Auvare – any number of houses of correction. Yes, given herself up and shopped the man into the bargain. But he knew she wouldn't.

'May I ask one more thing?'

'Shut the fuck up and drive.'

SIXTY-EIGHT

Inès Laborde had earlier challenged Darac to picture her mother callously slaying a defenceless young woman and a good half-hour into questioning Madame Zoë Laborde – convinced though he and Bonbon were of her guilt – he was indeed struggling to visualise her committing such a spectacularly brutal act. In contrast, the story of her almost tragicomic expedition to see with her own eyes her husband and his lover together, a tale of increasing disorientation, humiliation and physical injury – *that* he could picture easily.

Darac gave Bonbon a look. It was time to play their killer card.

'You love your daughter, Madame?'

The question clearly threw her. 'Of course I do, Captain.'

'And her love for you is just as obvious. As is her antipathy toward your husband.'

'Can there be any surprise at that? He has never loved her. In fact, he is incapable of loving anyone. Poor Samira would have found that out in time.'

She was well rehearsed, alright. Or was it as simple as that? In criminology circles, it had been known for some time that murderers in Zoë's position sometimes came actually to believe in their innocence.

'You know, Madame, I think you understood early on that the very implausibility of the story you were going to tell about what you did on the evening Samira was killed would give it an odd kind of strength.'

Zoë's colour was up but she still looked confident. 'What are you talking about?'

Bonbon set down the incriminating typescript in front

of her.

'Before we go any further, perhaps you should examine this document. You'll recognise it as a transcript of your chapter for the book *Boss Women*.'

Zoë shrugged. 'Alright.' She read the opening paragraph. 'And?'

'You don't recognise your daughter's hand in it?'

'No. I wrote it.'

'You conceived it, certainly. But Doctor Laborde actually did the typing. And she did so as part of your plan to murder Samira Padar and incriminate your husband as her killer.'

Zoë blanched. 'Really, I understand how overworked you people are, Captain but you're overlooking all the evidence.'

'I'm afraid not, Madame. Indeed, I'm certain further evidence will come to support the charge of premeditated murder we are going to bring against you and your daughter. Haematological evidence, especially.'

No confidence now. Panic.

'What do you mean – against me *and* my daughter?'

'Well, Inès did volunteer to type this up, didn't she?'

'No! *I* typed it. Every word!'

'Every word and space? Look again.'

Zoë's eyes skated frantically over the page, and the next one and the next one. 'This is nonsense. Nonsense! You're trying to trick us. Me, I mean.'

'At first, Doctor Laborde herself didn't spot she had used Anglicised punctuation throughout. But when she did, she freely admitted doing so.' He indicated the recorder. 'It's all on there. I'll play you the relevant sequence.'

'No!' In an exact reprise of Inès's reaction earlier, Zoë slumped on to her elbows, her head in her hands. 'No, I don't want to hear it.'

'As complicated as your plan was, you had complete confidence in your IT skills to make it happen, didn't you?

The last thing you could have imagined is that your brilliant scientist daughter would make a mistake in completing what was a much simpler task. It's quite a thought that but for a few misplaced punctuation marks, you might well have got away with murder. And seen your husband go down for it.'

'I… do not wish to comment further.'

'See if this changes your mind. By your actions, Madame Laborde, you have made your dutiful, loving daughter an accessory to murder. That is a crime for which she will pay…'

'Stop it! Stop! Alright, it was me and me alone who did it. Inès believed what I told her about… seeing them together. She had no idea what I intended to do. *I* didn't, myself, really.'

'But you did murder Samira Padar and try to incriminate your husband for the crime, did you not, Madame?'

She looked lost and when she spoke, her voice had the enduring sorrow of the ages percolating through every syllable. 'Oh, yes. You see, she pitied me, Captain. Pitied! Of course, *she*, the love of his life, she was too good for him. Me? No. I wasn't good *enough*. I'd suspected it for a long time but I didn't know he "despised" and "laughed at" me behind my back. But it was when she referred to me as "poor, poor Madame Zoë." That was the final straw. I wanted to kill him but I realised he would suffer far more if I killed her. With my background, the rest – making it appear he had done it – that was easy for poor old me to do.'

And the defenceless young woman she had so callously battered to death? What about *her* suffering? Darac's blood ran cold. 'In one sense, there's nothing poor about you is there, Madame Laborde? As the publishers of *Boss Women* understood, you are an extremely bright, articulate and successful woman.'

'If you say so.'

There was no time for delving deeper into the issues. Establishing exactly what happened was the priority. 'Perhaps you would help us with how you accomplished what you did on the evening. Here's what we believe…'

Darac recounted the scenario that he, Bonbon and Flaco had put together earlier. 'Is that largely correct?'

Zoë seemed in a trance now, and when she spoke, her words emerged in a slow monotone stripped of all pain, guilt, blame or accusation.

'Oh, yes. Except that from where I was hiding, I could actually see Gilles talking to Eric Cauvin at the gate before he drove off. That's how I knew exactly what time I had to set the hands on Samira's watch. I chose two minutes before – 10.30. It wasn't a guess, as you thought. Then I hit it with the rock.'

'And you did that to make it appear your husband was providing himself with an alibi for the time of her murder.'

'Uh-huh. And there's another thing you missed. Yes, I got Samira to give me a lift back to my car but if I'd parked it in the builders' yard, Gilles would have spotted it when he turned up there later. I didn't know he was going to set up that rendezvous with Samira beforehand, of course. I was just lucky I'd parked where I did.'

'Which was where?' Bonbon said.

'Oh, further along the lane off it – before it turns into the hidden path back to the Stade.'

'One final thing,' Darac went on. 'When you returned to the lane after dumping Samira's body in the water jump, you had two vehicles to deal with, didn't you? We know what you did with yours – you drove it home. What did you do with Samira's? There wasn't time to drive it anywhere.'

'There was, actually. I drove it around the corner on to the street. Fifty metres at the most. Walked back to mine and drove off.'

'But we combed the area, Madame. Extensively. There's no sign of her car.'

'There wouldn't be. I left the keys in and the driver's door unlocked, you see. I knew someone around there would have it away. And quickly, too.'

Darac shared a look with Bonbon. Sending out an invitation to the local car thieves to remove the vehicle for her? It was the second simple but ingenious solution to a problem they had encountered in the past 24 hours. And they had been simpletons not to have thought of it.

Darac let out a long breath. 'And now let's look in detail at the killing itself.'

SIXTY-NINE

About half-way up rue Malonnière, Granot turned into a *cul-de-sac* in which he hadn't set foot since he was a child. Squeezed into its far end was what had once been the home and premises of Jacques Baulois et Frère, cobblers, whose speciality was re-soling and heeling shoes "while-u-wait." Or if you were in luck, while-u-went home and your mother returned later to pick up the work done.

Although the place appeared to have been uninhabited for some years, he knocked at what used to be the side door to the Baulois's living quarters and waited. No response. Imagining a gentle push would open it, he tried the door but it was tight in its frame and nothing gave. It was only then that Granot noticed the door's spring latch lock was a current design and appeared to have been fitted recently. Derelict though it was, the building was more secure than it looked. Someone had been busy. He looked around. No one. Producing a defunct credit card retained for the purpose, a quick waggle in the lock and he was in.

In the light from the open doorway, he caught sight of a contorted cable hanging from the ceiling, a bare bulb dangling on the end of it. He found a switch. The bulb flickered into life, faltered and died. Pity. He closed the door behind him and with the beam from his torch cutting a swathe through the dank-smelling gloom of the ground floor, he picked his way around piles of debris looking for any sign that Terrevaste had been there. There was none.

So far, at least.

In the far corner of the room, a flight of stairs carpeted in a bizarrely exuberant floral pattern led to the upper floor. Broken glass crunching under his boots, Granot moved carefully towards their foot and trained his beam on each rodded tread in turn. They looked secure enough but would they hold *his* weight? There was only one way to find out. A smell assailed his nostrils at that moment. Sweetish and putrid at the same time, it was a reek like no other. Granot winced. There was a corpse somewhere up there. He knew it. But there was still reason to be hopeful. The body in question may not have been human. A rotting rodent could give off a stench out of all proportion to its size. Listening out for every creak and groan, Granot clamped his hand over his nose and gingerly began the ascent. There were no sounds of crunching now. The stair carpet felt spongy underfoot. Dampened. Soddened even. Blood? Lots of it?

His beam picked out Terrevaste's shoes first, their laces double knotted for safety. The man was lying on his back, eyes open as if staring intently at the ceiling. Around the ripped open flesh of his neck, a collar of dried blood was crawling with insect life. Granot peered at the wound and for a moment he was high up on Boulevard Blanqui gazing at the breached dam that had been Ludo/Medot's throat. Map would confirm it in time but Granot had no doubt this was Malraux's knife work.

He straightened to make the call, tucking the torch under his arm but it slipped and the careening beam picked out Darac. And then Darac with Frankie. Darac with Frankie and Lily. The *nounou*, Mariette. Noëmi with Lily wearing a yellow bonnet. Chantal and Martin Darac. A baby buggy. The yellow bonnet again. Photographs – the wall behind the corpse was lined with them. Faces. But street scenes, too: the gated entrance to Place Saint-Sépulcre; the twisting *ruelles* that linked it to rue Neuve and the Babazouk; the street entrance to the Promenade des Arts Car Park. And there was a handwritten sheet. Names. Lily's carers. Addresses. Phone numbers. A timetable. Granot's heart was racing. He understood the whole thing. He stabbed a key on his mobile. And prayed he wasn't too late.

SEVENTY

They were standing among thinly spaced palms planted in pavement. At their backs, lusher greenery stretched in a graceful S-curve towards the shimmering azure of the *Baie des Anges*. Their attention was on the darkened space across the street. The down ramp into the subterranean gloom of the Promenade des Arts car park seemed to Cassie like the maw of hell.

Malraux had an entirely different view of the situation. Since realising his dream required everything to go like clockwork, he kept running over the plan. It was the most he had had to say to Cassie since he had arrested her in Marseille just over 18 months ago. With having to keep up appearances for passers-by, it made him seem almost normal.

'So, Madame Tardelli – you're about to meet Darac's stepmother at last.'

'Yes.'

'Picture it. Get it clear in your head. She'll come off the Avenue St-Jean Baptiste on our left there and keep to the far lane before turning down left again into the car park.'

'Supposing she sees us as she drives up? She only needs to glance to the right.'

'She won't. She'll be concentrating on making the turn down to the left. It's tight. Needs attention.'

'Supposing—'

His peeling face hardened. 'Shut up!' His condition meant that people tended to stare at "that poor man." An approaching couple was doing so now. He gave Cassie a smile. 'No supposing, alright, bitch? Do as I tell you or I'll cut you like the others.' His gaze slid to the junction with the avenue. 'She's here.'

Her knees turning to jelly, Cassie didn't look.

'She's slowing … She's doing as I said… Not looking over here… She's made the turn down. She's… in. Right. I'll go over it one last time. We cross the Traverse. We go around the corner into Boulevard Risso and there, we wait. Let's do that now.'

As nauseous as she felt, Cassie wanted more than anything she had wanted in her 36 years of life to kick off her high heels and run for it.

'And remember, Carmen. If you get this right, you'll live. If you don't, you won't.'

Yes, she wanted to run but even if she could, she daren't. Her only chance was to go through with at least the first part of it.

'Got that?'

'Hm.'

Somehow, Cassie managed to make it to the waiting point without stumbling or throwing up. The achievement gave her little solace and in case she was in danger of forgetting the mortal danger in which she had put herself, a black panel van bearing the crest of the coroners' office was parked at the kerb alongside. Applied to someone else's situation, it might have been funny.

'In about five minutes, the stepmother will show up on foot. The kid will be bundled up in the buggy. We approach. Me one step behind. Now – what's your line?'

'Uh…' She couldn't remember it. 'It's…'

'Come on! It's just a few words!'

'Sorry. I'm no Dédé. I'm nervous.'

'It would have to be you who looks the spit of Tardelli's wife. Jesus!'

'Please. I'll think of it. Just give me a moment. Yes, yes! I've got it.'

'Spit it out.'

'First, I smile and say, "Oh hello, Chantal. Fancy bumping into you." She knows all about Noëmi Tardelli and has no doubt seen photos of her so she'll probably say something in reply there.'

'Like?'

'Like, "It's Noëmi, isn't it? Frankie has told me loads about you. Lovely to meet you after so long." '

'Better. This is better. What else might she do?'

'Hug and kiss me. She's a very warm person.'

'And that would be ideal for me but if she doesn't say or do anything, what do you say and do next?'

'I offer my hand, introduce myself as Frankie's friend Noëmi and say I've been meaning to call her.'

'Yes, exactly. Was that so hard?'

Along the boulevard, a squad car whooped in the distance. Somewhere in the direction of the Caserne Auvare. Malraux heard it, Cassie noticed. But it didn't seem to worry him. Perhaps he could tell it was going in the opposite direction.

'Here she comes. Buggy and all. Baby still asleep by the look of it. You know what to do.'

Don't think about the baby Cassie told herself. But she couldn't help it. That little yellow-bonneted thing touched what was left of her heart. Had Malraux sensed she was weakening? Staring coldly into her eyes, he pulled back his jacket to reveal the knife.

The squad car whooped again. Louder. And was that a second vehicle?

Chantal was almost on top of them. Malraux loudly cleared his throat.

'Uh… Cassie spluttered. 'Hello.'

Chantal beamed. 'Noëmi! At last we meet!' She let go of the buggy's handle grip and while kisses of greeting were exchanged, Malraux shoved the women aside, wheeled the buggy quickly towards the black van's side-loading door and slid it back.

Noises off. Drawing his knife, Malraux held the blade centimetres over the sleeping bundle as he frantically scanned the street.

A voice from his right: 'Put the knife down,' Darac said. 'This gun is loaded.'

Granot, directly in front: 'You may remember I'm a crack shot, Malraux. Drop it.'

Frankie from the left: 'I don't want to shoot you, Christian. But I will unless you set down the knife and step away.'

Behind them, a tide of blue uniforms flooding on to the boulevard began sealing off the crime scene as if they had been rehearsing the move for months. Darac stared hard at Malraux. Some of that flayed look was his condition, wasn't it? But he could see the man was rattled, astonished even, that his plan had failed so quickly. How could it? How could we all have been here, ready, waiting? You left all the evidence behind, you idiot. That's how. Not for the first time, Darac thanked his lucky stars for Granot's instincts and know-how.

'Know this,' Malraux called out. 'I have nothing to lose. Nothing! Six months to live is all I have. Shoot me if you want to. But if you do, I'll rip this little flower you care so much about to pieces before I even start bleeding out. So back off and then she's going to come for a little ride with me. Back off!'

'You're not going anywhere,' Darac said, moving almost imperceptibly towards him. 'There's no way out.'

'Stay where you are. I'm warning you.'

'Listen to him, please!' Cassie shouted. 'He'll kill her! He's mad!'

'If I am mad, it's your mother who did it to me, Darac. She climbed out of her grave. Did you know that? I saw her. She knew I'd tried to kill you and would have done if that bitch Flaco hadn't turned up. Your fucking mother cursed me, Darac. That's why my skin went like this. Falling off in clumps. She put a curse on me!'

While Malraux had directed his words exclusively at Darac, Frankie and Granot had moved closer in.

Darac was a poor shot. But proximity to the target was a great leveller. 'You are clearly deranged, Malraux. You need help but to get it, you must give yourself up. So I'm going to give you one last chance.'

'No. I'm giving *you* one last chance.'

'Five seconds to put down your weapon, Malraux. Starting from now. Five…

The man stood rock still.

'Four…'

He began blinking repeatedly.

'Three…'

Still no move to set down the knife.

'Two…'

Drawing screams first from Cassie, Malraux thrust the knife into the buggy's plump heart and, slashing wildly, proceeded to destroy its contents.

No shots rang out. But a baby's cry was heard and her mother holstered her weapon to go and tend to her.

The joy that surged through Frankie at holding her daughter in her arms once more was almost too much to bear. It took some time but finally, some coherent thoughts came. 'Thank you so much, Mariette,' she said, just about keeping it together. 'I am sorry for the loss of the doll.'

Mariette smiled. 'She wasn't family. Lily will need a new bonnet, though.' She squeezed her foot. 'Won't you, darling?'

'I'll ask Patricia. I'll think she'll knit her a new one.'

'Chantal's here, Frankie.'

She turned. 'It's… not usually like this. Honestly. You alright?'

'I need a stiff drink. I can tell you that.'

'You shall have one. You played your part brilliantly, by the way.'

'We've got Officer Flaco there to thank for that. She briefed me superbly. Quite a surprise to find her and Mariette standing by Martin's space like that. But it all worked out, thank God.'

Flaco was in the process of taking into custody one Carmen Luisa Portet a.k.a. Noëmi Two.

'Just a second, Yvonne. I'd like a word with her.'

'Captain.'

'We've met before, Carmen.'

'Cassie, please. Only *he* called me that. He and my mother.'

'By the *chocolatier* on Gubernatis it was, last Friday. Though it seems much longer ago.'

'To me too. Please, it's important you know I meant no harm to your baby. None.'

Lily stirred but went back to sleep.

'I need to be careful what I say here. You certainly called out a warning and that will go on the record.'

'I *had* to warn you. He killed the officer who came looking. He killed my friend Dédé, too.'

'Actually, he didn't kill Denise. But he did kill her killer *and* an associate. Among those and other charges, he'll also be held on suspicion of murdering the surveillance officer you mention.'

'I saw him do it, Madame. Stabbed him in the throat as if it was nothing. I *saw* it.'

'We'll have the opportunity to talk through everything later but in the meantime, I must know something.'

'I want to tell you *everything*, Madame. The photos, the roster and the other things in the place? Did you find them? Is that how you knew what he was planning?'

'They were found, yes.'

'Before he ran off, he ordered me to dump it all but I didn't. I left it so you would find it. *And* I left the prescription with his name on. I left it all deliberately, Madame.'

Frankie knew that had Granot not instantly grasped the significance of what he'd found, units from the city and beyond would now be searching for the baby she was holding tightly to her breast. Cassie had clearly been part of Malraux's plan to abduct Lily but if she was telling the truth, she was also instrumental in foiling it.

'Thank you, Cassie,' Frankie said, as neutrally as she could manage. 'Listen, we know *why* Malraux wanted to exact revenge on my husband but...' She braced herself. 'He could simply have waited for him in the dark one night and stabbed him, couldn't he? He could have stabbed me. Or thinking that the greatest pain he could inflict on us was to kidnap our daughter, he could have snatched her away from one of her carers at any point. You called Malraux deranged and that's clearly correct. But he's also cunning and resourceful. Why all the elaboration? Why the charade with your disguise and so on?'

'Because I resemble Madame Tardelli so closely, his original plan was to fool one of your baby's carers into handing her over to me without a thought that anything might be wrong. Then when he'd got well away from the area, he was going to call you. It was evil and insane – Dédé and I knew it from the beginning. But we were caught like fish on a hook.'

'How was this original plan to have worked?'

'Dédé used to be an actress and she was going to play the part of someone who knew MT well – that's what we called Madame Tardelli in our notes and messages – so when a carer who had never met her before showed to hand over the baby, Dédé was to chance by and in greeting us, come out with personal stuff designed to underline that *I* was MT. We knew the chances of there being a carer who hadn't met her before were slim at the beginning. And by the time he had learned enough about them to drill it into our heads, they were slimmer, still. Eventually, there was just one carer left still to meet MT – your husband's stepmother.'

Stepmother. It was obvious now. 'For stepmother, read SM in your messages?'

'Yes. We didn't think any part of his plan would work but some things did.'

'Such as?'

'Whenever Malraux learned that SM and MT were going to meet at last, he was pretty successful at taking steps to prevent it.'

'How did he learn that?'

'From watching. Eavesdropping.' Cassie hung her head. 'Sometimes, I'm afraid, he learned it from Dédé and me. He gave us these hearing aid-like things. You can make out what people are saying even quite quietly to each other from metres away.'

'So Denise overheard my conversation with SM in *C'est Ici!* last Friday – the day I bumped into you later?'

'Yes, Madame. I'm sorry.'

It chilled Frankie to realise how easily her personal space had been breached. 'And she reported that conversation to Malraux. What did he do then?'

'He called SM's frail old next-door neighbour to say he thought his dog had got into her garden and could he come and look? He can read people, Madame. He can identify their weaknesses and strengths. So, as he knew she would, the neighbour rang SM in a panic and asked her to pop round to sort it out. SM agreed, as he knew *she* would, and so the pair still hadn't met by the time you saw me.'

'With that being the case, how close did he come to putting the original plan into action?'

'Very close, we thought but then Dédé was killed and

everything changed.'

There was much to get through later but Frankie needed to know one more thing now.

'If the original kidnap plan had succeeded…' She braced herself once more. 'Where would he have taken my baby?'

'We… weren't supposed to know. But Dédé overheard him on the phone one day. There's a farmhouse somewhere in the Luberon. Secluded. Difficult to find. Near Carpentras, she thought he said, but she couldn't be sure. That's where he would have taken her. You see, he wanted you, your husband, the poor carer involved… *everyone* to suffer for as much as possible, for as long as possible.' She began to weep. 'He made me go along with it, Madame. I was scared. I couldn't get away from him. He controlled everything I did. But now the nightmare is over, I'll say all this in court. I will.'

'That is duly noted.' Feeling exhausted, suddenly, Frankie gave Flaco a beckoning nod. 'Thank you, Cassie.'

'Madame, just once, may I see your baby close to?'

She thought about it. And turned Lily momentarily towards her.

Cassie smiled. 'Thank you.'

'Off you go now. We'll see you later.'

On the street, Darac waited until a raving Malraux was thrown into the cell van before he turned to embrace Granot. Unable to hold back tears, his words emerged in a barely intelligible slosh of syllables. A transcript would have read: 'Thank you, man. Thank you. But for you, this would have ended very differently. We can never repay you. Never.'

'You could start by relaxing your hold,' Granot said, his words emerging in a constricted croak. 'You're crushing my windpipe.'

SEVENTY-ONE

The Babazouk night was a wondrous thing. From comedy to tragedy, all human life was there. Following the dramas Darac and Frankie had been part of earlier, the evening had brought everything from profound reflections on life, death and the supernatural to heightened emotional outpourings. With Lily safely asleep in her cot, the couple had curled up on the sofa to put the last remaining touches to the picture of their day.

'We must review our security arrangements for Lily,' Frankie said, her contralto tones sounding silkier that ever in Darac's ear. 'Without allowing a maniac like Malraux to dictate how we live, and without making everyone involved with her care paranoid, we must tighten things up.'

'Absolutely agree. It won't take much, you know.'

'Lord, we were *so* lucky, weren't we? I believe Cassie when she says she deliberately left the photos, the roster and the prescription. Do you?'

'I'd like to think so. Of course, she could have had no idea how long it would take us to discover her handiwork.'

'But thank God she did leave it all. And thank God dear Granot found it when he did and realised so quickly what it all meant.'

'And when he called it in on his phone, consider the importance of the very first thing he said. I'm paraphrasing but it went something like: "Before we go any further, it is absolutely crucial that we maintain radio silence about this." He couldn't have *known* Malraux was able to listen in to part of our comms network; he just thought that he *might* be able to. And sure enough, that proved to be the case. Malraux could have heard the control unit mobilising everyone to the scene, Frankie.'

'It doesn't bear thinking about.' She pursed her lips. 'Considering Cassie's part in preventing the abduction, and her enforced subjection to a raving lunatic, what sort of sentence do you think she's likely to get?'

'There's mitigation, certainly, but there'll be a deterrent aspect to the sentencing as well, you would think. I don't know. Something else I don't know, or rather don't understand...'

'Yes?'

'Don't you think Malraux took a hell of a risk leaving poor old Terrevaste where he did? He'd dumped the bodies of his two previous victims nowhere near where he'd killed them.'

'It would have been a bigger risk trying to get a body with its throat cut out of the building in broad daylight. He couldn't draw any kind of vehicle up to the place, remember. The *ruelle* outside is too narrow.'

'Is it? Ah, I hadn't realised that.' The image conjured thoughts of Zoë Laborde pushing her bike along the hidden path to the Stade, Samira's bleeding body entombed in a Gianluigi Vera garment bag slumped over the handlebars. Darac exhaled deeply and, as he often experienced in the aftermath to a murder investigation, became acutely aware of his own life breath. And Frankie's, too. In celebration of it, he kissed the corner of her mouth and nothing was said for some minutes.

'Zoë and Samira, Paul. Talk about them.'

'Zoë's confession interview, Frankie.' He shook his head. 'I almost lost it when she said it was Samira's pity for her that had pushed her over the edge. Gilles Laborde is a shallow, controlling, mendacious, hypocrite, right? And though he went through a tough time during interrogation, it's difficult to feel much sympathy for a tosser like him.'

'With you all the way.'

'So what *do* I think?' He took a moment. 'Put it this way. If Zoë's reaction to everything she'd seen and heard had been to take a pair of scissors to the designer suit she'd given Laborde a couple of days earlier – I would probably have cheered. If she had opted to assault, or even kill him, I may not have countenanced it but I would at least have understood. Alright, Samira may not have been a *saint* in this thing but bludgeoning her death for a liaison she tried desperately to end and about which she expressed a deal of sympathy for Zoë? No.'

'Actually, Zoë's anniversary gift did play a part, didn't it? There's something particularly horrible about her using the garment bag to transport Samira's body to the dumping site.'

'Absolutely. But Samira's murder wasn't just hideous and undeserved. It's difficult to square it with the perpetrator. Think of the chapter Zoë contributed to *Boss Women*. She writes that from shop floor to boardroom, a pervasive culture of misogyny flourished in the company she used to work for. She felt powerless to counter it, she says, and that was one of the principal reasons she wanted to strike out on her own.

'Now look at Samira. Here was a young woman who spent her entire life battling more extreme forms of the same malady. Her earliest misfortune was to have been born into a family who recognised that her burgeoning beauty could be exploited for gain. Theirs, not hers. And why did the Padars perceive the need? Perand managed to get out of Dilip that for years, the family business has been ill-served by its boss *men* – the elders pulling the strings.'

'What about its women? I always thought a powerful matriarchy was a feature of life in that country.'

'Samira aside, the power of the women appears to have been confined exclusively to the domestic sphere.'

'I can see where you're going with this. Knowing and believing all she did, why didn't Zoë feel a deep enough connection with Samira to at least spare her life?'

'Exactly. Where was the sisterhood? That Samira was regarded as no more than a bargaining chip by her family was cynical enough. To beat her to death as a way of getting even with a philandering husband? Even to a woman like Zoë, Samira still had no value of her own. I find that very difficult to fathom.'

They talked things over for another half-hour or so.

'Bedtime,' Frankie said. 'Come on.'

They set off hand-in-hand. 'Oh, I nearly forgot again – what did Agnès want to see you about after the team meeting?'

'Oh, she asked me what I thought about succeeding her as commissaire.'

Darac stopped in his tracks. 'What did you say?'

'I said how sincerely flattered I was to have the endorsement of a woman for whom I have the greatest respect, admiration and love. But that we had plans which rather ruled out my accepting such a full-time role. For a few years, anyway.'

'Ah.'

Looking in on Lily was always a beautiful thing for her parents. Tonight, it was loaded with such an acute awareness of her preciousness that neither could say a word.

In her cot, Lily kicked out a foot and slept soundly on.

Thursday, May 1st

SEVENTY-TWO

The seven members of the Didier Musso Quintet rolled into Cambridge in a buoyant mood. The two UK dates they had played so far had been an unqualified success and everyone appreciated that Ridge had had the band's welfare uppermost in his mind when he'd organised the tour on such a travel-friendly basis. Less time spent on the road meant more time for rest and recovery and, practically unheard of on tour, the prospect of a spot of sightseeing. For Darac though, the Cambridge gig presented an altogether different prospect.

He had arranged to meet Inès Laborde in her apartment.

The minibus set them down alongside a broad greensward right in the heart of the city.

'I take it the palace with the pepper pot domes is our hotel, Ridge?' Didier said, flashing drummer Maxine Walda a crafty wink as they began unloading the luggage and instrument cases. 'Right?'

'Let me see.' Ridge's gravity of mien was never more apparent than when considering a question. 'You're getting a grand between you for tonight's gig, right? Taking into account the hire of the bus, your *et ceteras* and your *je n' sais pas quois* … No, Monsieur *Tête Aérienne*, it's not. We're along the way there.'

'Just checking. Where are you staying, by the way?'

'With your fans from the Marsden gig a few years ago – Steve Randall and his wife. He's one of the guys who runs the club.'

'Sweet. How many CDs have we sold on the tour so far, by the way?'

'Our cup runneth over.'

'Which comes to?'

'Plenty.'

'One helluva expanse of grass, huh?' observed trumpeter Jacques Quille, surveying the sward as if worried he might suddenly be called upon to mow it. 'Grass and cyclists.'

'They call it Parker's Piece,' Englishman Dave Blackstock said, swinging his sax case on to his shoulder.

Luc Gabron seemed impressed. 'They named this after Bird? Cool.'

Darac was ready to head off to his appointment but first, he took Ridge to one side. 'The Vault,' he said. 'When's the sound check?'

'Six o'clock.' He knew all about Darac's other gig. 'Go carefully, now. But be on time, Garfield.'

SEVENTY THREE

Inès and Sue Talbot's flat was on the first-floor of a modernist housing block no more than a ten-minute walk away. Introductions made and remade, the first thing Darac noticed on being shown into to the sitting room was the piano, a hand-annotated score of a piece he knew well – Erik Satie's first 'Gnossienne' – open on the stand. He glanced at the opening phrases, intrigued at the imposition of tempo markings, bar lines and other instructions on what had been written in free time by the composer. And then he realised Sue was re-imagining the piece for a small chamber group, musicians possibly less used to such liberties than say, the DMQ would have been. It didn't seem the appropriate moment to comment.

His Francophone tones to the fore, Darac began lightly, if fatuously, in English. 'This corner position is nice. Although the view is not… classic Cambridge, I suppose. Not what one imagines, I mean.'

'Actually, pet,' Sue said. 'It's a famous street in Cambridge folklore is this. Mainly for the number of boozers it used to have. Pubs, that is. Oh, please sit wherever you want.'

Darac gave Inès an enquiring look. Whatever Sue had just said, he had understood about as much of it as he would one of Inès's scientific papers. No translation was forthcoming but Inès told Sue to "lose the Geordie" – whatever that meant – and to think "received pronunciation" – whatever that was.

'This any better for you, Captain?' Sue said, enunciating her words more clearly.

'Much. Thank you.'

Holding hands, the couple sat down on the sofa.

Inès made a show of their intertwined fingers. 'This

doesn't disturb you?'

'Expressing the love and support you feel for each other? Not at all.'

'Paul,' Sue said, 'if I may call you that? I should warn you that I've become quite a fan of your band and I shall be at The Vault this evening. Is *that* alright with you?'

'Yes you can call me Paul and yes it is alright to come this evening. I'd be delighted, in fact.'

'Good, because apart from looking forward to the music itself, I want to pick your bandleader's brains about a few things.'

'He has only the one brain but he will do his best.'

'I'll go back to Geordie if you're going to be cheeky, pet.'

Darac smiled. 'We do the sound check at 6 o'clock so come then by the means... by *all* means but if you are free this afternoon, Didier will probably be free, too. May I take your number?'

'You alright with this, Innie?'

'Sure. I've got some work to be catching up on, anyway.'

'Does Didier speak English?'

'If you talk only music, he speaks it quite well. Our tenor player, Dave Blackstock, he is totally bi-lingual and he will be happy to translate if he is present. In a crisis, our manager, Ridge Clay, is fluent but difficult to understand in either language. In a bigger crisis, if I am present, I will try, also.'

'Thanks, man.'

'I report that we have listened to some of your music, too. It's impressive.'

Sue's face lit up. 'Really? You think so? What in particular? Tell me. I'm vain.'

'We loved your suite for the quartet. And the solo piano pieces. Especially the one called *Glade*.'

Sue and Inès shared a meaningful if uninterpretable look. 'Yes, I must say *Glade* is a favourite of mine. Isn't it, Inès?'

'Oh yes.'

On another day in another place Darac could have spent an enjoyable few hours talking music with the talented and amusing Sue, but there was another point to his visit.

'Inès, if I may call you that?'

'You may.'

In preparation for their conversation, Darac had looked up a number of key terms in his dictionary. 'Shall we continue in English so you both... understand at the same moment?'

'Thank you, yes. Go for it.'

Sue squeezed Inès's hand, Darac noticed.

'So... I saw your mother last week, Inès.'

Tears came immediately. Darac let them run their course before saying anything further.

'I understand you are in touch with her every day so you know she is well.'

'As well as could be expected under the circumstances.'

'Indeed.'

'Do you have any news on a date for her trial?'

'No. But I have to tell you that whenever it does, she is certain to receive a life sentence and that however... I'm sorry... *Elle se comporte?*'

'She behaves.'

'She behaves – yes, thank you – there will be no possibility of parole for 18 years.'

'The lawyer told me that, too.'

'I'm sorry.'

Sue drew her fiancée to her and some moments elapsed before Inès felt able to continue.

'Captain, I am so desperately sorry that in order to punish my shit of a father, my mother saw fit to commit the horrible crime she did. There is an explanation for it, of course. An explanation rooted in things I care about. *But* there can be no defence, clearly. None. I know that. *She* knows it. I want *you* to know that we know that.'

'I do.'

'And I also want to thank you – *we* want to thank you – for what you did to ensure that I received no more than a caution for my part in what happened that night. I had no idea what my mother was planning to do and you believed that. And then you made the public prosecutor believe it.'

'Justice was done, Inès. That's what matters. And on that note, I must go.'

They shook hands and at the door Sue followed suit before thinking better of it and kissed Darac on both cheeks.

'Strange… circumstances in which to meet a fellow musician, Sue.'

'True. But I'm glad we have.'

'*Moi aussi*. See you later.'

SEVENTY-FOUR

The sound check completed, Joe Henderson's 'Inner Urge' struck up on the PA as the band began to file back through the concert room to the bar.

Alto sax ace Trudie "Charlie" Pachelberg turned to Darac. 'The place is a different shape but steps down from the street to the foyer, lowish ceilings and soft lights? Reminds me a bit of the Blue Devil.'

'Proper cellar jazz clubs. There's nothing like them for vibes, is there? Great sound in here, too.'

Luc Gabron had a typically wry observation to add. 'Check out the chairs. I reckon there's a good few gardens around where there's nowhere to sit.'

As they headed for the bar, Sue Talbot and interpreter-in-chief Dave Blackstock were the group's tail-end Charlies.

'First alcove on the right is for the band!' she called out as they crossed the foyer. 'Do you think they will have got that?'

'Leave it to me,' he said, masterfully. '*Mecs? A droite*! That should have done it.'

Once ensconced, the talk was all music, clubs and tours and it almost came as a surprise when fast-moving club MC Steve Randall shot by, radio mike in hand.

'*Dix minutes* to show time, Didier.'

'Ten, Steve? *Super.*' He turned back to Sue. 'I will send you this file and if you… *moment*, Dave? *Comment dit-on, envoie-moi le tien?*'

Dave leaned in. 'He's basically saying he'll show you his if you show him yours.'

'Got you.'

Show time. As Darac checked his tuning, Steve began his spiel to the sell-out crowd.

'Welcome everyone to the fourth of this season's gigs here at The Vault. I was lucky enough to catch the DMQ on their previous tour to this country. They knocked us out then and if their sound check just now was anything to go by, they are going to reach even greater heights tonight. First — a spot of housekeeping. The music is sure to catch fire but in the unlikely event the venue goes up in flames, your exits are…'

As the announcements continued, Darac completed tuning and with the volume control on his instrument still turned to zero, he ran through a few phrases of his go-to warm-up piece, *Limehouse Blues*. All set, he picked out Ridge in the audience, chatting and laughing — *laughing*? — with Sue in the second row. Luc had spotted this too and catching Darac's eye, the pair shared an incredulous look.

'… And the assembly point is outside the Friends' Meeting House in Jesus Lane. So, without further ado…'

Steve gave Didier a nod and led by Luc's walking bass, the band eased into a slow-cooking strut under the announcement.

'… Please welcome Didier Mussso on piano.' As the applause began, Steve glanced at his notes. 'Jacques Quille on trumpet; Trudi Pachelberg on alto; Dave Blackstock on tenor; Paul Darac on guitar; Luc Gabron on bass; and Maxine Walda on the drums. That's the seven, yes *seven* members of the fabulous… Didier Musso Quintet!'

As the welcome ovation rose a decibel or two, Darac had the happy thought that playing gigs on tour was the only time he knew he wouldn't be hoiked off the stand to attend a crime scene. But then, with the applause still ringing out, Sue left her seat and slipped nimbly forward.

'A message from Granny O, I think Mister Clay called her. I'm to tell you there's been a murder upstairs.'

'What?'

'Yes, the coffee was not to his liking and he'd like you to go and investigate.'

Darac's eyes met Ridge's as Sue went to re-join him and with the band sharing the joke, Luc's walking bass slowed to a stop, Didier counted them in, and they tore into their opening number.

It was around midnight when Darac climbed into bed and checked his phone. The hotel hadn't lied. – the wi-fi password worked and the connection appeared strong.

'How did it go today, darling?'

'The meeting with Inès Laborde or the gig?'

'Start with the gig.'

'A triumph. We would still be playing for them now but for the local rules and regs. Sold a lot of CDs, too.'

'I'm delighted. How wonderful to be able to bring such joy to people.'

'I haven't given up hope that you'll join us for a number or two on the stand one of these days. Audiences would love you.'

'As mother used to say – still says, in fact – we'll see.'

'Ah! Weakening.'

'Paul? We'll see.'

'And how is our Lily-belle this evening?'

'Don't know. She's out with Fabien and the boys. A rave up in Dignes, apparently.

'That's funny because according to my *Cot-Cam* link, she's sleeping soundly no more than four metres away from you at this very moment.'

'Really? Well, that's the mothers of today for you.'

'Seems so.'

'Tell me about Inès.'

'It's obviously incredibly difficult for her. But I think she'll get there. For one thing, she has the love of a good woman going for her – something I know quite a lot about.'

'Sweetie... Ooh – speaking of good women, Agnès collared me on my way home. Come next January, I know who is likely to be stepping into her slingbacks, as it were.'

'Our new commissaire? This is huge. Who is it?'

'Wouldn't *you* like to know.'

'Yes. I would. Spill!'

'Oh, was that Lily? Better go, darling. Love and big sloppy kisses!'

'Not so fast!'

He switched back to *Cot-Cam* and as he suspected, Lily was fast asleep. Frankie appeared, smiled innocently and mouthed something that had no connection whatever with commissaires past, present or future.

Oh, me too, sweetie, he mouthed back.

But then she held up a handwritten card reading: *And Agnès's choice is...* She turned it.

Darac stared at the reveal. Now *that*, he thought, might just work.

END

DARAC MYSTERY SERIES
BY PETER MORFOOT
AUTHOR'S NOTE

When I began devising what became the Captain Darac Mystery series, I knew what I *didn't* want for my central character. To be authentic, any character must have flaws but I determined Darac would not be a slave to his. I determined he would not always make the right moves in an investigation; nor would he solve cases over a chat in a bar.

I conceived him as a strong-minded individual but, attesting to the essentially collaborative nature of police work, I needed him to be a whole-hearted team player, also; an interesting dynamic and one that gave me the pleasurable task of creating a permanent cast of supporting players for him. This led to Darac's genesis as a "poète policier," a term derived from a resonant assertion by award-winning writer and, to Anglicise his rank, chief superintendent of police, Philippe Pichon: "A poet can be a policeman and a policeman can be a poet." But which art form for Darac? I felt that jazz with its tension between structure and improvisation would give me the most relevant and interesting possibilities.

The setting for the series? With its vibrant light, the spectacular Alpes Maritime mountain range at its back and that celebrated azure coastline at its feet, Nice is as beautiful as any Mediterranean resort. But it's also a multi-ethnic city of almost half a million souls. And are there serpents in this particular paradise? Ask Darac, Commissaire Agnès Dantier and the other officers of Nice's Brigade Criminelle.

A senior police officer who also plays jazz in a high-quality group, a significant player therefore in two different sorts of team, was someone I was looking forward to putting through his paces on the page. Unlike some of his fictional counterparts, Darac is a character drawn to living not so much on the edge as on the borderline; a man who chooses to position himself at points of junction or collision with the world. And in the six novels of the Darac Mystery series thus far, he has encountered plenty of both.

SOME BACKGROUND READING

French Criminal Justice
      Jacqueline Hodgson, Hart 2005
Investigating Homicide Investigation in France
      Charlotte Harris, Taylor and Francis 2013
The French Intifada, The Long War Between France and its Arabs
      Andrew Hussey, Granta 2015
The Discovery of France
      Graham Robb, Picador 2007
La Vie en Bleu, France and the French Since 1900
      Rod Kedward, Penguin 2005
Past Imperfect, French Intellectuals 1944-1956
      Tony Judt, New York University Press 2011
Hunting the Truth
      Beate and Serge Klarsfeld, Farrar, Straus & Giroux, 2019
The Secret Life of France
      Lucy Wadham, Faber 2013
Wild Words
      Kate Hodges, Portico 2021

PLAYLIST OF ARTISTS AND NUMBERS
REFERENCED IN *A DEATH IN TIME*

Grant Green: 'Idle Moments.' From the album of the same name, this is the guitarist at his liltingly after-hours best.

Charlie Mingus: Black Saint and the Sinner Lady. Lush, raw, wild, sophisticated – Mingus's complex compositional approach speaks to Darac's instincts and this set for an 11-piece outfit is one of his favourite albums.

Clifford Brown: Killed in an RTA at the age of 25, Brownie's influence on trumpet virtuosi is still felt 70 years later. Allying lyricism and adventurous improvising to a prodigious technique, 'Joy Spring' from the Alone Together album is a typical example of his genius.

Julia Hülsmann Quartet: En route to the scene of a brutal murder, Darac arms himself by recalling phrases from the atmospherically beautiful 'Snow, Melting' from In Full View.

Donna Summer: The disco classic 'I Feel Love' provides the seamy aural backdrop to Julien Baille's encounter with Dilip Padar.

Françoise Hardy: An album of the beloved singer's lower-octane hits is playing at the Labordes' anniversary party. 'Le Temps de L'Amour' is in the air.

Joe Henderson: 'Inner Urge' was the title track of the 1966 Blue Note album which saw the tenor sax-man venture into more adventurous territory – an approach Darac always favours.

Bill Evans Trio: Blue Devil Jazz Club Supremo Ridge Clay is not alone in rating all three takes of Scott LeFaro's tune 'Gloria's Step' from Sunday Night at The Village Vanguard as a high-water mark in live trio jazz.

Kenny Barron and Dave Holland: The Art of Conversation. Piano and bass here combine to create an album Darac regards as superlative in every way.

Kenny Barron, Dave Holland, Johnathan Blake: Without Deception. For Darac, adding drummer JB to the mix "just made the magic happen in a different way."

Django Reinhardt: inspirational swing era guitarist whose unsurpassable technique was honed in the Paris club scene of the 1930s. Darac warms up for every gig by playing phrases from Django's 'Limehouse Blues.'

Charlie Parker: Along with the unprecedented speed and precision of trumpeter Dizzy Gillespie, alto sax legend Charlie laid all the groundwork for Bebop and built on it subsequently. The Didier Musso Quintet's fleet-fingered altoist Trudi Pachelberg is nicknamed "Charlie" in his honour.

Erik Satie: pianist and composer whose spare lyricism continues to inspire many a jazzer. Nice's own accordion king Richard Galliano has recorded his 'Gymnopédies' and 'Gnossiennes' on more than one occasion.

ACKNOWLEDGEMENTS

Without the love and perceptive insights of my wife Liz, tackling this sixth Darac Mystery would have been a far tougher call. As always, Rob, Clare, Katey and Bryan proved ideal companions along the way. Beginning with the first novel in the series, *Impure Blood*, the sagacity and all-round support of Lisa Hitch, Susan Woodall, Alex Carter and that doyen of booksellers, Richard Reynolds, have been invaluable. A big thank-you also to David Gower and the team at Cambridge Modern Jazz Club.

Further afield, thanks are due to Boris Blouin and Jacky Ananou. I owe a particular debt of gratitude to Commandant Divisionnaire de Police, Jean-Baptiste Zuccarelli of Commissaire Foch in Nice. For her many kindnesses and for her translation work both from texts and during live interviews with officers of the Police Nationale, special thanks to Katherine Roddwell. Finally, warm thanks to my publisher Robert Hyde.